T0179578

Titles by Christine Feehan

The GhostWalker Novels

GHOSTLY GAME	RUTHLESS GAME
PHANTOM GAME	STREET GAME
LIGHTNING GAME	MURDER GAME
LETHAL GAME	PREDATORY GAME
TOXIC GAME	DEADLY GAME
COVERT GAME	CONSPIRACY GAME
POWER GAME	NIGHT GAME
SPIDER GAME	MIND GAME
VIPER GAME	SHADOW GAME
SAMURAI GAME	

The Drake Sisters Novels

HIDDEN CURRENTS	DANGEROUS TIDES
TURBULENT SEA	OCEANS OF FIRE
SAFE HARBOR	

The Leopard Novels

LEOPARD'S HUNT	WILD CAT
LEOPARD'S SCAR	CAT'S LAIR
LEOPARD'S RAGE	LEOPARD'S PREY
LEOPARD'S WRATH	SAVAGE NATURE
LEOPARD'S RUN	WILD FIRE
LEOPARD'S BLOOD	BURNING WILD
LEOPARD'S FURY	WILD RAIN

The Sea Haven / Sisters of the Heart Novels

BOUND TOGETHER	AIR BOUND
FIRE BOUND	SPIRIT BOUND
EARTH BOUND	WATER BOUND

The Shadow Riders Novels

SHADOW FIRE	SHADOW KEEPER
SHADOW STORM	SHADOW REAPER
SHADOW FLIGHT	SHADOW RIDER
SHADOW WARRIOR	

The Torpedo Ink Novels

BETRAYAL ROAD	DESOLATION ROAD
RECOVERY ROAD	VENDETTA ROAD
SAVAGE ROAD	VENGEANCE ROAD
ANNIHILATION ROAD	JUDGMENT ROAD
RECKLESS ROAD	

The Carpathian Novels

DARK MEMORY	DARK CURSE
DARK WHISPER	DARK HUNGER
DARK TAROT	DARK POSSESSION
DARK SONG	DARK CELEBRATION
DARK ILLUSION	DARK DEMON
DARK SENTINEL	DARK SECRET
DARK LEGACY	DARK DESTINY
DARK CAROUSEL	DARK MELODY
DARK PROMISES	DARK SYMPHONY
DARK GHOST	DARK GUARDIAN
DARK BLOOD	DARK LEGEND
DARK WOLF	DARK FIRE
DARK LYCAN	DARK CHALLENGE
DARK STORM	DARK MAGIC
DARK PREDATOR	DARK GOLD
DARK PERIL	DARK DESIRE
DARK SLAYER	DARK PRINCE

Anthologies

EDGE OF DARKNESS
(with Maggie Shayne and Lori Herter)

DARKEST AT DAWN
(includes Dark Hunger *and* Dark Secret*)*

SEA STORM
(includes Magic in the Wind *and* Oceans of Fire*)*

FEVER
(includes The Awakening *and* Wild Rain*)*

FANTASY
(with Emma Holly, Sabrina Jeffries, and Elda Minger)

LOVER BEWARE
(with Fiona Brand, Katherine Sutcliffe, and Eileen Wilks)

HOT BLOODED
(with Maggie Shayne, Emma Holly, and Angela Knight)

Specials

DARK CRIME
THE AWAKENING
DARK HUNGER
MAGIC IN THE WIND

RED ON THE RIVER
MURDER AT SUNRISE LAKE

BETRAYAL ROAD

CHRISTINE FEEHAN

BERKLEY ROMANCE
New York

BERKLEY ROMANCE
Published by Berkley
An imprint of Penguin Random House LLC
penguinrandomhouse.com

Copyright © 2024 by Christine Feehan
Excerpt from *Dark Hope* copyright © 2024 by Christine Feehan
Penguin Random House supports copyright. Copyright fuels creativity, encourages
diverse voices, promotes free speech, and creates a vibrant culture. Thank you for buying
an authorized edition of this book and for complying with copyright laws by not
reproducing, scanning, or distributing any part of it in any form without permission.
You are supporting writers and allowing Penguin Random House to continue to
publish books for every reader.

BERKLEY and the BERKLEY & B colophon are registered trademarks
of Penguin Random House LLC.

ISBN: 9780593638781

First Edition: August 2024

Printed in the United States of America
1   3   5   7   9   10   8   6   4   2

For Samantha.
Thank you for always coming
through for me over the years.
You manage to make my hair look
amazing no matter the weather.

FOR MY READERS

Be sure to go to christinefeehan.com/members to sign up for my *private* book announcement list and download the *free* ebook of *Dark Desserts*.

I also have a Feehan Pet coloring book in ebook form just for fun for those who enjoy coloring. It features many of the pets in our family. Sign up for the book announcement list, join the community, and the coloring book is free to download. The community is behind a wall to keep out spammers.

The third surprise is an amazing book with crossword puzzles and all kinds of fun things to do, also in ebook form. Sheila English has worked on it for such a long time so we could give it to community members.

Join my community and get firsthand news, enter the book discussions, ask your questions and chat with me. Please feel free to email me at Christine@christinefeehan.com. I would love to hear from you.

ACKNOWLEDGMENTS

I need to give special thanks to my son Caedyn Feehan for Maestro's song declaring his love for Azelie. Thank you to Diane Trudeau, without whom I would never have been able to have gotten this book written under such circumstances. Brian Feehan for making certain he was here every day to set up the pages I needed to write in order to hit the deadline. Denise Tucker for handling all the details of every aspect of my life that were so crazy. And to my amazing, invaluable researcher, Karen Brownfield Houton, you are a miracle to me! Thank all of you so very much!!!

TORPEDO INK MEMBERS

Viktor Prakenskii aka *Czar*—President

Lyov Russak aka *Steele*—Vice President

Savva Pajari aka *Reaper*—Sergeant at Arms

Savin Pajari aka *Savage*—Sergeant at Arms

Isaak Koval aka *Ice*—Secretary

Dmitry Koval aka *Storm*

Alena Koval aka *Torch*

Luca Litvin aka *Code*—Hacker

Maksimos Korsak aka *Ink*

Kasimir Popov aka *Preacher*

Lana Popov aka *Widow*

Nikolaos Bolotan aka *Mechanic*

Pytor Bolotan aka *Transporter*

Andrii Federoff aka *Maestro*

Gedeon Lazaroff aka *Player*

Kir Vasiliev aka *Master*—Treasurer

Lazar Alexeev aka *Keys*

Aleksei Solokov aka *Absinthe*

Rurik Volkov aka *Razrushitel/Destroyer*

NEWER PATCHED MEMBERS

Gavriil Prakenskii

Casimir Prakenskii

Fatei Molchalin aka *Rock*

PROSPECTS

Glitch

Hyde

SIBLINGS WITHIN THE GROUP

Viktor (Czar), Gavriil and Casimir

Reaper and Savage

Mechanic and Transporter

Ice, Storm and Alena (Torch)

Preacher and Lana (Widow)

TEAMS

Czar heads Team One

> *Reaper, Savage, Ice, Storm, Transporter, Alena, Absinthe, Mechanic, Destroyer*

Steele heads Team Two

Keys, Master, Player, Maestro, Lana, Preacher, Ink, Code

OLD LADIES

Blythe, Lissa, Lexi, Anya, Breezy, Soleil, Scarlet, Zyah, Seychelle, Ambrielle

BETRAYAL
ROAD

ONE

Azelie Vargas became aware of the whispers and giggles, and she looked up to see her three favorite seniors gesturing wildly toward the window. They were matchmakers, those three. They came into the coffee shop, every day at the same time, and ordered the same drinks and pastries. Sometimes Azelie treated them, knowing they were on a tight budget.

Penny Atwater had been best friends with China and Blanc Christian for nearly sixty years. They still lived next door to one another in San Francisco homes that shared a wall. None of them drove. They'd taken the bus everywhere as children growing up and then later continued to do so as adults. All three referred to themselves as widows and shared a love of dancing. Blanc had been a professional ballroom dancer and had taught in a studio with her sister, China.

Azelie loved their passion for life. She wasn't so certain of their enthusiasm for finding her a romantic partner. Still, they made her laugh because they wore bright clothes and had such a joy for living. The three referred to themselves as "the merry widows" and then would laugh with such enthusiasm it was difficult not to join them in their merriment.

Two gentlemen, Doug Parsons and Carlton Gray, had been

neighbors with the three women for over forty years. Their houses were on either side of the merry widows' homes. They often came into the coffee shop around the same time as the three women, sitting with them and reminiscing about funny or poignant times from their past. Azelie enjoyed listening to them. She suspected most of those coming to the coffee shop did as well.

The coffee shop wasn't a trendy one. It was a mom-and-pop organic coffee shop, so the prices were a little higher. But everyone who frequented it was loyal. Azelie went there to study for her classes or read. Sometimes she worked on the book she was currently writing. She'd been lucky enough to have three books published and had a contract for a fourth. They were moderately successful, which meant she made some money on them. Not a lot, but it helped to pay for her college classes.

The man the three seniors were all atwitter over stood on the sidewalk just outside the coffee shop. He'd come in twice before with another man. Both times the women in the shop— including her—were rendered speechless at the sheer beauty and power the two men exuded. Even Shaila Manger, the owner, came out of the kitchen to ogle the men. Her husband, David, simply laughed good-naturedly, not in the least upset that his wife of thirty-eight years found the two men hot.

Personally, Azelie did have a bit of a crush on the taller of the two men. Just looking at him took her breath away. She was careful not to stare when he had come in with his friend. In fact, she kept her gaze glued to her laptop. That didn't stop the three seniors from gesturing wildly and giggling like schoolgirls. The men had to have noticed—they would have been blind not to—but she refused to acknowledge the matchmaking or the fact that the women had managed to ferret out the names of the newcomers.

Naturally, it was Mr. Gorgeous and Powerful that was coming into the coffee shop alone today. She would have been perfectly fine if his friend Lazar Alexeev had come in. Her body didn't have the slightest reaction to Lazar—but

Andrii Federoff, holy cow, she'd gone up in proverbial flames. That had never happened to her. Not once. It was disconcerting and just a tiny bit horrifying that without even trying Andrii could set her body on fire.

Azelie had never seen a man quite like Andrii before. He was tall with broad shoulders and so much muscle through his arms and chest she didn't know how his shirt could contain it all. His hair was a true black streaked with silver. The silver didn't make him look older, but his eyes did. He should have had gray eyes, but the color was lighter than gray, so he appeared to have silver eyes. When he looked at her, she had the mad desire to do anything he asked of her. Not a good thing. She wanted to be independent, and over the last couple of years she had worked hard to suppress the need in her to nurture and serve others.

Clearly, she hadn't succeeded—yet. Not with the seniors who she bonded with. There were also the parents she helped out occasionally in the park she frequented. And now there was Andrii. She was staying far, far away from him.

She had gleaned from the conversation she'd overheard between the two men that Lazar lived close, and Andrii was visiting because he had business in San Francisco. She'd never seen Lazar in the coffee shop, but that didn't mean he wasn't there at different hours than she was. He was probably considered good-looking—at least the merry widows, the owner of the shop and a few other females ogled him when he was there with Andrii.

Lazar had a build similar to Andrii's in that he had wide shoulders and a thick chest and arms, giving him an appearance of power. His hair was dark, and he wore it slicked back and neat, much neater than Andrii's shaggy hair. His eyes were hazel and at times looked amber to her. There were freckles all over his face, which should have detracted from his looks but only seemed to enhance them—at least to the other women.

The moment Andrii entered the shop, she was acutely aware of him in the room. She didn't have to look up to know he was there. She knew exactly where he was every minute. He had such a presence. She sat at her usual table, a small one for two people only, toward the back of the shop. She had a good view of the windows and could see two streets, as the coffee shop was on a corner. Instead of looking at the views—or at Andrii—she brought up the book she was currently reading. She hoped the novel would keep the butterflies from fluttering in her stomach.

With one finger, Azelie pushed back the glasses threatening to slide from her nose. The thick black frames annoyed her when they insisted on falling right when she was reading something exciting. She loved books and the adventures they could take her on. It wasn't like she was ever going to be leading a wild and crazy life, so reading about exotic places and heroes and heroines appealed to her—especially ones that were monogamous. And happy endings were always important, no matter if there was murder, mystery or mayhem.

It was impossible to shut out the giggles of the merry widows. For no reason at all, color swept up her neck into her face. She was certain the women were gesturing wildly toward her. Sighing, she glanced up over the top of her glasses, blinking rapidly several times to bring her surroundings into focus. Her gaze collided with a pair of eyes more liquid silver than gray and very intense. His lashes, very black and thick, didn't take away from his chiseled features. The fact that he wore his black hair longer, and it was streaked with fine threads of silver, only enhanced the entirely masculine vibe he had going. As far as she could tell, there wasn't an ounce of fat anywhere on him.

Her stomach clenched. Her sex clenched. Her entire body wanted to seize. He was intimidating just because he was so gorgeous.

"Would you mind if I join you? As you can see, the shop is filling up quickly."

She blinked up at him again, trying to catch her breath. Just looking at him made everything she had want to run. She had to look away, afraid she'd make an utter fool of herself if she tried to speak. She looked around the coffee shop. It was nearly empty.

"Zelie."

His voice was smooth. Like the brush of velvet against her skin. She'd never heard a voice like his before. Not ever. He had the kind of voice that made her shiver in anticipation of . . . what? Hot blood rushed through her veins and under her skin, coloring her face a bright red. There was no controlling that wild blush any more than there was controlling the flutter in her sex. And *Zelie*? No one called her Zelie. It was always Azelie. But she liked the way he said Zelie. Still . . .

"How did you know my name?" To her horror, her voice came out small, not at all like she wanted to sound. A whisper. As if she were inviting him to be intimate with her. She never sounded like that. She might avoid men, but when she spoke to them, she was decisive.

The table was small, and he moved the chair close to her—too close. His thigh brushed along hers. Warm. No, hot. She was suddenly very aware of herself as a woman, every nerve ending springing to life. He was definitely a man.

"The barista calls your name when your order is ready," he said simply. "I'm Andrii Federoff. I couldn't help but notice the beautiful woman lost in her own world."

No one called her beautiful. She wasn't beautiful. She was . . . ordinary. Mousy even. There wasn't a single thing remarkable about her. Not that she was complaining. The fact that no one noticed her helped her to disappear into the woodwork, where she could observe those around her without having to participate.

"Azelie Vargas," she managed to get out without making more of a fool of herself. She couldn't drink her coffee; her hands were shaking too bad. She threaded her fingers together tightly in her lap, wondering why a man as gorgeous as Andrii would choose to sit with her.

"What are you reading? It must be very interesting to have you so completely absorbed in the story."

She tried to fight the blush but was unsuccessful. "I enjoy a variety of novels."

He remained silent, his silver eyes moving over her face like twin lasers. He looked a little moody. Disappointed. Definitely aware she'd dodged his question and not happy about it.

She lifted her chin. She didn't know him. What the hell did it matter if he judged her? "I enjoy reading romance. Happy endings. Stories about men and women communicating and forming families. Being faithful to each other."

Immediately, those strangely colored eyes turned to a liquid silver, approval lighting them. The change sent little darts of fire shooting straight to her sex. Why in the world did his approval of her matter so much? It made no sense when he was a complete stranger, but her entire body responded just to the look in his eyes.

"I've seen you typing. Do you write your own stories?"

His voice was remarkable. She'd never heard anything like it. She felt as if he were wrapping her in velvet. Azelie nodded. He continued to stare at her with his light-colored eyes, burning right through her, exposing her every secret.

"Yes," she whispered. "I do write stories. It's difficult to make a living as a full-time author, so I work at a local club as a bookkeeper to make ends meet." She had absolutely no idea why she blurted out that information, but it just came flying out of her mouth. "I've worked there for years, but had hoped I could quit eventually. That isn't looking too good."

He nodded. "You're published, then?"

"Yes. I've sold three stories so far—romantic suspense—and I've contracted for one more. I'm hoping when I turn that one in, they'll offer me another contract. So far, the books have sold fairly well." She took pride in that. She wasn't a bestseller, but she was definitely midlist. That didn't mean she could quit her day job. She just couldn't make enough money being an author. She understood the cost of paper and ink kept rising.

She also had tried self-publishing. That hadn't worked

out for her. She wasn't good at marketing. On top of that, a trend had started where readers returned books after they read them, and authors had to return the money. She couldn't pay her bills. Many authors went under. She was fortunate in that she had a good-paying day job, but having that possibility hanging over her head was daunting. She didn't have the nerves for it. She needed the buffer of a publisher.

"I find it interesting that you work as a bookkeeper and you write novels. It's unusual to do both."

She nodded. "I know. I think my brain is always at war with itself." She flashed him a small smile. "What do you do?"

"I work in security. It's not nearly as interesting."

His voice literally sent chills down her spine. She was grateful she was sitting because she was afraid she might not be able to keep her legs from trembling and she'd fall right at his feet. She really hoped those strangely colored eyes of his couldn't see right into her. She'd never, not once in her life, had a reaction to another human being the way she did to him.

"In novels, the man working security is always interesting."

One dark eyebrow shot up and his lips curved into a slow smile. No teeth, but that almost smile made her stomach somersault. "Have you ever written a hero working security?"

She moistened suddenly dry lips as she shook her head. Again, there was silence, and she knew he was waiting for her to speak. "Not yet."

That earned her a flash of his white teeth. Her heart nearly stopped. She forced her gaze to the to-go mug she had carefully picked up and now held between her palms.

"I don't suppose you would describe him as looking like me?"

She dared to tilt her head to the side and allowed her gaze to drift over him, making certain to start from the neck down. She couldn't look into those mercury eyes, especially if he was looking at her with that focused intensity. "Neck tattoos,

broad shoulders, a thick chest, all muscle. If I described my
hero like you, my readers would think I was relying on for-
mula writing." She laughed because she couldn't help it. He
was beautiful. A gorgeous man who had no business sitting
with her.

"Why are you laughing, Zelie?"

"I'm afraid you sat down at the wrong table, Mr.
Federoff."

"Why are you so certain of that?"

She gestured toward him, from the top of his head down
his chest, grateful the rest of him was hidden. She was finally getting to a place where she could speak to him without
making a total fool of herself. She was fully capable of speaking her mind or speaking the truth, but only if she didn't
think too much about the rest of his body.

She pushed her glasses back on her nose. "You have to
know what you look like. Even what you sound like. Men as
beautiful as you are don't give women who look like me a
second glance. I have no idea why you decided to sit at this
table, but it's absurd. Did the merry widows talk you into
sitting with me?"

His eyes had gone hot silver. Gleaming silver. Mesmerizing. She couldn't have looked away if she wanted to. "Women
who look like you? What do you look like?"

His voice made her shiver, as if she had said something
that truly annoyed him. It didn't show on his face, so she
couldn't exactly say what it was that made her think he was
disappointed and even angry, but she knew he was. The silver
eyes glittered. Moved over her face. Dwelled on her mouth.
Dropped lower. He seemed to be able to look right through
her boxy sweatshirt to the body she hid from the world.

He leaned toward her. "I'm going to do you the courtesy of
telling you the truth since you're so honest with me. As for
the merry widows, as sweet and funny as they are, I would
never sit down with a woman I wasn't interested in."

His voice made her shiver. Those eyes had come back up

to hers and held her gaze captive. He was *interested* in her? She didn't know what to think of that.

"In case you hadn't noticed, I have scars. Not all women find that attractive. Evidently, you do, which is good for me. Your hair is unbelievable. For a man with my tastes and needs, your hair is a fucking miracle. I think you have one of the most beautiful faces I've ever seen. Every emotion you feel is transparent. Right there. You have incredible eyes. I would know exactly what you were thinking or feeling just looking into your eyes. I've been in this coffee shop numerous times and fantasized far too much about having your lips wrapped around my dick. Just looking at your mouth makes me hard. You have tits and an ass, something that I look for in a woman. You also have brains. You're not afraid of speaking your mind, yet you're the kind of woman a man like me needs. Women like you don't come along that often."

She wished she was offended by his plain speaking, but she had gone damp. Her breasts ached. Her mouth even watered. Color crept under her skin, and there was no way to slow her quickened breathing, so she didn't try to hide her reaction to his assessment of her.

"What the hell do you think is wrong with your looks?"

He didn't raise his voice at all. If anything, it was lower than normal, but all the same, his tone was a demand for her to answer him.

She moistened her lips. The minute she did, her gaze dropped to his lap and the heavy bulge outlined against his dark jeans. Her heart thudded a desperate beat, a wild drumming that pounded through her clit.

"I do have a lot of hair," she conceded. "It's thick and wild and isn't very tamable. My eyes are too big for my face. My lips are too much. If I wear lipstick, especially a bright color, I look . . ." She broke off abruptly.

Sometimes when she was alone at night, she applied a bright red lipstick and wore the only club outfit she had, which she would never dare to wear in public. She would stand far back from the mirror and walk slowly toward it. She turned even redder thinking about how she performed in front of the mirror. She loved to dance. *Loved* dancing. It was right up there with reading.

Andrii smiled at her, his gaze on her mouth. "I can imagine how you would look and what every man seeing you would want you to do. I would love to walk into a club with you on my arm. You're so fucking sexy. I like the idea other men would know you're mine."

Azelie could tell he was waiting to see if he'd shocked her or put her off with his crude, explicit way of speaking, but her entire body responded to it. That was her dirty little secret. He had evidently taken the time to study her long enough to figure her out. To realize she was the type of woman to respond to a man like him.

"By all means, Zelie, keep going. What else do you think is wrong with your looks? Why do you hide your tits behind those ridiculous shirts? And your very nice ass in those baggy pants? What is the purpose?"

She tried to stay still under his demand for an answer. She was ashamed of her desire to be anonymous. She had her reasons. She didn't really need to share everything with him. The bare minimum would do. "I've been working as a bookkeeper for one of the local clubs since I was sixteen. It wasn't exactly legal when I started because I was underage. It just sort of happened. The bookkeeper unexpectedly quit right before an audit, and the owner, Alan, needed someone. I'm really good with numbers. Really good. Really fast."

"How did this Alan know about you?"

"My brother-in-law knew him. He told Alan about me. Quentin always called me the whiz kid. He told me to wear really baggy sweats and work during the day, to never go to the club at night. So that's how I started wearing these clothes to work."

She gave him a tentative smile. She was telling him the truth. Quentin, her brother-in-law, had gotten her the job, and he had been the one to insist she wear baggy sweats.

"This club owner trusted a kid to fix his books when he was being audited?" There was disbelief mixed with incredulousness, as if Andrii wanted to believe her, but the idea was so absurd, he just couldn't.

Her smile widened. "It wasn't like he had anyone else. He didn't have time to find someone professional. Alan had less than forty-eight hours. I was taking classes at the college, and Quentin wouldn't let me go. I worked nearly the full forty-eight hours straight."

"I take it you were able to fix the mistakes his accountant had made?"

She laughed; she couldn't help it. "The point was to keep him out of prison. I managed to do that. Alan's accountant had a big grudge against him. He had an interest in the clubs. There are actually two clubs, and they make a *lot* of money. With his partner out of the way, he might have managed a takeover."

"Was the accountant a full partner?"

Azelie shook her head. "He had been embezzling. That was blatant. Alan trusted him. He didn't pay much attention to the books. He does now."

"Do you ever work at night?"

"I work whenever I need to, meaning if I'm behind or the boss calls me in for something, I'll go in at night. I don't like to. The clubs are very popular, and both are always packed. The clubs are mostly empty during the day, so it's easier to work when no one's around but the security guards. They know to leave me alone. Even Alan sleeps in late. I can have the place to myself."

"What club is it you work for?" He reached out and ran one finger down the back of the hand curled around her to-go mug, as if the temptation of touching her was too hard to resist.

"The Pleasure Train." She rolled her eyes. "The name is so ridiculous, I laughed the first time Quentin told me about it. I can't believe how many people go there."

"I've gone there a few times with friends of mine," he admitted.

"You have? The upstairs, the Pleasure Train, is a dance club. The floor beneath it is the Adventure Club for the much more adventurous." She already knew which floor he'd visited with his friends.

The pad of his finger slowly stroked back and forth along the back of her hand. "Most of those men claiming to be Doms are playing roles, Zelie. They're acting out parts, playacting. Nothing more. It isn't a lifestyle for them or their partner."

She nodded. "I've been around them enough to have learned they're only there to have fun."

"You haven't ever participated at the club, have you?"

Was there an edge to that soft voice? A hint of steel? A dark thrill crept down her spine. She suddenly had the premonition that he could be very dangerous. "I've walked through every room many times and never once felt the slightest inclination to join in the fun," she admitted. It was true. She wasn't into games. She didn't play.

"I think it would be a good idea to keep it that way."

She wasn't certain what he meant by that. He held a fascination for her no other man had ever managed to do. It was disconcerting and a little frightening. As a rule, she wasn't the least intimidated by anyone. She could not care less what they thought of her.

"Full disclosure, I have met your boss, Alan Billows, on more than one occasion. However, I don't know your brother-in-law."

"Quentin is dead," she said. Azelie pressed a tight fist against her stomach, where that knot of anger was, holding it in. Keeping it there. Knowing it was bright and hot and fresh as the day the murders had occurred.

"Zelie," Andrii murmured, his tone that stroke of velvet. "I'm so sorry."

"He murdered my sister, my nephew and my niece and then killed himself. My sister and I tried to shield the children, but he shot me three times." She pressed her hand to her chest. She could still feel the pain and horror of those last moments with her family.

She didn't know why she'd told him. But then she didn't know why she'd admitted to fixing Alan's books for him so he wouldn't go to prison. She'd never told anyone, and she knew Alan would beat her within an inch of her life if he found out. The fact that Andrii had met him and had mutual friends with him didn't bode well for her, yet she just kept blurting out intensely private and very personal details of her life to him. She *never* did that. Not even to the merry widows, and she liked them. She couldn't say she was great friends with them because she was reserved around everyone . . . yet not so much around Mr. Gorgeous and Powerful.

Andrii was silent, his eyes going slate, then completely silver. He cupped the side of her face with one palm, his thumb sliding very gently along her jaw. "What a terrible tragedy, Zelie. Have you talked about this with anyone?"

She gave a short shake of her head because she hadn't. She couldn't lift her lashes to look at him. They were wet. She didn't allow herself to cry over her family. The rage was there, and it kept her going. Kept her alert to every pitfall.

"Talk to me. I'm a good listener."

His voice was so dangerous. Low and imperious. Gentle and almost tender. Hell. What did it matter if he knew the entire story? It wasn't as if it were a secret.

"My sister, Janine, was ten years older than me. She married Quentin, and they seemed happy enough in the beginning, at least I thought they were. I lived with them after our mother died. I don't remember my father. My mother drank a lot. And she was pretty violent when she drank. She seemed to forget she had children, or she just didn't care. In any case, Janine mostly took care of me until she moved out."

Azelie pushed the to-go mug away from her and stared steadily out the window. "Apparently, Quentin liked to play at the club, and he played without Janine. She worked; he didn't. He ran around on her a lot. Suffice it to say, she was sick of it."

Bile rose unexpectedly. She hadn't expected to be so affected by relating that terrible tragedy in her past when her life had changed forever—even though the memory was always so raw and ugly when she allowed herself to think about it.

"The night before it happened, I was studying in my room. I had a huge final the next day in one of my classes. I also had to put a couple of extra hours in on the books at work. Alan said he'd gone over them and added in income from one of the vendors he'd forgotten, but he'd done it incorrectly and messed everything up. In any case, I knew I had to get up around four in the morning. I had already set my alarm and was in my pajamas but was up studying. Janine came into my room and I could tell she was really upset."

A huge ball of acid threatened to choke her. For a terrible moment she couldn't breathe. Andrii transferred one hand to the nape of her neck, his fingers strong as they massaged her there.

"Take a deep breath. You don't have to tell me anything else if you can't, Zelie." He indicated the bottle of water on the table. "You need to drink that. A slow sip. You're here with me. Safe. You're not anywhere near that man or what he did to you or the ones you love."

Azelie was grateful he didn't use the past tense when he referred to her loving her deceased family. She did still love them. She would always love them. She took the bottle of water he pushed into her hand and drank from it. The cool water did help ease the blockage in her throat. The fingers massaging her neck never stopped moving.

She'd felt alone for a very long time. Nobody had touched her since her sister had died. She didn't want anyone to get close to her. She moistened her lips. "She came into my room that night." Her voice was husky with pain. "She came in and lay down on the bed right next to me. I had my books strewn all over the bed, and Janine kind of pushed them onto the floor, and we both started laughing. And then she started crying. That's when she told me she had to leave Quentin before her self-esteem was completely gone and she could never look her children or me in the face or at herself in the mirror again."

Quentin had been gone again that evening, as he had so many other nights when Janine had told her she'd had enough. She had everything in place for all of them to leave. She was taking the children and she wanted Azelie to go with them. They would move out of the house to a smaller place Janine could afford on her own. She hated that Azelie had had to contribute or they couldn't afford the rent in the neighborhood where Quentin insisted on living. Azelie had told her of course she would go.

"By that time, I didn't like Quentin or his sense of entitlement. I despised the fact that he cheated on my sister and didn't work or contribute financially."

Janine was very much like Azelie—she had a personality that needed to nurture others. She enjoyed taking care of her man. She didn't mind that she was the one earning the money or that she cooked the meals and cleaned the house. Even after the children came along, it had been Janine who took care of them. Quentin, more and more, spent time with Alan at the club. He came home drunk, reminding Azelie of her mother when she would show up belligerent and stinking of alcohol.

"He must have realized Janine was taking the children and leaving him. I don't know if he saw the suitcases or what tipped him off."

She pressed her fingertips to her mouth, shocked that she kept talking to him when she was so careful not to talk to anyone. It didn't help that he knew her boss. She had a distant relationship with Alan, but she was afraid of him. After doing his books for so many years, she knew he was a criminal. Not just a common petty criminal, but he was involved in things she didn't want any part of. She didn't want to know about them. No one generated the kind of money he had, especially the way the payoffs came in, without being super dirty. The kind of dirty she feared could get her killed.

She *never* should have told a virtual stranger that she'd fixed Alan's books. What kind of power did this man have that she was blurting out intimate details of her life to him?

She wanted to run from the coffee shop and hide in her tiny studio apartment.

"Zelie." He said her name softly, in that velvet voice that seemed to turn her inside out. "You've been through a lot for one your age. I can't change the past, but I can do my best to make your future as safe and as happy as possible."

Azelie had no idea how to respond. She didn't believe anyone could keep her safe. If a man could kill the woman and children he was supposed to love and cherish, how could she ever believe in anyone? Her father had abandoned her. Her mother had done the same, just slower, choosing to drink herself to death. Azelie had lived with Quentin from a very young age, yet he had attempted to kill her along with her sister, niece and nephew. There were no feelings there. None. She didn't—couldn't—allow herself to believe in anyone. That way led to disaster. She was barely keeping her head above water emotionally as it was. Keeping to herself was the most intelligent strategy she could have.

"I've got work to do this afternoon and promised a friend of mine I'd go to a club with him tonight. Tomorrow, around five-thirty, will you meet me here?"

She didn't answer him. Couldn't. How could she agree when she wasn't certain she could resist him?

"Let me have your phone number, and I'll give you mine." He already had his cell out and was looking at her expectantly.

Azelie had no idea why she complied, but she found herself exchanging information with him.

"I'd like to take you to one of the nicer restaurants. Wear a dress for me. Something short and clingy to show off your beautiful figure." He tipped his head to one side, his eyes going silver. "With your coloring, you could pull off red. Or deep purple. Vibrant. Your hair is gorgeous. Wear it down. Smoky eyes. Silver would look beautiful on you. Surprise me."

He stood up, towering over her. She couldn't speak. Couldn't make a sound. He was the most intimidating, gorgeous man she'd ever encountered, and she just wanted to stare at him forever.

"Zelie." He leaned down. Two fingers slipped under her chin and raised it very gently, but decisively, forcing her head up. "Say you'll meet me here tomorrow at five-thirty. I have to leave, and I can't be late."

His voice moved over her skin like the brush of velvet.

She wanted to shake her head and say no, but he mesmerized her. She wasn't certain why it was important to her to please him—but it was.

"Yes."

"Good girl." He touched her lower lip with the pad of his index finger, turned and sauntered out.

Touching her lips with trembling fingers, she stared out the window as she watched him walk down the sidewalk. Very carefully she stood up, deliberately turning her back on the sight of him. What in the world was wrong with her? Why had she agreed to meet him for dinner? She had actually agreed to wear a dress for him. She had temporarily lost her mind.

He really was like a mythical hero in one of the books—the romance books she read. She secretly wanted a home and a man who would love her. She'd learned not to give in to her needs, and she wasn't about to allow a man—a stranger—to shatter her hard-won feelings of independence and courage. She deserved everything she'd fought for, and she wasn't taking one step back. Not one. It didn't matter how gorgeous he was. Or what kind of voice he had. It didn't matter that he affected her the way he did. She had to stay on her present course.

The moment the door to the coffee shop closed behind Andrii, the merry widows rushed to Azelie's tiny table, the three of them giggling like schoolgirls. Penny fanned herself.

"You just struck *gold*," China said. "We tried to hear what

you were talking about, but he speaks so low. So do you."
She made it an accusation.

"Did he ask you out?" Blanc wanted to know.

"Give us the details, girl," Penny insisted.

Azelie found she didn't have to say very much. She wasn't
about to tell them she'd made a total fool of herself, but she
did admit Andrii had asked her out. That sent the merry
widows into a fluttery frenzy, allowing her to sit back and
wonder how she'd gotten herself into such a mess.

TWO

"What do you think, Maestro?" Lyov "Steele" Russak, the vice president of Torpedo Ink, asked. "We're under the gun with this one. You don't have a lot of time to get the job done if Billows is holding prisoners. We don't know if he's gotten in a new shipment of victims, but we need to find out."

Steele might be one of the younger members of the club, but he was highly intelligent and a skilled surgeon and, most importantly, he had developed his abilities to be able to heal with his mind and hands. Married to Breezy, he was the only member of their club besides their president with a young son.

Two hundred eighty-seven children were taken from their parents and placed in a school run by a high-powered man. He had their families murdered, and those children were to be shaped into assets for their country—taught to be assassins. The instructors were sadistic pedophiles who grew crueler as they were encouraged to treat the children any way they desired. Only eighteen survived the vicious abuses of the school. At least they believed only eighteen survived. Recently, a nineteenth survivor had joined them.

His name was Rurik "Destroyer" Volkov. Destroyer was a large man covered in prison tattoos, as he'd spent a great deal of time in one of the worst prisons in Russia. He was still learning to be a part of the Torpedo Ink world.

The club members were in their meeting room, where they often met when discussing club business. The room was large, with a bank of windows on one side allowing views of the ocean. The table was huge, oval in shape and made of solid oak.

Torpedo Ink had purchased the old paymaster's building in Caspar to renovate into their existing clubhouse as well as the surrounding land. The compound was extremely large and was surrounded by a high chain-link fence. Razor wire on top of the fence and tall rolling gates gave the appearance of a fortress. The side yard was a full acre with views of the ocean, and held fire pits, benches and the beginning of gardens. Most of the meadow was still wildflowers and brush, but they were slowly taming it.

The common room was very spacious. A long curving bar with a gleaming oak finish was on one side of the room. Stools were pushed up to the bar. In the center of the room were tables and chairs. On the opposite side from the bar and in front of a gas fireplace comfortable chairs and couches were positioned for conversation. The bedrooms were in the back part of the building, where most outsiders were never invited.

Andrii "Maestro" Federoff shook his head at Steele. "You know these kinds of relationships aren't built overnight. It takes time to build the kind of trust needed between us for me to get the information we want."

"We need to find these women if Billows is holding them. We know he trains them as sex slaves," Steele said. "If he has victims and they're auctioned off before we can get to them, we don't have a prayer of ever getting them back."

Andrii was well aware. He wouldn't have gone along with this assignment if the stakes weren't so high.

Viktor "Czar" Prakenskii, the president of Torpedo Ink, Maestro's motorcycle club, studied his hard features. Maestro kept his expression a mask. No one wanted Czar's scrutiny. He had a way of seeing into a man or woman and knowing their secrets. Maestro had too many secrets he couldn't afford to expose.

"How hard is this going to be for you?"

The question was put to him in a mild, almost casual tone, but Maestro wasn't deceived. He'd been around the club president since they both were young children. Czar had saved his life on more than one occasion. Maestro was still undecided about whether that was a good thing. On some days, especially when he was around Czar's children or Steele's son, there was a lightness in him he vaguely recognized as happiness. His music gave him peace. He lived for his music. And there was his affinity with wood. At times just being in a work environment, hands on wood, gave him close to the same peace as music gave him.

"Maestro?" Czar pressed. Czar was a big man and very strong. His blue-gray eyes often could turn a liquid silver when he focused wholly on someone. His hair, worn long and usually pulled back at the nape of his neck, was black but streaked with silver.

Maestro knew he was taking too long to answer. Just thinking about Zelie sent strange waves of euphoria snaking through him. He didn't like the foreign sensation.

Maestro lifted one dark eyebrow, a smirk appearing briefly. "Easy target. She isn't going to be a problem. I made the approach. The connection was solid immediately." His smirk faded. "I'll say this much. She's gorgeous, intelligent and the real deal. That combination doesn't come along very often. In fact, I've never seen it. Not ever. Not once in all the women I've been with."

There was a stunned silence. The other members seated in the meeting room exchanged long shocked looks. "You're really attracted to her," Lazar "Keys" Alexeev blurted out.

Keys was his best friend. Together they played in the band Crows Flying. They owned a construction business, 287 Construction, with the two other band members. Keys and Maestro guarded Steele whether he liked it or not—and he didn't like it. They made it their business to keep him and his family safe. Keys had wide shoulders, dark hair and hazel eyes. He looked fit, his arms bulging with muscle that was more genetic than built in a gym.

"She got me hard as a fuckin' rock," Maestro admitted. "She didn't do anything but sit there looking at her tablet, with the sun shining through the window hitting all that hair."

Czar frowned. "That could be a problem for you, Maestro. Finding someone who fits with you and knowing you're deceiving her can take a toll."

Maestro's gut tightened unexpectedly. He didn't know why Zelie affected him the way she did. He didn't trust women or outsiders. He couldn't imagine anyone ever changing his mind. His childhood and teenage years had been horrific, thanks to the many betrayals and, worse, him losing those he cared about because they refused to listen. They refused to acknowledge anyone else's expertise.

He'd seen that trait in a few of the women his Torpedo Ink brethren had chosen for partners. He could never—would never—be able to put up with that type of what he considered reckless and willful disobedience. He knew he was a control freak when it came to anyone he cared for. The fear of losing them was so strong that he often said and did things that even his sisters and brothers in Torpedo Ink didn't understand. How could they, when he barely understood how he had become the way he was?

"She's a mark, Czar," Maestro reiterated, more for himself than Czar. "We have no idea if she's involved. This is the first time we've had solid information on anyone high up in this trafficking ring. How long have we been working on it? Two years? Three? How many women and children have been lost because we couldn't find names or places to look for them?"

All members were present as usual when they were deciding on something important. They might follow Czar, their president's, lead, but the policy was that everyone had a voice. The original members of Torpedo Ink had been joined by two of Czar's birth brothers, Gavriil and Casimir. Stamped with the Prakenskii looks, both had been held and trained in Sorbacov's schools of horror. The schools they attended weren't quite as bad as the one Czar had been taken to, but they suffered their own horrors, and more than once, Gavriil had been brought to Czar's school as a threat.

Torpedo Ink had one newly patched member, Fatei "Rock" Molchalin. Fatei had been with them almost from the beginning. He'd gone to the same school in Russia that Gavriil had attended. He didn't have the obvious muscle many of the Torpedo Ink members had, but he was strong and could always be counted on. They'd begun calling him Rock because he was the one they had learned over time they could count on. He was a quiet, intelligent man, and had proved his loyalty over and over.

"Unfortunately, he's right," Code said. Code was their main source of information. He could handle computers the way race car drivers drove on a speedway. When Code had been brought into the basement of the school where the other children were, he had been thin and frail, his eyes weak. Czar had recognized the genius, tenacity and loyalty in him. Code was a survivor and extremely valuable to Torpedo Ink. He was anything but thin and frail now. He had developed the physical strength to match his enormous intelligence. It didn't take much for him to get on the scent of a trail and track down whatever the club needed. But the hierarchy of the trafficking ring had eluded them. They were able, at times, to stop auctions and free the women and teens used for prostitution against their will, but those successes seemed few and far between.

"If we can't utilize this information and get to Alan Billows before he sends out the next batch of sex slaves he could be training, they'll be lost. We won't be able to get any of them back," Code added.

"But we don't know if this girl—woman—is involved," Alena "Torch" Koval objected. "Shouldn't we get more information on her before we destroy her self-esteem? We've learned the hard way that we should be more careful of how we handle human beings."

That was Alena. She tried to be tough, but she was soft on the inside. She'd given Maestro the premature silver streaks in his hair. Alena, like all of Torpedo Ink, had been trained to be an assassin. She was good at her job but lacked the toughness the rest of them had. She had compassion and empathy. Unfortunately, that could get her killed.

Alena was a beautiful woman, in Maestro's opinion, both inside and out. With her curvy body, platinum hair and icy blue eyes, she was striking. Coupled with her fast thinking and compassionate heart, she was extraordinary. Maestro thought of her as a younger sibling, a sister he protected even though she didn't believe she needed it. Younger birth sister of two Torpedo Ink members, Dmitry "Storm" Koval and Isaak "Ice" Koval, she owned the Crow 287 restaurant. Alena's ability to cook was undisputed.

Maestro tried to be fair. "I believe we need to act on the information we have. It took us too long to get it, and if we miss this opportunity, we may not get another one." If he was being honest with himself, he wanted to spend time with Zelie. He also wanted to do the right thing if Billows was holding prisoners.

"I watched her pay for two different orders for a couple of women who clearly needed it and couldn't afford it. She didn't make a big deal of it and did it anonymously. She often treats the older women who refer to themselves as the merry widows," he conceded.

"I looked into her financials," Code said. "She doesn't have much, but she's still generous to others. We've had eyes on her for three weeks, and she consistently helps the homeless, seniors, new mothers, and single dads. Most of her money goes to pay for her school, and living in San Francisco is expensive, even in a small studio apartment like hers."

Maestro found that last bit of information regarding single fathers irritating, which made no sense. "On a different day, I saw her help an older lady when the woman was confused, and two teenagers were laughing at her. Zelie gave them a look that said 'back off' and took care of the woman, making certain she had her purse, glasses and food."

Alena sighed as she drummed her fingers on the end table beside the comfortable chair she occupied. "She doesn't sound like the kind of woman who would be involved in a human trafficking ring." She tilted her head to look up at the president of their club. "You tell us all the time that we need to find a way to fit into society. That we should keep learning to be better people. Taking this poor girl's life apart and destroying all trust, to get information she may not even have, doesn't sound like we're progressing to me."

"Alena." Maestro spoke as gently as possible. "I know you've experienced betrayal time and again. It hurts, but it can also make you strong. I'm not going in with a bulldozer. We know she has information that could be vital to us. She's central to getting inside the underground rooms situated below the nightclubs. She has keys to those rooms."

Maksimos "Ink" Korask, their resident and extremely popular tattoo artist, weighed in. He had wide shoulders and dark hair. His body was covered in tattoos, mostly of animals and birds. Ink was a phenomenal artist and had an affinity with the animals tattooed on his body. He owned Black Ink Tattoo, a popular tattoo parlor in the small town of Caspar.

"We've spent more than two years trying to get names, anything at all, to help us find a way to break this ring. If Billows has women trapped in those rooms below his club, we need to get them out of there. We also need answers from Billows."

Savva "Reaper" Pajari and his younger brother, Savin "Savage" Pajari, were the sergeants at arms for the club. Savage rarely spoke, but when he did, they all listened. He shaved his head to keep his blond curls away. He had shockingly blue eyes, and his very appearance often was enough of a deterrent when other bikers wanted to cause fights in the Torpedo Ink Roadhouse, a bar the club owned and operated.

"We can't interrogate Billows until we know where those

keys are kept. Breaking into the underground rooms hasn't been a viable solution. Too many risks. We need the keys. Hell, we don't even know where the entrance is. Maestro, do you believe you can get them from her?"

Maestro had no doubt that, given time, he would be able to search for the keys and make a copy when he found them. Zelie would have to trust him enough to allow him to roam freely in her studio apartment. They'd already searched her living space multiple times when she was out but hadn't found the keys to the rooms below the club.

"I told you, give me the time and I'll get everything we need from her. She's extremely susceptible to me." He didn't add that he was also susceptible to her, but somehow, he must have given it away.

Steele gave him a hard look. "You need me to send Keys in?"

Maestro allowed himself to appear a little disconcerted. "Why would you do that?"

"You reacted to her. You've never reacted to any woman."

"She's a fuckin' mark, Steele. For all we know, she could be the brains behind this operation. I'd be shocked, but she's smart enough. She's into their books. I don't see how she could see their books every day for all these years and not know what's going on. Maybe not the trafficking, but she knows this owner is dirty. She actually told me that the first time she ever did the books for Billows she kept him out of prison, and she was only sixteen."

There was silence for a moment. Czar shook his head. "Sixteen years old and she's cooking the books for one of the worst criminals we've come across."

"I think she's a genius when it comes to numbers and patterns," Maestro admitted. "How else could she manage those books at such a young age?"

Steele sighed. "That's one more strike against her, Maestro. She's intelligent enough to keep Billows safe from IRS scrutiny, and she's worked for him for at least seven years. It seems a little far-fetched that she doesn't know."

"I disagree, Steele," Alena objected. "She's looking at numbers. She doesn't necessarily know where the money is coming from."

"There has to be some accounting." Kir "Master" Vasiliev was their treasurer and a genius with numbers and making money. Code would steal it from the targets they chose to go after, and Master invested it, making them even more money. He was tall with dark hair and ripped the way most of them were. He'd recently married Ambrie, and that, Maestro had to admit, had turned Master's life around. "You don't just have numbers without some explanation."

"Before Billows has her come in to work on the books," Lana "Widow" Popov backed up Alena, "it would be easy enough for him to make shit up."

Lana was gorgeous; there was no getting around her looks. Tall, with a curvy body and shiny black hair like a raven's wing, she had a way of walking and talking that was pure seduction. She was tougher than Alena, although the same age. Her birth brother, Kasimir "Preacher" Popov, was older than she was and extremely protective of her, not that Lana ever wanted any of his protection.

Czar sighed and swept a hand through his hair. "There are good arguments for both sides. Maestro, you're the one who will have to put in the work and be with this woman day and night. You're the one setting her up. There's always a danger in that. If there's anyone in this room who understands the damage betrayal can do, it's you. No matter how many times you tried to save the girls in that school, it was impossible. That took its toll on you as well. I don't want you taking this assignment if it will make things worse for you."

Maestro shrugged. "I don't feel I'm in jeopardy in any way."

He honestly didn't know if that was the truth. He knew it would have been true in any other circumstance, with any other woman. He believed they needed to find where the kidnapped women and children were being taken. He wanted to find out how to get to them before they were sold if Billows was holding prisoners. He absolutely believed in what they were doing.

He'd been imprisoned for years, from the time he was a child, at the mercy of sadistic pedophiles. He knew what the life of a sex slave would be. He'd seen it. Lived it. The purpose of Torpedo Ink was to eliminate as much trafficking as they could. They found pedophiles, took back their victims, returned them to families or took them in if they had nowhere to go. The pedophiles were eliminated, sometimes in not-so-nice ways.

Maestro wasn't a man to take an interest in outsiders, particularly women. He partied hard at times but walked away quickly from any entanglements. He didn't *feel*. That was the bottom line. He'd never met a woman who got under his skin—until Azelie.

Shadowing Zelie these past few weeks, watching her closely, hearing her soft laughter as she teased the merry widows and their gentlemen friends, gutted him. She had slipped into his veins, the fire burning slow until he found himself thinking about her night and day. That was unlike him, and anything out of the ordinary raised an alarm. He didn't trust emotions—not his anyway, not when it came to women.

Maestro gave the president of Torpedo Ink a look of complete confidence. He felt confident in his ability to manipulate the situation. Zelie was younger than him by a good ten years. He was very experienced when it came to women. She had no experience when it came to men. A man like Maestro could chew her up and spit her out.

When he thought too much about this job, a tiny nagging emotion he couldn't identify but didn't like surfaced. Was it shame? He knew betrayal. He had lived a lifetime of betrayal. Women weren't to be counted on. Neither were most men. He told himself this woman wasn't any different from the ones who had betrayed him over and over. She deserved whatever happened working for a slime bag like Alan Billows. He knew she was intelligent. He couldn't get sucked into feeling sympathy for her because she'd lost her family in much the same way he'd lost his and the others in Torpedo Ink had lost theirs.

Young women and children were being ripped from their homes, trained as sex slaves and sold to the highest bidder. Torpedo Ink had to find them. Maestro believed that. It was the vow they'd taken together. Yeah, they had a code they lived by, but that code was between the club members. Anyone involved in trafficking of any kind was fair game.

Czar pinned Maestro with his piercing gaze. "You're willing to see this through."

"No problem." He did his best to sound casual when that weird emotion nagged at him. "I'm looking forward to it." That was the truth. He wanted a chance to spend time with Zelie. Really get to know her in every sense of the word. "I haven't been around a true submissive in years. I'm sure that's the only reason my body responded to her the way it did. It gave me a rush like I haven't experienced since I was a kid." He didn't think she was submissive, more a woman who needed to care for her man, to please him. That was even more intriguing to him.

Steele and Keys exchanged a long look. Maestro noted both expressions held apprehension. Even alarm. The others knew him, but not like Keys or Steele. Keys and Maestro guarded Steele and his family, which often meant they stayed in his home and interacted with him on a regular basis.

"Explain, please," Fatei "Rock" said.

Maestro exchanged a look with Savage. Savage knew exactly what he was talking about. "I can spot a submissive a mile away, even if the woman isn't aware she is one. In Zelie's case, she must know she's a pleaser. A nurturer. She's too intelligent not to recognize those traits in herself. She doesn't think of herself as submissive, and she doesn't mind pleasing the people she loves or even likes."

"Would it follow that if she liked Alan Billows, she would please him by assisting him with his trafficking ring?" Fatei asked.

"Not necessarily," Savage denied. "A submissive isn't necessarily passive or docile. Oftentimes they are very intelligent and don't go along with just anyone. They might avoid confrontation, but they don't give their submission easily."

Maestro continued the explanation when he read confusion on Fatei's face. "A submissive doesn't just turn over their trust to anyone. One has to work at earning it."

"So, what you're saying is you would get this woman to fall in love with you?" Fatei asked.

"Not necessarily," Savage denied. "It's possible for a submissive to spend time with a dominant, give him her trust, but neither falls in love. They can have a long-distance relationship where they meet up every month or two and both are satisfied because their needs are being met."

"A sexual relationship only?" Fatei pressed.

"For the most part," Maestro agreed. Instinctively, he knew Azelie would never turn over her trust to any man without being in love with him. He felt it prudent not to mention that.

"In your school, with all the training they put you through, you must have seen submissive girls," Savage said.

It was Gavriil who answered. "Our school wasn't exactly the same as the one you attended, Savage. There was training in sex, admittedly all kinds of sex, but it was simply part of the curriculum and not the central theme. We weren't subjected to pedophiles on a daily basis, female or male. We had instructors who enjoyed inflicting pain, but it wasn't necessarily sexual. We weren't exposed to submissives long enough to learn about them or why they are the way they are."

Savage again answered. "It's rare to find a true submissive, one willing to give her trust to you more than sexually. It's even rarer to find someone truly competitive and have that woman give you her complete trust. If she falls in love with you and you're like I am, you know you have gold. The treasure. You do whatever it takes to keep her and give the best of you in return."

Maestro wouldn't have revealed so much information to everyone, but then he tended to keep his mouth shut most of the time. He came alive when he played his music or when he worked with wood. Sometimes, when he was around Czar and Blythe's children, he found a way to be much more forthcoming, but it was never with information he felt was personal.

He had no trouble sharing his opinion and did so often. He just felt like there was no place for emotions in discussions. When others felt passionate about subjects, he knew he wasn't going to change their mind—so what was the point of expressing his opinion?

"Do you believe Azelie would be open to having a sexual relationship without any commitment on your part?" Lana asked.

Maestro's heart dropped. That was the last question he wanted to answer. The policy had always been the members of Torpedo Ink didn't lie to one another. They didn't use their gifts on one another, only *for* one another.

Silence stretched out and tension rose. Maestro finally sighed and shook his head. "I doubt that she's capable of a relationship only involving sex. I don't know for certain; that's just a gut feeling. I only just made contact with her."

"When are you seeing her again?" There was concern in Czar's voice.

"Tomorrow night. I've made reservations for dinner at a romantic restaurant with a view of the Bay. It wasn't easy to get that reservation. I had to throw quite a bit of money their way to be first in line for a cancellation. Fortunately, one came up and I was able to get us in."

"Do you know what kinds of food she eats?" Alena asked. "Is she vegetarian?"

Code answered. "No, she does enjoy fish, and the restaurant is renowned for its fish menu. I gave Maestro all her preferences."

"We went over the most romantic restaurants with the best menus that she might enjoy," Keys added. "We didn't leave anything to chance."

"Although I almost blew it," Maestro admitted. "I asked her

out and told her what I'd like her to wear and realized after that if she wasn't spending money on extras, she wouldn't have a cocktail dress and shoes for the occasion. That would just give her an excuse to get out of going to dinner with me. I'm certain she's looking for one."

"How did you handle the problem?" Fatei asked.

"Sent her an apology and bought a dress and shoes and asked Ice to provide jewelry. The dress will look killer on her. Very feminine, silver, clingy, but good taste. She'll look sexy in it, but I'm hoping she won't feel on display."

Lana's eyebrow shot up. "You aren't testing her right off the bat?"

"Everything is a test with a submissive, Lana," Maestro said. "If she chooses to wear the dress and heels for me, she's passed the test. She doesn't dress this way as a rule. In fact, she covers up her figure. Asking her to wear the dress and heels is going to take her out of her comfort zone. If she wears them for me and doesn't cancel, I think I have a very good chance with her. She's a pleaser. She should want to do the things I ask because she wants to make me happy. That's how it works."

"It's bullshit," Alena protested.

"It has to be done if we want the information," Czar said. "I don't think any of us like it, but that doesn't mean we aren't going to do it. We've had to do much worse things in order to survive or to take back women and children."

"That's true," Alena agreed, "but I thought the point of moving here and putting down roots was to learn to be better people. How does destroying this young woman make us better, Czar? Do we have the right to decide, before we know whether or not she's involved, to potentially destroy her? We know she lost her family and how. We know she was shot several times. After what we put Anya through with an interrogation, and Seychelle, not accepting her the way we should have, haven't we learned anything?"

"Babe," Maestro said gently. "You know we need this. I'll do my best to handle her with kid gloves."

Alena shook her head and looked down at the table. "You have strong opinions when it comes to what a woman's place should be. You're like Savage when it comes to meting out punishment. Forgive me for being blunt, Maestro, but your past with women is horrific. I wouldn't want to believe that you might take out your very justified anger on a woman who did nothing to any of us."

There was silence again. Alena continued to stare at the gleaming oak that made up the top of the table.

"Honey, look at me." Maestro's voice was velvet soft, but compelling.

Reluctantly, Alena's gaze met his. She looked miserable, and he could see the guilt in her eyes over her all-too-real fear.

"I swear to you, I'll do my best to handle this situation right. I'm not looking to hurt anyone, especially this woman."

Alena swallowed and nodded.

"That's it, then," Czar said. "If you need any help, let us know."

"If I get in with her, we'll need a club to go to, one we can control," Maestro said.

"I'm working on that," Code assured him.

Maestro stayed for a short period of time visiting with the others before he walked out. He was already packed to make the ride back to San Francisco. Keys would be going with him. They would have backup from Mechanic and Transporter. Eventually, when needed, the others would come.

Keys was already outside, leaning against the chain-link fence, regarding him with exasperation. "Cut the crap, Maestro. I've been on this mission with you for the last few weeks studying this woman. We both know she's more than a mark for you. If you do this, you're going to lose her, and you can't afford to do that."

"We don't know if she's involved or not."

"We've watched her for three straight weeks helping little kids and old people nonstop. She's generous and caring. You really think she's involved in human trafficking? And why is she taking college classes the way she is? She'd have money if she was involved, wouldn't she? She's barely getting by, even writing her books," Keys pointed out.

"Maybe. And maybe she's smart enough to hide her money. I'm telling you, just talking to her, she's far more intelligent than Alan Billows," Maestro said. He rubbed his jaw with the pad of his thumb. "She's scary smart. Soft and sweet and scary smart."

"Listen to you. I've never heard you like this. Or seen you like this over a woman. You can't blow this, Maestro. You know how it is for us. Women just don't come along for the kinds of people we are."

"I'm not about to get led around by my dick like Czar and Player and, hell, even Savage," Maestro declared. "I know women can't be trusted. I'm not going to be the mark here."

"Is that what you think?" Keys asked. "You need to really think about this before you take it any further."

Maestro sighed. "I did think about it. We both separately went into the coffee shop several times. She didn't react when you went in. She nearly dropped her coffee and couldn't stop looking every time I went in. At no time did she show interest in any other man. It's me or it's no one, Keys. It's my job because she reacts to me. And as much as I don't want to admit it, I wouldn't want you or anyone else to seduce her. I don't think I could take it, and that's me being real."

"Maestro, she told you very personal details about the night her family was murdered. Those are things she wouldn't have told to someone else. You know that. You can't seduce her, betray her and then think you can have the kind of relationship you need with her after it's all over. If you want this woman, you're going to have to come clean with Czar and Steele and tell them the truth."

Maestro pushed off the fence. "What the fuck is the truth, Keys? That I expect a fairy tale? I think I'm getting a happy ever after? I don't believe it for a minute. I'll do the job, and the only way I can do it is to go all in."

"Czar has the happy ever after," Keys pointed out.

"I'm not Czar." Maestro stayed silent, letting the ice in his veins make its way to his heart. He couldn't afford to think too much about the sound of Zelie's voice when she told him about her family being murdered. He had glaciers surrounding his heart. It had to stay that way while he worked. "Tell me what you would do, Keys. Women and children are being trafficked. No one's looking for them. Someone has to stop these people. This is our first real lead. We don't know whether she's part of the pipeline or not, but we know her boss is."

"You saw her. You heard her," Keys persisted.

"Yeah, I did," Maestro admitted, trying not to sound as bitter as he felt. The taste of blood was in his mouth. He felt the sharp blade of the knife as it retreated from his body. The hot lash of the whip as it tore strips of skin from his back. The burn of shame and humiliation for once again trusting a female. Betrayal tasted bitter.

THREE

With shaking hands, Azelie opened the box that had come unexpectedly. She had texted Andrii that she was sorry, she wasn't going to be able to make their dinner date. She hadn't told him she didn't have the clothes to wear to an upscale restaurant—but she didn't. She'd gone through every single item in her closet and realized even if she knew for certain she wanted to go, she couldn't.

The worst of it was—she did want to see him again. She wanted to spend time with him. He'd texted her back asking for an address where he could have a delivery made. Thinking he was sending flowers, she gave him the address of her building. A part of her knew she shouldn't, but she didn't want to cut ties with him.

The box had arrived at four, an hour and a half before they would have gone on their first date. Heart beating too fast, Azelie stared at the large rectangular box for several minutes before she managed to get the courage to open what clearly wasn't flowers.

Her breath caught in her throat when she moved the tissue paper aside to reveal a shimmering silver minidress.

There were heels, stockings, garters, earrings, a necklace and a note.

> It occurred to me I took too much for granted. I wasn't thinking about anything but the chance to spend time with you. I really would like to see you tonight. Please wear this for me. I'll come by your building at five-fifteen to pick you up. M

Silver sequins sparkled as Azelie carefully lifted the dress from the box. It was beautiful. More so than anything she'd ever worn. It was also more daring than anything she'd ever considered wearing. The dress had a plunging neckline leading to a twist in the fabric at the waist. Fully lined, with a deep V back, the fabric would cling like a second skin, showing off her body. She'd never done that before either. The label in the dress simply read, Label 287.

Her breath caught in her throat. She had often looked at the clothing from Label 287, but she had never bought anything, not even the most casual blouse, although she longed to. The fabrics were always soft, and each design looked sensual. The designer only sold limited editions of her work. If you didn't order immediately, you might not get your choice because there was a high chance of each piece being sold out within days or sometimes even hours. She couldn't justify spending the money when she needed it to stay in San Francisco and continue going to school.

The garters looked sexy, and the stockings were silk. The heels were shocking. Silver glitter-covered leather. She recognized the brand immediately, although she had never owned a pair and only knew about them because Janine had been saving her money for shoes from that designer. The slim band of glittered leather buckled around the ankle. The stilettos were at least four inches high, closer to five.

Then there was the jewelry. She didn't own jewelry and had no idea what real jewelry was or how to tell the difference.

That was probably a good thing because if the drop earrings were real diamonds she would have fainted. The necklace was a silver choker with sparkling diamonds she hoped weren't real.

Nested in the bottom of the box was a barely there scrap of underwear. Just looking at it made her mouth go dry and her heart beat even faster. She desperately wanted to try the dress on, to see how she looked and felt in it.

Telling herself she didn't have to go through with the date, she dressed carefully. She'd already taken a long bath, the way she often did on her day off from school. She was grateful she'd bathed in scented water. She had to admit, just putting on the thong, garters and silk stockings made her feel sexier than she'd ever felt.

The dress clung to her body like a second skin, emphasizing her abundant curves. She had often tried to lose weight. She worked out and ran every day, but her body had curves. She didn't lose weight the way she wanted, and eventually she decided with her body type, she'd just cover up. The dress showed every curve. She couldn't wear a bra with the dress, and the plunging neckline showed the high rounded curves of her breasts.

After she did her makeup with the smoky eyes Andrii had requested, Azelie stared at herself for a long time. She didn't look slutty the way she feared she might. She looked sexy—almost beautiful. Certainly not the way she normally looked.

She did her lips in a rose-petal red and then allowed her hair to fall in its usual mass of wild curls and waves down her back and around her face. She didn't like that she couldn't see the earrings when they were so beautiful, so she pulled the sides of her hair up and fixed them in a fancy twist. She thought that might complement the dress and show off the beautiful earrings.

For the first time in her life, she thought she looked beautiful. Even sexy. More than anything, she wanted to go to dinner with Andrii. That would mean she would have to pay him back for the dress and shoes. She could give the jewelry back to him unless it was costume jewelry—in that case she was going to keep it, even if it was on the expensive side. It would be wonderful just knowing she had the dress and shoes in her closet.

How was she going to get to the coffee shop? She didn't want to chance riding the bus in the dress. She'd probably get robbed. She could wear a long coat and her tennis shoes and change. She picked up the note and read it again. He had a definite masculine scrawl. He'd signed it with a single letter. Not *A*, but *M*. What did that mean?

The last line told her he'd come for her at her apartment building. It probably hadn't been the best idea to text him her address. She knew better than to trust any man with her safety, but somehow her need to see Andrii again superseded common sense. She glanced at the clock. He would be arriving soon. She didn't really have the time to tell him not to come, that she wasn't going after all.

She searched through her closet for a decent coat or sweater to wear with the dress. She had nothing. A puffy jacket and vest. That wasn't going to go with the outfit. She didn't want to ruin the look. She stared at herself for a long time debating and, in the end, decided she would go without a coat. It was San Francisco at night, which meant it would be cold, but she was willing to hope the inside of the restaurant was warm enough.

She picked up the little glittery bag that contained her ID, credit card and emergency cash. She was smart enough to know if things didn't work out, she might need to find her own way home. No matter how attractive she found him, Andrii was a stranger. She had already broken enough of her rules just agreeing to go out with him.

Azelie texted him that she would be waiting downstairs. She didn't want him coming up to her apartment. For one thing, he was obviously far wealthier than she was. She didn't want him seeing her tiny space. And she didn't want to forever picture him there. Or smell his cologne. Maybe it wasn't cologne—maybe it was his natural scent. Whatever it was, she found Andrii Federoff intoxicating.

She tried not to obsess over the man as she took the elevator down to the first floor. She couldn't help trying to dissect why she was so enamored with him when she wasn't attracted to other men. When she was with him, she felt like she was under a spell. His voice mesmerized her. Sadness lurked in his eyes, and it felt very genuine to her. She found herself wanting to do whatever it would take to make him happy.

He was plainspoken, telling her exactly his feelings and what he found attractive about her sexually. She heard honesty in his voice. He might have sounded crude, but she had the feeling he did that deliberately to see if she would be offended. She had considered, for one brief moment, pretending to be. But if he was being honest with her, she wanted to be just as honest with him. She admitted to herself that the things he said to her sent heat waves through her body.

She reached the first floor to wait by the door for a car. She should have texted him to find out what he was driving. It was difficult to find parking in San Francisco. She had a space in the lot at the apartment building where she could park a car if she owned one, but she preferred the bus system so she wouldn't have to try to find parking everywhere she traveled. She'd been using buses and the BART system for so long she knew the various connections and stops without looking at maps.

She hadn't been waiting more than three minutes when a BMW pulled up to the front of her building and Andrii stepped out of the car. Instantly, Azelie couldn't breathe. He was incredibly gorgeous in a dark suit. The jacket emphasized his wide shoulders and deep chest. When he moved up the walkway toward the building, his gait was so smooth he appeared to be gliding—or prowling like a great jungle cat.

Azelie had no idea why she was so susceptible to him, but she couldn't take her eyes off him. Draped over one arm appeared to be a full-length coat that clearly was too small for him. Her heart accelerated and a million butterflies took flight in her stomach. He was too thoughtful for words. She didn't think men like him really existed. In her world, they never had.

She stepped out the door of the building just before he reached it, watching his face, needing to see if her appearance pleased him. Andrii's eyes softened and his mouth curved into a smile. Not only was there approval in his eyes, but the way his gaze drifted over her body and returned to her face filled her with a strange pride. His eyes had darkened with intense sensual desire. For her. All for her. She wasn't used to a man's entire focus or admiration, and she felt color sweeping up her neck into her face.

"You look beautiful."

His voice, that compelling velvet voice, played over her skin like the touch of fingers. Goose bumps rose. Her sex clenched. She even went damp. She found herself blinking up at him, unable to speak.

He cupped her chin and tilted her face up toward his. "*Solnyshkuh*, when I give you a very sincere compliment because you are truly the most beautiful woman I've ever seen, it would be nice if you acknowledged it."

His thumb slid along her chin, featherlight, sending flickering heat streaking through her veins. He was truly deadly when it came to seduction.

Azelie swallowed the tight knot in her throat. "Thank you, Andrii."

Immediately, she got a warm look of approval that added a hard knot of desire to the emotions already roiling inside her. She decided honesty was the best policy, even if it was embarrassing.

"When I look at you, or you speak to me in that voice you have, sometimes I find it difficult to breathe, let alone speak." She made the admission in a low tone, but she kept her gaze fixed on his. It was important to see his reaction to her honesty. If he looked amused, she would turn and go straight back to her apartment.

His eyes went from gray to liquid mercury. His expression softened even more. Her heart stuttered at the look of complete approval and desire in his eyes. She had made him happy with her admission.

"Telling me that must have been difficult for you," Andrii said. His voice was always low, even when he sounded commanding, creating an intimacy between them. "Thank you for being so honest with me. When you don't answer me, I'll be more cognizant of giving you time."

He held up the black coat. It was full-length, slim, long-sleeved, straight cut with a tailored neckline. The coat was double breasted with two slanted in-seam pockets. The front closure was enhanced with a wide tone-on-tone belt with a large gold buckle and gold eyelets. The adjustable cuff tabs were gold buckles matching the large one on the belt.

"You aren't allergic to wool or cashmere, are you?" he asked. "I should have asked before I brought this coat. It was just so perfect for you, and I worried you might get cold."

Azelie knew that coat had to cost the earth. It was from that same famous designer, Label 287, which she could never afford in a million years, but then she couldn't afford the dress or shoes. Now she worried that the earrings and necklace might be real.

"I'm not allergic to anything but bug bites," she admitted. She struggled with herself to tell him she couldn't accept the coat, but he was already holding it out for her to put her arms in. She wanted that coat even more than the dress and heels. It was one of the most exquisite items of clothing she'd ever seen.

Andrii wrapped her in the coat and then stood in front of her, cinching the belt. He pulled her long hair from the back of the coat so it flowed down nearly to her waist. He stood regarding her with an approving eye. "That coat was made just for you."

"It's beautiful." She managed to find enough air to get the declaration out, when her lungs felt raw and burning. "I can't thank you enough for the clothes and jewelry. I didn't have anything suitable in my closet and would never have been able to go with you."

Andrii wrapped his arm around her waist and began to walk with her toward the car. Just having his arm around her made her feel safe. Walking with him felt right. He was taller than she was by quite a bit and made her feel almost delicate when she'd always felt awkward. He opened the passenger door for her and handed her in carefully.

The car was pure luxury and warm. Maybe it was the coat. She wasn't certain she'd ever want to take the Label 287 coat off. It made her feel so different, like she had stepped into an alternative world. A fairy tale. Girls like her didn't get happy ever after, and they didn't meet men like Andrii Federoff. She made up her mind to enjoy every single second with him. She wasn't going to waste time on worrying that he might find a way into her closely guarded heart. Just for this one night, she was going to be that fairy-tale princess.

He drove the way he talked and walked. In complete command. Soft music played, a surprising mix of older songs by Frank Sinatra and Perry Como. She didn't think anyone else listened to them. She had a passion for singers from the past.

"I love the music." She managed to tell him without stuttering.

"I play the piano, the guitar and a few other instruments," Andrii disclosed. "I'll admit I particularly love older music, all kinds. This mix is a favorite when I'm driving."

She hugged the information to herself, feeling as if he had bestowed a gift on her. She sensed that he didn't talk about himself much. He had concentrated on her, asking questions when they'd been in the coffee shop, but she didn't know anything about him.

"Do you play in a band?"

"I have three brothers—more like foster brothers; we were raised together. We all play instruments, and we get together and gig sometimes in bars. I go to piano bars and play. Music is soothing to me."

"If you only play occasionally, that clearly isn't your regular job. You said you worked security. Is that what you do full-time?"

She felt very brave asking. He wasn't a man who would want anyone prying into his business. She must have sounded hesitant because he glanced at her, sending a reassuring smile.

"*Solnyshkuh*, we're getting to know one another. I'll let you know if I would prefer not to answer a question. You have every right to do the same. I'm very interested in pursuing a relationship. We can't do that if we don't know each other."

She sent him a tentative smile. "I don't want to make you uncomfortable with questions."

His eyes warmed, going from that piercing, intense silvery color to a softer gray. Her answer, as sincere as it was, meant something to him.

"I own a construction company along with those three brothers. I enjoy working with my hands. Sometimes I design furniture just because the wood speaks to me."

"I'd love to see something you created," she said. "Music and designing furniture. You have the soul of an artist. Security must be your fill-in work."

She'd made that a statement, so he didn't correct her. In any case, finding human traffickers was more on Code. The rest of them just went on the rescue missions.

"Are you concerned about asking me questions because you don't like to answer them?"

Azelie frowned, thinking it over. Eventually, she shook her head. "It isn't that, although I don't tell very many people my business." She hesitated, but he shot her a look that told her he knew she was hedging. "I don't talk to anyone about my business," she admitted. "After my family was killed, there were so many reporters and cops coming around. I'd been shot multiple times and was in the hospital. I couldn't get away from them. I just kept my mouth shut, hoping they would eventually give up and go away."

"You didn't have anyone to protect you?"

His voice had dropped another octave, sending a shiver of awareness down her spine. He wasn't happy that she'd been alone, and no one had watched over her. His voice hadn't really changed, just seemed more intimate, more intense. She wasn't even certain how he did it, but she knew with absolute certainty that her simple explanation had sent a wave of anger through him.

"No. I have no other family. Janine and the children were everything to me." She twisted her fingers together in her lap to keep her hands from shaking. She didn't like thinking about that time in her life, let alone talking about it.

"I can understand why you wouldn't want to disclose your past to just anyone. It must hurt to talk about it." He dropped one large hand over her hands, stilling them. "Do you have nightmares?"

Azelie pressed her lips together, debating whether she wanted to answer that question. He was a man filled with confidence. She felt she appeared weak beside him. She wasn't weak. That was an illusion. Others took her quiet nature for weakness, not strength. She believed there was strength in silence. In getting others to talk while she listened—and remembered. She had an excellent memory. Too good. It was impossible for her to forget the smallest detail of the night her brother-in-law had murdered her family.

"Zelie?"

Again, his voice was velvet soft, but when he looked at her, there was the merest hint of disappointment in his eyes. She detested disappointing him. It made no sense that she seemed to need to please him.

"Yes, I have nightmares."

"Often?"

She bit her lower lip and then forced herself to answer. "Yes."

"Every night?" he pressed as he turned into the parking lot of the Waterfront Restaurant.

The Waterfront building was located at Pier 7. Renovated from an old longshoremen's bar, the building dated back to

1894. It was very San Francisco with its old beams and wood.

The valet parking allowed Andrii to open the car door and help Azelie out. The restaurant had spectacular views of the bay, Bay Bridge, and Treasure Island. The atmosphere inside the restaurant was old, eclectic and comfortable. They were seated immediately at a table for two in a more secluded location with a stunning view of the water.

Andrii helped her out of the coat, although a part of her wanted to cling to it. The only thing that made giving up the warmth and comfort of the coat worth it was seeing the way his gaze drifted over her. The way his expression changed, softening the hard edges yet carving sensual lines deeper. The way his eyes heated with desire and what she identified as pride in her.

Andrii handed her beloved coat to the host as he held out her chair for her. She sat carefully. The dress was shorter than she had ever worn before, and when she sat, the tops of the garters showed. It looked sexy, but she wasn't certain if she liked the way several men in the restaurant looked at her so openly. She wasn't used to male attention.

Nothing escaped Andrii's watchful gaze. He noticed her trembling hand as she picked up the menu. Immediately, he placed his hand over hers. "What is it?"

It took a moment to decide whether to answer honestly. He waited for her, not attempting to hurry her. "I'm not used to so many men looking at me the way they are." The admission came out low and a little unsteady. Again, she maintained eye contact, waiting for his reaction.

"You're a beautiful woman, Zelie. Men are going to look, and they're bound to have reactions to the sight of your body. How could they not? It shouldn't bother you. It's natural. I'm pleased to be the man escorting you."

She resisted the urge to pull at the hem of her dress, but she did look down at the plunging neckline to assure herself that her nipples weren't on display.

As always, Andrii seemed to know what she was concerned

about. "Your tits are gorgeous, *Solnyshkuh*. I love the curve of them and your dress frames them expertly. If there was a malfunction and one slipped out, I would have the pleasure of tucking it back in for you."

His voice slid over her skin like the brush of velvet. Instantly, she was hyperaware of him, her body reacting to the suggestion of him physically touching her. Every nerve ending leapt to life. Her nipples hardened into twin peaks of desire, feeling hot, like twin flames. A knot of sheer lust formed in her stomach. Her sex fluttered. Clenched.

"You're with me, Zelie," he reminded her, his voice gentle. "Trust me to look after you. I am the one that asked you to wear the dress for me, and you did. It's my pleasure and honor to protect you. You wore it because I asked you to, didn't you? It isn't your usual manner of dressing."

Azelie pressed her lips together and nodded. "I did wear it for you," she admitted. "I like pleasing you."

"Does it give you pleasure to please me?" he asked.

A shiver of something far too close to desire went down her spine. It was a strange, intimate conversation to be having with a man—especially one she barely knew. On the other hand, she felt as if they were progressing toward something beyond what she may have imagined.

She nodded again, slower this time. Her mouth felt dry, and her lungs burned for air. Fortunately, the waiter returned, giving her a reprieve.

The Waterfront, located in Northern California, used fresh foods directly from farmer's markets. The restaurant offered a wide selection of local seafood.

"I'd like to order for us," Andrii said.

Her eyes met his above the menu. It would be interesting to see what he would order for her. Just the suggestion made her feel cared for. She loved seafood, but she was never decisive when it came to ordering. There were so many items that looked good. She didn't want to go too expensive either. He'd provided her clothes, which cost enough already. Mainly, she wanted to be in his company.

"I'd like that," she agreed. The waiter stood beside her, closer than she preferred, and she knew he could look straight down the plunging neckline of her dress.

Andrii reached across the table for her hand, giving her added reassurance. He clearly had studied the menu. "We'll start with your crab cakes and oysters. We'll both have the salad of young leaves. For the entrees, for my lady, the hand-made seafood linguini, and I'll have the halibut. For dessert we'll share the strawberry shortcake and the peach and blackberry crisp. The lady will have the pisco punch and I'll have an old-fashioned."

Andrii handed the menus to the waiter, still holding on to her hand. One thumb ran over the back of her hand, brushing lightly. He adjusted his hold, so his thumb could slide over her inner wrist. She knew if he found her pulse, it would give away the secret of her accelerated heart rate.

"You will have to get used to men admiring the way you look, *Solnyshkuh*. I can't take my eyes off you. I would expect that other men would look and lust after you."

"What does *Solnyshkuh* mean?" She couldn't quite get the pronunciation perfect.

He gave her one of his rare genuine smiles. "It is Russian for 'little sun.' A term of endearment in my homeland. I'm a citizen of this country now but lived there during my childhood and teenage years. I didn't make the United States my home until a few years ago. I traveled quite a bit before deciding to settle here."

She hugged that information to her. "And what is a pisco punch? I've never had one before and don't have the slightest clue as to what is in it."

"The drink is made with BarSol Pisco. It's produced from the fermentation of one hundred percent Quebranta grapes."

"So it's a wine."

His thumb slid along her inner wrist, keeping her all too aware of him.

"Yes, a wine. The drink is made with Lillet Rouge. That's a blend of cabernet sauvignon and merlot grapes with lemon and orange brandies. It also has quinine and a botanical infusion."

Her heart jumped. She wasn't used to drinking alcohol. She didn't want to get drunk on one drink and mess everything up.

"The drink also has lime and pineapple gum syrup. If you don't like it, you don't have to drink it. We can get something else. You seemed up for an adventure, so why not try new drinks?"

His thumb continued those brushstrokes over her pounding pulse. She inclined her head, afraid she was going to burst into flames any moment. Electricity seemed to spark over her skin with each slide of his thumb.

"Before the waiter interrupted us, you were about to tell me if pleasing me gives you pleasure," he reminded her, his gaze holding hers captive. "I think it's an important question, and I would like an answer."

She knew a nod wasn't going to cut it. He wanted a verbal response. She had no idea if she was humiliating herself by telling him the truth, but she felt she needed to. It was the only way there was any chance of a future relationship. She honestly didn't think she could hold Andrii's attention for long, but already, she found herself falling under his spell.

"Yes." The admission came out barely discernible. Color crept into her face. "I want to make you happy, and when I do the things you ask me, I can see that you're happy."

"Even when those things I ask are difficult for you?"

She thought that over carefully before answering. "It gives me more pleasure because it's a hard decision, and when I overcome fear for you, that seems to bring you greater joy. That's what I want for you."

"Do you get the same pleasure from doing what other people in your life ask of you?"

Her eyebrow shot up. "Other people? I don't have other people in my life. If you mean men, I don't date."

He looked satisfied at that statement. "Men such as Alan Billows. You're what now? Twenty-two or three? You've known him going on at least seven years. Do you try to please him?"

Azelie did her best not to make a face. Andrii had admitted he knew Billows. She didn't want him repeating anything she said to the man. "I would prefer not to talk about him," she finally said.

"May I ask why?"

The pad of his thumb swept over the pulse on her inner wrist. She couldn't look away from his eyes. They had lightened to that intense silver. He still had that soft, gentle tone, intimate and warm, but something in his eyes reminded her of a predator. That silver seemed to pierce through any veil she tried to hide behind. She feared every secret she had was exposed to him.

"You know Billows," she pointed out. "And he's my boss. I don't talk about him to anyone. It was a fluke and wrong of me that I admitted I work for him and that I helped keep him from getting into trouble with the tax investigators."

"Do you believe I would betray your confidence?"

At the sound of disappointment mirroring the look in his eyes, her stomach twisted into hard knots. She detested hurting him. Was she really afraid he would tattle to Billows?

The waiter brought the appetizers and drinks, once again choosing her side of the table to serve the food from. She felt more self-conscious than ever, and she almost tugged at the hem of her dress to cover the exposed tops of her silk stockings. As if he knew what she was thinking—and he probably did—Andrii shook his head. That small gesture was enough to keep her from fidgeting and giving away the fact that she had little confidence in herself as a woman.

Andrii waited until the waiter had left the table before he persisted in getting his answer. "Zelie, this is extremely important. Do you believe I would betray you by telling Billows anything you say?"

She shook her head. Just the way he looked so disappointed in her gutted her. "No, I'm just not used to discussing him."

"I wondered why he didn't help you after you lost your family. Surely, he must have come around to the hospital to see you."

"No, we don't have that kind of relationship. Alan is moody. One time he can be rude and abrupt, another time funny and charming. He also can be very intimidating. Not in the way you are, but more as if he might hurt you if you don't agree with him. I stay away from him as much as possible. That's why I do the books when no one is around. I told him I could concentrate better that way. If he needs to speak to me about anything, the meeting is very brief."

"You would prefer not to work for him," Andrii stated and indicated the food. "He isn't a friend, Zelie. I met him a few times because when I'm in the city, I like to play occasionally."

She didn't like the idea of him with other women, so she didn't respond. Instead, she tried the crab cakes and then the oysters. The food was amazing.

"You were going to tell me about your nightmares," he reminded her, changing the subject. "How often you have them and whether it interferes with your sleep."

Azelie wasn't sure it was true that she'd started to tell him about her sleepless nights. He'd asked the question, and it appeared as if he was determined to get an answer. She knew if she said she didn't want to discuss it, he would accept the limitation, but he would be disappointed. She'd already not only disappointed him but offended him.

"I have nightmares nearly every night. I'm afraid to go to sleep. I often play music or listen to thunderstorms to lull myself to sleep. Sleep never lasts long."

"Have you spoken to a therapist?"

"Yes, when it first happened." She took a cautious sip of the drink. To her shock, it was delicious. "This is really good."

His smile was slow and this time lit his eyes. It didn't last long, but her heart sang at his reaction.

"The food is too."

"Trusting me to look after you has its rewards," he pointed out.

"Yes, it does," she agreed.

The rest of the evening was magical for Azelie. She found the longer she was in his company, the more relaxed she became. The view was so spectacular that she kept getting caught up in staring out the window. They talked mostly about her. He asked her questions regarding the merry widows and their two gentlemen friends. He seemed so interested in everything about her, down to the smallest detail. How long she'd known the merry widows, why she chose to go to the small coffeehouse rather than one of the larger chains.

The conversation continued on the drive home, although mostly on her end. Each time she wanted to ask him a question about himself, he got there before her, asking her something new about her life. She really didn't want the night to end, fearful that she might not see him again. He hadn't indicated one way or the other that he wanted to see her again when he pulled up in front of her building.

Azelie reached up to remove one earring. "You've given me the best night of my life, Andrii. Truly. I don't know anything about jewelry, but the coat, dress and shoes are designer. I have a terrible fear these might be real." She held out one earring dripping diamonds. "If you give me your address, I can send you the dress and shoes. If you don't mind, I'd like to keep the coat but will pay for it."

She hoped she had enough in her savings to pay the price, but letting that coat go meant giving up everything he'd given her. Gifts. Beautiful gifts. She didn't get birthday or Christmas presents when she was young. The money went for food and for the children. She contributed what she could for them. To receive such an enormous gift, like the clothing Andrii had provided for her to wear out, brought her to tears. Of course she couldn't keep the items; they were far too expensive. But the coat . . .

Andrii sat very still, his expression an unreadable mask.

His eyes went that glittering silver she found herself fearful of. She didn't know what triggered the sudden rising tension in the car, but she felt it. Oppressive. Dark. Ominous. She tried to explain further.

"Seriously, I had the best time with you. It's been magical. I don't want you to ever think you have to spend money on me for me to be happy. It makes me happy just to spend time with you."

Unfortunately, that only seemed to make things worse. The tension in the car thickened. Her stomach churned. She had no idea why she was upsetting him, but it hurt. Physically hurt. She felt sick. She'd had the best time she'd ever had, and yet he seemed to be angry with her.

"When I buy something for you, Zelie, you don't throw it back in my face." He got out of the car and walked around to the passenger side, yanking open her door. There was thunder on his face. Disapproval.

She had definitely triggered his temper, but she had no idea why. Not just his temper, but his smoldering disapproval. He looked at her as if she were a complete stranger. He did help her from the car, ignoring the earring altogether, but he didn't put his hand on her back or touch her at all when he walked her up to the door. He was silent as she put in the security code and stepped inside, turning to thank him again. He was already walking away. He didn't look back, or even at her, when he got behind the wheel of the car. She knew because she remained right at the door watching until he drove off.

FOUR

He'd blown it big-time, all because he couldn't keep it together. Maestro needed to feel the wind in his face and his colors on his back. He needed a reset. Grounding. Torpedo Ink grounded him. His Harley-Davidson Iron 883 grounded him. He'd purchased the machine in 2017. Black leather seat, parchment cream paint, blacked-out chrome and trim with black-and-gold music note stenciling—his ride felt like home to him. Mechanic and Transporter had turned the Harley into a road rocket.

He made the ride back down the coast to Caspar, even though he needed to stay in San Francisco. That was how fucked up Zelie had managed to get him. He wasn't physically attracted to women without ordering his cock to cooperate. That was part of his extensive sexual training back at the school of hell. His cock didn't seem to get that message around her.

Maestro had to ask himself if Azelie Vargas could have been trained in the art of seduction. He knew better. That was the sad truth. He knew she was innocent when it came to men. She was no seductress; he was simply that susceptible to her. If he had any sense of self-preservation, he would get as far from her as possible. Tell his club it was too dangerous for him to go anywhere near Zelie.

A relationship with him was equally as dangerous for her. He wasn't a nice man. He never would be. He could be gentle when needed, but he didn't know if that was who he was or if he'd trained to deceive everyone around him. Deep inside, there was an explosive assassin willing to cut throats without warning. Willing to do whatever it took to get the job done.

Swearing, Maestro pulled up to the house he had purchased with his share of the money the club had taken from the billionaire president of the Swords club. He had been the primary criminal in an international human trafficking ring. He had also inherited billions when his older brother died. Torpedo Ink, meaning Code, had managed to siphon the money from all his accounts, even the ones he thought well hidden.

Maestro had discovered the property when the members of the club had all been assigned to go house hunting. Czar wanted them to put down roots in the Caspar/Sea Haven area. He didn't think sleeping at the clubhouse was best for them. Those without partners tended to do so even though they'd each purchased a house. They were used to guarding one another's backs. His job, the way he saw it, along with Keys', was to guard Steele, their vice president. He spent a lot of time sleeping at Steele's home. That meant his house was empty.

What was there to go home to? It was a cool house, but it wasn't a home yet. He'd watched Breezy transform Steele's house into a home. Anya had done the same for Reaper's house. There was no question that each of his married brothers or those with partners had homes instead of houses. Maestro was intelligent enough to know it didn't matter how cool the house was, or how much he liked the design; living alone, for someone who had spent their entire life with others, didn't work.

The unique design of the house had drawn his attention

immediately. The roofline was sharply slanted so that it appeared to cover the house like the wings of a bird. The house itself was all glass and wood. The glass allowed the light in, and the wood spoke to him. Gave him that semblance of peace he needed. The ceilings of the single-story house were extremely high, with banks of windows and oddly shaped but cool tubular skylights allowing the light to come in from every angle. Fortunately, the glass was self-cleaning, or he would have spent his every waking minute trying to keep up with the dust or dirt from the trees and garden. Or the salt from the sea.

The house was situated in a perfect location for him. He had views of the ocean, although he wasn't as close to it as some of the others. He liked the location because he was partially in the forest. Various species of trees were abundant on the property. There was a garden area.

His deck surrounded the house and gave plenty of opportunity to entertain, not that he was a man who invited others over for barbecue. When he wasn't with Keys or Steele, or at the clubhouse, he played music. He wrote music. He could spend hours sitting at a piano. He had a beautiful piano in his house, one perfectly tuned and adjusted. It was the first thing he'd purchased for the house.

He needed the solace of his music. That was just as important as the ride on his Harley. Maestro didn't ever try to fool himself about what he was. Or who he was. He knew he was controlling. He also knew any woman living with him would feel suffocated under that tight control. Men like him, with his personality, didn't find women who would stay. Who could love them despite their flaws.

He opened the large front double doors and stood there a moment, admiring the craftmanship of the design and the impeccable work that had gone into building the house. The doors opened straight into an enormous room, revealing the high ceilings and woodwork as well as a step down to the seating area in front of the fireplace. The wall of windows and glass sliding door leading outside to the deck were visible, giving him a partial view of the trees while standing at the front door.

He moved inside and closed the doors behind him. There was only one place he wanted to be—seated at his piano. Thinking of Zelie. Writing a song for her. Deciding, once he was back to normal and could use his brain to think things through, whether to take a chance on finding a real relationship with her. That was if he hadn't already blown his chances with her.

The moment his fingers were on the piano keys, and as he flooded the room with music, he could breathe again. His mind calmed. The chaos in his head receded along with the howling demons. He allowed himself to go through the time he had spent with Zelie moment by moment. Azelie Vargas could be the perfect woman for a man like Maestro.

He had excellent recall, and he examined what he'd learned about her. She was giving. A pleaser. Her pleasure was in pleasing him. She had worn the clothes he'd sent to her, even though they made her uncomfortable, because he'd asked her to. Each time he had reassured her with his touch or voice, she had responded positively.

She was generous with others even though she didn't appear to have much. She actively pursued higher education, and she'd been honest when she spoke of Billows' strange mood swings. He'd noticed those same shifts in disposition each time he'd met the man. Granted, it was only a couple of times, but the man had been jovial and friendly one day and standoffish the next.

He went over every detail of their conversations. Several times she hadn't wanted to tell him personal things, but she had when he just simply looked disappointed. The thing was, he hadn't been playing her—he *was* disappointed. He not only found himself intensely attracted to her physically, but he wanted to know everything there was to know about her. Strangely, he had an overwhelming need to protect her. To keep her safe. To make her happy.

Being with him would never be a picnic, and she

deserved so much better. That was one of the many things he had to face. If he managed to convince her to take him on, was it even fair to her? The answer was no. Still, he was selfish enough to take into consideration how he would feel if he didn't try with her.

Maestro wasn't used to having emotions, let alone the intensity of these feelings he had for Azelie. He hadn't trusted her or his own emotions. The moment she attempted to return the earrings to him, he had been horrified at his reaction to her. He wanted her with every cell in his body. He wanted to keep her. To make her his exclusively. Alarm rushed through him, so much adrenaline he couldn't control it.

At the same time, he wanted to be away from her, desperate to convince himself she was a betrayer like every other woman he'd known—with the exception of Alena and Lana. Out for themselves. Greedy and conniving. Or unable to follow the slightest command because their egos refused to acknowledge that he might know more about security than they did.

The music flowed through him, a soft, intimate melody, and he could hear the lyrics building in his mind. His music never lied to him. If it told him she was real, she was. The longer he played, the more he felt her wrapping herself around his soul. It was a frightening sensation for him, and yet he didn't stop playing. He needed to feel her close to him. Imagine her in the house, turning it into a real home. Imagine her waiting for him at the door. Giving him her angelic smile. Giving him whatever he asked for.

He acknowledged to himself he'd never had the same feeling for another human being. He wasn't a coward. If she had the courage to face him, to answer personal questions and go that far out of her comfort zone for him, he couldn't do less for her.

He'd vowed never to pursue a woman or trust one outside the club, and he had good reason, but he realized he wasn't willing to give Zelie up. Not without a fight. That was the bottom line. He needed to see her again. He had to know if there was any chance at all for him to have a real relationship with her. The idea of cutting her out of his life so abruptly without even giving them a chance was unacceptable to him.

"Where does that leave us?" he murmured aloud.

He played for another five minutes without stopping, listening carefully to the perfectly pitched notes telling him he was on the right track. He waited for the answers, the music freeing his mind as his fingers flew over the ivory keys.

Maestro had a very important job to do. He couldn't blow it by placing Azelie in danger. That meant he couldn't tell her what he was doing. If he was going to work at a real relationship, he would have to tell her after they got the information needed and he knew she couldn't possibly be held accountable by Billows. He didn't have to play her. He could be real, himself, and hope everything worked out between them. The moment the mission was accomplished, he would come clean.

Azelie would like that he helped find trafficking victims. She would understand why he didn't tell her what he was there for. She might not like that he had initially approached her because he was on the job, but once he explained that the attraction was very real and he wanted, even needed, a continuing relationship with her, he was certain she would be understanding.

Once he made up his mind that he was going to pursue her and do his best to tie her to him, he swung around on the piano bench, blinking to try to clear the memories from his brain. The moment he stopped the flow of music, his past tried to crowd in. The betrayals. The tortures. The rapes. The very ugly deaths. Every girl, every woman, starting with his mother and aunt, had betrayed him.

He hadn't known anything else. Without Czar, Keys and Steele, he would never have survived those early days. The psychological torture was far worse than any of the physical tortures he had been subjected to during his childhood and teenage years. He didn't want those doors opened to his past, not when he had found a woman who might actually be someone amazing and compatible with a man like him.

He locked the house and went to his Harley. He wasn't that surprised to see Savage sitting on his 2015 Night Rod Special. The motorcycle was all black with dull gunmetal-gray trim, blacked-out chrome and the image of a dripping gray skull. It had one more adornment that Maestro—and all the other club members—had thought he would remove. For his birthday, the Red Hat ladies, a group of older women, had gotten Ice to make them a form of a hat in rubies and diamonds. They had no idea those gems were the real deal, but they'd had Mechanic and Transporter weld the hat onto the bike. No one thought Savage would take the prank so well, let alone keep the gleaming hat on his stark bike.

The prank had been played on him by Jackson Deveau, a deputy sheriff. He'd made the suggestion to the women. Not understanding that no one touched a man's bike, they had happily made Savage an honorary member of their club. For some unknown reason, Savage had allowed the decoration to stay. He was used to it now, and it would have looked strange not to have the embellishment on his bike.

"Keys let me know you had come home for the night," Savage greeted. "Just checking to make sure you're doing okay."

"Thanks. I appreciate it, although you should be home with Seychelle. If I had a woman, I wouldn't be away from her if I could help it."

Savage shrugged. "Seychelle worries. She worries, I take care of it. As soon as she heard you'd driven to Caspar tonight and would have to turn around and head back to San Francisco, she was afraid something was wrong. She wanted me to check on you as much as I needed to. Heard the music. You have a gift, Maestro."

Maestro threw his leg over his bike to straddle it. The moment he did, he felt familiar peace slipping over him. "I can lose myself in music. I don't always feel the passage of time."

"Haven't heard that song before. You played it over and over, adding to it."

"I was writing a new piece." He hesitated, but Savage had managed to find happiness, and he was a sadist when it came to sex. He also was controlling and had no problem punishing his woman if she disobeyed him. She did so often, but never over safety issues. Maestro thought she might like those punishments just a little too much. When Savage and Seychelle were together, the chemistry between them was electric. He wanted that for himself.

Savage just sat on his bike, seemingly in no hurry to rush away. He didn't probe, just waited to see if Maestro was going to talk.

"I had a difficult time believing Seychelle would stay," Maestro admitted. "I made life hard for you by giving you the wrong advice. She took the things I said to her wrong, but I shouldn't have said them."

"I was at fault, Maestro," Savage corrected. "Not you. I was in the relationship with her, and I didn't act like it. Unfortunately, I'd never been in a relationship. I didn't know what to do to fix things between us. In the end, I turned to Czar and Blythe. I also encouraged her to talk to her friends if she was concerned about the nature of our relationship."

"Her friends?" Maestro asked.

"She's very close friends with a lot of the women in the Red Hat Society. I don't want her to ever feel alone. We have a unique relationship, one that can be hard on not just her body but her mind. I learned to listen to her. To hear what she needed or wanted. It took a while for me to get it, but she's the most important person in my life. She sacrifices a lot for me. I want to make certain that she knows she's loved."

"How do you do that?" Maestro asked. "I don't have a clue."

"It took time for me to hear her. She needed to feel she was my partner. She doesn't ask about club business, but I know she worries if I'm gone, so I make certain Czar fills her in on my status, so she knows I'm alive and unhurt."

"How do you find the balance of control and giving her

freedom?" Maestro asked the question whose answer most eluded him.

"I think the thing I learned about being in a relationship that was the most helpful was that it is important, even essential, to communicate clearly. I made certain Seychelle knew what she was getting into every step of the way. I told her about myself, what happened to me and why I am the way I am. I told her it wasn't going to change. I needed a certain type of sex, and I would enjoy her fucking up, so I would have the excuse to punish her. I also explained what kinds of control I needed to have in my life to stay sane."

Maestro winced. He didn't spill his guts to anyone, let alone a woman. He wanted her to follow him blindly. "Don't know if I can do that," he admitted.

Savage shrugged. "I wouldn't have been able to talk to another woman the way I do her. I realized almost from the first time that I met her that Seychelle was the one woman I wanted, even needed, in my life. I was willing to do whatever it took to keep her with me. I fucked up several times and was lucky enough that she stuck it out. If you aren't willing to give her everything, she isn't the one for you, Maestro."

Maestro continued to sit on his Harley, the familiar leather seat creaking when he shifted his weight. Of everyone in the club, Savage was most like him. He needed control to survive and to keep everyone around him safe. Not only had Seychelle accepted that control, but she seemed to thrive in the relationship. There was no doubt that she loved Savage. It was in everything she said and did as well as in the expression on her face. She didn't try to hide the way she felt about her man.

"I want Azelie," Maestro declared. "It's difficult to believe we stand a chance, but I know if there's one woman I want to be with, it's her. I keep looking for something wrong, waiting for the betrayal. I'll always be testing her. Controlling every move in our relationship. What woman can live with that?"

Savage gave him a humorless smile. "Don't you think I asked myself the same thing a million times? Before I met her, I'd already been preparing to take a ride over the cliff. I knew eventually I'd hurt someone. I have cycles—you've seen them. When I'm bad, I need Seychelle to ride those out with me. Trust me, Maestro, the things I do to her aren't for the faint of heart. Fortunately, I'm able to work with her so she gets off on it—eventually. Whatever you're asking of Azelie is not ever going to be as bad as what I've asked of Seychelle."

Maestro knew Savage told the strict truth about his sexual needs. He was aware of the things Savage needed in a relationship. Maestro was a natural dominant, and he enjoyed various kinks when it came to sex, but hurting his partner wasn't something he needed to get off. He might use a flogger or a whip, but again, it was more of a control issue, asking his woman to do something she would be uncomfortable with just to please him. How fucked up was that? Still, even knowing it was wrong, he was aware he would demand and enjoy it if his woman was willing to please him when he asked for bondage. He would need confirmation of her devotion on a daily basis. Was that any better than the things Savage needed?

"You have to make up your mind if you want her, Maestro," Savage reiterated. "If you do, you not only have to walk a fine line with this mission, but you'll have to talk to her. Open up about your past and let her know why you're so fucked up."

Yeah, that was the one thing he wasn't certain he could do. Yet Savage had. Absinthe, one of his Torpedo Ink brothers, had to ask his woman to play roles; kitten, librarian, all sorts of fucked-up things, and she did it for him because he'd told her the worst of his childhood. Ice was an exhibitionist. Storm got off on being a voyeur. Ice was married to a wonderful woman. Maestro was certain Ice had told her what he'd been through. Storm was still single, but Reaper, Savage's birth brother, had Anya. It had been a real shit-storm with Reaper making mistakes, thanks to the rest of them giving him very poor direction.

Maestro was guilty of giving poor counsel to Savage. He probably had given the worst advice of all of them. He had even given Steele crap advice, and Breezy was as sweet and accommodating as any woman could be. Maestro tended to view all women as egotistical rebels, unable to obey when their safety was a concern just because they wanted to prove that they were equal to a man. Protecting his woman shouldn't mean he didn't see her as an equal. They had different strengths. Everyone had different strengths.

"I don't know what I'm going to do," he admitted. "I do know I want her in my life. I'm going to think about the things you've said, Savage, before I contact her. I blew it with her last night. Everything was so perfect, too perfect. I kept waiting for the stab in the back. When she tried to give back the earrings, I panicked. I swear, I can face bullets any fucking day of the week, but looking at her earnest expression and hearing her say she didn't care about things, she just wanted to spend time with me, I lost it."

"Let's head into Sea Haven. Hannah Drake Harrington opens her tea shop early. We can grab coffee and something to eat. You can't drive back to San Francisco without getting coffee in you. You've been up all night."

Maestro agreed and started up his Harley-Davidson Iron 883. Savage's Night Rod Special roared to life. The two took off, riding along the coastal highway toward Sea Haven. Once again, peace settled over him, the early morning fog enfolding him like a gray blanket. The sun shot through the fog, sending streaks of orange-red light over the water in a dazzling display. The wind played with the surface of the water, sending white foam and diamonds into the air and over the bluffs.

Maestro tried to keep his thoughts away from Zelie, but it was impossible. He had no idea why she had made such an impression on him. Why he couldn't get her out of his thoughts. Why he couldn't stand the thought of never seeing her again. He knew he should cut off all contact with her. He might not be a sexual sadist, but he had flaws. Damage. It was very real and lasting. He wasn't a man who would put up with his woman defying him. Like with Savage, there would be consequences, punishments. He knew most women would never put up with a man like him. Not long-term. The worst was, he would enjoy those punishments a little too much because it meant she cared enough about him to give him the things he needed.

He wasn't like Savage and Reaper, men who women sympathized with. Their scars were physical and the trauma to them so deep they never failed to garner the attention of women. It wasn't as if Maestro hadn't been physically tortured or raped, but his trauma was far more psychological. Unseen. The scars were there, just not as noticeable. He was softer inside. He was a musician, an artist with a poet's soul. It embarrassed him that he wasn't as tough as he thought he should be. Sorbacov seemed to have had a gift for knowing what would harm each child the most. He had been able to see into Maestro when others, to this day, couldn't.

He wasn't upset with his Torpedo Ink brothers and sisters. He'd developed a tough shell. He'd had to in order to survive. If anyone saw into him, it was Czar. The others took what he said and did at face value. Unless it was Keys. Keys seemed to read him, to see into his bullshit performances.

Comparing himself to Reaper and Savage all the time made him come up short. It wasn't as if he ever shirked his duties. He was an assassin, and there was no hesitation when he killed, but the kills haunted him. The victims, no matter how deserving of death, visited him at night.

How did he explain himself to a woman like Azelie without sounding like a pathetic loser when he really was a monster? Sorbacov specialized in creating monsters. Maestro knew he could explode into violence easily. It had become second nature, no matter that the instincts hadn't been natural to him.

The town of Sea Haven was very quiet so early in the

morning. The street was mostly empty, and they had no trouble finding parking directly in front of the tea shop called the Floating Hat. The sign was a hat made of wood. The name Floating Hat was intriguing, but other than the cups that looked like hats in the windows, and the bells shaped like hats on the door, the shop had nothing at all to do with hats.

The Floating Hat was not only a tea shop but an organic bath and lotion shop. With bay windows on either side of the door facing the street, when one first looked, the shop appeared to be on the small side. The shop was really quite spacious, spreading out behind the bay windows and going back the whole depth of the building. Behind the counter, there was at least one more room and another exit.

One window held the intriguing hat-shaped cups, an assortment of teas and stacked caddies of delicious-looking scones and pastries. The other window held lotions and bath products. The division was the same in the shop, with products for sale on one side and tables and chairs, as well as a few booths, on the other side. Most tables were for two to four people, but there was one larger table that could handle at least six. The tables were a distance apart from the other half of the store, creating a feeling of openness.

Savage pulled open the door to the shop, setting the hat-shaped bells chiming, announcing their presence. A woman looked up from the counter and Maestro recognized her immediately. She sometimes worked at the roadhouse bar. She was learning bartending from Anya and Preacher.

"Sabelia," Maestro greeted while Savage nodded at her.

The woman was tiny, like a little pixie—or a woodland fairy—with her wealth of shiny black hair and eyes that should have been too big for her face. When he'd first met her, she never smiled, and with her long black hair and small features, at times she appeared witchy to him. Now, seeing her smiling and hearing the welcome in her voice, he understood that she knew she had a safe home with Hannah and Torpedo Ink. He realized that had changed Sabelia, giving her happiness and perhaps some peace. That showed in her laughter and lighter expression.

"Anywhere is fine." Sabelia motioned toward the tables. She sent Savage a wry smile. "I know you're not fond of tea. Do you want your usual coffee?"

Savage gave her a thumbs-up as he headed toward what all the Torpedo Ink members considered a prime table. The table gave them the advantage of seeing the windows and the door, and they could keep an eye on the back exit without being seen. Everyone else wanted tables by the windows, but they didn't care to present a target to anyone looking in. They stayed alive by being careful.

Kasimir "Preacher" Popov sauntered in as if he owned the place. Preacher was Lana's older birth brother. He had very curly hair and wore it on the longer side. He was the club's chemistry man. He had other well-developed gifts as well. He worked at the roadhouse as the head bartender and manager of the bar. Hannah Harrington was working with him to teach him more about the natural products and what they could do. There may have been a little magic mixed in, but if so, Maestro didn't want to know about it.

Preacher greeted Savage and Maestro, and rubbed his knuckle on top of Sabelia's head as he swept past her to go behind the counter. "I'll make my drink this morning, Sabelia."

"Good morning to you too," Sabelia said. "I don't recall Hannah hiring you to work here, but if she did, that makes me your boss."

Preacher gave a little dramatic shudder. "You're already bossy as hell. I'm not stupid enough to allow you free rein to boss me around."

Sabelia arched a winged black brow. "I work for you at the Torpedo Ink Roadhouse. Does that mean I'm braver than you? Because you're sounding a bit like a coward."

"You're looking to get yourself in trouble, little girl. Keep it up and you'll find yourself over my knee." Preacher sounded perfectly amicable.

She narrowed her eyes at him. "Try it and you'll have the cops knocking on your door."

Preacher laughed, his eyes lighting up, indicating he felt genuine amusement. "That's an empty threat if I ever heard one. You despise law enforcement."

She tilted her chin. "I don't despise them," she clarified, "but I don't trust them. So, no, I wouldn't call the cops, but your favorite truck would be filled with frogs. Slimy ones. Toads. Big giant toads."

Preacher threw back his head and laughed aloud. "That isn't an empty threat, but it still might be worth the pleasure I'd get from spanking your ass."

Sabelia stuck her nose in the air. "I'm ignoring you this morning. Everything was quite pleasant until you came along. I refuse to change my good mood just because you're a blight on society and the bane of my existence."

"You two need to get a room," Savage suggested.

"I don't need a room," Preacher said. "I'll lock the doors so she doesn't get embarrassed when her customers come in."

Sabelia's pale skin flushed red. "You two aren't funny at all. For your information, Savage, Preacher thinks of me as a baby."

"An *obnoxious* baby," Preacher confirmed.

"Maestro?" Determinedly, Sabelia turned to him. "What are you looking for this morning?" she asked.

"Clarity," he answered honestly. "Tranquility. You make the blend of tea for me, Sabelia. And three of your orange cranberry scones."

Sabelia laughed softly. "I don't see how any of you can put away that many scones and look the way you do. If I ate like that, you'd have to roll me out of here."

Preacher came around the counter and smacked Sabelia on her ass. She yelped and spun around, glaring at him. He glared right back.

"We had an agreement. You weren't to talk or think negative things about yourself anymore. No liquor and no ugly thoughts."

She rolled her eyes. "Fine, but you keep your hands to yourself, or I'm retaliating by practicing with Hannah on your truck."

Preacher didn't appear impressed. He made his way back behind the counter. "The agreement stated there could be no retaliation if you were punished for either of those two things. You always keep your word."

Sabelia's breath hissed out in a long slow exhale. "I think I'm going to need to drink whatever kind of tea I make for Maestro for my own tranquility."

Maestro gave her a sympathetic grin. Preacher and Sabelia had a strange chemistry between them. Enemies, but the physical attraction between them couldn't be denied. He had no idea why Preacher hadn't acted on it. He certainly ran men off in the bar if they made a play for her.

"I'll buy your cup of tea, Sabelia." He poured sympathy into his voice, knowing it would irritate the shit out of Preacher.

Sure enough, Preacher looked up, glaring at Maestro. "She doesn't need you to pay for her fucking tea, Maestro."

It was all Maestro could do not to burst out laughing. "Just helping the lady out." Preacher didn't swear much. When they were children, he looked after Lana like she was his child. He couldn't prevent the abuse she suffered, but he made certain all the kids down in that torture chamber of a basement knew Lana was under his protection. He didn't want them swearing around her, and they respected his orders—for the most part.

"Don't annoy me," Preacher warned.

Sabelia rolled her eyes. "I live to annoy you. Don't get all grumpy because someone wants to do something nice for me." Her implication was that Preacher didn't do nice things for her.

"I'm never grumpy," Preacher denied. "Get to work before your boss comes in and finds you flirting outrageously with your customers."

Color swept under Sabelia's pale skin. Her long lashes

fluttered as she glared at Preacher. "I don't flirt with customers. That would be you."

"Sabelia," Savage interrupted. "I find this all very enter-
taining, but if I don't get coffee soon, I'll be the grumpy one."

"Coming right up, Savage," Sabelia swept past Preacher,
going straight to the coffeepot.

Maestro's phone vibrated. He pulled the phone from his
pocket and glanced down, inwardly wincing as he read the
text message from Azelie.

I had a wonderful time with you, Andrii. I'm sorry I hurt
you, but I can't keep the clothes and jewelry. You can
pick the box up at the coffee shop. I am keeping the
coat. I looked on the website at Label 287 but couldn't
find the amount I owe you for it, so I've emailed the designer asking. I'll pay you back as soon as possible.
Thank you again for a wonderful time, but clearly, it's
best if we don't see each other again.

FIVE

Two days had gone by since her date with Andrii, and Azelie found herself more upset than she had realized she could be when she barely knew the man. She hadn't gone back to the coffee shop after giving the box of clothing, shoes and jewelry to the owners, Shaila and David Manger. They promised to text her when Andrii came in to pick up the box. The text had come in that morning.

She still hadn't gone to the coffee shop because she didn't want to answer any questions. She knew the merry widows would ask her how her date had gone. What was there to say? *He was perfect until he wasn't*? She'd blown it, but she didn't know how? She felt sad. Bereft. The intensity of her emotions made no sense and raised another red flag for her. She had no business dating a man who brought out such overwhelming emotions in her.

Her phone dinged, letting her know she had a text message. She didn't want to look because she knew it wouldn't be from Andrii, or worse, it might be, and then she would have hope. She knew she was ruled by emotion, but she'd tried very hard to be more logical. Swearing off Andrii was logical. She couldn't prevent herself from looking. The compulsion was too strong.

Coming up now. Open the door for me.

Her heart stuttered. Andrii. Already in the building. How did he get the code? He was on his way up to her door, and she was dressed in her ridiculous but very comfortable tank and drawstring flannels. She was barefoot and had no idea where her slippers were.

She caught up her phone and tried to hastily text to stop him from coming to her apartment. Her home was too small, and he would leave his presence everywhere. His scent would linger. She would dream of him, not that she didn't already dream of him. Erotic dreams. She didn't know which were worse, nightmares or erotic dreams that left her burning for him.

Before she could text, he knocked. She found herself hurrying to the door, one hand on the dead bolt.

"I don't think this is a good idea, Andrii," she said without opening the door. Her voice sounded strangled. Husky. Her heart pounded with trepidation and excitement.

"It's the only idea, *Solnyshkuh*. Unlock the door."

His voice. Soft but commanding. Compelling. Goose bumps whispered along her skin and crept down her spine. She was so susceptible to him. Her hand was on the dead bolt almost of its own volition. Her brain wasn't catching up.

"I'm not dressed," she announced as she cracked open the door.

Opening the door was a mistake—a huge one. Looking at him standing there, dressed casually in dark jeans and a tee from a Queen concert stretched tight across the heavy muscles of his chest, took her breath away and robbed her of her ability to talk.

Very gently, Andrii put one hand to her belly and moved her back into her tiny living space, allowing him entry into the apartment. He closed the door behind him. In one hand he had a large rectangular box that was twice the size of the one she had so carefully taped up and given to the owners of the coffee shop to hold for him.

He immediately placed the box on the small coffee table she'd bought at a secondhand store. She rather liked that coffee table, with the inlaid tree of life in wood and the glass top covering it. There were a couple of small chips in the wood on the edges, but she had found the perfect match in wood stain and covered them. The box took up nearly the entire table.

She moistened her lips with the tip of her tongue, trying to find the right words to get him out of her space before it was too late.

"Andrii." She detested that she sounded hesitant.

"Before you decide to throw me out, Zelie, let me apologize for my atrocious temper. My lack of control really hurt your feelings. That's the last thing I ever wanted to do."

Azelie couldn't take her eyes off of him as he moved around her small apartment easily. Even though he seemed to glide with only air under him, he took up all the space. Eventually, after going through the open-floor-plan kitchen area and sitting room and looking at the bed in the small space that was her bedroom, he flung himself into one of the two comfortable chairs she'd found at a garage sale. They both had thick cushions and were in fantastic shape. They were made with a forest-green leather that went perfectly with the coffee table.

She hadn't expected an apology or an admission of a bad temper. He seemed so calm and in control, it was difficult to imagine that he had a temper.

"Did I scare you?" he asked when she remained silent.

She swallowed the first three things she wanted to say. None of them were true. Finally, she shrugged. "I wasn't afraid you would hurt me physically." That was true. It hadn't occurred to her that Andrii might hit or slap her.

"I'm grateful you see into my character enough to know I would never abuse you in that way. You didn't exactly answer my question. What are you afraid of? I know you're attracted to me. I know you would like to try a relationship with me, but now you're very reluctant, and you're looking for reasons to throw me out without listening to me."

She couldn't help herself. The smile came out of nowhere because she had the childish desire to stick her fingers in her ears to keep from hearing his voice.

He leaned forward, his eyes going soft. "Baby, give me the reasons so we can talk them out. I know I want to do this with you. I want you to have the same resolve. I know I blew it for us, but I'm asking you to give us a chance to get back on track."

Azelie struggled with her answer. She wanted to be honest, but it would be giving him too much. In the end, she could only be who she was and answer him with the truth. "I can't afford to have you rip out my heart, Andrii. I don't like to admit it, but the truth is I'm still very fragile. It makes sense to protect myself from heartache. You're a heartache waiting to happen."

"Why do you say that? My temper?"

She shook her head. "It isn't that. A man like you can't possibly be with someone like me without getting bored. You'll move on eventually. I'm the investing type. I would put everything I am into the relationship, including my heart, and when you walked away, I'd be shattered."

"Now that right there would earn you a punishment if you were mine."

The way he said it, in that low, firm voice, sent butterflies winging in her sex. Her stomach clenched around the sudden knot of sheer desire. Her physical reactions to his declarations were frightening, but it was the emotional one that shocked her. She felt so much happiness it was astounding, joy bursting through her and radiating outward to every cell in her brain.

"What does that mean?"

He sounded like he really cared about her. She did her best to shake off the spell he was mesmerizing her with. She shook her head and held up her hand to stop him from uttering another word in his velvet voice.

"We don't need to go there. I'm not doing this with you. I'm trying to be polite and state it as nicely as possible, but I feel it's best if we don't see one another again." There. Perfect. She got it out without stumbling over the words.

Andrii's eyes went liquid silver, and her stomach did a drop right from a roller coaster. A somersault. She watched him stand, his height and wide shoulders, along with his dominant personality, instantly shrinking the size of the room.

"You aren't walking away from me," Andrii declared.

She turned her back on him to walk to the door. She had taken two steps when the next thing she knew she was across the living room floor, her back pressed against the wall beside the door and Andrii tight against her front. She felt every muscle in his chest. Her heart stuttered as she gripped his Queen tee in her fist and tilted her head to look up at his face. Up that close he appeared even more masculine and intimidating. The dark bristle on his face, the strong jaw, the aristocratic nose. That mouth. So incredibly sensual.

She was aware she was alone with him in her apartment, and no one knew he was there. She'd been crazy to open her door. Crazy. Silly. Even if she screamed, she wasn't certain anyone would hear. What was wrong with her that she was fixating on his mouth when she should be screaming for help?

"Step back, Andrii." Her voice was a mere thread of sound. She couldn't make her voice sound decisive and commanding.

His hands cupped her face, his touch exquisitely gentle. Looking down at her, the silver in his eyes softened to a gray, giving him the look of a man feeling tender toward his woman.

Her stomach did a slow roll seeing that look. Every single cell in her body woke up, came alive, went on full alert. There was so much caring in that look.

"I can't do that, *Solnyshkuh*." He whispered his denial to her, his thumb sliding over her right cheekbone, tracing the contour gently.

She forced herself to keep her resolve. This man was gorgeous. He was also dangerous. Not just because he could look like a predator very high up on the food chain, but because she knew he had the capability of capturing her heart. If he did that and left her—which was inevitable—she would be shattered. She was far too fragile for a man like Andrii Federoff.

"You have to go." She tried to be firm.

"You don't want to throw me out," he said softly. Too softly.

His tone sent shivers of awareness down her spine. It sucked to be so susceptible to him. Azelie just didn't have physical reactions to men. Any man. The fact that the chemistry between them sizzled, was so strong it was nearly tangible, was frightening.

"I do," she insisted. There was silence.

She knew he was looking down at her with those eyes of his. It would be a mistake to look up at him. His thumb slid along one cheekbone, tracing the curve. He didn't say anything. She sighed.

"Okay, I do want you to stay," she admitted. Why she told him the truth when it was embarrassing, she didn't know. "But you still have to go, Andrii."

"Thank you for telling the truth when most women wouldn't. You don't play games, Zelie. That's one of the hundreds of things I love about you."

She detested that when he complimented her she melted inside. Especially when he used that voice of his. His voice should be outlawed. *He* should be outlawed. She needed to grow a spine.

"I need you to go, Andrii, and not come back. Take whatever you brought with you." That was definitely firmer, even though she whispered.

He rubbed the pad of his thumb over her lower lip, sending

a million sparks dancing over her skin. Heat rushed through her veins to pool low and wicked.

"I need you to explain why you're so afraid of me, *Solnyshkuh*. You've already conceded that you know I'm not a man to beat a woman. Punish my woman when she fucks up, yes—beat her, no."

She inhaled sharply, eyelashes fluttering in the hopes that he couldn't read her expression. Should she even ask? She didn't dare chance prolonging their conversation. She had to get right to the point. Still, she couldn't help herself.

"Punish her?"

"You," he clarified. "I'm spelling it out quite clearly that I want you to be my woman."

She tilted her chin. "You aren't making a great case for yourself, throwing around words like *punish*."

"We'll get there. Right now, tell me what you're most afraid of." He poured command into his voice. He didn't raise it, but it was a definite order.

Azelie refused to be embarrassed. She had the truth on her side. "Men like you don't stay with women like me, Andrii. And I'm not built for flings."

His hands once again cupped her face, forcing her head up.

"Look at me." There was steel in his voice.

He waited until she raised her lashes and met his slashing silver eyes. Instantly, there was that same roller coaster wreaking havoc in her stomach.

"I want an explanation of what you mean. Exactly, Azelie. Men like me? Women like you? What does that mean?"

He never called her Azelie. Never. Right from the first meeting he had called her Zelie. He wasn't happy with her. She fought to overcome the rush of fear that she'd displeased him. She kept her chin tilted.

"You want me to tell you the truth, don't you?" she challenged. "That's what I'm doing. I don't have to like it and neither do you, but nevertheless it's the truth."

His thumb slid along her chin, featherlight. Sensual. A

hint of power. Azelie had no idea how he could convey so much in a simple touch.

"You haven't explained, and I have no idea what you mean." She lowered her lashes, unable to meet the building desire in his eyes. "You're gorgeous. You walk into a room and women throw themselves at you. Clearly, you have a lot of experience. You're dominant, overwhelming and you know how to use your voice to get what you want."

A faint smile came and went so quickly she wasn't certain she really saw it, but for that brief second, her heart stammered.

"That's a beautiful thing to say about me, *Solnyshkuh*. Thank you."

He would steal her heart easily if she wasn't careful. That was the one thing she couldn't afford. She knew herself very well. She was doing her best to get a tough exterior, but since the deaths of her sister and the children, she felt disoriented, alone, and far too fragile emotionally. She didn't have anyone to lean on, although the merry widows treated her like a long-lost relative.

"I mean it too, Andrii. Everything about you is appealing. I can't imagine any woman not being drawn to you. But you're way out of my league." There was regret in her voice. She couldn't keep that out, regardless of how hard she tried to sound indifferent.

His thumb slid over her bottom lip, his silver gaze holding hers captive. "What do you mean by that? I don't understand why you think I'm out of your league."

Her heart was stuttering just being under his blazing, sensual gaze. How could he not see the difference in them? He looked at her with such puzzlement she was certain he really didn't know what she was saying, although he seemed to see inside her. He appeared to know things about her natural instincts and character no one else saw.

"Look at me. I'm nothing special. I'm not in your league because men as gorgeous as you might go slumming and find someone like me to be with, but you don't stay."

His face darkened and the color of his eyes lightened even more. She powered on, determined to get it over with so he'd leave.

"You'd get bored and move on. I'd be left with a shattered heart because I don't know how to cope with that."

He was silent for a long time. Too long. The disappointment in his eyes gutted her. She despised the displeasure and unhappiness he conveyed.

"That's how you see me, Azelie? As a man who would break your heart? Not treat you with the care and consideration a treasure like you deserves? Because I know what a treasure you are."

She shook her head, not believing him despite him sounding perfectly sincere. Did he honestly believe he would stay?

"Do you see me this way because of my temper? Because I hurt you when I left so abruptly? That wasn't treating you with tenderness and care. You have no idea what I'd do to fix what I broke between us. I know I was in the wrong, and worse, I also know that there will be times when I lose my temper. I would never hurt you physically, but I can't promise I won't inadvertently say or do something that hurts you emotionally. If that happens, Zelie, call me on it. Don't let my temper, which I promise I will do my best to overcome, keep us from a relationship."

He still wasn't seeing the whole picture. She was going to have to spell it out for him and really embarrass herself. Again, she tilted her chin at him, trying to give herself courage. "My reluctance isn't about your temper, which is atrocious by the way. It's about your looks versus mine. Your experience versus mine. My personality, which will wear on you after a while, right along with the differences I just stated."

Andrii's eyes went that slashing silver color. He was seriously displeased. "Right there, what you just said to me, would earn you a punishment. I'd put you over my knees so fast your head would spin."

She gasped and found herself gripping the tee stretched tightly across the heavy muscles of his chest.

"I don't like the sound of that."

"First, baby, you don't ever talk about yourself that way. If you feel insecure, we can work on that. You're beautiful, inside and out—you're beautiful. If anyone is getting a poor bargain here, it's you, not me. The likelihood of you wanting to leave me is far higher than the other way around."

She heard the sincerity in his voice and saw it in his eyes. He was either the world's best actor or he believed what he was saying. To hear him calling her beautiful with such true admiration made her glow inside. There was no way to squash the blossoming joy—or hope. Still, she had to be careful. He wanted a commitment, and she wasn't sure of him. It was probable she would never be certain of him. That was more on her than him.

"There are no guarantees in life, Zelie. None. No one knows what's going to happen years from now, but I believe in commitment and loyalty. I'm not a man who would be unfaithful. Loyalty is everything to me. To betray you in that way goes against every code I have."

He sighed and gently slid his palm from her cheek to her neck, then along her shoulder and down her arm, never losing contact with her skin. Her sex fluttered again. The bottom went out of her stomach as a thousand little sparks danced over her entire body. His long fingers settled around her wrist like a handcuff, but very gently.

She couldn't help reacting to his gentleness. It was so at odds with his strength and dominant personality. The way he touched her with such reverence and care was the opposite of the dark lust and sensuality carved deep into his features and moving in his eyes. The combination was both exhilarating and intimidating.

Azelie didn't try to hide the shiver of awareness or the way his touch could turn her into a puddle of desire or the way his voice affected her.

He tugged on her wrist, leading her across the room to the two chairs she had. She'd found them at a garage sale. The forest-green leather chairs went perfectly with her little coffee table. They were also in great condition and extremely comfortable. She'd been lucky to get them for a steal because it seemed like no one else wanted to take a chance on the color.

Andrii seated himself in that casual way he had, not relinquishing his hold on her, but exerting pressure on her wrist until she tumbled onto his lap. He scooped her legs up to drape them across one of the arms of the chair while his arm supported her back.

"I gave a lot of bad advice to a couple of my brothers on relationships. My heart might have been in the right place, but I didn't know what the fuck I was talking about and shouldn't have said anything. It wasn't until I laid eyes on you that I began to realize what a dick I'd been."

That was the last thing she'd expected him to admit. She liked that Andrii had no problem confessing his screwups to her. She couldn't help but admire him for it. When he made mistakes, he owned them and seemed to readily apologize.

"Since I'm confessing my sins, *Solnyshkuh*, you may as was well know that I stalked you for a few weeks before I made my approach."

That admission sent her pulse racing. If she relaxed, she would melt into his body. As it was, she was aware of his reaction to her. He didn't try to hide the fact that he was aroused. His scent surrounded her so that every breath she took, she inhaled him. She took him inside, where he wound himself around her organs and branded his name into her bones.

"You did?" She squeaked her question.

"I did." There didn't seem to be an ounce of shame in his confession. "I spotted you one morning when I was crossing through the park to get to the coffee shop a friend had told me about. The sun shone on your hair, and I'd never seen that particular shade of auburn. I'd never seen hair so thick and wild. You have no idea what that did for me. To me. I'm not a man who has reactions to women the way I've had to you."

She had to admit she liked that.

"You were wearing a pair of jeans, old and faded. The denim clung to your body like a glove, accenting your hips and ass. I will admit I've had quite a few fantasies about what I would do with you if you were mine. But just being physically attracted doesn't mean we'd suit."

She knew that probably better than he did. She didn't point it out because he didn't like her saying—or thinking—anything derogatory about herself.

"You were pushing a child on a swing, and at first, I thought she was your little girl, but then a woman came over and the two of you talked for a minute before she picked up the child and walked off, looking back to wave at you. The little girl blew you kisses, and you blew one back to her."

"That was Betsy and her mom, Abigail. Abigail is going to school to become a hairdresser. I met her in the park. She was sitting on a bench watching her daughter play, but tears were running down her face. I couldn't help myself; I went over to her to see if I could help. We struck up a friendship, and I watch Betsy when Abigail's mother can't and I'm not in class myself."

Andrii's arms tightened around her. "I watched you taking care of that woman and her daughter. There was also a man with two sons you sat with in the park for a little while. He left, and you took over watching the boys until he came back. He didn't return for nearly two hours."

"That was Bradley. His wife died in childbirth and left him with twins, Luke and Teddy. They're five now and a bit of a handful. He's trying to date again, but he works two jobs. Sometimes his sitter falls through, and he can't get home to be with the boys when they get out of school. I fill in for him too."

"I noticed Bradley looking at you like he'd prefer to date you."

She didn't respond.

"Zelie? Has he asked you out?"

His voice was low and compelling. Insistent on an answer. Azelie nodded. "Several times. I didn't want it to be weird between us because I kept turning him down, so in the end I lied to him." She knew she sounded mortified because she was. "I really hate lying, but he needed help, and if I kept turning him down, it would get awkward."

"Your lie?"

She should have known he would insist on knowing what she'd told Bradley. She twisted her fingers together. "I told him I was in a relationship already and very much in love with my partner."

Azelie turned her head so she could look straight into his eyes. "I really don't lie, Andrii. It just seemed kinder." She knew lying would be a huge problem for him. She shouldn't be apologizing. She should be happy he would think she was a liar, but she couldn't bear for him to think that of her. She also didn't want to see his disappointment in her, but she wasn't a coward. She believed, in this instance, she'd done the right thing. "Bradley's children need someone to be with them in the interim if their regular sitter is ill or has something she can't get out of, like a medical appointment. It doesn't happen that often, but it's important that the boys have someone they trust to look after them. I don't go to his home, and I made that clear. I watch them in the park, or if it's bad weather, we go to the rec center."

"I understand why you believe you did the right thing, but it's important to me that you're always truthful with me, even if you're afraid it might hurt me." His palm cupped the side of her face. "You don't believe you're in my league, and you're right, *Solnyshkuh*. You're so far above me it isn't funny. If I were a decent man, I'd walk out just like you want me to and leave you to find a good man."

Azelie couldn't look away from the darkness and deep sorrow in his eyes. He was telling her the truth as he saw it. She had developed a sense of radar ever since her family had been murdered. Even before, she had become concerned when she was around her brother-in-law. At the time, she thought it was because she didn't like the way Quentin treated his wife and children. He'd grown selfish and overbearing, using drugs and drinking quite a bit. It hadn't occurred to her that she often avoided certain people because they felt off to her. Andrii might feel dangerous and even powerful, but he didn't feel at all the way he portrayed himself.

"I'm not easy. I'll never be easy. I'm not even a good man, and you deserve so much better, but the truth is I have no intention of giving you up. I'll work hard to make you happy. I believe that we're right for one another and that I can do that—make you happy."

"Andrii," she cautioned, not sure what she was going to say to protest. She didn't want to protest. She wanted to be his. She just wasn't sure she had enough trust in her to develop the kind of relationship he needed.

As if sensing her hesitation, he continued. "I'll keep you safe. I'm not a man other men want to fuck with. I don't ever want you to think I wouldn't put your safety first. As dramatic as it sounds, I'd take a bullet for you. I'd kill for you if that was necessary."

She tried to find a smile, but at the mention of him taking a bullet for her, the shocking pain of metal tearing into her flesh, the terror, the memories of the long road back surfaced.

Again, he seemed to know what she was feeling. His arms circled her and pulled her tight against his chest. She felt surrounded by a fortress. He was that strong and sure.

"I'm sorry I triggered a bad memory when I was trying to reassure you, baby."

"It isn't your fault," she admitted readily. "I still haven't gotten over what happened."

"You won't. How could you?" His voice was that soft, soothing velvet that stroked over her skin like the finest of paintbrushes. "You can't expect to ever get over something like you experienced. You learn to live with it, Zelie. When the nightmares get bad and you're having a difficult time, you can talk to me. I've got things in my past, not the same, but similar. I understand lasting trauma."

"You think we can do this," Azelie said. "But I don't have your faith. Not because of you, but because I can't seem to trust anyone. Not even the merry widows, and they've been so good to me. Consistently good to me. I still can't talk to them about my brother-in-law and what he did. I'm not just trying to save myself heartache; I'm trying to save you too."

His hand came up to fist in her hair, the fingers threading through the thick, luxurious strands. He gave the lightest of tugs, sending fiery tingles of awareness through her scalp.

"Right there, Zelie, that's what I'm talking about. I know you're trying to look out for me. Do you realize how rare you are? I've never had that. Never. Not even from my parents or relatives."

Her heart hurt just hearing him. Her parents hadn't been the best, but she had had Janine. Her sister had treated her with love and kindness. She'd never acted as if taking on Azelie was a burden. If anything, Janine had made her feel as though she was a great help to her, that she needed Azelie and felt lucky to have her living with them.

"I'm so sorry, Andrii. Some people shouldn't be parents." She gave him a small smile. "But then neither of us would be here, so I guess in the end, we should just make the most of our lives. That's all I'm trying to do, just live the best life I can without hurting anyone."

The color of his eyes softened to an intense gray. "I watched you, and yes, I know I sound like a creepy stalker, but I realized in the time I paid attention that you are an extraordinary woman. That was just observing you. Being with you just assures me how right I was."

"Andrii, I can't make decisions. I despise making them. I'm good with numbers, but I don't especially like the work. It's the only thing I am good at. I can make decisions without hesitation when it comes to numbers, but anything else,

I'm a wreck. I worry about everything. You see me being nice to a couple of people and think I'm worth something. I'm not."

"I asked you not to make disparaging remarks about yourself."

"I'm trying to get you to see the truth about me."

"All you're doing is sealing your fate, *Solnyshkuh*. You're telling me you need me. You won't have worries when you're with me because I'm willing to take those on for you."

She couldn't speak. His declaration was obviously sincere, but she found herself too attracted. Wanting to give him everything. She'd be so lost in him.

"Don't look so scared, Zelie. Trust me when I say I'll take care of you."

The pad of his thumb swept gently, tenderly, over her cheekbone, and then traced her lips, setting her heart pounding and sex fluttering.

"I'm just as distrustful as you are. We both have good reasons for being the way we are. Let's do this together. Say you'll try for me. Commit, Zelie."

He mesmerized her, a predator cornering his prey, yet she didn't want to escape. As much as she feared she would be swallowed by him, he was the only man she had ever been attracted to, physically or emotionally. "All right." She whispered her capitulation because there was no way to make her voice any louder.

A slow smile softened his hard features. It didn't make him look any less dangerous, but it made him even more attractive.

"You should be outlawed," she said. "Seriously, Andrii, I'm not certain I can think straight around you."

"I'm going to fuck up," he warned softly, his thumb still moving over her bottom lip. "That temper you saw, it gets away from me. When it happens, you'll need to know my anger isn't at you. When I'm upset with you, we'll talk about it. Calmly. Without anger."

She swallowed hard. Was she really going to commit to a relationship with a man who admitted he had a bad temper?

"You're looking scared again."

Her cell phone played a few bars of Sheb Wooley's "Purple People Eater." She scowled before she could school her expression, but she made no move to answer.

Andrii's brows drew together. "Who is that? Clearly, you don't want to talk to them."

"That would be my boss, Alan Billows. He knows I have class tomorrow. I told him I couldn't come in for a meeting tonight, but he doesn't take no for an answer."

"I'll tell him no for you."

She found herself laughing. "You probably would. I need the job until I finish school and can get another one."

She wasn't certain it would be that easy or smart to walk away from Billows, but she wasn't going to tell Andrii that. She changed the subject instead. "What's in the box?"

SIX

Andrii debated whether to allow Azelie to get away with the change in subject. It wasn't in his best interest—or Azelie's—for Billows to find out they were dating. He didn't want more attention on Azelie from Billows. The man was a psychopath, and he was deeply involved in human trafficking. If the information Torpedo Ink had worked so hard to acquire was correct, Billows trained women and teens as sex slaves before they were put up for auction. He didn't like the thought of Azelie anywhere near the man.

Azelie was a gorgeous woman, whether she wanted to think so or not. She wore baggy clothes to hide her curves, but she had them. Any man who looked at her—and they would look—would be able to guess what was under her sweaters and hoodies. Her jeans clung to her body lovingly, and all that was without mentioning her face. She had beautiful skin that glowed and was rose-petal soft. Her eyes were large, vividly blue, and heavily lashed. Then she had all that wild hair.

Billows trafficked women. He would be able to assess Azelie's worth easily. The fact that she was a pleaser would go a long way to adding to her value. The man needed her for her skills in manipulating his books, but if he felt threatened, he would turn on her in an instant. In some ways, being with Andrii would be a protection for her. Men like Billows recognized immediately when there was a threat. At the same time, Billows might feel he was losing control of Azelie. Bookkeepers could be replaced.

"You aren't returning the dress and shoes to me, are you?" Azelie asked.

Her finger crept up to her bare ear. She didn't wear jewelry as a rule. She didn't even have studs in, although her ears were pierced. Andrii loved the little shells of her ears.

"Yes." He poured firmness into his voice, all the while keeping his tone low. He moved around her to pull the tie from the box and lift the lid. "I don't want you to give back any gift I give you, Zelie. It's a little hurtful, although I appreciate that you don't want to use me for my money."

She bit down on her lower lip as she took a step back. "Do you have money?"

"Yes."

"You said you were a contractor and that you played in a band," she protested. One hand went defensively to her throat, and she gave a little shake of her head. "And that you did security."

Andrii could see that the idea he had money really bothered her. She wasn't after him to see what she could get from him. That felt good. He'd known she wasn't all about money, but it was good to have it reaffirmed, to know his instincts were working.

"I am a contractor, and I do play in a band. I also work in security," he crooked his finger at her as he sank back down into the chair he'd occupied. "Come on, baby, there's nothing in here that's going to bite you."

She didn't move even though he'd used a compelling voice, the exact tone she was so susceptible to. Andrii was a little shocked at the genuine amusement welling up in him. As a rule, he didn't experience intense emotions. If he had them, they were usually negative rather than positive. He realized, almost from the moment he began studying Azelie's character to get close to her, he felt things much more deeply. He also found himself genuinely happy, as if by discovering a woman like her existed, there was hope for him after all.

"I don't want you to buy me gifts, Andrii." Azelie took another step back.

The room was tiny. The entire studio apartment could fit into the closet in the master bedroom of his house—and his house wasn't nearly as large as some of the other homes Torpedo Ink members had purchased. All he'd cared about was privacy and room for his piano and other musical instruments.

"If you keep backing up, you're going to hit the wall. Then I'm going to come to you, and you'll be scared all over again. What's the point?"

"You don't have to come to me."

Her voice was a little whisper, a thread of sound. Her eyes had gone wide and her face pale. She really needed to stop stroking her throat with trembling fingers or he was going to pick her up and carry her to the bed he'd been all too aware of. Or just take her right there against the wall. He didn't want to do either of those things.

Azelie deserved a courtship, getting to know him, becoming comfortable with his demands and way of life. She needed to believe that he would take care of her, do whatever it took to make her happy. To do that, to build the trust needed in their relationship, especially when she'd experienced trauma and betrayal at the hands of someone she loved, he had to take his time with her, not just jump into a demanding sexual relationship.

It was clear to him that she was very wary. He wasn't about to lose her through stupidity by going too fast. Pushing her too hard. He wanted a lasting relationship. He didn't know how any woman could have a relationship with him, but he was going to do his best to try to make it work.

"I would have to come to you. Haven't you figured out yet that I can't resist you?"

"I don't think you're seeing the real me, Andrii. I worry about that."

"You're rather adorable when you're stalling. Come over here and we'll talk about this, but I want to show you the things I chose for you. And no more protests. I enjoy choosing dresses and shoes for you. I know where I'm planning on taking you, and it was fun to envision what you would wear."

Andrii poured sincerity into his voice. He was telling her the truth. He had enjoyed shopping for her. Planning dates. Thanks to Code and three weeks of shadowing her, he was aware of her schedule. The only person who could throw a monkey wrench into his plans was Alan Billows scheduling unexpected meetings at the times Andrii had chosen to take her out.

"Come on, *Solnyshkuh*. Come here to me."

He kept his gaze steady on hers and saw that first moment of capitulation—that sweet surrender to his command, even though she was still wary. Still scared. She thought she wasn't brave, but it took tremendous courage to choose building a relationship after what she'd suffered.

She'd been knocked down hard and yet she was taking a chance with him. She was leery and trying to talk them both out of it, but even with her reluctance and probably every warning bell she had shrieking at her, she came to him. She chose him. She was getting to his heart, and they hadn't even started. The idea was terrifying yet exhilarating.

Azelie crossed the short distance and stood in front of him, her large blue eyes fixed on his as if at any moment he might bite her. He had a dark desire to do just that. Put his mark on her any way he could, brand his mark into her bones so she would know she belonged to him and never want to leave. He was shocked at the strength of his want—no, need.

Andrii wasn't a man to trust feelings, especially ones so intense, yet the longer he spent in her company, or watching her—even the surveillance films of her—the more it felt right and necessary to be with her. He knew it was crucial to gain her complete trust, and it had nothing to do with his assignment. She was his one chance at redemption—at happiness. He knew better than to trust her, but despite his knowledge of women, his mind was already made up.

"Don't look so leery, baby," he advised softly. "Come see if you like the clothing I chose for you. If you don't, I want you to tell me I got it wrong."

He lifted a pair of blue jeans out of the box. One pair appeared vintage, a faded blue. He knew they would fit her body like a glove and should be very comfortable because he'd made certain they weren't going to be skintight on her. They would show off her shape without making her uncomfortable. That was important to him. He put the denim aside.

"There are two pairs. One is black." He placed that pair of jeans on top of the other one and pulled out a soft blouse. The material stopped just short of being transparent. If she wore a black bra, which he'd included, beneath the light crimson, it would be sexy as hell. There was a black sweater to pair with either of the jeans, which went beautifully with the crimson blouse. There was also an equally soft off-the-shoulder sweater in a dark ash blue. It would also go with either pair of jeans. He could tell by her expression that she'd expected sexy cocktail dresses. That would be coming, but not yet.

"What do you think?"

She touched a sweater. "Beautiful." She breathed the word in a whisper. "Andrii, you have amazing taste. I love them. Thank you so much."

"We aren't quite done. I'm returning your silver dress and shoes, along with the jewelry. You may need those for another evening out. The jeans are for a couple of dates I have planned. I'll tell you when I'm surprising you, and you can choose what you'd like to wear. I might suggest one or the other, but that doesn't mean you have to wear what I suggest."

"Again, thank you, Andrii. I'm sorry I hurt you when I tried to give back the clothing. I'm uncomfortable with you giving me presents. I'm not with you to get anything."

"Which is why I choose to give you things. It makes me happy. Not only that, Zelie, but it was obvious to me that you had no idea I had money. It feels good to have a woman who wants to be with me for me. Not for what I can give to her."

He pulled out a royal-blue skirt that fell to the ankles in a series of long ruffles. The matching-colored top was a camisole that came to a V at the waist, hugged her breasts, but again was more sensual than showy. It was a classy outfit. He'd paired it with a soft pair of leather boots in a darker blue. A wave of ruffled leather crept up the back of each boot.

Andrii watched her face as he shook the skirt and camisole out to show her. Her eyes went wide and soft. Her lips parted, her expression showing absolute delight at the clothes. He was grateful he'd taken the time to search for the exact color and style he wanted for her. It had taken an extra day to get them to her, and Lana had helped him find the right boutiques to shop in, but that look was well worth his time.

When he pulled out the boots, she shook her head, covered her face and burst into tears. It wasn't exactly the reaction he was going for, but he'd take it. Setting the boots aside, he lifted her into his lap and pressed her face into his chest.

"What is it, *Solnyshkuh*? Talk to me. Let me make this right." He kept his voice low and soothing as he brushed kisses into the thick mass of wild hair.

She struggled to pull herself together. He liked the way her fists gripped his tee. He rubbed her back and massaged the nape of her neck, waiting patiently for her to stop crying. It didn't take long. Her lashes were wet and spiky surrounding her liquid-filled eyes, changing the color to a deeper blue.

"No one has ever done anything like this for me, Andrii. It's too much. Too overwhelming. I don't know why you're being so kind to me."

"Baby," he objected.

"No, you don't understand. I don't know what to do to thank you. Or to even things between us. I don't have a clue how to give you this amazing feeling you've given me."

He bent his head and rubbed the bristles of his short beard along her wet cheek. "I told you, Zelie, giving you gifts and watching your face to see if you like what I chose for you makes me happy. I'd know if I got it wrong. A large part of our relationship will be about trust, communication and my ability to read you."

Her long lashes fluttered and then he was looking directly into her eyes. "Why would it be necessary for you to read me?"

"I told you, babe, we're going to have a unique, intense relationship, and I'll need to know instantly when you're not happy with anything I ask of you."

Her eyes moved over his face, studying him carefully. She had a way of looking at him with a little bit of hero worship. There was no doubt that she was attracted to him. She didn't bother to try to hide it, although he knew it embarrassed her that she was so open with him. That was a good part of her personality that he loved.

"What kinds of things are you going to ask of me?"

"We're going to shelve that for a little while, just until you get to know me more. I've told you enough to intrigue you, but at the same time, you're freaking out just a little. I don't want you to get to the point where you're ready to run again."

Her chin went up and color crept up her neck into her face. Those blue eyes glittered like twin jewels. "I didn't run, Andrii. You did."

He couldn't help the grin that welled up out of nowhere. "There you go, calling me out on my shit. You're right. I acted like a child."

"I'm not trying to bring it up, Andrii. You apologized, and as far as I'm concerned, the incident is behind us, but it's important to me that when we discuss any issue, we get the facts correct. You implied I ran from you when it was the other way around," she reiterated. "I don't know what I did wrong other than try to give you back the clothes and jewelry."

"You scared the holy hell out of me, baby," he admitted. He was going to have to avoid many questions she would eventually ask, so he was determined that he would give her truth whenever possible, even if it made him look bad. "I have just as many trust issues as you do, and when you appeared to be so perfect for me, I struck out at you to drive you away. The moment I was in my ride and tearing down the freeway, I knew what a mistake I'd made."

The soft look on her face told him he had done the right thing in confessing. She really had forgiven him and put his entire idiotic reaction behind her. That only reinforced his belief that he'd found a woman he had a chance of being compatible with.

Using the pad of his thumb, he gently wiped at the wet trails on her face. "You have amazing skin, *Solnyshkuh*. It's even softer than it looks."

Her long lashes fluttered again. "You're going to have to stop giving me compliments. I don't know what to do when you say nice things about me."

Words mattered to her. She was a woman who dealt in words. The world might think she was all about numbers if they knew she did bookkeeping, but Azelie heard music in words. She wrote stories that played in her head. She saw the world differently because of her affinity for words. He loved that about her.

"Babe, you'll have to get used to me telling you the truth about yourself." He rubbed his jaw along the top of her head. Strands of her hair caught in his beard, binding them together. It was ridiculous how much he liked that. He was supposed to mesmerize her, keep her focused and centered on being with him, yet he was fast falling under her spell. It made no sense to him, and panic flooded his system for a brief moment before he could get it under control.

"You bought me three outfits." Her voice was soft, creating intimacy between them.

"I've planned three outings for us." He stroked caresses down the back of her head, deliberately tangling his fingers in the thick strands. Her wild hair was sexy to him, especially because she had such an innocent aura clinging to her. "I tried to find things I think you would enjoy. When is your next free day? It can be anytime during work hours, up until nine. The place I want to take you to closes at nine."

"I have my classes tomorrow. And I have to call Billows back and make an appointment with him."

Maestro could hear dread in her voice. It made him want to take her back to Caspar with him and stash her somewhere safe until his club had taken Billows down. Having her in the line of fire was becoming abhorrent to him, and they were just getting started.

He needed her keys. Various Torpedo Ink members had looked through her studio apartment, which was very small, and yet they hadn't found them. The members of his club were very adept at finding objects hidden in people's homes, no matter how big or small the place was, yet they had been unsuccessful despite several attempts. She didn't appear to carry keys on her person.

Was it possible she didn't have the keys, and Billows admitted her to his underground office when she made an appointment with him?

As if Billows could hear his thinking, the intercom blared. Azelie leapt off his lap, a look of alarm on her face.

"It's him. Billows. I should have answered him." Her fingers went up to her throat, stroking nervously. "It would be better if he didn't see you, Andrii. He's not always rational."

The fact that she tried to protect him endeared her to him even more.

She went to the intercom. "Yes?"

"Let me the fuck in," Billows demanded.

"No. We had an arrangement, Alan. I agreed to continue working for you, but you weren't to come to my home or try to intimidate me."

Andrii could see that she was shaking, but her voice was very steady.

"I agreed to that nonsense when I thought you'd be reasonable." There was a distinct threat in his voice.

It was all Maestro could do not to go downstairs and lay down the law to Billows regarding his woman.

"What have I been unreasonable about?"

"I'm not standing outside arguing with you over this. Open the fucking door."

"I'll come down. We can talk in the lobby." She lifted her finger from the intercom and hastily rushed over to the tiny closet to pull out a puffy jacket. "I'm sorry, Andrii, this won't take long."

"He sounds angry."

"He almost always sounds angry," she agreed.

"Will he get violent with you?"

Azelie shook her head. "I've known him going on seven years. Believe me, he knows if he did, I'd quit."

Andrii didn't want her to quit. That might trigger Billows into kidnapping her and forcing her into his training program for the women and teens he trafficked.

"I'll just go downstairs with you and make sure he doesn't treat you with disrespect."

Azelie reacted exactly how he knew she would. "No, absolutely stay up here, Andrii. He won't be pleasant to you if he thinks you're dating me."

Every cell in his body went on alert. "Why would Billows be ugly if he found out you're dating me? Has he asked you out?"

Andrii was older than she was by a good ten years, but the age difference between her and Billows was double that or more.

"Not like that, not as in trying to take me to dinner. He just acts proprietorial over me. Not like a daughter or sister, just as if he owns me."

She covered her clothing with the puffy jacket. "This shouldn't take long, Andrii."

A part of him felt like laughing at the firmness in her

voice. She was dictating to him, insistent that she would face
Billows alone. He recognized she was protecting him. She
knew his inclination was to go with her and she didn't want
that. She knew Billows was a criminal. She might not know
about the trafficking, but she knew his books were indica-
tive of a very dangerous man. Andrii doubted if Billows
would allow her to leave him. He'd traffic or kill her first.
She knew too many of his secrets.

Azelie might be an introvert and a nurturer, but she was
highly intelligent. She had to have realized she was in trouble with Billows. She made no attempt to quit despite his
mood swings, mostly, Andrii was certain, biding her time,
getting through school. She had to have an exit plan. He
knew it wouldn't work. Billows would track her down. He
couldn't afford for her to be out in the world, a possible informant to law enforcement.

Azelie took the lift down to the entrance. Andrii took the
stairs. He was fit and he could move with both speed and
stealth. He wasn't about to leave her alone and unprotected
with Billows. He'd gone from playing her to protecting her
in two meetings. Even if things didn't work out between
them, he would see she was free of Billows.

Tonight, he wanted to see the interaction between the
woman he considered his and her boss. The two had known
each other for nearly seven years. If he was lucky, he would
learn vital information, such as where the keys would be to
the underground rooms and how to get inside them unde-
tected. Code had gotten the blueprints for the three-story
building, but Billows had managed to conceal rooms beneath the Adventure Club, which was beneath the Pleasure
Train Club. Those rooms weren't on the blueprints. Torpedo
Ink knew the rooms were there, just not how to get to them.

Azelie had opened the door to allow Billows into the foyer.
There were a couple of chairs in an alcove across from the
stairs. As if she was wholly confident, she turned her back
on her employer to lead the way.

From his vantage point, Maestro studied the man his club

knew to be a huge cog in the trafficking wheel. He looked to be about forty-five. His hair was thick and sandy colored. Although he was slim, his suit showed off his physique, a man with muscle hiding beneath the smooth lines of his jacket.

Maestro had met him a couple of times, going to the Adventure Club, spending enough money and acting the dominant enough to be noticed. That had been the point. The owner came out to meet with the "big spender." Maestro played up his Russian accent even though he rarely spoke with an accent. Billows had introduced himself and appeared friendly at the first meeting. In the second meeting he'd been more reserved and abrupt. At the third and last, Maestro had felt an immediate threat, as if two predators vying for top position had crossed trails and only one could survive.

"I'm not certain why you couldn't have waited until I got out of class, Alan," Azelie ventured, seating herself across from her boss.

"I told you it's an emergency. I need you to fix the problem tonight. All you had to do to prevent my coming here was answer your damn phone."

Maestro didn't like his tone. The man sounded threatening, ugly even. It didn't seem to faze Azelie. She looked at her boss calmly, not even blinking at the building tension between them. Maestro would have to always remember that his woman would hold her ground under any circumstances if she believed she was in the right.

"I told you that I have school tomorrow. I study before I go to class, particularly if there is going to be a test. I don't always have my phone on me. I don't during class, and I don't when I'm studying. I watch children sometimes, and I rarely have my phone on during those times."

"That's bullshit, Azelie. You're to be available whenever I need you."

Azelie lifted one eyebrow. "We had a deal, Alan. In fact, I have it in writing, signed by you. School is important to me, and there wasn't to be any interference with my classes or studies. I get your books done. I've never once failed you. I don't understand the sudden emergency. If you somehow found out you're going to get a surprise audit, you should have told me this afternoon. At night I study. You know that."

"I know you get paid a hell of a lot of money to push numbers around."

"Actually, I don't. We talked about that too."

He leaned forward. "What does that mean? I know how much you get paid."

"I don't get paid what a regular bookkeeper gets paid. If you had someone else doing for you what I do, you'd be paying them thousands."

He opened his mouth, closed it, sat back, folded his arms across his chest and pressed his lips together, glaring at her. Maestro studied his expression. Billows didn't like what Azelie had just revealed to him. He had to have known the going rate for a bookkeeper like Azelie. Basically, she cooked their books. She tracked down lost money for them. She laundered it into legitimate businesses. According to Code, she barely scraped by.

What the hell? It was impossible for Billows not to know what she got paid, but Maestro was a master at reading people—it was what kept him alive. Billows believed Azelie made far more money than she did. Did he have another bookkeeper? Was he setting Azelie up so it appeared she was skimming cash from the books?

"Let's start over, Azelie," Billows finally said. His tone wasn't exactly conciliatory, but he clearly wanted her to be on the same page with him.

Azelie smiled at her boss and inclined her head—princess to riffraff. Her smile didn't reach her eyes, but it illuminated the beauty in her face. Maestro didn't like the satisfaction gleam creeping into Billows' expression. A man training trafficking victims for the sexual assault that would end up being their lives should have been able to read the falseness of her expression. Either Billows was so arrogant he believed she was into him and wanted to please him, or he didn't care enough to learn to read others. That made him stupid and even more dangerous, in Maestro's opinion.

"I'll see to it that you receive the proper amount of money for the work you do." Billows sat back in the chair and regarded her with shrewd eyes.

To Maestro, the man looked cunning. There was a cruel edge to his mouth, and far too much interest in his gaze when he looked at Azelie.

"I don't know why you aren't receiving what you should be, but I'll fix that immediately."

"I appreciate that, Alan, but my not going tonight isn't about the money. School is extremely important to me. When my classes are over tomorrow, I'll come straight to the club. You know I've never once let you down. I *need* these classes and I can't reschedule them."

Billows scowled at her, openly showing his displeasure. Maestro paid attention to Azelie's reaction. Had Andrii been the one upset with her, there was no doubt in his mind that she would be uncomfortable and would try to find a compromise. Instead, she appeared serene but implacable.

"How late will you be tomorrow?"

"My last class gets out at four. So basically, all day. I don't even have time for lunch. On my break between classes, I'll study for the tests I'll be taking. So, after four, I'll grab something to eat and come straight to the club."

Maestro noted that she wouldn't have time for lunch. He would find out where she was going to be and bring her something to eat. Someone needed to look after her, and he wanted to be that someone.

Billows' scowl deepened. "Azelie, I've told you it isn't a good idea for any of our customers to see you. We might not be open, but staff arrives and sometimes others come with them. If they like to play in the Adventure Club and you're spotted without a protector, things could go wrong for you. Someone might stalk you."

Maestro found it interesting that Billows appeared to be somewhat protective of her, yet he hadn't visited her in the hospital when she'd been shot. She'd nearly died and was hospitalized and then in rehab for several weeks. If Billows did visit her, Code hadn't found evidence of it, and Azelie had indicated that her boss hadn't come to see her. There had been no protection from press or police.

He also thought it strange, if Billows was concerned for her, that he didn't volunteer to bring her lunch or say he'd have something waiting at the club for her. He didn't want her seen by customers. Was that for her protection? Or was the reason sinister? No one would recognize her if she disappeared.

"I can use the private entrance on the ground floor and come down to the offices. I'll wear my hoodie and keep my face shielded," Azelie offered. "Hopefully, no one will see me."

Billows rubbed his jaw and then shook his head. "I'll come get you around six. It's much darker then."

Maestro's heart did a slow stutter. He didn't want Azelie alone in the car with her boss. The man could take her anywhere. Make her disappear.

Azelie appeared to think it over, and then she was the one shaking her head. "Everyone knows you, Alan. They know your car. If you showed up at the club with a woman in a hoodie, even if they couldn't see my face, you know everyone would be talking. Speculating. You can't go anywhere without celebrity press taking photographs. I think that would bring too much attention to you—and me. I'm used to taking the bus, even in the evening."

She sounded sincerely concerned about bringing undue attention to Billows. Maestro was a little in awe of Azelie's acting skills. He would have to always watch her carefully. He never wanted to miss a single cue, which would clue him in on what she was thinking or how she was feeling.

He knew he was born with instincts, and he'd honed them into a superb skill set. That had been done for survival. When one needed to understand and read the enemy, or any potential enemy, it made a great incentive to work hard. He also had done psychological studies at an early age to better understand and manipulate his enemies. When he was a child, he hadn't been able to spot those willing to betray him, but he sure as hell could now.

Her boss looked pleased. He should have been worried about Azelie going out at night, but instead, he focused on her statement, taking it to mean she was looking out for him. Maestro knew better. His very intelligent woman didn't want any part of getting in a vehicle alone with Billows. Again, Maestro had to wonder how Billows didn't pick up on that.

"I have tons of studying to do tonight, Alan, before I can go to bed." Azelie stood and instantly Billows followed suit, allowing her to lead the way to the door. "I'll see you tomorrow evening," she added as she opened the door for him, stepping back to give him room to exit.

Billows nodded, looking pleased with the outcome. He sauntered down the walkway to his car. Azelie closed the door, which automatically locked, but she stood watching Billows until he entered his vehicle. Believing her safe, Maestro swiftly raced up the stairs and let himself back into her apartment. He quickly arranged the clothes and shoes by outfit. He hadn't shown her the sexy underwear, but he placed the lingerie on the chair as well. The little boxes of jewelry were set beside the lingerie. He hoped she wouldn't notice until he was gone.

When Azelie entered, he was seated, but he stood up. "How did it go?"

She shrugged. "I'm going to meet him after my classes. I get out at four or four-thirty and should have enough time to get home, eat something and change before I have to be there."

"That makes for a long day. When is your lunch break at school?"

"One-thirty, but I don't have time to pick anything up. I'll take some crackers with me. I usually sit outside. The campus has quite a few trees and I enjoy feeling I'm surrounded by nature. I have a semiprivate spot I like to claim where I can just sit and relax before my next class."

"How will you get to the club?"

"I use the bus system all the time."

Deliberately, he raised an eyebrow. "I'll come by and pick you up."

Looking alarmed, Azelie shook her head, an unconscious movement. "I don't think that's a good idea, Andrii. Alan was acting weirder than usual. I never know what mood he's going to be in."

"Do you think I'm afraid of this man?"

"No. But you don't really know him. I screwed up and admitted to you that I started working for him when I was barely sixteen. I even told you what I do for him. Clearly, he's into criminal activities. I know he's all over the celebrity sites and is considered an eligible bachelor, but he isn't a good man."

"Neither am I." Maestro wanted her to keep that in mind. "Still, if you don't want to be seen with me, I'll just hang back and make sure you're safe."

"There isn't any reason. You can't get into the offices. It's a labyrinth down there and there are security measures everywhere, including guards. As it is, I think he would kill me for talking to you about this."

"That's why you haven't left the job."

Again, she shrugged. "I just want you safe. I'm going to be fine, but you need to be safe. That's important to me."

Maestro heard the sincerity in her voice and read the determination on her face. He couldn't help feeling a little overwhelmed by her concern. His brothers and sisters in the club looked out for him, but the way she was anxious to stand in front of him felt huge. Important. Better than good.

"All right, baby, have it your way. Save the day after tomorrow for us. I have somewhere special I want to take you. I'll text you with details."

He wasn't leaving without the taste of her in his mouth. That was most likely a huge mistake, but it didn't matter. He needed the taste of her almost as much as he needed his next breath. Shaping his palm around the nape of her neck, he gently pulled her closer, sliding his thumb along her soft skin, tracing her cheekbone.

"*Bog*, but you're beautiful," he said. He meant it. She was a beautiful woman, but he didn't mean the outside of her. There were a lot of gorgeous women in the world, but he'd rarely met one with her character.

Her long lashes fluttered and then lifted, and he was looking into wild blue. Shy. So endearing. He could see desire in all that blue. He wanted that look to always be there for him. That meant he had to earn it. He had to step up. She was worth it.

He ran his thumb over her bottom lip. "You remember who you belong with, *Solnyshkuh*. I was born to be your man."

That meant something to her. Faint color crept under her skin, and her eyes took on a glow. He didn't wait a moment longer, his palm tightening around her neck when he leaned down to brush his lips over hers.

The earth moved under him. The room spun away. There was nothing but the two of them. He had kissed women. Hundreds. Maybe more. A requirement of his training. Since he'd been a free man, kissing was off-limits. Kissing was too intimate, and he didn't enjoy it—or want it. Now it was a need. An addiction. An obsession. *She* was his obsession.

She tasted as sweet and innocent as she looked. Strawberries and champagne. Strawberries and cream. Strawberries and fire. The longer he kissed her, the hotter the flames burned through his veins. She melted into him, her body pressed tight against his so he felt every feminine curve. So he was aware of the exact way they fit together, as if she'd been created just for him. There was no hesitation on her part. She might not be experienced—and she wasn't—but she was the best he'd ever had. Would ever have.

Her arms slid around his neck, and she surrendered to him wholly. Gave him everything. Offered him the world, and he didn't care what kind of dick he was—he was taking what she was offering, and he would treasure her, do his best to keep her happy. And he would protect her with his life.

He poured possession into his kiss. Gave her fire for fire. Held her as close as possible without breaking her with his strength. She felt perfect to him.

Maestro lifted his head just enough to rest his forehead against hers. "I've never had perfection. I didn't know it even existed."

"I'm not perfect."

"You are for me." He pressed his lips against her forehead and then each temple. "I had no idea I had it in me to feel this way about anyone. When I think of some of the idiotic advice I gave my brothers or said to their women, I'm thoroughly ashamed of myself. I'm sure when you meet them, they'll tell you all about it and I'll look like a dick."

"You aren't a dick."

"I am, baby. I just hope that side of me stays hidden until you're sure of us and you can trust me to make up for my foul temper, controlling ways and idiocy when it comes to a relationship." He forced himself to do the right thing. "I've got to go before it's too late."

Her arms tightened around him, and she looked up at him with the most amazing expression—one of near adoration. He didn't deserve it, but he was going to take it.

"What if I don't want you to go?"

The blush of her skin was like a rose blooming to him. She was so beautiful he ached inside. She was embarrassed to ask him to stay, but she still gave him that.

"I don't want to go either, *Solnyshkuh*, but you aren't ready. The kind of relationship I want with you is based on trust, not sex. Although we're going to fuck a hell of a lot. When you trust me enough to live with my flaws, I'll take care of you, baby."

A little shiver had gone through her body at his crude declaration, but she didn't pull away. If anything, she moved closer, clung tighter, held on. "Perfection," he murmured and didn't dare risk kissing her again. He had always been a man with control, but she seemed able to rob him of that iron discipline he'd learned in the school from hell. "I'm leaving now, Zelie, but I'll see you tomorrow."

He turned abruptly and walked out before she could remind him she had classes all day and an appointment with Billows. Before he could lose his resolve and stay to fuck her all night. To hold her close and let her in further.

SEVEN

China Christian caught Azelie's hand as she made her way to the counter at the coffee shop. "Tell us. We're *dying* to know. We know you went out on a date with Mr. Hottie. Sit here, honey. We've waited for *days*."

Blanc Christian nodded. "At our age, that kind of anticipation could take years off our lives, and we can't afford it. I'll get your drink, and you just park yourself right here."

Penny Atwater patted the chair beside her. "We snagged the best table so the four of us could sit together."

"Did you have out-of-this-world wild sex?" China persisted.

"China Annabelle Christian," Blanc chided, sounding shocked. Then she leaned forward. "Well, did you? Was he to die for?"

"Is he as good in the sack as he looks like he would be?" Penny asked, her voice a little breathless.

"I am not the kind of woman to kiss and tell." Azelie did her best to keep laughter from bubbling to the surface, but it was impossible when the three women looked so crestfallen.

"I'm getting her drink," Blanc said, rising. "Sister, you work on her. I'll never be able to sleep again if she doesn't give us the 411."

Azelie laughed. "You three are horrible."

"No, dear." Penny shook her head solemnly. "We need to live vicariously through you."

China's eyes were dancing with glee. "It's so true, Azelie. I was a beauty in my younger years and could have my pick of men. Your Andrii would have been my number one choice. I would have done anything to make him mine."

Blanc had hurried back after putting in the order for Azelie's coffee. "What did I miss? Seriously, Azelie, I can't afford to lose any more sleep over this. I know you gave Shaila a big box and asked her to hold it for your man. He came in a couple of days ago to retrieve the box."

"We *begged* Shaila to open it and peek inside," China continued. "She wouldn't do it."

"I even tried to bribe her and David," Penny admitted. "They said absolutely not."

"I'll have to thank them for keeping my confidence," Azelie said, using her primmest tone. "At least *they* have morals when it comes to other people's business."

Blanc wasn't in the least offended. She waved her hand in the air as if shooing away a bothersome fly. "Morals be damned," she stated. "You have to live this life, Azelie. Grab on with both hands. That man is the kind of man who will give you hell, but hold on tight to him because the dance will be worth it."

"Or he's the kind of man who will cut out your heart and leave you with nothing." Azelie shared her worst fear. "I don't have it in me to go from man to man. And he isn't the kind of man who can leave a woman unscathed if he left, at least a woman like me."

There was a small silence while the merry widows digested that information. It was the most information about herself she'd confided to the women in all the years she'd been coming to the coffee shop. They seemed to be taken aback by her revelation.

Shaila called out Azelie's name. Blanc immediately rose and hurried to the counter to get the iced latte that they all knew was Azelie's favorite drink. Azelie had cash out to pay her back for the coffee, but Blanc shoved it back across the table at her.

"You buy us coffee often," Blanc said firmly. "I think we can afford to buy yours once in a while."

"Are you afraid of Andrii?" China asked gently. There was no hint of amusement in her tone. She was very serious.

"No, not like that. I think it's possible he would hurt someone if he thought they were upsetting me. He's a little on the overprotective side. But . . ." She trailed off.

The three women waited, showing extraordinary patience when Azelie hadn't realized they were capable of such a thing. All three had sobered at her confession. A part of her felt warm and wished she had been able to connect with them on a more personal level sooner.

"Tell us, dear," Penny insisted. "You have us to look out for you."

The Christian sisters nodded in agreement. "We're very experienced," China added. "Between the three of us and the era we grew up in, we've seen and become very knowledgeable about the ways of men. And we're very good at confidentiality, despite the teasing we just subjected you to. What you tell us remains with us."

Azelie gripped the latte. Her reluctance wasn't about trust. She had come to know the three women fairly well, at least their character, and she was certain they would always act with her best interests at heart. She had observed them for a long time and knew the affectionate way they teased one another. She was grateful that she was considered their friend. Her reluctance was about getting too close. Caring too much. Putting them in danger. Losing them.

Blanc leaned close to her. "We might be as old as dirt, Azelie, but our minds are sharp. We're always going to be on your side."

"You can't be so nice to me," she said. "I mean it. I act tough, but I'm not."

The three women burst into radiant smiles. It was Penny

who addressed that statement. "Dear, we are very aware of what a soft heart you have. Why do you think we're so protective of you? I always wanted a daughter—or, in your case, a granddaughter. I have neither. I lost the love of my life long before we ever thought of making babies together. There was never another man for me, at least not one I wanted permanently in my life."

China patted her hand. "Do you know why I was named China and my sister Blanc? Our parents were addicted to heroin. They thought it would be hilarious to name their children after their drug of choice. In those days there weren't many protections for children, certainly not the way there are now."

A fist of apprehension knotted in Azelie's stomach. Pressure was suddenly severe in her chest. She had suffered intense trauma, and it had been very public in the news. Her brother-in-law murdered his wife and children and attempted to murder her as well. There had even been accounts of her mother's abuse, done in her drunken rages. They knew. These women who had never once indicated they knew who she was, had never brought up her past.

"Our parents 'gifted' us to their drug dealer," Blanc disclosed, and reached for her sister's hand. Penny laid her hand on Blanc's shoulder. "That abuse started when China was twelve and I was eleven. It didn't end until Penny's father stepped in. He was in law enforcement, and Penny told him what was going on. By that time, we were fourteen and fifteen." She glanced at Penny and blinked away tears.

"We rarely talk about it," China said. "Penny's father died saving us. She has forgiven us, but to this day we find it difficult to forgive ourselves."

"There was nothing to forgive," Penny interjected. "I was the one who went to my father and told him how your parents treated you. I told him about the drug dealer and the arrangement with your parents. He was horrified. He took it upon himself to investigate. Those were our choices, not yours."

Azelie's heart felt as if it were pounding out of her chest. Her mouth had gone dry. There was a lump in her throat making it difficult to breathe.

"Our parents found out about the raid, that it was going to take place. We were both with the dealer," China continued. "My father had a friend in the department, one who more than once had exchanged information for us. He called my father and asked for us in exchange for date and time of the raid. My parents rushed to inform their dealer. They wanted to take us home quickly so they wouldn't lose their prize possessions in making money for their drugs."

"How terrible," Azelie murmured. She pressed her hand over her aching heart. "I've never understood how people can abuse their children that way. My mother beat me and more than once threatened me with a knife, but I don't think she considered selling me. She did see me as a rival for men's affections. I was lucky to have Janine, my older sister."

"We didn't have anyone, not a single relative," Blanc added in a hoarse whisper. She cleared her throat. "When our parents arrived, pounding on the door, at first Marty, that was the dealer's name, refused to answer. He was furious that they would bother him when he and his customers were having fun with us. There was a lot of shouting back and forth. Swearing. Marty even shot at the door. My parents had weapons, and they shot back through the door. At that point, Marty dragged China away from one of his men and put her in front of him as a shield."

"Blanc was screaming at Marty to let me go. Marty had three men with him and four customers. Chaos ensued when he finally yanked open the door and my parents were pointing guns at him and he was pointing guns at them and his soldiers were yelling that they'd heard our dad say the cops were on their way," China said.

"Then the cops were in the house, and Marty opened fire on them," Blanc continued in a much stronger voice. "They broke in through the back and kitchen doors."

She reminded Azelie of herself and the way she distanced

herself if she had to repeat the story of her brother-in-law massacring her family. Azelie felt more connected than ever to the three women, and she felt privileged that they were telling her of their past when they didn't have to.

"Our parents forgot all about Marty keeping me in front of him as a shield," China continued. "They opened fire on the cops. I saw Blanc go down to the floor with blood on her chest. I thought she was dead. Marty's men stepped on her and kicked her when they ran. Our father went down and then our mother. Marty kept firing at the cops. The sound of his gun was so loud by my ear I couldn't hear anything."

Subconsciously, she rubbed at her ear, and then she hugged herself. "I was certain I would die, and it didn't matter if Marty shot me. Someone was going to sooner or later, and I didn't want to live without Blanc. I fought Marty, throwing off his aim. I was able to break away but ran right between Marty's men and the cops, with both sides firing. Penny's father jumped out of the line of cops and tackled me, but he was hit from both sides."

Azelie heard the sob in her voice, but China kept it together. Penny put her hand on China's shoulder.

"He saved my life, Penny," China whispered.

"I know he did. He was a man everyone looked up to for a reason. He wanted you to live. You and Blanc."

"And your mother . . ." China broke off with a little shake of her head. She lifted her fingers to her trembling mouth. "She was the most extraordinary woman I've ever met. Bar none, the most extraordinary."

Blanc nodded her agreement. "She took us in when no one would. She claimed it would be a temporary shelter, but she gave us the first real home we'd ever had." She lifted her gaze to Penny's. "She would sit on our beds with Penny when we had nightmares. She rocked us like we were babies and told us nothing was our fault, and we were worth everything. She believed that, and she made us believe it."

"Her name was Annabelle Foster, and we both took her name for our middle names," China continued. "We wanted to honor her. She knew a judge who made our name changes legal."

"My middle name is also Annabelle," Penny added. "Her name ties us together as sisters. Maybe not by blood, but of the heart."

"That's so incredible. I wish I'd had the opportunity to know her," Azelie said, meaning it. "Thank you for giving me such a gift as sharing your past."

"It's important that you know you can trust us, Azelie," Blanc said. "Obviously, we read about you in the papers, just like most of the people here in San Francisco. It was all over the news. We don't want you to feel alone."

"If Annabelle were here right now, she would tell you that you deserve to live your life," China assured her. "She would tell you that you took a tremendous knockout, but standing up and getting on with your life honors the ones you lost."

"She believed everything she said to us," Penny said. "She drilled it into the three of us that life is to be lived. To be experienced. It isn't always easy, but when it's right, it's a thrill ride."

"She also told us to be brave, to reach out to others worthy of our friendship with an open heart," Blanc added. "Her advice has never steered us wrong. You have a good heart, Azelie. You also need to trust your instincts. What do they say about Andrii?"

She put her latte down and tried to answer honestly. "Everything in me wants to be with him. I'm afraid though. I don't know what he sees in me. When we're together and he's talking to me, it's almost overwhelming how drawn I am to him. I fell too far too fast. I can't seem to help myself when I'm around him. I think I'm going to throw him out, but he starts talking in that voice he has, and I'm totally mesmerized." She took a deep breath and made her confession. "I can't help but want to make him happy."

Penny frowned. "You want to make him happy. Does he feel the same way? Does he try to make you happy?"

"He's spoiling me. If he takes me somewhere, he thinks

he has to bring me clothes and shoes and jewelry. He brought the most beautiful coat I've ever seen. When I wanted to pay for it, he was upset with me. I don't want him to think he has to buy me things. I'm not interested in him for his money."

"That was the box you had Shaila and David hold for him," Blanc guessed. "The clothes and jewelry were inside."

Azelie nodded. "I felt I couldn't keep them. He wasn't happy. He showed up with more gifts."

"Dear," Penny leaned close to whisper. "Did you tell him you were interested in having sex with him?"

Azelie felt color creeping under her skin. "Unfortunately, he can read me like a book. Seriously. I look at him and melt. There isn't any hiding that."

"Does he take proper care of you in bed?" China asked. "If he's selfish, end it, honey, no matter how much you're into him. He needs to be more interested than you are."

"Sadly, I don't think that's possible," Azelie confessed. "I tried to tell him there were hundreds of reasons why we shouldn't be together, but he countered every one of them."

"He knows his own mind. That's good," Penny said. "You want a man who knows what he wants. Too many men are always looking for something shiny and new. Or they are 'finding themselves.' You'd think at a certain age they would know what they want and who they are."

"Penny, dear," Blanc said gently. "You mustn't be bitter."

"I'm grateful the old codger found himself with a younger woman," Penny said. "Fourteen years of cooking and picking up after him, watching him quit job after job because he decided he wasn't appreciated, it got old fast."

"Your husband left you for a younger woman?"

"He didn't want to leave. He wanted an open marriage, so I'd continue to support him while he ran around finding himself. What he didn't realize was I was happy to see him go. Happy to let his car model pick up after him. He was going through his photography phase, and clearly, she thought he had money. He didn't. I do really recommend prenups. Especially the cheating clause."

"She had to prove he cheated in court," China said. "He was ridiculous enough to demand a court ruling on the pre-nup. Sadly for him, his cheating was very blatant. He went to hotels and was photographed because his little darling wanted the publicity. They were caught in compromising situations several times."

"I'm so sorry, Penny," Azelie murmured. "I don't have words."

"I'm not. Truly. That's why I say trust your instincts. If I'd followed mine, I wouldn't have wasted so many years with him. Right from the beginning I knew he was a worm, but I was certain he would blossom into a wonderful man." She gave a snort of self-derision. "Once I shed that snake, I had the time of my life. I just followed my mother's advice and stood back up, more determined than ever to live my life fully. I grabbed on with both hands and I rarely looked back."

"That's when she acquired all her excellent knowledge of men and their various kinks," Blanc said solemnly. "If you need answers to any question regarding sex, just ask Penny."

Rather than take offense, Penny laughed, breaking the tension that had built up with the revelations the Christian sisters had made.

"I became an official groupie for an entire summer, following a very popular band around. It was the most fun I'd had in years." There wasn't a sign of remorse in her voice or her expression.

"You refer to yourselves as the merry widows," Azelie pointed out. "But it sounds as if you didn't lose your husband to death."

The three women exchanged a long, amused look and then burst into laughter. Penny nearly knocked over her coffee, she was laughing so hard.

"I'm officially a merry widow because I killed my husband off in fifty clever ways without actually killing him. It was an amazing journey of retribution and recovery. It was China's idea."

China nodded. "We played a game thinking up heinous ways to do in cheating husbands, wrote the ideas down and burned them in a solemn ceremony. When we reached fifty, we were feeling quite merry. Hence the name."

The women burst into laughter again, and Azelie joined them. "How do you top that?"

"Now we play cards with Doug Parsons and Carlton Gray," China said. "Neither one of them is anywhere near as good as we are, but we let them win unless money is on the table."

"Once Doug had a little too much to drink and wanted to play strip poker," Penny said and burst out laughing all over again at the memory. "We made sure he lost every hand."

"I'm sitting at a table with some badass women," Azelie declared.

"You're one of those badass women," China said. "You just have to believe in yourself."

Azelie glanced down at her watch. "I have to catch the bus. I don't want to be late for class. I have a very tight schedule today."

"Promise you'll talk to us later," Blanc said. "We want to know you're safe. And happy."

"We mostly want you to know we're here for you," Penny said.

Azelie shrugged into her backpack and caught up the latte. "Thank you all. I'll see you later." She didn't have too much time before the bus would show up. Hurrying along the street toward the bus stop, to her dismay, she spotted Alan Billows in his sporty little BMW. He was parked directly across from the bus stop, talking on his cell phone.

As Azelie approached the corner, Billows looked up and beckoned to her. She shook her head and indicated her watch and then the bus stop.

Billows scowled darkly at her. "Get in the damn car, Azelie. I don't have all fucking day to wait around for you. I'll drive you to school."

"I have to take the bus." That sounded lame even to her own ears. She tried to look calm and all smiles as she waved to him.

"Azelie?" A woman's voice had her spinning around. The woman was tall and curvy, absolutely gorgeous with her sleek, shining black hair, perfect skin, dark eyes and lush lips. "I'm sorry I was late." She winked at her. "We have time to study on the bus together."

She came close. "I've seen you around the campus. Is that man bothering you?" She whispered the question, her back to Billows.

The last thing Azelie wanted to do was to have this woman who was trying to help get on Billows' radar. He could be ugly and vindictive when he didn't get his way.

Azelie hastily texted Billows that her study partner was there, and they'd planned to ride the bus together to work on their project. Billows didn't answer, but roared off, his expression a mask of fury.

"Thanks," Azelie said, meaning it. "I'm Azelie Vargas."

"Lana Popov," the woman introduced herself. "I have seen you around a couple of times, although I don't think we have any classes together."

Azelie would have remembered her. The woman was gorgeous. Perfect hair, skin, teeth, figure. Azelie couldn't find a single flaw in her. Lana made her feel a little mousy. The bus drove up and the door opened. Both women climbed on, Lana following Azelie to one of the middle-row seats.

"Should you have called the police?" Lana asked. "Is he some kind of stalker?"

Azelie considered how best to answer. The woman had been kind to a stranger. She had deliberately pretended they were friends because she thought Azelie was in danger. She didn't want to lie to Lana, but she didn't want her probing any deeper. It was never a good thing to get on Alan Billows' radar.

"No, he's just the most annoying boss in the world."

Azelie kept her tone light, as if Billows amused her. "He doesn't understand the concept of days off."

Lana laughed. "I know a few people like that. Obsessed with work."

"I keep telling him the days I have school. He agreed to let me have those days off, but now he wants me to come work whenever it suits him." Azelie heaved an exaggerated sigh. "Really, thanks again for rescuing me. It was quick thinking."

"I sent up a prayer to the universe that you wouldn't ask me who the hell I was. You're quick on the uptake."

"You threw a lifeline, and I caught it. He would have made me late for my class, and I have an important test first thing. I don't want to miss taking it. The policy is that if you fail, no makeup unless by prearrangement."

"Harsh," Lana said. "I'm glad I'm not in that class."

Ordinarily, Azelie would have smiled at her and turned away, content to be quiet and turn inward, fearful of having friends in her life. But Lana's laughter, the cool confidence she exuded as well as what appeared to be genuine friendliness had Azelie wanting to follow the merry widows' advice. She wanted friends. She wanted to be connected to others. Now was the time; all the signs seemed to point in that direction.

"What are you majoring in?" That seemed a safe enough question. If Lana asked her, she could talk about how her brain was always so conflicted.

"Fashion design. I particularly enjoy designing unique articles of clothing for young teens, ones that are misfits in school and don't have much. My goal would be to sell high-end to those who can afford it and make clothes to give to teens at a nominal fee or be able to waive the money altogether."

Azelie was impressed. "That's amazing. Really amazing. I swear, if you ever get your business off the ground and need backers, I'll find a way to help you, even if I have to take out a personal loan. That's a very worthwhile ambition.

I'm good with numbers; I could do your books for free or something just to help you out."

She meant it too. Every single word. She wrote down her name and cell phone number. "Stay in touch with me and hopefully you achieve exactly what you envision."

Lana accepted the Post-it Note and put it in her backpack. "Thank you. I intend to make my business a success. It's nice to hear that someone else thinks it's a good idea."

"It's a *great* idea," Azelie enthused.

"What are you majoring in?" Lana asked.

"Not something that will help others the way you plan to do—certainly not that concrete of an idea. I love to tell stories. I want to get better at that craft, but I do have a weird brain. I see in patterns, in numbers, so logic is always at war with my creativity."

"Words can be very powerful. Stories touch people and seem to find the ones who need to hear them. I love to read. It's one thing I'm passionate about," Lana said. "I like happy endings, even if the stories involve murder and mayhem. I never want the hero or heroine to cheat, and I have to have a romance in the story. Seriously, the authors I read bring all kinds of real-life issues to their stories. They've helped me, and I can't imagine that they aren't helping others."

"I prefer writing romance for those very reasons," Azelie said. "I detest stories where the man's wife is a nag and un-attractive to him, and his mistress is awesome. I want to show that men and women can live together and love each other while going through years of ups and downs. That a wife can be sexy and loving, and the man can think she's attractive even when she's nine months pregnant or just had the baby and is exhausted every minute of the day."

Lana gave her a high-wattage smile. "See, you do have lofty goals. I'll be purchasing your books one day."

The bus lumbered to a stop, the doors opening. Azelie glanced at her watch. "I've got to run, but hopefully I'll see you again soon. Thanks again for your help today."

Sprinting across the parklike campus, she contemplated

what the merry widows had told her about living life. About standing back up after getting knocked down. They certainly had stood back up again and made the most of their lives, even to the point of making tragedy in the form of cheating husbands humorous.

She made a vow to herself she would take more chances. That meant she would give herself into the relationship with Andrii without reservation. She was an all-or-nothing person, and if she committed to him—to them—she would go all in. That meant trusting him. The idea was frightening and yet exhilarating.

There was something about Andrii besides his blatant sex appeal that called to her. She caught glimpses of a man who had seen too much, been through too much. He knew firsthand what real trauma was. There was wariness in his eyes at times when he looked at her.

She had no doubt that he desired her and he'd made up his mind to have her, but a part of him was worried that she might shatter his heart. He was doing his best to go slow and guard his heart. Although, she found herself a little amused and hugging the knowledge to herself that his going slow was like a bowling ball being hurtled down the alley straight at her. Their ideas of slow were two different things.

Her classes seemed to fly by. Probably because she was testing, and she found the material interesting. At her lunch break, she made her way outside. Even when it was cold or foggy, she preferred to get out of the building and be outside. Today was a glorious day in San Francisco. The weather was perfect. The sun was out and there was a small breeze rather than a roaring wind.

As she approached the small grove of trees she had found that gave her some privacy, she was shocked to see Andrii sitting on the bench surrounded by what appeared to be take-out bags. The wonderful aroma of Thai food made her stomach growl. She halted a few feet from him, but he stood, towering above her, coming straight to her.

"What are you doing here?"

"You said you didn't have time to get food between classes. If you're taking tests all day, you need fuel. I brought you fuel." He flashed a grin that sent her heart into overdrive. "Thai. I think you mentioned you liked Thai on our first date."

He continued to advance until their bodies were so close his scent surrounded her, drowning out the Thai, the sea, the flowers and trees. All she could do was inhale deeply and take him into her lungs. He was potent. An aphrodisiac. There was no resisting the man, not when everything about him appealed to her. Not when their chemistry was so off the charts, she felt electrical sparks leaping back and forth between them.

Andrii cupped her face between his palms. One thumb slid in a caress over her jaw, tracing her bone. A shiver of awareness slid down her spine. She couldn't find her voice; she could only stare rather helplessly up at him. Then the pad of his thumb slid over her lower lip and his eyes darkened to that sensual gray that caused a mini-explosion in her sex.

She wasn't a sexual person. At least she'd never believed she was. She thought about sex, imagined and fantasized, but she didn't have reactions to men. Standing in front of Andrii with the tips of her breasts pressed into his chest, she had a major reaction, and there was no hiding her arousal from him.

"Babe, you see me, what do you do?" He murmured the question, his tone as mesmerizing as he was.

She blinked rapidly, hoping to activate her brain cells. He induced brain fog, smothering all rational thought so she was reduced to a mass of overactive sexual cells.

"Babe?" he encouraged.

"Melt at your feet." Her hand came up to cover her mouth. "I said that out loud, didn't I?" Sadly, she knew she sounded and looked breathless because he robbed her of her ability to breathe.

"It isn't safe for you to be so fuckin' adorable, Zelie. Or

sexy. Not here where we're out in the open, and I have to protect you from me."

"Protect me?" She echoed his declaration like a parrot. She was stuck on adorable and sexy. "I think it's okay not to protect me from you." If he meant more kisses, she was all for that.

Andrii shook his head, his expression soft. "I'm going to kiss you because I *have* to. I spent all night thinking of you. When I finally fell asleep, I dreamt of you."

Her stomach did a slow roll. He was such a beautiful man. He might think he wasn't, but she knew he was. She saw inside to the heart of him.

"I dreamt of you too," she admitted, feeling the color rising under her skin and sweeping up her neck into her face.

His eyes went soft, adding another loop to the roller coaster that was her stomach. He bent his head to hers and took her mouth. She melted into him just as she had when he'd kissed her before. When he kissed her, the entire world changed. Shadows receded. Colors grew more vivid. Lightning and thunder mixed with explosive, colorful fireworks. She came alive, her entire body on fire, melting into his.

"We're stopping," he said gruffly. "It's the only safe thing to do." He took her hand and led her beneath a tree where he'd set out a blanket to cover the ground. "What kind of dreams did you have about me, baby?"

She was still caught in the foggy brain induced by his kisses and stupidly answered, "Erotic dreams." The moment the truth slipped out, she clapped her hand over her mouth as if she could take it back. It was mortifying to know she had no control around him.

He flashed a grin at her, one that was truly heart-stopping. He had to stop, or she wouldn't be able to concentrate on her next test—she'd be too busy daydreaming about him.

"I'm certain your dreams were pretty tame when compared to mine." He indicated for her to sit on the blanket, then he dropped down beside her and placed the white carrying bags between them. "We aren't discussing our dreams while you eat your lunch because if we do that neither of us is going to be worth shit the rest of the day."

That was *so* true. Azelie nodded her understanding and concentrated her attention on the white boxes he pulled from the bags. The aroma made her stomach growl in anticipation.

"You said these tests were important. So, fuel first. You don't have much time, and it's important for you to eat."

Her heart contracted, and that roller coaster in her stomach was on full loops. He was *such* a sweet man. The best of the best. She had no idea how she'd gotten so lucky, but she was going to give him everything he ever wanted or needed.

She sent him one emotion-laden look from under her lashes. "Don't ever tell me you aren't a good man, Andrii. Not ever again."

He flashed her another one of his heart-stopping grins. "Doesn't mean we aren't going to be discussing dreams in the future, Zelie. We're just putting that on pause for today."

He handed her a box of the most delicious Thai shrimp, along with chopsticks. She sat in the sun with him, fueling for her tests and enjoying every bite. It was perfection.

EIGHT

Azelie used the private side entrance that was for employees only. Not all employees. One had to have a special micro-chipped card to gain entrance. An armed guard sat in the hallway behind a desk supposedly to check IDs. She knew he was there to ensure no one took that small left corridor that led beyond the underground Adventure Club. The door was built seamlessly into the wall, impossible to see. If one didn't know it was there, the entrance to the underground offices would be difficult to find even when looking for it.

The guard looked up as she approached. It was always the same. He recognized her, she knew him. His name was Bobby Aspen, and he'd been working the security in that corridor for as long as she'd been working for Alan Billows. At sixteen, she'd been silly enough to find the intrigue exciting—thrilling even. She wanted to help her sister by paying for her own clothing and also to give something to Janine toward the household expenses. If she was being hon-est, she had wanted to show off. Few people had her skills, and even fewer had them at her age.

"Hey, Bobby," she greeted and pulled back the hood of

the sweatshirt she wore so he could see her face and clearly identify her. "How are you?"

"I'm good, but Sandra has a nasty virus," he said. "Being a schoolteacher, she gets every single illness those kids bring to the classroom."

Sandra was his wife. They didn't have children, and after getting to know Billows and understanding the extent of his criminal activities, Azelie thought it was a good thing he didn't have a large family. Anyone associating with Billows lived under a threat—including her. Maybe *especially* her, since she had been doing his books for so many years. She knew if she quit, she would have to disappear for a while. She knew too much about their activities. Not really what they were doing so much as that the amounts he brought in were massive and came from illegal activity.

Over the years, she'd been in the office working while Billows had visitors, seedy men dressed in suits. They smiled at her when they greeted her, but their eyes were speculative and moved over her face and body, leering and giving her the creeps. Billows had hustled them from the office she was working in and later would come back to reprimand her for not locking the door. He had a policy that she was never to lock the door. It was a direct order, but the few times she had locked the door after he yelled at her, he seemed to change his mind.

She detested Billows' mood swings. She detested him, but she'd learned to stay calm and act friendly and a little spacey, as if she didn't have too much in the brain department. She knew he had begun to believe she was gifted when it came to making his books look legitimate, but he also believed she wasn't quite bright in any other field.

"Tell Sandra I hope she gets better," Azelie told Bobby.

Bobby lowered his voice. "He's in a mood and he's texted four times to see if you're on your way down." There was concern in his tone.

Whatever the problem was, Billows was *really* acting out of character. He had never come to her house before or waited by the bus stop for her. Something was really wrong. Clearly,

Bobby thought it was unusual for Billows to text him about her arrival time or he wouldn't feel the need to warn her.

"Thanks." She lifted her hand at him. "Let him know I'm on my way." She gave Bobby a vague smile. She knew from experience not to trust anyone no matter how friendly they seemed. If Billows employed them, he bought that loyalty and kept it through fear and money. She'd learned that much about him.

Billows tended to surround himself with men like her brother-in-law. Yes-men. Men who had addictions and failings and could be taken advantage of. It seemed to be Billows' specialty to spot men and women he could use.

When she'd first been shown the door that fitted so seamlessly into the wall, she thought it was super cool. She'd been so excited to discover that beneath two dance floors was a maze with hidden rooms. The idea of it sounded so much like spies and fantasy. To a sixteen-year-old, the concept of secret passageways, guards and special IDs was intriguing.

"Fantasy versus reality," she murmured as she started down the narrow steps lit only by LED lights. "Not so fun when you know your boss is creepy."

She had been working alone in the office one night when she heard screams. She had worked up the nerve to investigate, even though Billows had ordered her to stay in her office and go nowhere else. She'd never once broken his rule until she heard someone screaming. It had sounded like a woman in pain, and she couldn't just ignore it.

The office she always worked in was soundproof. The entire floor was soundproof. Above them, music played constantly, and customers played in the lavish dungeon-themed Adventure Club. Above that were more music and even more customers, dancing and talking in the Pleasure Train Club. Despite the amount of people and noise above the office, it was absolutely quiet in the underground maze. That was why hearing someone scream was so shocking. And frightening.

Azelie had leapt up, knocking over her chair. She was ashamed that it took a few seconds to force her terrified brain to stop panicking and allow her to move. She had never been shown around to the other offices. She knew there were hidden doors and cameras everywhere. Billows would know she'd run out of her office into the corridor rather than heading back up the stairs. He would be able to view the security tapes even if someone wasn't monitoring and informing him she was breaking the rules.

The screams increased in volume, sending chills down her spine. She ran toward the sound, but it was abruptly cut off. The ensuing silence seemed worse than the screams. She found herself facing three walls as the corridor dead-ended. That meant there had to be hidden doors in the wooden panels. Whoever had screamed was behind one of the walls.

"What the fuck are you doing, Azelie?" Billows sounded furious. "You aren't to leave that office."

She leaned against the wall, one hand supporting her, her palm seeking to reassure the woman when she had no chance of finding her. She found herself trembling.

"I'm sorry, Alan." She was conciliatory immediately. "I heard screaming. A woman." There was no point in denying it. "She sounded hurt, in pain. I rushed out to find her, to help, but I don't know my way around and I got lost."

His fingers bit deep into her arm, his grip hard enough to leave bruises. "Call me next time you think you hear something. This entire floor is wired."

He began walking her back toward her office.

"I don't know what that means."

"It means if you step wrong, you could set off a bomb."

She paled, the color draining from her face. "Do you mean you have active bombs down here? If I accidentally set one off, would it kill the people above us?"

Billows' fingers bit even deeper. "Don't you dare get hysterical on me. I was watching a fucking horror movie in the office next to yours and I had the door open a crack. You heard the screaming and, like an idiot, didn't bother to text me to see what was happening."

He was lying. She knew he was lying. Worse, that woman

had *stopped* screaming. Azelie had no idea who she was or where she was. If she called the police and they came and searched the maze, they might set off bombs. She wanted to go home and pull the covers over her head and pretend she'd never met Billows.

He practically flung her into a chair, his face a mask of anger. She knew he could feel her trembling; there was no way to stop it. He hadn't answered her question about the bombs. She absolutely believed him that there were bombs. What was he doing besides rearranging his books to make his businesses seem legitimate?

"I'm sorry, Alan," she said, pouring contriteness into her voice. She didn't feel contrite. She just felt scared. "I won't leave my office again."

"You'd better not." He sounded menacing.

Now, each time she descended the narrow stairs to the office where she worked, the atmosphere beneath the dance floors always felt tense and oppressive. It felt sinister and dark, as if a thousand ghosts cried out for her to join them.

She ignored her overactive imagination and headed straight for the office she always used. The door was open, and Alan Billows was waiting for her inside, one hip to the desk. His dark eyes jumped to her face as she pushed back the hood and shook out her hair.

"Someone has been stealing from us," Billows announced as she entered the office. He waved her toward the chair behind the desk. "I need you to find out who, and I don't want you to leave until you have."

To give herself time to think of a response that wouldn't trigger his temper, Azelie moved around him to do as he wanted, seating herself at the desk. The computer was already running, the books open for her to inspect.

"Alan, of course I'll do my best to see who is stealing from you, but I'm a numbers person. Just looking at the books probably won't initially give me answers. I'll be happy to work on it until I find the culprit, but it could take weeks. Or more. Depending on how clever they've been."

"Then you'll stay weeks or more," he snapped.

He began pacing, his movements quick and angry, much like a trapped tiger. She forced air through her lungs, refusing to give in to panic. Billows was very angry. The atmosphere in the room felt sinister. Ominous. A giant storm ready to break right over her head.

"I understand your anger. You work hard for your money, and no one has the right to steal it from you. I'll find them, Alan, but I need to go home when I'm tired. I don't sleep well anywhere else. To do this for you, I have to be alert."

Billows abruptly stopped moving, swinging around to stare at her. Her stomach dropped. There was far too much speculation in his eyes. Something else as well. Lust maybe. Certainly interest in her as a woman, not just his bookkeeper. His steady stare was unnerving, but she forced a pleasant smile as she pulled a notebook from her backpack.

The weird thing was, she'd seen that look a few times before. Not often. Mostly he was terse and dismissive. He didn't spend a lot of time with her. Usually, he barked orders and left. She was uncertain why he would have sudden bouts of interest in her. She didn't flirt. She dressed in baggy, shapeless clothes. No makeup.

"Why didn't you allow me up to your apartment?"

It was the last thing she expected him to ask. Her heart accelerated at the dark shadows creeping over his face.

"Did you have someone up there?"

His tone indicated she had better not have had someone in her apartment. Worry for Andrii sent a shock wave of panic through her mind.

"I'm quite capable of making someone disappear," he added.

He wasn't joking with her. She kept her expression serene, with effort. She'd practiced the look a million times in her mirror after hearing those screams coming from somewhere in the complicated maze of secret rooms. Her eyes met his, and she made certain she had a look of inquiry.

"Alan." She kept her voice gentle and sweet. Deliberately,

she acted as if she didn't understand. "That isn't something you should say to me when I'm looking for the criminal stealing from you. I know he might deserve whatever he gets, but I can't know about it. It wouldn't be safe for you."

He frowned and took a step closer to the desk. "What is it with you? I don't like bitches as a rule. I have a hard time getting you out of my mind."

Her heart continued to accelerate. Her mouth went dry. That wasn't good. She'd begun to suspect he was looking for more than a working relationship, although he never dated anyone for more than a week or so. His women didn't last.

"Perhaps you could refrain from referring to me as a bitch. I am not a dog, nor am I in heat. I'm your employee, and you're skating very close to a pet peeve of mine." She stuck her nose in the air and regarded him steadily with as much annoyance as she could muster.

What could have been a smile touched his mouth. "A pet peeve? Damn, woman, that's it right there. That attitude you have. We can talk about that later. Right now, I want to know about the other night. Why you didn't let me come upstairs."

She sat back in her chair. He was expecting her to say she had company, and she feared if she admitted Andrii was there, Andrii would mysteriously disappear. She had to give him something or he would get angry. She decided on a partial truth. And she was going to give it to him without attitude because he seemed to like attitude. She didn't want him thinking about her, let alone liking anything she did.

Her lashes fluttered, and she took a deep breath, letting him see it disturbed her to tell him. She wanted to give the impression of reluctance and a little bit of shame.

"I haven't gotten over it." That was the stark truth. She would never get over witnessing Quentin murder Janine and her niece and nephew. She would never get over the trauma of the three bullets tearing through her body. Still, she poured embarrassment into her tone.

His eyebrow lifted. "Gotten over what?"

Andrii would have known immediately without making her

say it. Billows was that obtuse. Really? She wanted to get up and walk out. But then, she'd wanted out for years. She knew that wouldn't happen with consent. Billows would threaten her and possibly kill her before he would allow her to quit.

"Quentin murdering my sister, niece and nephew. Shooting me three times, attempting to kill me."

His eyes lost the blaze of anger. "You were still a kid."

She decided to act as if she was powering through. She allowed her eyes to shimmer with tears before she dropped her gaze from his, as if hiding her shame. "I don't feel safe when anyone's in my personal space." That was true, and she hoped he believed her. Everything she'd told him was the strict truth.

She caught at the drawstrings on her hoodie and twirled them nervously around her finger. "I don't even invite women friends to my apartment. I'm not ready yet." She wasn't certain she would ever be.

She hadn't invited Andrii, but once he was there with her, she hadn't been afraid for her life, more for her heart. Fortunately, Billows dropped the idea of thinking someone was in her apartment.

"That makes sense, Azelie." He seemed much more relaxed, the harshness and cruelty fading from his expression. "You aren't going to get over something like that quickly."

"It didn't stop when I was in the hospital. There were so many reporters and cops forcing me to relive it over and over. I have nightmares. If someone came up to my apartment and could see where I keep everything, I would never be able to fall asleep." That was true as well—with the exception of Andrii. She didn't know why he was the exception when danger emanated from him. She felt physically safe, just not her heart. She desperately needed to guard her heart from him, but she knew it was impossible.

"You realize, working for me in the position that you do, adding someone else into the mix would be seriously dangerous for them."

Billows stated it casually, as if it was a foregone conclusion that she would never date anyone.

She forced herself to meet his gaze. Again, he had a strange look in his eyes. This time he looked possessive. She had no idea what that was all about, but she didn't like it.

"I'm far too busy to add anyone into my life." She was. That was the truth as well.

Studying Billows' hard expression, she suddenly was terrified for Andrii. She would have to convince him she was too busy or not interested. But she wanted at least one night with him. Just one. It would have to last her a long, long time. She wasn't going to take chances with his life. Billows was a criminal, and by his own admission, he was willing to kill people.

That made her think of the woman who had screamed. Billows could say he was watching a movie all he wanted, but she didn't believe it. She hadn't believed his explanation then, and she didn't believe it now. If anything, she was more certain than ever that he had hurt someone while she was working in her office.

She refused to put Andrii in danger, not even if he was her one chance for a perfect relationship, or as perfect as one could get with both people having issues. She wasn't going to take all the blame. She knew she was screwed up after what Quentin had done. Her parents had started her down a road of mistrust and her brother-in-law pushed her over the edge. But she saw things in Andrii's eyes when he wasn't guarding himself. Bad things. He definitely had issues, so no, she wasn't going to shoulder all the blame for being the only one screwed up.

"It's good you don't want to put anyone else in danger, but I think it's time you had someone looking after you."

Her heart jumped, began to race. She worked at breathing normally, at settling her pulse. She had to handle this just right. "I'm quite capable of looking after myself, Alan. I've been doing it since Quentin took my entire family from me."

"That's not quite true," Billows disagreed. "I've been looking after you, making sure you're safe when you go running around that park in the evening. I'm going to put a stop to some of the things you do that are dangerous. You don't seem to have any real concept of self-preservation."

Her brows drew together. "You're my boss, Alan. You're not my partner. No one tells me what I can or can't do."

"That's about to change." He made it a statement.

She didn't pretend to misunderstand his meaning. "Getting into a relationship with your boss is *always* a bad idea. When things go south, and they always do, you no longer have a job." She used her primmest, snippiest voice.

Billows burst out laughing. His reaction was totally unexpected, and for the first time, she could see why so many women were attracted to him.

"Right there is why we're going to have a relationship."

She'd forgotten he liked attitude. Mostly, she was amenable and preferred pleasing those she cared about, but she had no trouble expressing her opinion when she didn't like something or thought the other person was wrong. Being in a relationship with Alan Billows was so wrong.

"We are *not*. I'm not risking my job, and you have a bad reputation with women. I'm sorry to say this, Alan, but you're never with a woman for more than five minutes. Gorgeous women. Models. Actresses. You date celebrities and heiresses. I'm none of those things. They couldn't keep your wandering eye from straying, so there would be zero chance that I would keep your attention."

"We'll see."

"We won't see," she corrected firmly. "You need to let me get to work. This isn't going to be easy. If someone has begun to siphon money from your accounts . . ."

His dark scowl was back. "They took it. All of it. Drained the accounts. This isn't a little siphoning off of the profits. This isn't one of my business associates deciding to steal from me, skimming from the top. This is blatant, finding my hidden accounts and wiping them clean."

Azelie sat very still, her mind racing. No one should have been able to find his concealed accounts. They were buried under so many layers and companies, it would be a miracle for someone, even the Feds, to find them and identify that they were Billows'.

"Alan, if they wiped out every one of your hidden accounts, they targeted you specifically. Do you have enemies? Someone who would want to destroy you and your businesses?"

He shrugged. "No one gets where I am without stepping on people. The answer would be yes, I have multiple enemies."

"Ones capable of hiring someone elite with a computer?"

"Yes," Billows said. "Strange thing is, they didn't touch my legal business accounts, only the ones where I stash the money from illegal businesses."

She dropped her forehead into her palm. "I'm not elite on a computer, Alan. I am with numbers, but not with tracing someone that good. We should find someone to help us." Deliberately, she aligned herself with him in the hopes he wouldn't go ballistic on her and insist she could find the culprit. She could not. Whoever had done such a thing was far, far better than she was on a computer.

She dared to raise her gaze to Billows' face. He was beyond an ordinary storm and had gone straight to a level-five hurricane. His face was flushed, eyes dark and scary, and he was actually gritting his teeth.

"That's bullshit."

Azelie knew she had to make him understand, even if it meant his wrath would descend directly on her head. She feared it already had with the way he was looking at her.

"I wish it was, Alan. There are some very gifted individuals who stay in the shadows. They don't work for the government or anyone else unless they are paid a great deal of money. They have skills far beyond what I have. Sometimes their skills exceed anyone the government employs. They hack their way in and out of very secure websites. At times they work together. Again, I don't have those kinds of skills and I never will have them."

"You fix the books and come up with solutions in the shortest amount of time possible. I've never seen anyone with your skills." He was back to pacing, quick angry steps, his glare directly on her. "When there were shortages before, you found how much and where that leak was coming from."

She shook her head. "I'm telling you, it isn't the same thing. I have a gift for numbers. I can see patterns in the numbers that make sense in my brain, but I don't have an affinity with computers. Some people are good on a computer. A few are great, even rarer are the ones who can do just about anything on them. Whoever did this to you is one of those people. I'm not one of them. If you have enemies, they could have hired the person or people. It wouldn't be cheap. It's possible I can start looking into some of those you say are out to harm you. I might see payments going out to someone."

"You do that," Billows snapped.

"Just know it's possible someone hacked your accounts on their own. These people like challenges, and they like to see if they can do what might be considered impossible."

"I don't care how it was done. I want the money back, and I need to know who my enemies are. Find them."

Azelie knew there was no making him see reason. He was incensed over the loss of his money. She couldn't blame him. He thought his ill-gotten gains were safe in anonymous offshore accounts hidden beneath layers of companies and misdirection. The money should have been safe, and most wouldn't be able to trace it back to Billows. She had a sinking feeling whoever had taken the money knew exactly who they stole it from. The fact that they hadn't taken a cent from his legitimate businesses was worrisome to her. She was surprised Billows hadn't questioned that further himself.

She knew Billows was shrewd and cunning. At times, he exhibited knowledge in areas she was rather shocked he knew anything about. Other times, he appeared to be totally obtuse. Whether he just affected ignorance or whether he really couldn't understand didn't matter. He insisted on everything being his way, and he didn't seem to care how he made that happen.

"I'll get to work, then," she told him, hoping he would go away. Deliberately, she turned her attention to the computer.

Billows didn't leave her office. He continued to pace, casting her speculative looks as he stalked from one side to the other of the relatively small room.

She pretended to be engaged in her research, but who could possibly work with a lethal tiger in the room? She was terrified that at any moment he would erupt into violence. Even though it had been months since she had heard the woman scream, she thought of it often. The sound echoed through her mind whenever she was alone in the office, but it was worse when Billows was there.

She thought of the woman and what could have been happening to her. It wasn't sounds of pleasure the unknown woman had been making. The screams were animalistic, as if she suffered great pain. Billows' anger toward Azelie when he discovered her trying to hunt down where the horrendous sound was coming from made her feel as if he had something directly to do with the woman's pain and fear.

Azelie didn't like being alone in the soundproof office with only Bobby as a witness to her entry. She was acutely aware she could disappear, and no one would know where to look for her. She knew from experience that a man who supposedly loved his family could turn on them in a moment. Billows was inherently cruel and selfish. She had no doubt that he would beat his wife and do so casually if he ever married. Being in the small room with him was distracting and a little terrifying.

She finally sighed and looked up. "I can't concentrate with you in here, Alan. I need to be able to pay attention to the numbers and names. Time stamps when money arrived or disappeared. You're going to have to leave."

Azelie forced herself to be firm with him. She poured confidence into her tone and carefully adjusted her expression. All the practicing in front of her mirror would hopefully pay off.

There was silence as Billows stopped his relentless pacing and once again swung around to confront her. She couldn't read his expression very well. He didn't look quite so angry, but he was frowning. He also had that same look in his eyes that told her he was looking at her differently than he ever had before. She *really* wanted to go home and maybe hide under her bed.

"It has occurred to me you didn't understand what I was telling you, Azelie. It's important you are perfectly clear so there are no mistakes made."

It was her turn to frown. She pushed back away from the desk and turned fully to him, folding her hands on her lap so she could twist her fingers tightly together.

"What did I misunderstand? I thought I was on the same page with you trying to find who stole your money."

He shook his head and settled one hip on the edge of the desk, too close to her. She was grateful she'd already pushed her chair back. There was a small distance between them, but she doubted if she could outrun him. She went through the weapons on the desk she had available to defend herself with. A stapler. It was heavy. She could wrap her fingers around it like a fist and clock him in the head. She went over the maneuver several times in her mind, never once looking at the stapler. She didn't want to give the impression of being nervous, or that she might lunge for that weapon.

"I'm not talking about the money. I want you to look into it, but you're right. I need a computer expert to figure out who stole that money from the accounts. That isn't your gift."

She hadn't expected him to acknowledge that he needed someone else. He sounded grim but resigned. She braced herself for what was coming. She had a very bad feeling.

"I'm talking about you needing a man to take care of you.

And I want to make it very clear that the only man you're going to have in your life is me."

Her heart jumped and then went crazy. She was in so much trouble. She pressed her lips together to keep from blurting out the *hell no* that pounded through her brain.

"I thought we agreed that would be a bad idea. I'm not looking to lose this job anytime soon." She forced her eyes to meet his. "Do you have someone else you want to do the books? Have I let you down and you didn't say anything?"

Swift impatience crossed his face. "No one else is going to touch the books. That's been your job for the last seven years, and it will always be yours. I think you get that you can't just walk away after working with me all these years. You know more about what I do than anyone else. It wouldn't be safe for you to decide to leave."

There it was—a clear threat. She didn't pretend to misunderstand. Her chin went up and she glared at him. "I don't appreciate the threat, Alan. I've always been loyal, and I don't understand where all this is coming from. Why after all this time you suddenly feel the need to threaten me. I've gotten you out of trouble more than once. I found the people who were supposed to be loyal to you, skimming money off the top, and reported it to you." Mostly, she'd done that just in case he was testing her. That would be like him. She didn't like that those people had disappeared. She felt the weight of responsibility for them, although he could have simply fired them. She hadn't heard in the news about bodies appearing. "Why the sudden problem with me?"

He was silent for so long that she didn't think he would answer. He just stared at her, and she didn't like the way he was doing it. Again, he had that speculation and a little too much lust, as if he suddenly saw her differently. She wanted to pull her sweatshirt around her and check to make certain her body wasn't on display. She sat quietly, keeping her fingers twisted tightly in her lap, her mind on the stapler and going through the steps she would take if she had to use it.

"I don't have a problem with your work, Azelie, but let's

be real. You've grown up, and you look . . . well . . . the way you look. I'm surprised that some man hasn't tried snatching you. It will happen though. We both need to face the fact that you're not going to spend your life alone."

She frowned. "The way I look? I've always looked this way. Men aren't falling at my feet, Alan. Nor do I want them to. I'm going to school and working. I babysit a couple of children when their parents are in a jam. I write because it's important to me."

He didn't ask what she meant by writing or what she wrote. He fixated on one thing only. "I don't like that you watch kids for Bradley Tudor. He's single and he definitely wants to fuck you."

Her heart accelerated again. He knew about Bradley, even his last name. He'd been watching her—or he'd hired someone to do it for him. That wasn't good. That was putting Bradley in jeopardy. The twins had already lost their mother. They didn't need to lose their father, and the threat was there. She feared for Andrii now. Had it been reported that she was seeing him? She'd gone out with him. Did Billows know, and that was what this was all about? Her breath caught in her lungs and refused to move. It took her a moment to calm herself so she could sound natural.

"You're very much mistaken, Alan. I think Bradley is dating someone. We have no interest in one another. If he feels differently, he wouldn't get anywhere, because I don't look at him that way. You know what happened with my sister and her husband."

Deliberately, she pressed her hand to the one scar close to her heart from the bullet that had nearly ended her life. "I have no wish to be with anyone right now. I like my life just the way it is." That wasn't just a half-truth, it was a lie. A blatant lie. Since meeting Andrii, she desperately wanted to take a chance with him. To see if she could possibly have a real relationship. Now she knew, in order to protect him, she didn't dare continue to see him. She just didn't know how to tell him.

"I'm just letting you know, there had better be no dating. When you're ready, you'll be with me."

She rolled her eyes and turned back to the computer.

"Do you hear me?"

"I hear you. We can take this up again at a future time. Just not now."

He seemed to take her at her word and walked out, allowing her to breathe.

NINE

It hadn't been difficult to attach the device Mechanic had engineered onto Azelie's hoodie. It wasn't detectable with normal equipment, which was what made the tiny camera so perfect. Even when Azelie went through the security screens, that hidden camera would never set off the alarms.

She went through a side entrance and then stopped at the desk of a guard. "This is why we can't find the offices," Maestro said to the other members of Torpedo Ink watching the situation unfold as Azelie made her way into the lion's den. "The door is hidden in the wall panel. I've been there several times. I have an affinity with wood, and I didn't find it."

"You weren't exactly running your hands over the wall," Keys pointed out. "We didn't have time, and we were ensuring no one could see us."

Wood spoke to him in ways he didn't understand. It always had. He touched it for any length of time and memories crowded in. Emotions long lost after others had touched the wood or worked with it. He saw and felt things others had no possibility of seeing. It was a strange gift to have, and one he was thankful for. Trees could be extremely old. Patient.

Serene. Strong. They stood against vicious storms and sometimes endured fire, drought or flooding and survived.

Over the years, Maestro had learned a lot from wood he'd come into contact with. But there was always a downside with any gift. Sometimes it was seeing all the ugliness the trees had witnessed or the pain of the saws cutting through them. Sometimes the drawback was extremely simple, such as having to have his hands bare when he touched the surface. That meant fingerprints. DNA. His cells left behind.

When Torpedo Ink was on a mission that would likely include blood, violence and death, they always wore thin gloves. The gloves were really just a thin coating of barrier cream covering skin, impossible to detect. The fingerprints were not their own.

"She didn't unlock the outer door with a key. She used that same keypad we used to break in," Preacher pointed out.

"The fact that Billows has a guard sitting right in the hall entrance speaks volumes," Czar said. "You were in the right place."

The club members were gathered in the Airbnb they'd rented in preparation for raiding the nightclub to find the victims sent to Billows for training. They were certain the women would be held there if Billows had any victims at the time, but they had no blueprints to show them the underground offices. That was unusual. As a rule, Code was unstoppable with his computer. He was patient and meticulous and persevered until he got results. He hadn't found the blueprints of the underground offices. They knew there were rooms below the two floors housing the Pleasure Train and the Adventure Club, but they had been unable to get inside them.

Code had managed to find Billows' illegal accounts, powering through the layers of companies and diversions to find what they needed. He'd drained those accounts, making Torpedo Ink much wealthier. It was standard when they went after criminals to take their money. That enabled them to divert attention, so they had more of a cover when they physically went after their targets. It also ensured they had whatever funds they needed in their fight to stop human trafficking and pedophiles.

"Look at that guard," Ice pointed out. "He can't read her at all. She's all smiles and politeness, but that's the last place she wants to be."

Maestro agreed. "She's guarding what she says."

The audio was astonishingly good. Azelie spoke in a low tone, but they could hear her clearly. They heard the guard warning her that her boss was in a lousy mood.

"Notice how carefully she chooses her words when she answers him. She doesn't trust that man," Lana said.

"Her brother-in-law got her involved when she was sixteen," Maestro added.

"Once in, she isn't getting out unless they kill her," Master said. "Not with what she knows."

"It's clear she's very aware she's walking a tightrope," Alena added. "She must be living under so much stress every single day."

"He's got eyes on her," Storm reported. "Not all the time, but one of his men sits outside her apartment and follows her to the park occasionally."

"Man by the name of Andrew McGrady," Code chimed in. "He's a real peach. Domestic violence charges with nearly every girlfriend. Bar fights. Breaking and entering. He's got a rap sheet the size of Texas."

Maestro had clocked the man the first day he began following Azelie, but Billows' investigator was lousy at his job. Most of the time he was looking at his phone, not paying attention to his surroundings. Maestro hadn't once been seen by him. He'd even walked next to the parked car. Maestro was a man people noticed, yet the investigator had been playing a video game on his phone and hadn't even looked up.

"I could have killed him multiple times," Maestro pointed out.

"Same here," Storm agreed. "He doesn't bother following her most of the time. I think he's bored out of his mind."

"Good for us, bad for him," Mechanic said. "Although it's a pain in the ass having to keep a lookout for him."

"When we move, he'll be the first to go," Storm said.

Maestro shook his head. "The goal is to keep Azelie safe while we're getting those women out and getting information from Billows. We can't risk tipping him off." He looked directly at Czar. "Maybe coming clean with her and asking her outright for her key and a map of the underground is the way to go. We could move her to a safe house until it's over."

"That's not your head talking, Maestro," Czar said. "If Billows doesn't have women down there, but you find evidence he trains them there, we missed a shipment. There is bound to be another coming immediately. We don't want those women to be shipped somewhere else without our knowledge. We need to see this through."

Alena and Lana exchanged a long look. "What if she isn't safe now, Czar? Can we risk that? Look at her. She's holding herself in check but just barely. Mechanic programmed heart rate monitoring into that camera as well as audio. You can see she's terrified."

"She's been living that way for a long time," Czar said. "I know it's rough, but she's under our surveillance. We're not going to let anything happen to her."

"I just would like to point out that she's alone in that hallway with that guard and scared out of her mind," Destroyer said.

Czar sighed. "We put a lot of effort into this before we got any kind of a lead. Years of work. This is it, all we've got. We can put it to a vote to abort the mission and pull her out of there, which is fair. She doesn't deserve to live the way she's living. And she's Maestro's. That makes her ours. Before you vote, weigh the consequences to the other women lost to trafficking that we know we'll never get back against the fact that leaving her would be like leaving Blythe or Soleil or Anya. Seychelle or Zyah. Any of our women."

There was a long silence. Maestro broke it with a sigh of resignation. "I want her out of there. I'm not going to lie, I want her out more than I want my next breath, but I want her out for myself. For my peace of mind. I know damn well I'm never going to find another woman like her. No one else is going to do it for me. Do I want to protect that? Fuck yes."

Savage nodded. "I would feel the same way if it was Seychelle hanging out in the danger zone."

Reaper, Ice and Player murmured agreements, as did Master.

Maestro shook his head and then ran both hands through the sides of his hair. He had to do the right thing even though it went against everything his mind screamed at him to do. "But it wouldn't be what Azelie would want. She would put those women first every time. She'd be pissed beyond hell if she found out we'd sacrificed other women to get her out. She would tell me she's worked there a long time and knows how to handle Billows and she could work there for several years more if that's what it took. She may be soft inside like Alena, but just like Alena, she's got a core of absolute steel."

Azelie looked small and fragile to him and to the others. But he knew her now. "She would never agree to be put somewhere safe if that meant jeopardizing other women's freedom. And she wouldn't forgive me for taking that decision out of her hands." He knew that to be true, and it was the most difficult thing for a man like him to tell his brethren and sisters.

For years he had advocated that women obey their men when it came to matters of safety. He'd said it shouldn't matter what the woman said or did. She should be punished for not trusting her man to make the right decision. She should always follow his lead. He'd not only advocated for that shit, but he'd also believed it. To some extent, he still believed it. He needed his woman to allow him to lead. He needed control. But after watching Azelie with others and seeing the way she was with him, he also knew their relationship had to be about trust.

Like Maestro, Azelie had known betrayal—the ultimate

betrayal by a family member. Someone she loved. She'd lost everything she valued. To be her partner, he had to always give her reason to trust him. That meant he had to know her. Read her smallest cues. It was important to provide what she needed for her happiness if he was going to keep her.

Maestro was a man who looked at himself closely. Kept himself in check. Knew what he had to work on about himself and what he needed in his life to keep those around him safe. He was dangerous, and when he was dangerous, that meant lethal. Azelie made him even more lethal. He had never expected a miracle. A gift such as she was. Every instinct in him was to wrap her up in Bubble Wrap, keep her in a safe room, never let her leave his side, but that wasn't going to make her happy.

He struggled to find a balance between his intense personality and needs and her gentle independence. She wanted to stand on her own two feet, when he wanted her to depend on him. Needs versus wants. He absolutely knew Azelie would never forgive him if she thought other women suffered because he took her out of play.

"You're saying you want to leave her where she is." Czar attempted clarification.

"Fuck no! That's the last thing I want, but that's what she needs. I'm asking every one of you to be vigilant if we leave her there. The moment we have the information from Billows we need, and if we manage to find the victims, we'll get her out of there. Hopefully, she won't be in any danger once Billows is gone, and I can just come clean with her."

There was another long silence. The other members of Torpedo Ink stared at him in astonishment. He couldn't blame them. He'd been spouting so much shit for years, voicing his opinion of women and what they should or shouldn't do, none of it good. He was telling them he thought they should do just the opposite of what he'd always proclaimed should be done.

"Maestro." Alena's voice was soft and soothing. "Are you feeling all right?"

"Steele," Keys said to their resident doctor, "you should check him out immediately."

Maestro gave them the finger when the snickers started.

"Are you certain, Maestro?" Czar asked.

"We've got eyes on her," Code pointed out. "We keep someone on her all the time."

"I want her out," Maestro reiterated. "But if I choose that path, it will be for me, not her, and not the other women caught up in this mess. She wouldn't forgive something like that."

"You going to be able to live with this choice?" Savage asked. "Think about it, Maestro. Things can go to hell fast. We all know that. We've lived through it."

He *had* been thinking about it. He'd been thinking of nothing else. It wasn't as if he could move in with her, lock himself to her side. He had the feeling Billows would sweep her up the moment he realized she was with Maestro.

"I know what can go wrong. I'm putting a tracker on her tomorrow when I take her out."

"She knows his entire business. She might not know what he's doing, where that illegal money is coming from, but if she turned on him and talked to the Feds, he would go down fast," Master said. "What I'm saying, Maestro, is that Billows might decide to kill her, not traffic her."

"What the fuck is wrong with all of you?" Maestro demanded. "I'm finally trying to do the right thing here, not for me, but for those women we're looking for and for Azelie. You're all trying to talk me out of it. It isn't going to take that much."

But he'd lose her. He'd have to go to the grave never admitting the truth to her. The lies would stand between them for the rest of his life. She would always know something was wrong because she had intuition, awareness. Especially when it came to him. She saw inside him where few others ever did. That was part of the reason he had leapt with both feet down the path he was taking them on. She *saw* him—the real man under his armor—and she was okay with that. She even seemed to admire that man. Definitely she wanted him.

Maestro was not only certain that Azelie was attracted to him physically—the chemistry between them was off the charts—but convinced she could love him. He'd never once thought that of another human being. Not even his Torpedo Ink brothers and sisters. They were loyal and protective toward him and even affectionate, but it wasn't what Czar had with Blythe. Or what Savage had with Seychelle. He needed what Savage had. A woman willing to love him despite his many flaws.

"Do we want to put it to the vote?" Czar asked again. "If Maestro is right, and he reads people better than any of us, he will lose his woman if we take away her ability to choose to help."

"She isn't choosing," Lana pointed out. "No matter which way a vote goes, she isn't choosing, we are."

Maestro knew that was true, but he also knew what her choice would be.

"Can't risk pulling her out or letting her in on what we're doing," Reaper stated. "Sorry, brother, she may look in control when she's talking with Billows, but she's scared out of her mind. Anyone with a brain should be able to see that. Billows is an asshole."

That much was true as well.

"He sees only what he wants to see," Mechanic said. "He wants a behavior, and he uses threats and intimidation to get his way. He does it with his employees as well."

"When we work something this hot, we can't afford to bring in an untried person," Steele agreed. "I'm sorry. Maestro, I'm with you. I think if we lose this opportunity, we're not going to get it back. You know how I am with Breezy. I don't want her out of my sight. I lost my mind when I first had her back. And I'm not much better now, although I'm trying to give her freedom." Even as he said it, he winced visibly. "She understands when we communicate. If Azelie

is the woman you think she is, it's my belief she'll understand the reasons why you left her in play without telling her
what's going on."

There it was. Steele was one of his closest brothers. He
and Keys guarded the vice president and his family. Steele
didn't like having them watch his back so closely until
Breezy and Zane, his son, came back into the fold. When it
came to needing control, Steele was right up there with Savage and Maestro. He was over-the-top protective and needed
to know where his woman was at all times. Breezy gave him
that. Maestro was fairly certain Azelie would give him that
same consideration without freaking out or thinking he was
doing it just to control her. She would recognize he was working hard to overcome those needs that had been ingrained in
him since his childhood.

"I'm making the call," he decided. "She's mine. I'm asking for everyone's help in keeping her safe until we get this
taken care of."

"She going to be okay that you played her?" Gavriil
asked.

"She'll be pissed." He amended that. "Hurt. She'll be hurt
at first, but once I explain it to her, she'll understand. She's
like that. Hate hurting her for any reason, but we need the
information Billows can give us to get to the next level. We
also need to get those women out before they're sold."

Czar indicated the screen to Code. "Keep playing it. We
need to see where the door is and how she got in."

"It isn't a key," Master observed as they watched Azelie
stand in front of the wooden wall. "Anyone count how many
steps she took?"

"Seventeen," Alena said. "She doesn't have a long stride
either."

"I've got her stride down," Maestro assured them as they
all kept their eyes glued to the screen.

Azelie stopped in the hall, facing the wood. She took something from her pocket, palmed it, and then adhered her hand
to a spot on the wall among the intricate carvings. Her fingers

were splayed, and she pressed whatever was in her palm tight against the wall.

"Her fingerprints are being scanned," Code observed, moving closer to the big screen. "Look at the color around each finger. It's faint, but it's there. There's some kind of electronic plate there, and her fingerprints are critical."

"I can lift her prints," Maestro said. "That won't be a problem. But it's more than her prints. Whatever she palmed is also being scanned. That's what I need to find. I have to know what that is."

"My guess is a chip of some kind," Code said. "That's what it has to be."

"He's got two kick-ass clubs that are full every night," Player said. "Both clubs bring in massive amounts of money, but he isn't satisfied. He doesn't have that kind of security on either of the clubs, which is insane."

"Not if you're training women as sex slaves and intend to sell them to the highest bidder," Czar said. "You need a large space where you can hold them where no one can find them. You need another space to train them, and then you must have a setup for an auction. After that, you still need to ship them out without getting caught."

"Hence the rooms beneath his underground Adventure Club," Transporter said. "And the extra security."

The door slid open, and Azelie stepped into a narrow staircase lit only by LED lights. Those LEDs were dim, throwing off enough light to illuminate the stairs and that was it. The stairs seemed to have walls close on either side. Azelie descended cautiously.

"Her heart rate doubled," Code reported.

Maestro found his heart rate accelerated right along with Azelie's. Her descending that steep staircase in such poor lighting gave off the feel of a very real horror film. Ominous. Sinister. Downright evil. He'd lived in a hell. All of Torpedo Ink had. They'd come from brutal torture, pedophiles for instructors. They were forced to become assassins at a very early age and became outstanding at it. Still, seeing the darkness as she descended slowly felt the same to him as the thousands of times he had been forced into the basement dungeon located below the school where he grew up.

"Mine has as well," Alena reported.

"You're not alone," Lana confessed. "I hate this for her."

Azelie turned to the right at the end of the stairs. They caught a glimpse of another corridor to the left, but once she made that turn, it was impossible to see anything but what was directly in front of her.

"She's doing something with her hand," Ice said. "Go back a couple of frames, Code."

"The hand she's holding the chip or whatever it is," Storm agreed. "See, right there, she fished in her pocket and took out a chain. A necklace of some kind."

She appeared to do it automatically, but she turned her jacket slightly, just enough for the camera to see her push her hand into her pocket and come up with a chain. It was long and made of what appeared to be silver.

"You see that before?" Czar asked.

Maestro shook his head. "She has jewelry on her nightstand in a little box but no necklaces. It's cheap stuff. Cute but cheap. I couldn't find a safe."

"I thoroughly searched her apartment three times," Keys said. "I didn't see that chain either. Or find a safe."

Azelie hesitated briefly just before an open door. She pushed what appeared to be a tiny square into a pendant hanging on the chain. The pendant looked like a small envelope charm. She put the chain around her neck and then dropped the pendant inside her clothing.

"That's what you're going to be looking for, Keys, when I take her out tomorrow night," Maestro said. "We get that, we're in."

Keys studied the picture frozen on the screen. She had placed the chip in the envelope charm so quickly, her hand shielding the item, but at least they knew where it was. It was a matter of finding where she kept the necklace.

"We'll need eyes on her all the time. She doesn't have a safety deposit box at the bank, does she?" Czar asked.

Code answered. "No. And she would always need access to that part of the key. Billows seems to call her randomly. This crisis is most likely because he's been informed his money has disappeared from his various accounts and no one can trace it. He's acting out of character from what Aze-lie told Maestro."

"No shit. I'd be flipping too if fifty million dollars disappeared into thin air," Master said. "A little more than fifty million," he corrected, "but who's counting?"

"I think Billows is. He made bank with trafficking," Transporter said.

"And a few other illegal businesses," Code said. "The man knows people. Has the information we need. When we make our move on him, we need to be certain we keep him alive until we have a chance to get that information." He glanced at Destroyer and then Savage.

Savage grinned at him and held up both hands. "Some men are pansy asses. They give up before we can extract the information. Just sayin'."

Maestro knew he was full of shit. They all did. Savage didn't like pedophiles or traffickers. He made that known to them immediately and he did so in extreme ways. He knew how to keep an informant alive and make them suffer the worst pain imaginable, but there were times when his disgust and need for vengeance outweighed his desire to allow the informant to talk.

Savage had it particularly difficult as a child. Intellectually, Maestro knew they all had suffered tremendously, but to him, what happened to Savage was some of the worst. They had turned him into a sexual sadist, unable to get off without causing his partner pain. Hell of a thing for any man to live with, especially when you loved the woman more than life. There had been a time Torpedo Ink had worried they would lose him. They'd come close until Seychelle had entered into his life. Maestro almost managed to fuck that up with his idiotic advice to the two of them.

He ran his fingers through his hair in agitation. What was he thinking? How was he supposed to do the right thing for his woman when he didn't have a clue about relationships? He detested most women. He didn't believe a word coming out of their mouths. They seemed to delight in betraying their man. The only good ones were the ones married to his brethren and Alena and Lana. The rest of the world of females seemed fucked up to him. Or maybe he was the one fucked up. More than likely, he was.

"Maestro." Czar used his low, commanding voice. "We're going forward with the recording. Has anyone else noticed that it's eerily silent? We can't hear her breathing, and we should be able to, shouldn't we, Mechanic?"

Mechanic was the king of gadgets. He continually came up with new and unique designs for keeping eyes and ears on their enemies as well as communication devices.

His head went up alertly. "Damn it, the lower she goes into that hellhole, the more the audio is affected. He has it soundproofed down there, but I didn't think that would matter."

"Jamming device?" Transporter asked, moving up beside his birth brother.

Maestro stopped with the introspection, his heart clenching hard in his chest. Azelie's heart rate had accelerated. The camera was still sending that data, and they could see the shadows of grays in front of her as she approached the office. What they couldn't do was hear anything.

Billows waited for her, pacing back and forth. He swung around and snapped something at her, but she wasn't looking directly at his face, so they couldn't read his lips. She made her way to the desk and sank into an office chair. That was bad. The camera was pointed at the computer, not at Billows, and they didn't have audio.

Mechanic swore under his breath. "Sorry, Maestro. I thought we'd have it all when she went in."

The worst of it was, there was no doubt that Azelie was frightened. She held it together, but Maestro couldn't see her. He could only read her heart rate, and at times it was frantic. Once, she changed positions in the chair, shoving away from the desk, and they caught a glimpse of Billows coming close.

"The discussion is a long one," Lana said. "I can't see her directly, but I've caught several glimpses of her reflected in the computer screen. Can you enhance that, Code?"

Maestro looked to Code, the miracle worker. Code immediately tried to adjust the screen on the scene he'd frozen. He stepped closer as if that would get him what he wanted—her safety. Could he leave her hanging out there virtually unprotected to finish what they'd started more than two years earlier? Did having relationships make you indecisive?

"I'm sorry, Savage," he murmured aloud. "Really sorry, brother. I'll go to Seychelle and apologize to her."

"You did apologize to her, multiple times, Maestro," Savage reminded him.

"Yeah, I know, but I didn't mean it the way I do now," he admitted. "I told her I was sorry, and I was, but it was because I hurt her. Seychelle isn't a woman who ever deserves that kind of hurt. She didn't think I wanted her with you. I'm sorry for making her feel that way. I was trying to save the two of you, keep her from getting hurt when things got extreme, but I still didn't understand."

Savage touched him briefly on the shoulder. Savage rarely touched anyone other than Seychelle unless he was interrogating them—and no one wanted to be the man Savage was questioning. It was shocking to Maestro that Savage gave him that brief moment of affection and reassurance. And it meant a whole hell of a lot, especially when he felt so confused and frustrated.

Maestro didn't do well in the world of confusion or frustration. It was the reason he always maintained control and demanded it in his life. It was safer for him and everyone around him. Not knowing whether to allow Azelie choices when her life could be in danger was maddening. He was a decisive man. He was in charge.

He guarded their vice president for a reason. Every move was instinctive and precise. He could easily run an army if need be. His brain worked at high speed to solve puzzles, particularly problems that put those he cared about in jeopardy. Yet now, when he needed clear thinking the most, he found emotions hampered him.

"I can see her reflection much clearer on the screen," Lana reported. "What about everyone else?"

All of them could lip-read, but Reaper was particularly adept at it. He appeared totally absorbed as he stared at the screen.

"She's telling him she doesn't have the skills to track money that was stolen from the accounts. She's being upfront with him about what kind of specialist he needs."

It was all Maestro could do to keep from laying his hand on the screen. He wanted to touch her. To hold her close. In the reflection, her expression appeared surprisingly serene, but they had the evidence of a pounding heart to clue them in to the fact that she was terrified.

"Look at that woman of yours holding it together," Reaper said, awe in his voice. "She knows he's an asshole and dangerous, but she's standing up to him. I have no idea what he's saying to her, but she's not letting him walk on her."

"Can you tell what the conversation is about?" Lana asked. "It seems intense."

Reaper shook his head. "She turned her head, and I can't see her mouth anymore. I suspect she's looking directly at him."

"Another spike in her heart rate," Code reported. "Big-time."

"I'm looking as close as possible at her reflection in the screen," Reaper said. "I can see the side of her face, but there doesn't appear to be a change in her expression. That woman is pure ice." He grinned at Maestro. "You've got your work cut out for you living a lifetime with that one."

"I can read her." Maestro was confident he could. She might try to hide from him, but he was too adept at reading people. It was a gift, instincts he'd developed and honed over the years. He didn't miss the slightest nuance when he was with others. He knew when someone lied. He knew when they were uncomfortable. He knew when women were attracted to him. He was always aware of the most dangerous man in the room and kept his eye on him. He knew who was a bully and who was the real deal.

He'd started out learning the hard way about deception and betrayal. After years of living with both deception and betrayal on a regular basis, it wasn't difficult to begin to see the signs in people the moment he met them. He had been so ready to condemn Azelie, and yet, despite what she'd gone through, she was honest. A ray of sunshine in his dark world.

"She has a protective streak in her a mile wide," he informed the others. "She actually tried to protect me from Billows. No doubt, she will again."

Lana and Alena flashed him a smile. Savage scowled. The others exchanged worried looks.

"Spit it out," he invited.

"You can't have your woman standing in front of you, Maestro," Savage counseled. "I'm serious. You're going to have to stop being the good guy and make it very clear she's to do what you say. She's in a very dangerous position and she needs to understand you're the man to trust. What you say goes."

Maestro didn't need to be reminded. "Not a pussy, Savage. And I'm not whipped. I'm still feeling my way with her. I trust her, but she isn't there with me yet. Her instincts are to run."

"Girl's got good instincts," Alena murmured. "You can be overbearing, Maestro, sweet and gentle, but you're always going to want your way. That can be trying to independent women."

"She's a pleaser," Maestro said. "She thinks for herself,

but she likes to do things for others. If I can find a way to win her trust completely, I'll have it all."

This time he did touch the screen, his touch as gentle as Alena had claimed he was. There was a lump in his throat and a fist of heat in his gut just looking at her.

TEN

"I thought we were past this," Maestro said, leaning down to cup Azelie's face between his palms.

"I told you not to come here, Andrii."

She not only sounded terrified, but she looked it as well. It was all Maestro could do not to pull her tight against him.

"He has people watching me." That came out a whisper.

Maestro straightened to his full height. "Are you talking about the idiot who parks across from the complex, pulls out his phone and plays games on it? Babe, I clocked him the first time I was following you like the worst of stalkers. He's never seen me, and he won't. I've had my friend looking out for you when I couldn't be here, and that idiot never saw him either."

"You have someone looking out for me?"

She had beautiful eyes. When she looked up at him under that thick veil of lashes with a mixture of trepidation, desire and interest, his heart melted. Damn, but she was adorable.

He slid the pad of his thumb along the full curve of her bottom lip. It felt like silk. "Yeah, baby, I'll always have someone looking out for you when I can't do it myself. I'm not taking chances with your safety."

Her long lashes fluttered. "You're taking chances with your safety, Andrii. Billows is very dangerous. I've always known I would need to find a way to get out from under him, but I'm beginning to suspect he's far worse than I originally thought."

"Get ready while you're talking to me. Jeans, comfortable shoes, the blue top. We're in a time crunch."

"I can't be seen with you in public. He might find out."

The fear was real. He could see it on her face. In her eyes. Her lips trembled. He wrapped his palm around the nape of her neck. "I want you to trust me to take care of us. He isn't going to see us together. I want to take you out, *Solnyshkuh*. It's important to me. I planned for this, and I think you're going to love it. We can talk while you get ready." Deliberately, he ran his thumb along her high cheekbone, tracing it gently, feeling her shiver in response. "Can you do that for me?"

Her little studio apartment was small enough that if she dressed in her bathroom, they would have no trouble hearing each other.

She reacted to his voice, the one he used that was velvet soft yet compelling. He'd become a master at using that tone. The fact that Azelie responded to it every time was not lost on him. And she didn't want to disappoint him.

Maestro could see the conflict in her eyes—the need to protect him warring with her need to please him. Her teeth bit into her bottom lip and then she capitulated, going to the small closet to pull out the clothes he'd brought for her a couple of days earlier. She disappeared into the bathroom but didn't close the door all the way.

"I need to tell you something about Billows, Andrii. It's important."

"I'm listening, Zelie."

He was. He was also moving around her apartment looking for the necklace that held the key to the underground rooms.

"Months ago, when I was in the office, I heard a woman scream."

His head went up sharply and he froze, turning toward the bathroom. "A woman screamed?" he echoed, willing her to keep talking.

"I'm not ever supposed to leave my office when I'm working, and I never have. The offices are located directly beneath the Adventure Club."

He heard the rustle of clothing as she donned the pair of jeans he'd chosen for her. He found himself feeling warm and even happy, liking that she was wearing something he'd given her. He wanted everything she wore to be from him. He'd never thought about purchasing gifts for anyone until he'd laid eyes on her.

"Keep talking, Zelie. I'm listening."

"It's soundproofed down there, and I think, but I don't know, that the entire floor is taken up with various rooms. I've never explored because it's strictly forbidden. Cameras and motion detectors everywhere. Around two-thirty in the morning a couple of months ago, while I was working, I heard a woman scream. I'm not crazy, I know what I heard. She sounded in pain. Agony. It was terrifying, especially since I had been told never to go anywhere but the office, but I couldn't just leave her."

Maestro's heart clenched hard in his chest. She was so damned courageous. But she'd just confirmed the suspicions Torpedo Ink had about those underground rooms hiding trafficking victims. They were definitely held and trained below the Adventure Club before they were auctioned off.

She came out of the bathroom dressed in the vintage blue jeans and ash-blue off-the-shoulder sweater he'd gotten for her. The denim hugged her curves, and the off-the-shoulder sweater was perfect, sexy and innocent at the same time, just the way she was. His cock hardened just looking at her.

"You're so fuckin' beautiful, Zelie," he said. It was the truth. Absolute truth. He caught up her jacket. "You'll need something to take notes with, your laptop and your glasses unless you're wearing contacts." He was certain she didn't wear colored contacts. Her eyes were just that blue. "I've got everything else under control."

That got him another flutter of her long lashes and a quick smile that lit her eyes. "What are you planning?"

"You'll see. Hustle, baby. And we're going to finish talking about the woman you heard once we're on the way."

"We can't exit the building together, Andrii," she cautioned as she allowed him to take her hand. "I'll go out first and make sure Billows' man is nowhere around."

"No, you won't," he denied. "He's gone for the night. My friend saw him drive off and he hasn't been back."

"Your friend?"

He took the keys to her apartment from her and locked the door. "Shit lock, babe. We'll have to get you a better one."

"I have a chain."

He looked down at the top of her bent head in exasperation. "Do you think a chain would stop me if I kicked your door? News, baby, it wouldn't."

"I wouldn't expect you to kick down my door."

There was that hint of amusement in her voice. Despite everything, she'd still found something to laugh about and teased him with it. His ray of sunshine.

"You've met my friend a couple of times. At least you saw him with me. We went into the coffee shop together. His name is Lazar. We've known each other since we were boys. He was in the same school I was in. I'll tell you about that later."

He opened the car door for her and then rounded the hood to slip into the driver's seat. He didn't want them to be late. This was a special surprise that he was certain would mean something to her.

"Tell me about the woman, Zelie."

There was silence. She twisted her fingers together in her lap, portraying nerves. He reached over and laid his palm over her restless fingers, driving with only one hand. That had been practiced like every other skill he had. He was nowhere near Transporter's level, but he knew how to drive a car.

"You're safe with me, baby. Take a deep breath and tell me what happened."

Out of the corner of his eye, he saw she had turned her head to look at him. Assessing. He remained silent, waiting for her to decide. She'd brought the subject up for a reason. She just had to let go of her fear of Billows and tell him.

"I heard her scream and went to investigate. It's really dark down there and it's a maze. The hallways end and you're just looking at walls. I'm sure there are ways to enter more corridors and find rooms, but I don't know how. I tried to follow the sounds, and then all of a sudden, she just stopped. Really abruptly. That was worse than the screams."

Azelie crossed her arms over her chest, hugging herself. Maestro was aware of the shiver running through her body. He touched her shoulder, reminding her he was with her.

"You're doing great, Zelie. I know this is difficult to relive, but you had a point to this you wanted to make. It's scary, but you're safe with me."

She turned those vivid blue eyes on him. "But you're not safe with me, Andrii. I get that you're a badass in your circle, but I think Billows is involved with the Mafia." She sighed and rubbed her temple as if she had a headache. "I think he's part of it, or something very similar. Whatever it is, it's bad. His enemies disappear." She whispered the last.

His gaze slid to hers. She was looking up at him with fear. With dismay.

"He can't ever view you as the enemy, Andrii."

His heart clenched in his chest. Softened. *Bog.* This woman. She lived in the lion's den, but she worried about him, not herself.

"Are you safe?" He asked the most important question.

Her teeth tugged at her bottom lip for a moment. He was grateful she didn't just assure him. She thought it over first.

"For now. I won't be if I try to leave, which is why I've never given Alan the slightest inkling that I'm going to leave. He believes I'm working there to pay for my school and that I'll always work for him. I want him to believe that."

"You got in young and now you can't get out." He made that a statement.

She inclined her head. "That's true. I had no idea what I was getting into when Quentin first introduced us. It seemed like fun, and I was a bit arrogant in those days, knowing I was good at something most adults couldn't do." She gave him a faint smile. "The hubris of the young."

She was still young. A baby. She certainly had learned quickly.

"I'm working on an exit plan," she volunteered.

Azelie had a tendency not to share anything about her life, but with him she disclosed personal things. He loved that. He loved that she gave him that. That intimacy was important to him. He needed her trust even when he hadn't fully earned it.

"Tell me about it," he invited.

She hesitated. Rubbed her temple again as if the headache might be more persistent than nagging. "It isn't fully formed yet. Billows is so difficult. Moody. I sometimes wonder what personality I'm going to get when I see him. One moment he's matter-of-fact, another time he's rude and abrupt, and then he's acting possessive and almost jealous."

Alarm bells went off. Red flags. What the hell? Maestro felt possessive toward her, but Billows had no cause to exhibit that trait. Jealousy? Is that why Billows had a man on her? He wanted to ensure she didn't date?

"He acts possessive and jealous? Is he into you?" He kept his voice mild, casual even, when he wanted to rip the man apart. He detested that he had to stay in the shadows and not claim Azelie. Not show Billows she was under his protection.

"He never was before. Last night and when he came to my apartment, he seemed . . . different. And he was parked by my bus stop near the coffee shop, waiting to offer me a ride to school. I was lucky a woman who goes to the college saw me and recognized I was uncomfortable. She played it off as if we were studying together. I don't understand him, and I don't want to understand him. I'm just keeping my head down until I can get out from under him safely."

"Babe." He waited until he felt her eyes on him. He glanced her way, letting their eyes meet. Letting her see what possessive really was. "There is no safe way to get away from Billows. You're going to have to let me handle that."

Her breath caught in her throat. It was audible, and the tension in the car grew so tangible you could cut it with a knife. She began to shake her head. "No, no, absolutely not. You have to promise me you'll stay away from him. Promise me, Andrii. Nothing can happen to you."

She hadn't added "because of me." She'd simply stated, "nothing can happen to you," as if he was what mattered, not how she'd feel guilt afterward if Billows harmed him. She was killing him. So perfect when nothing ever was. He needed to talk to her. Make her understand what kind of a man she was dealing with. She might decide to bow out before they even got going, but he wouldn't be taking off. He would make certain she got away from Billows safely. Billows didn't have long to live, but that wasn't something he could confide to her.

"You didn't find the woman." He went back to the original topic. They were close to their destination, and he wanted to get as much information as possible to pass on to his brothers.

"No. Once she stopped screaming it was impossible to find her. Billows came out of nowhere, furious with me that I left the office. I'd never seen him so angry. Frankly, he scared me. When I told him about hearing a woman screaming, he told me he was watching a horror movie and he'd left the door to his office cracked open. Does he think I'm incredibly stupid?" There was disgust in her voice. "That was no movie."

"What do you mean he scared you?" Removing one hand

from the wheel, he wrapped his long fingers around her wrist. He needed to touch her. Needed that connection.

"He can get intense when anyone crosses him. And he told me there were bombs down there, built into the floor." She lowered her voice even more.

"Do you think he was trying to scare you? To keep you from wandering around down there?" He was damned certain that wasn't the case. At least he had that information, and it would be critical for their mission to know about the floor being wired.

"I believe him, Andrii. I asked if a bomb were accidentally set off, would it be powerful enough to harm the innocent people in the clubs above that floor, but he didn't answer me. That's how ruthless he is. That's why it's so important that he doesn't know about you. I really think this is going to have to be the last time we . . ."

"Stop right there, Azelie." He poured command into his voice. Firm. Calm. Kept his voice low. He wasn't a shouter, and he never would be, but he could take control of a room filled with people with his voice alone. Another gift he'd worked at for years.

Again, her breath caught in her throat, the sound audible. Her large eyes fixed on his face immediately. She stopped speaking, pressing her lips together.

"I'm not going to stop seeing you. You aren't going to stop seeing me. I think you need to take a closer look at me, baby. You don't seem to get who I am, and that's important going forward. Do I look like a nice man to you? Really see me, Azelie, not who you're fantasizing over in your head."

Her long lashes did that fantastic fluttering thing they did that made him harder than a fucking diamond. His jeans were too tight for his body. It felt marvelous. Exhilarating. Real. For the first time in years, he felt alive. His woman. She didn't even know she could put steel in a cock that had been trained to never respond unless he commanded it. She took him over with that innocence in her gaze.

"I don't fantasize."

He lifted one eyebrow. "Babe. You do."

She pressed her lips together. Yeah. She knew she did.

"I'm going to tell you something about me, something that might scare you, Azelie, but I hope instead of that, it reassures you."

She flashed him an uneasy, anxious look. "I'm listening."

He had the urge to kiss that haughty look right off her face. Instead, he gave her raw truth. Ugly truth. "I was born and raised in Russia. When I was a boy, my mom wanted nice things. Really nice things. She didn't have a way to get those things unless she sold herself—or sold me."

Azelie choked. She hadn't expected him to share intimate details of his life. The genuine distress in her eyes made him feel as if she saw into him. She did that to him. Made him feel as if he mattered. As if he was someone other than the monster they'd shaped him into.

"I'll tell you the entire story someday, but not tonight. Tonight, I'm just going to say I was eventually taken to a school run by criminals and pedophiles. They were instructed to turn the students into assets for the country by shaping us into assassins. We were forced, at a very young age, to learn how to kill and to do it in many ways. I was a very good student, Zelie. Excellent, in fact, as were the other survivors of that school. Out of two hundred eighty-seven of us, only eighteen survived. Well, nineteen, although we weren't aware he had survived until recently. The point I'm making is that Billows may be a first-class criminal and a depraved lunatic, but he doesn't have the skills or experience that I have when it comes to killing human beings."

He took his eyes off the road long enough to see the shock and horror on her face. He waited for her reaction, a part of him certain she would condemn him. Liquid turned the blue of her eyes to a deep-sea blue. Tears sparkled like diamonds on the ends of her long lashes and then spilled over, tracking down her face.

"Pull over, Andrii," she whispered. "Criminals? Pedophiles? Two hundred sixty-eight deaths? Only nineteen survivors? That's insanity. Your life has been insanity. Pull over. I need to . . ." She broke off abruptly and put her hand on his thigh.

She was crying for him. Tears. Real tears, not crocodile tears. She was as genuine as it got. How the hell had he, of all people, managed to find a woman like Azelie? It made no sense. She made him humble.

"Baby, don't cry for me. That happened a very long time ago."

The tears continued to spill over and run down her face. He had a fierce desire to pull over and sip at those tears. He couldn't remember a single person ever crying for him. Still, they had somewhere important to be.

"You'll ruin that makeup it took you all of three minutes to apply," he teased her, hoping to avert more tears. He wanted to get her to their destination.

She lifted her chin at him. "I don't think where we're going is nearly as important as what you just told me."

"It's important to me, *Solnyshkuh*." He kept his voice soft but firm. This was a very significant moment whether she knew it or not. He knew it was.

She wanted him to talk to her about his past. He wanted to take her somewhere special. He'd planned the date out carefully, and it was important to him. Mostly, what was critical was if she recognized that going on the date meant something to him and she put his desires before her own.

He continued to drive, very aware of her palm burning a hole through the material of his jeans to brand his thigh. He was aware of time passing and how quiet she'd gotten. The entrance to the mini-mall was directly ahead. He turned into the large parking area that ran around the outside of the stores.

Trees, shrubs and flowers were in brick planters all along the center of the lot. Around the sidewalks were more plants, neatly kept, some in wine barrels. Tables and benches provided eating and resting places in various alcoves between stores, cafés and restaurants.

"If that's what you want to do, Andrii, and it's important to you, then we're doing it. I'm not going to insist you talk about something that is clearly distressing."

Relief washed over him. Triumph. He hadn't been wrong in his assessment of her. His desires mattered to her. He parked the car and turned to face her. Just looking at her took his breath away. The fact that her soft skin was still wet with tears and the hint of liquid kept the blue ultrabright in her eyes sent heat coiling through his veins.

"Thank you, Zelie. I know it's important to you that we talk, and we will. It's important to me as well, but I have a surprise for you, and we can't be late, or they won't let us in."

She studied him for a moment and then looked around her. "Where are we?"

"Concord. We're going to Celine James' master class on suspense."

Maestro was grateful he was looking directly at her. Azelie didn't have a poker face. Shock. Disbelief. Excitement. Tears. There it was. All his. He may have found the perfect gift for her, but in receiving it, she filled him up, gave him what he'd never had before. He had thought he was empty and devoid of all feeling, even the capacity to feel, and yet that look on her face, being with her, changed everything.

He cupped her face between his palms, his thumb sliding through the wet trails on her face. "We've got to hurry, *Solnyshkuh*. They're locking the doors right at seven."

"Kiss me." She whispered the invitation, her voice soft with promise.

He pulled back immediately. "Can't give you that, baby. I start kissing you, we won't get in. I want you to have this experience. I'll give you a different one when I take you home."

A little shiver went through her body, and the blue of her eyes darkened with desire. He liked that a fuck of a lot. She wanted him. She was shy about it, but the chemistry between them was raw and visceral. He felt electricity sparking over his skin, keeping every nerve ending alive.

"Let's get going, baby." He dropped his hands and deliberately exited the car to get away from temptation. He wasn't going to be able to resist her for long. He was a man who had spent his entire life with discipline and control, yet with Azelie that control left him very quickly. He felt a little wild around her. Very predatory and dominant. Possessive and yet loving.

Loving. He hadn't known what that felt like. He hadn't told her the entire story of his mother and aunt and how they had betrayed a little boy. What they'd sold him into. What his life as a child and teenager had been. He hadn't known how to feel love until he'd found her, and it had happened so fast that he fell right off a cliff. Now he wanted her to leap off and trust him to catch her.

Maestro carried her pack to the door of the Barnes & Noble in Concord, where the master class was taking place. It was a new event, and the ticket price had been high, but aside from having the bestselling author there, the store had catered food and drink. They had limited room, and the author had insisted on each person having a comfortable space. All of that, including employees staying after hours to help, cost money. He would have paid any price to see that look on Azelie's face.

He spent the next two hours watching her. Savoring every look. Every word she exchanged with the author when the woman opened her talk up for questions. Azelie was intelligent, and the questions she asked were pertinent to what they were learning, not about the future of the Celine James books. Many of those in attendance wasted their time with the author asking about characters in her books and where she was taking her series rather than learning from her. Azelie was very focused on pursuing her knowledge, and her questions were direct.

Maestro found himself fascinated by her. He could watch

her all day and never get bored. She might have an affinity for numbers, a way to see patterns in them, but it was apparent, not only to him but to Celine James, that she was also very gifted with her creative side.

During the break, when they were getting food from the two long tables, Celine went right up to Azelie and began a private conversation with her. Maestro immediately took her plate and indicated she go with the author to a small table, and he'd bring her food as well as something to drink. One of the employees was already getting Celine food.

Once he placed the plate and glass in front of her, he removed himself to give them privacy, but he took a seat facing Azelie so he could read her lips and expression. He wanted to ensure Zelie was having a perfect experience. That was what was most important to him: that he gave her things she'd never had. Everything, including clothes and jewelry, but mostly experiences.

He had no doubt that once he took her to bed, she would want more, but he didn't want their relationship to be all about sex. He'd been with countless women. None had meant anything to him. He'd been taught to use sex to get close to a target. Azelie may have started out as a target, but she certainly wasn't one now.

He loved watching her face light up. His sun. He called her *Solnyshkuh*. His little sun. She was. He had never felt sunlight on him or in him. Azelie had changed that for him. He'd never noticed how good a woman could smell. Or how her curves were so completely feminine, and his body was utterly masculine. She was a shining light. Her smile lit up the room. Celine James was drawn to her not only because she was intelligent and talented, but also because she was a bright star.

The moment the author got up to make her rounds in the room, several other participants hurried over to crowd around his woman. Maestro wasn't certain he liked that. Two of the five were male. One had a very hungry look on his face. Maestro unfolded himself from the fairly comfortable chair.

The moment he did, he drew attention. Physically, he was a big man. Lots of muscle. Tattoos drifting up his neck. A few scars. He knew women found him attractive and most men avoided him.

The moment he stood, Azelie's gaze was on him. She'd checked with him several times during her visit with Celine James, her eyes on him and a lift of her eyebrow asking if he was okay. He had deliberately put off the vibes for others to stay away. When he did that, he might as well have been surrounded by a wall. He didn't want anyone to take his attention from Azelie.

It was important to him that she enjoy herself. If Celine had made her uncomfortable, he would have known, and he would have immediately shut down the conversation. Right now, it was important to him that the men move away from her, particularly Hungry Eyes. He didn't want to be the jealous idiot, but he had little trust in him.

She stood up in the middle of the small crowd that had gathered around her. Blue eyes fixed on him, she broke out into a welcoming, excited smile and practically flung herself into his arms. She gave a little leap at the end of her run and wrapped her arms around his neck, winding one leg around his thigh at the same time. Zero hesitation about showing the others in the room who she was with.

"Thank you, Andrii. This has been the best time *ever*. I can't believe you did this for me."

She lifted her face up to his and he brushed her lips lightly. The touch was featherlight, but he felt the jolt all the way to his soul. His cock reacted the way it seemed to whenever she was near. He fought for control, willing the threatening erection to stand down.

"We could go home," she suggested. "I could show you my appreciation."

He was tempted. How could he not be? She sounded shy and yet fearless at the same time. The combination of sultry temptress and sweet innocent was almost too alluring to pass up. The event had another hour and a half to go. Celine James had more to give to those who had paid to hear her advice. She planned on critiquing three pages of each of their works. Maestro wanted that for his woman.

He had the feeling Celine would be extremely impressed with Azelie's talent. He felt Zelie needed to hear others she respected praise her work. Azelie had grown up without compliments. No one told her she was doing a good job. No one gave her gifts or experiences. She fought hard for everything she had. She needed to know how others saw her. He wanted that for her. He loved her shyness, but he wanted her to have self-esteem, to see herself the way others around her saw her.

"You have another session with this author, and I think it's important. I have every intention of spending the night with you, Zelie. We'll have plenty of time for you to show your appreciation." He kissed the tip of her nose, giving her a reassuring grin when her expression told him part of her felt rejected. He had to remind himself she was as new to a relationship as he was, and she expected rejection just as he always expected betrayal. "I'm looking forward to it, *Solnyshkuh*. I want you to have every moment possible with Celine and get whatever it is you think is pertinent for your work."

Azelie nodded and reluctantly unwrapped herself from him. He was just as reluctant to let her go, his hands sliding over her as she stepped back. He held out his hand, and when she took it, he led her back to their table, where her pack and tablet were. Others were already moving to their places and pulling out their work in anticipation of the next hour and a half with the legendary author.

When they'd first arrived, Azelie was required to choose three pages of her work to send to Celine James to read. The other aspiring writers had already done so, and Celine had read their work and come prepared with her critiques.

The master class had been closed until Maestro offered enough money and used his voice shamelessly when pleading his case. Fortunately, the woman in charge was a romantic.

She was also very susceptible to his voice. The money helped as well. When Celine was contacted, she agreed to allow one more writer into the class and said she could read Azelie's three pages on her break.

Each person received feedback on their story. Maestro found the entire process interesting. The various writers worked in different genres, and yet the feedback Celine gave each was encouraging and seemed to him to be spot-on. She took her time going over each writer's entry, talking to them, appearing to be interested and focused and genuinely giving them tips and helpful guidance.

Maestro found himself respecting the woman. She had knowledge of her craft and shared it willingly. She was careful to be encouraging. He was good at body language and the least nuance of a voice. He could tell when Celine didn't feel a particular writer was very good. She gave them the same attention as the ones she was excited about. He admired her for her ability to find positive things to say while giving them helpful tips to improve their skills.

He was holding his breath when Celine focused her attention on Azelie. After each writer had been critiqued, they gathered their belongings and exited the building so the event planners could begin to break everything down to prepare for the following day's business. That meant that since Azelie was the last to be critiqued, she had the author to herself.

Azelie admitted to Celine she had previously had three books published and a contract for a fourth. The books were still selling well, and her sales had increased, but not significantly. She hadn't really done much social media or marketing on her own. The publishing house hadn't done much marketing on her behalf either.

Maestro found it interesting that most of Celine James' conversation with Azelie centered around marketing and the publishing business rather than writing technique. She praised Azelie's work and seemed quite taken with her. Azelie was animated, laughing and at times very engrossed in the things Celine told her.

It was clear to Maestro that her writing was extremely important to her. She might be getting a degree in accounting, but the creative writing classes she was taking were where her passion truly lay.

She was excited and happy, but the moment they got in the car and were headed back to her apartment, she went quiet on him.

"Babe, tell me what's going on in your head."

Her gaze touched his and slid away. "It's just that you're so amazing, Andrii. I don't know what I have to give you in return for everything you always seem to be doing for me. I don't want a one-sided relationship. I'm bringing a man like my boss into your life. You need to worry about him finding out about us before I can safely get away from him. That puts your life in danger."

"Zelie." He said her name quietly. They'd talked about Billows already. He was willing to share more about his life, but not in the car.

"It's more than that. I'm not experienced when it comes to sex." She turned her head to look directly at him. When his eyes met hers, he read her fears. "I don't know how to please you, and clearly, you're very experienced. I don't want to be a letdown for you."

He could see the disparity between their experiences was a major stumbling block for her, and he wasn't going to simply dismiss her concerns. The fact that his enjoyment mattered to her made him happy.

"We'll take care of your worry when we're home, and I can hold you while we talk. Is that acceptable for you?"

She nodded, but she did so with a little frown. Just that look made him want to smile.

ELEVEN

~~~

"All right, *Solnyshkuh*. We're home and you should feel safe." He used his gentlest tone but saw Azelie wince and realized his mistake instantly. She hadn't been safe in her home. She hadn't been safe with her relatives. None of them, not even the children, had been safe.

She paced across the room. It wasn't a large area, so there wasn't much space for her to get away from him. Maestro read her uneasiness without difficulty. He noted that she placed her backpack on a hook just inside the tiny utility closet. He would have to go through that backpack in an effort to find the key to Billows' underground rooms.

"Take your shoes and jacket off and get comfortable. If you want to change your clothes, I have no problem waiting." Deliberately, he bent to remove his motorcycle boots. He nearly always wore them, unless he dressed up to play the part of an affluent Russian. He had played many roles to get the job done. Usually, the job was assassination. He was extremely good at his work.

He didn't look at her, but kept his gaze on his boots, as if his feet hurt and he couldn't wait to get them off. His boots were very comfortable, but she needed to feel as if she were in control. When he had the boots sitting beside the chair, he stretched out his long legs with a sigh of relief.

She was instantly alert. "We shouldn't have stayed so long, Andrii. I stayed late because I was talking so much with Celine, but I should have been paying better attention to you." She hung her jacket in the closet and removed her shoes and socks, taking them to the bedroom and placing them inside another closet.

When she returned, she sent him a small smile. "This apartment is so tiny I've learned to utilize all available space. Everything I own has its place. If I leave my shoes or anything else out, I would eventually stumble over them in the middle of the night."

"You're wandering. Come over here."

She sent him a leery look from under her lashes, but she crossed the room to stand in front of his chair.

"I asked you to come to me, Zelie," he reminded her in his softest, most compelling tone.

She swallowed her nervousness and indicated with her hand she was close. "I'm right here."

"I see that, but when I tell you I want you to come to me, that means I want you sitting in my lap." This time he held her gaze captive. He refused to allow her to look away from him.

She pressed her lips together as if to keep from blurting something out, but she obediently stepped close to him. His long, outstretched legs forced her to straddle him. She felt small and curvy in his arms. The heat at the junction of her legs seared right through his jeans. He wrapped one arm around her back to support her, but mostly to keep her anchored to him.

"I believe you owe me something." He dipped his head to nuzzle her ear and then tug at her earlobe with his teeth. A small bite but it accomplished so much. Goose bumps rose on her skin, and she shivered. Her blue eyes darkened with desire.

"Owe you?" she echoed, sounding confused.

"Kisses, baby. You were going to kiss me to thank me for your surprise, and I had to shut it down to keep you safe. As it was, I had a hell of a hard-on with you winding yourself around me." He smiled at her and nipped her neck this time. "Seems my control goes right out the window when I'm with you."

Another shiver went through her body. She squirmed on his lap, right over his cock. He'd flared to life the moment his body felt the heat of hers. He lay beneath her, thick and long and demanding. Andrii made no move to hide his reaction to her.

"Kiss me, baby," he whispered—an enticement. Meant to be temptation. Was temptation.

Her hands slid up his chest and then she circled his neck with her arms, turning her face up to his. "I'm not sure I know how."

His heart melted at the whispered admission. Still, she tilted her face and brushed his lips with hers. Light. Barely there. The shock was electric. His pulse jumped. His heart slammed up against his chest. Flames raced through his bloodstream straight to his cock.

Her breath was honey and strawberries. Impossible. When she pressed her lips to his again, the tip of her tongue slid along the seam of his mouth. It felt like a living, burning flame. He gripped her hair, angled her head perfectly and took control. Honey and strawberries gave way to fiery whiskey. The flames rolled down his throat.

Azelie ignited. Detonated. Set him off. The explosion between the two of them was a fiery volcanic storm that built in intensity. The earth rocked beneath them. No joke. It happened. He hadn't known it could happen, that the world could spin and drop away when the one woman who was your other half kissed you.

She wasn't experienced in the least, but she followed his lead and surrendered herself to him completely. There was no holding back; she gave him everything. He took it without hesitation, although he hadn't planned to follow through, not until they had talked. He wanted her to know exactly what she was getting into with him before she surrendered her body to his keeping.

Maestro wasn't a man to share intimacy with anyone. Kissing was as intimate as it got, and yet once he had her mouth, the dance of their tongues, the heat poured down his throat, racing like a wildfire out of control straight to his cock. Every nerve ending was awake. He felt alive for the first time. Completely and utterly alive. This woman owned his heart.

He had to feel her skin. There was no going back from this moment. No stopping and slowing down. He was on a runaway freight train rushing down the tracks, and there was no way to put the brakes on. Thunder roared in his ears. Flames ignited in his belly and settled lower. A sinful dark craving rolled through him. Took hold. Those flames branded that addiction deep into his bones. Wrote her name on his heart.

He made short work of the off-the-shoulder top. Azelie didn't seem to notice. She was too busy trying to pull his shirt off, evidently needing the same thing he did—bare skin. Her lips feathered over his throat, leaving tiny flames behind.

"We're taking this into the other room." His voice sounded like a growl, but she didn't seem to notice as he stood in one smooth motion, holding her to him. She wrapped her legs around his hips as he made his way to the bed, grateful the room was so small, with his aching erection making it difficult to walk.

One knee on the bed, he lowered her bottom to the edge and quickly dispensed with her bra. She was wearing one he'd purchased for her, a sexy demi-cup that held her breasts lovingly. Any other time he would have focused on the sight, savoring the luxury. She had gorgeous breasts. Full and round, with nipples begging for attention.

He pushed her back until she sprawled out in front of him, her silky breasts jutting up at him as he grasped her jeans and panties to draw them down her legs.

"You take my breath away." It was the truth, and he needed to give her that when the trepidation was creeping back into her eyes.

"I'm afraid. Really scared, Andrii," she admitted in a little whisper. "Most of the time I feel alone and a bit lost, but when I'm with you, everything is different. I know better than to depend on anyone else, but when I'm with you, I can't help the way I feel."

"I'm not going anywhere, Azelie. I want us to have children, grow old together, the works. I'll do whatever it takes to keep you happy. I hope you can hear the truth in my voice."

He had to reassure her, give her that much. His teeth tugged on her lower lip and then nibbled down her chin. That sweet chin that beckoned him to use his teeth for just one moment. He pressed kisses over the pulse racing in her throat. He needed to feel the way her heart pounded, assuring him she was there, alive and in perfect tune with him.

"You have one foot out the door, baby. I don't blame you; I'm a bit much, and I know that. Still." He kissed his way over the upper curves and down the valley between her full breasts. She shivered in response as the bristles along his jaw rasped against that sensitive skin.

Her fingers bit into his shoulders as she struggled to decide what to do. Push him away or pull him closer? He read her easily.

"Tell me what's happening in your mind right now, *Solnyshkuh*." He swept his palm down her body from her breasts to her mound. All that satin-soft skin. Those feminine curves. "What are you afraid of?"

Her blue gaze searched his a little frantically. She gave the barest shake of her head.

"Be brave, Zelie. You're always brave. Trust me to catch you." There were little inviting drops of moisture caught in the fiery auburn curls guarding what he wanted. What he was determined to claim.

Cautiously, gently, he slipped one finger lower, swept it across her wet opening and went deep. He'd expected her to be tight, and she was, much tighter than he'd imagined. It was going to take some time to make her comfortable enough to take him. But she was hot and slick, her body reacting to his. There was no denying the chemistry between them.

She gasped at his invasion, her body jerking, but she settled when he turned his gaze on her.

"When I look at you, Azelie, when I see you like this, I feel like I'm drowning. I love the way your body responds to mine. I need that from you, and you give it to me without reservation."

He'd been doing his best to convince her they belonged together, try to get her to fall in love with him, but somewhere along the line, when he didn't even believe in love, he had fallen right off a cliff. Fallen hard. He hadn't even realized just how much emotion he felt for her until that moment.

He brought his finger to his mouth and sucked the taste of her off, all the while holding her gaze captive with his. A shiver went through her. He savored that moment. Let her see how much she meant to him. How much he desired her.

Very gently he nuzzled her breasts, once again using the shadowy bristles along his jaw to stimulate her even more. He slid both hands, fingers splayed wide to take in as much of her as he could, shaping her feminine body, the lush curves, narrow rib cage and tucked-in waist. Claiming every inch of her. Showing her she belonged with him. He knew she was afraid, and she had every reason to be, but he had every intention of going slow. Taking his time. Doing sweet and loving to ease her into their world together.

"Andrii," she sounded lost. "I don't know what I'm doing."

"That's the beauty of this, baby. You don't need to do anything at all but enjoy what I'm giving you."

Once more, he kissed his way up to her mouth. That

fantasy mouth. He loved kissing her, dreamt of kissing her, thought too much about it during the day. He poured the emotion he couldn't speak of down her throat. Giving that to her. Making certain she felt it. He hadn't considered that he would be the one to fall. He thought all along that he could hold back, that part of him would always remain aloof and above it. She would fall in love with him, and he would be safe from betrayal. From taking the chance that she would rip out anything that was left of his heart. There was no holding himself apart from her. Not a single chance. He was already gone.

He kissed her with real emotion, pouring his feelings for her into his kisses. He kissed her over and over, stripping himself bare, making himself totally vulnerable by showing her what she meant to him. He did so with what he was best at, only his kisses weren't practiced perfection. For the first time they were real and intimate and meant something.

Her mouth moved under his, surrendering everything to him. She caught fire, completely detonated. The chemistry between them was explosive. She didn't know it yet, but she belonged to him. She kept trying to pull back until he kissed her. It was then she completely gave herself to him.

His heart pounded. Thunder roared in his ears. Hot blood pumped through his veins. He caught fire right along with her. He found her nipple, tugging, rolling, catching her whispered moan in his mouth. He kissed his way to her breasts and then flicked her nipple with his tongue. Her entire body reacted to that brief, cautious takeover of her senses. He wanted to go slow and savor every reaction. He wanted to keep her in the moment, so she couldn't get into her head and feel fear.

She liked what he was doing to her, arching just enough to give him better access and her complete approval. He took the invitation, pulling one breast into the heat of his mouth while he worked the other, tugging and rolling her nipple, gently at first and then with increasing pressure. All the while, he was aware of her every reaction. Breathing. Squirming.

Moaning. He needed to know what she liked and didn't like. What she feared but would try.

He liked control in bed. He needed to know his woman would give that to him. Fortunately for him, his little wildcat seemed to prefer following his lead. The one way he knew he could tie her to him for sure was through sex. He'd spent years being trained to draw his partners to him, to keep them addicted, coming back for more.

Her nails dug into his shoulders as he spent time on her breasts, using teeth and tongue, at times rough and then so gentle, refusing to set a rhythm so she never knew what was coming. Her breath came in rapid little pants, and her legs moved restlessly.

Maestro didn't want their relationship to be all about sex. If that was the only way he could have her, so be it, but he wanted what was between them to be the real thing. He wanted to give her as much pleasure as possible because, to his absolute astonishment, he had fallen hard for her.

He swept his palm down the length of her, absorbing the feel of her silken skin. The feminine shape of her. His fingers stroked her sensitive mound as he followed the path of his palm with his lips, sipping at her skin. Kissing and nipping. All the while, his fingers played and teased along her mound. Skimming along her enticing lips, looking for her slick heat and telltale dampness where he slid one finger through fiery wetness, testing that she was as eager for him as he was for her. Not that he thought that possible. He felt as if he'd waited a lifetime for her.

Her feminine channel clenched tight around his finger. He felt the silken muscles clamping down, nearly strangling his finger, making his cock ache even more. It was disturbing to need her so much. To want her the way he did. He'd barely touched her, barely gotten started, and he was harder than he'd ever been in his life. Every nerve ending in his body was alive, on fire, desperate for her.

He lifted his head and looked into her eyes. She was completely innocent and yet he saw trust there. It was such a gift. Seeing that look in her eyes humbled him. He was asking a lot of her and would be asking more. On some level, she knew and understood that, yet she was still willing to give her body into his keeping.

He had fallen hard. So fast. Finding her was unexpected, and given the circumstances of their meeting, it came at the wrong time, but nothing mattered to him but her. Her happiness. Her pleasure. She robbed him of his breath. Each separate beat of his heart was for her. He had found something to live for. Someone who elevated him when he didn't think that was possible. He had been so far gone and yet there she was—his sunshine.

"I want us to always be like this, *Solnyshkuh*. The two of us."

His breath felt raw, his lungs burning for air. It was becoming a familiar feeling to him when she was nearby. Fire burned bright and hot, the flames licking over every nerve ending.

He wrapped his palm around her throat, feeling her heart beating in his hand. He continued sliding through her wetness with one finger, then brushed her clit, feeling her jerk beneath him in reaction.

"Tell me how that feels, Zelie. Do you like what I'm doing?"

Her gaze jumped to his, dark with heat. She nodded, giving him that. He read her body, but he wanted her to confirm she was growing desperate for him. He hadn't even started, but she needed to be at fever pitch to accept him.

"It's like the brush of a white-hot flame." She whispered the admission. "Amazing."

"Relax for me, *Solnyshkuh*. I've waited far too long to taste you. Kissing you sets up an addiction to your particular taste. I love the way you smell. I'm craving your unique flavor on my tongue."

He lifted his finger to his mouth and licked, his eyes focused on her, needing to see her reaction, tongue curling around his finger, savoring the honey and strawberry spice.

Color crept under her flesh, turning her silken skin to rose. She came up on her elbows, looking at him with a mixture of apprehension and heat.

"I don't know . . ." She trailed off, her gaze clinging to his, looking to him for reassurance.

He slid his palm from her neck, moved it gently over the full curves of her breasts to her belly, savoring the feel of her. She was as soft as any rose petal. Like silk. Splaying his fingers wide, his hand nearly took up her entire abdomen. He liked the way his hand, rough and scarred, looked against her skin.

"I promise, baby, you're going to like everything I do to you."

His gaze dropped to the scars on her body from the three bullets her brother-in-law had pumped into her when he did his best to murder her. One was very close to her heart. It was a testament to her strength that she had survived and to her indomitable spirit that she was such a bright, shining light.

Slowly, but relentlessly, he applied pressure until she complied with his order, letting herself fall to her back. Her gaze never left his. He loved her looking at him—to him—trusting him to give her pleasure when she felt vulnerable.

"Andrii." She whispered his name.

His heart accelerated, ached for her, an actual physical pain. He knew what she saw. Lines of lust and the possibility of love were carved deep because he felt both. Desire was stark and raw.

"I've got you, baby," he reassured her. "Just looking at you makes me hard as fuck. You can't know what that means to me. Natural. Real. Someday I'll tell you just what kind of miracle you really are."

Maestro stood at the end of the bed, looking down at the woman he knew was his. His entire life had been one of betrayal by women. His gut, his every instinct, told him she was different. She would stay. She could put up with his bullshit and insecurities.

Azelie lay naked; her gorgeous body with its generous curves was his. She was giving herself to him. He wanted to spend hours devouring her. Savoring her. Convincing her she couldn't live without him because he was that far gone already. He couldn't live without her.

He wanted to spend time, hours, days, weeks, hearing her call his name in that soft little whimper she had, the sounds at the back of her throat that drove him mad. He wanted to make her come for him over and over.

She was on the verge of flight half the time, so wary, so afraid what was between them couldn't be real. He knew her background, that the abandonment of her parents and betrayal of her brother-in-law had made her feel as if no one could really love her. He knew what that felt like—he often felt the same way. But how could anyone not love Azelie?

He started from the beginning again, kissing his way from her chin, down her throat, to the swell of her breasts. Soft. Silk. Perfection. He was lost in his exploration for a few minutes, giving himself the sheer pleasure of feasting on her, watching the way his tongue, teeth and the heat of his mouth kept tension in her coiling deep. He spent time at each of the scars, his tongue moving in a soothing, caressing motion, mapping them, holding her to him, savoring the taste of her, even as he memorized every inch of her body.

Maestro ran his palms from her belly to her thighs. Moved his hands down her legs to her ankles in a slow claiming. He wanted the shape and feel of her imprinted not just in his brain but in his bones. He wanted to know she would allow him to touch her anywhere they were. He wanted closeness with her.

When they talked, he wanted her in his lap. He needed to hold her close to him. Her kisses were pure fire, and he knew he'd never get enough of them. It was important to him to know she wouldn't mind if he slid his hand under her clothing to touch her bare skin. That need wasn't about ownership. He wasn't an exhibitionist, nor did he want other men to think his woman was his plaything. He wanted respect for her because she deserved respect. He knew he would need to touch her intimately at times, to stroke his fingers along her belly or hips, but not where others could see.

At the same time, it would never bother him to have his brethren close, even if he was making love to her. That was something he would have to discuss with her. So many things he needed her to understand. So many things she would have to put up with. What was he giving her in return? How was he ever going to make the two sides of their relationship equal?

Very gently he tugged her thighs apart, keeping them wide enough for his shoulders. He had wide shoulders. Very wide. She was gorgeous. A beautiful woman in need of what he could give her. He was going to take his time, ensure she felt nothing but pleasure. He might not have a lot to give her, other than his protection and this.

"*Bog*, but you're so beautiful. A gorgeous woman, Azelie. I have no idea how I got so lucky, but I'm not a stupid man. Fate handed you into my care, and I intend to keep you."

He saw the sudden flicker of indecision creep into her eyes. He couldn't have that, couldn't allow her to think too much. This was about feeling.

"I wonder how many times I can make you scream my name," he murmured, distracting her on purpose.

She shook her head, eyes clinging to his. "I don't scream, but I might whisper your name a *lot*."

She was serious. Somber. He bent his head to breathe warm air against her inner thigh. She gasped, and her leg jerked in his hand. He tightened his grip, holding her in place.

"Andrii," she whispered. Just as she'd said she might.

He met her startled blue gaze and gave her a faint grin. One that said he was in control, and she might not scream his name, but she would be pleading for mercy.

He'd had enough of being alone, of feeling as if he wasn't worth a damn. Azelie changed the way he thought about himself. He had no idea how, but he'd face death every single day to keep her.

"Stop making me wait," she demanded. Impatience was there in her voice. Anticipation. The blue in her eyes had gone royal.

He decided it was about time to put them both out of their misery. Bending slowly, he pressed his lips to the inside of her thigh and gently sucked. Sipped. Whispered how he felt about her, so the sound was muffled against her silky skin. Just touching her bare skin knotted his stomach, putting a fist of desire so large there that he was shocked.

He didn't feel sensations the way others apparently did. That had been tortured out of him when he was a kid. He'd had to be in total control of his cock because it was a matter of life and death—to him and his partner when he was learning. In one moment with Azelie, just inhaling her scent, just being close, simply observing her, his body came to life. Kissing her destroyed any control completely. They detonated together and his cock went into a frenzy of need for her. It was a little terrifying, as well as exhilarating, to feel as if he was truly alive.

He kissed his way up and down the inside of her thigh, occasionally stopping to suck gently. In places a little harder. He nipped. Swirled his tongue to soothe the brief sting. He wanted to leave his mark on her. He wanted her mark on his skin.

Azelie's breath came out in a hiss of need. She squirmed. Shifted her hips restlessly. A little moan escaped when he tightened his grip on her thighs in warning.

"I don't know if I can take this," she whispered.

"We're just getting started," he warned.

"I was afraid of that." But she stopped trying to retreat from him. Instead, when he tightened his grip, she seemed to widen her legs even more to accommodate him. Showing she wanted him as much as he wanted her.

Maestro kissed his way up her inner thigh, one small increment at a time until he felt the heat of the junction between her legs. Where she wept for him, beckoned and enticed with her feminine scent.

His cock felt like a monster, aching, hurting, desperate to be free of the material putting pressure on him. He tore down the zipper with one hand so that his engorged shaft and balls were free of the prison. Thunder roared in his ears. Lightning ripped through his veins. He took the time to free himself completely, shedding his jeans fast, grateful he'd removed his boots earlier.

The cool air on his body didn't alleviate the heat rushing through his bloodstream. It didn't give him back any of the control he needed. He found himself struggling to take his time. She softly moaned as he spread kisses from her thigh to the back of her knee and then back up to the little tangle of fiery curls shielding her slick lips.

"You taste like pure heaven, Zelie." He didn't lift his head to see her reaction. He didn't need to. Her body shivered and arced closer to his mouth, desperate for more. He took his time, knowing the anticipation would heighten her pleasure. He blew a steady stream of heated air, gentle but constant, and then when she was squirming, he licked at the fiery honey liquid. She whimpered and lifted her hips to him.

"So responsive, *Solnyshkuh*." Again, he didn't raise his head, too far gone himself to leave where he wanted to be most. He leaned into her, settling his mouth over her clit, tongue fluttering gently.

Azelie gasped, a small broken cry escaping. She jerked her legs and hips as if she might try to flee. He found himself smiling as his eyes met hers.

"Baby, we're just getting started. I plan on spending time right here." He blew more warm air. "Savoring the taste of you." He loved her taste. Was already addicted to it. "There isn't going to be any running."

"You need to hurry." Her little demand was whispered.

That was his woman. Rarely speaking above a soft sound. Even the laughter he was so addicted to hearing was soft, as captivating and enticing as it was.

"You need to know something about your man, Zelie. I'm the one in control here. I always will be. If I want to take my time, we're taking time." He swiped his tongue along that delicious slit that beckoned. "I definitely want to take my time and you need to be ready for me."

"I am ready for you." There was a plea in her voice.

"No, you're not. You just feel like you are. I don't want you to experience anything but pleasure, so we're doing this my way." He would have done it his way regardless, but he meant what he said. He had no intention of her feeling anything but sheer bliss. That meant taking his time and building her need slowly. Preparing her body. It was his good luck that his pleasure was all about bringing it to her.

"I've never felt anything like this," she confessed. "It feels so good it's a little scary."

His woman was giving him that starry-eyed adoration he'd come to look for. "You're in good hands, baby. Just keep trusting me. I'm going to make you feel a whole lot better."

He was just as addicted to that look on her face, the one that said he was incredible, the most amazing lover on the planet. They hadn't even gotten started yet and she was already certain of his abilities. But then she didn't have anything to judge this experience by. He intended that to never happen. He was determined to be her only. Ever.

Spreading her thighs wider, he shifted his weight, placing her legs over his forearms. One hand on her belly, fingers splayed wide to hold her still, he dipped his head and began his feast. Slow, delicious licks. Flicks with this tongue. Teasing her. A slow burn that built and built, sneaking up on her until it was a fiery inferno.

He was careful not to give her exactly what was needed to get her off. Very gently he brushed her clit with the pads of his fingers. He circled that sensitive little button and then replaced his fingers with his tongue. Azelie gasped and gave him that same little broken whisper of a cry when he curled a long finger inside her, finding her most sensitive spot and stroking.

Maestro pulled back when he felt the tightening of her body, the hot slickness. He replaced his finger with his tongue, a unique weapon that made her go a little wild. He plunged his tongue into her, withdrew, and did it again and again. Truthfully, he felt a little wild himself. He prided himself on control, yet he knew he was on the verge of tipping over the edge.

He loved her taste. He loved her response to him, the way she thrashed under him. The little whimpers and moans. The sight of her needing him. Her fragrance enveloped him, driving him nearly out of his mind. Her skin was rose-petal soft, flushed now with desire. When he moved one finger in her, the silken walls of her channel were scorching hot, her need growing for his full, painful cock.

Once again, he slowed things down, nuzzling her, running his nose along her inner thighs, all the while inhaling deeply to breathe her in. He wanted to keep her in his lungs forever.

"Andrii." Her little whisper was back. A moan. A plea. "You have to do something. I'm burning up."

He was burning up as well. Aching. Needing. But this was for her. "Have to make sure you can take me, baby."

Her eyes widened. "I can," she announced solemnly. Certain.

She was tight around his finger, and his cock was much larger than his finger. Her silken muscles tightened. She was coiled tight. Her body was flushed with heat, the flames dancing through her veins licking at her nerve endings.

The fire *roared* through him. Raged. He wanted to be inside her. Sharing her skin. Her body. Once more he put his mouth on her. Sucked. Flicked. Worked her hard, brought her so close numerous times until she was thrashing beneath him.

Maestro lost himself in her, in the wonder of her body. The miracle of real feeling. He used every bit of his skills, tongue, teeth, lips, fingers. Worshipping her. Losing himself in the exquisite taste of her. Her feminine fragrance. He would know her anywhere. Her soft skin. Like silk or satin. Then there was that emotion welling up, coming close to overwhelming him. Was that what love felt like? Because he'd never known that emotion, but what he felt for her was all-encompassing. He couldn't ever take the chance of losing her.

"Andrii," she wailed his name, her body close. So close.

He felt the tightness coiling in her belly. Her thighs went rigid as the scorching-hot silken muscles clamped around his fingers. This time he didn't stop.

"Andrii—" She broke off, her hips bucking with need.

"Let go." He made it a command as he flicked her clit and used his finger to stroke her sensitive bundle of nerves.

That scorching-hot tunnel clamped hard on his fingers, so hard his cock jerked in anticipation. She shuddered, driving her nails into his shoulders, scoring his skin. Her gaze clung to his as the first orgasm rolled through her. Her tight muscles fought to drag his fingers deeper. He bent forward, rubbed the bristles of his jaw along her breast, and then sucked her nipple into the heat of his mouth. Just as her body was beginning to settle, he bit down on her nipple, applying gentle pressure and then a harder nip, his tongue soothing instantly. Her body detonated a second time, this orgasm stronger than the first.

Maestro loved watching the helpless, dazed expression on her face. The shock. He heard the soft whisper of his name as she climaxed. Beautiful. Hot. For him.

She was ready for him, and he couldn't wait another moment. He pushed her knees up, placing each foot on the cover, knees wide apart so her thighs were open for him. His heart accelerated at the sight of her open and ready for him. Circling the thick shaft with one hand, he nudged his way into that hot, wet inferno.

Azelie's gaze clung to his, all that beautiful blue wide with shock as he shuddered with the exquisite sensation of the tight squeeze.

"Andrii," she whispered his name again, a kind of awe, wonder mixed with trepidation in her voice. Her small teeth bit into her lower lip.

"That's right, *Solnyshkuh*, Andrii. No one else." He leaned forward, nearly helpless to do anything else, needing to lick at those little tooth marks on her lip. His cock slipped a bit deeper into that scorching tunnel, her muscles seizing the sensitive head like a vise.

He could barely find his voice. Nothing in his life had ever felt so good. Heaven. Hell. He didn't know which, but he never wanted to leave.

"Stay with me, Azelie. Promise you'll try with me. Give all of yourself to me."

Her body squeezed and burned around the broad head of his erection. His cock throbbed with need, pulsed and jerked. He couldn't help himself; he pushed deeper until he encountered her barrier. Swearing softly under his breath, feeling her hot, sweet tunnel close around him, he leaned forward a second time to lick at her mouth, and then took her lower lip between his teeth. One shocking nip and he pushed past the barrier. She gasped at the burn, tensing. Every muscle taut.

"Relax for me, baby." It was difficult not to move when everything in him urged him to drive deep. "You're so fucking tight, Zelie."

He forced himself to go slow, sinking another inch into that tight fist of scorching flames. He didn't want to be rough with her, and he had to fight for control. Her lush body was producing a kind of rapture, pleasure he'd never experienced with any of the partners he'd had, not even as a teen.

"Relax, *Solnyshkuh*," he coaxed. "Give yourself to me. Trust me to make this good."

She took a deep breath. "I'm afraid you're making it too good. I feel as if I'm losing myself in you."

A feeling of utter joy burst through him. Triumph. "That's what you're supposed to feel. Let go and give yourself to me. You won't regret it."

Very slowly she widened her knees. He rubbed the tight knots on the insides of her thighs, using a circular motion. Always, he was gentle, cognizant of her fears. He waited for those inner muscles to ease just a little, enough for him to inch his way inside her. He stroked her clit with the pad of his finger, trying to ease not just the tightness of her body but also her fears.

He knew she was afraid she was giving him too much of herself, and she wouldn't be able to pull back if he let her down. His fingers stroked, circled. Eventually, the helpless pleasure eased the tension on her face and in her body.

"I've never given myself to a woman, Azelie. Not ever. Not one single time. Not until you. I've never taken time with one, didn't kiss, didn't give anything of me. I got them off, but that was the extent of what I did. You're so different. Everything about you, about us, is different."

All the while he spoke, he worked her body and pushed gently to allow his cock to invade deeper into those scorching-hot depths. The strangling vise robbed him of air. He licked at his fingers, not wanting to miss one single drop of her addicting honey. He was careful not to surge forward. There would be no powering through those tight petal-like folds.

Her body slowly gave way to his invasion, stretching to accommodate his long, thick cock as he relentlessly sank into her. He couldn't repress a groan. Sweat broke out as he held himself back from ramming ruthlessly into her.

"For you," he murmured aloud. "All for you." He was a man who had more control than most, needed it. Wanted it. But with Azelie, his control was threatened.

He'd never seen such a beautiful sight as his woman lying there, taking what he was giving her, his cock impaling her, stretching her. Each time she thrashed or lifted her hips in an attempt to get more of him, her lush breasts swayed and jolted. He began to make small thrusts with his hips, holding back power, setting a rhythm that rocked her with each stroke.

The pleasure was so intense it bordered on pain. Her body so scorching hot and tight, surrounding him with those silken muscles, squeezing down on his cock like the tightest of fists. She had to stay still, or he was going to lose all control. He pushed farther as he wrapped his hand around her calf and drew it around his waist. That simple move allowed him to sink deeper. His breath caught in his lungs as her tight muscles loosened enough to allow him to push forward, sinking deeper and deeper into her.

He drew her other leg up and wrapped it around him. "Lock your ankles for me," he commanded. His voice was deliberately velvet soft, but husky as he pushed forward again, this time burying himself all the way. He was surrounded by a fiery tunnel of silk, so tight the pain was exquisite. It felt as if her every individual muscle was wrapped around his cock.

Azelie's body pulsated. That pounding beat radiated up his shaft to his sensitive crown. Pleasure burst through him. Now he had to move in her; he had no choice. The slow slide withdrawing had her gasping. Her eyes widening. Legs tightening around him. Even her inner muscles grasped at him.

"We're going slow, baby, until you get used to me."

"I don't think I can wait for slow."

He loved that little admission from her and gave her one hard stroke, surging back into her, sending streaks of lightning through them both. She gave him a scowl when he withdrew slowly again.

"You'll like this," he assured her.

He set a slow pace, driving deep but moving through her hot channel with a leisurely slide, savoring the way her tight muscles grasped and tried to lock down on his cock. He made certain to press hard on the bundle of nerves as he moved with lazy strokes. Color spread over her satiny skin, turning it a delicious rose. He kept his attention on her sweet spot, building her need.

All the while he could feel the power building in his body, his own need gathering. His balls tightened, signaling he wasn't going to be able to hold out for long. He felt the force gathering in her body. Building. Always building. Fists of desire gripped his thighs. Her thighs tensed. He could see her breath catching in her throat. Her fingers dug into his shoulders as her delicate muscles, so scorching hot, locked down on his cock. He surged forward, hard. Several strokes. Over and over.

Azelie's eyes widened in shock. The breath hissed from her throat. She cried out softly as the orgasm tore through her. The grasping, greedy muscles felt like a scorching fist, taking him flying with her. He drove through that paradise another three times, but then it was impossible to move. His cock jerked and pulsed in the silken fist as her body milked his, flinging him somewhere he'd never been before. He had the sensation of floating in another realm, surrounded by Azelie.

Maestro collapsed over her, holding her tight, his heart pounding out the rhythm of hers. He could feel her heartbeat around his shaft as his own throbbed in his cock. Never had he ever felt the way he was feeling. Not the bliss. Not the emotion. She might not be tied to him yet, but she owned him. He knew that. He would never be free of her. He didn't want to be. He sent up a silent prayer to a higher power he wasn't certain he believed in that she was the real thing. That she would never betray him.

TWELVE

Azelie wrapped herself in her largest robe. She'd taken a bath in her tiny bathtub and now she had to face what she'd done. She should have asked Andrii questions *before* she had sex with him. Now she didn't know if she could bear to lose him. Still, she didn't want to go into a relationship with her eyes closed.

Andrii was a scary man. Not in the same way Billows was scary, but there was no denying he was dangerous as hell. Just because he was so unfailingly sweet to her didn't mean a relationship would work, especially with Billows looking over her shoulder and threatening anyone who came near her.

Andrii had been wonderful to her after having sex with her. He kissed her dozens of times, whispered how beautiful she was. How much she meant to him. How amazing she made him feel. He made her feel as if she were the only woman in the world. Still, that didn't excuse the fact that she should have asked questions *before*.

Her apartment was extremely small, but she made certain she was a safe distance away from Andrii. He seemed to be able to cast a spell on her, and she had to have a clear mind when she asked him very important questions.

He was seated in one of her two comfortable chairs, his legs sprawled out, feet bare, wearing just jeans and his unbuttoned shirt. His laid-back position and the way he was dressed suggested an intimacy level she wasn't sure she could cope with.

He had scars. A lot of them. Burn marks. Bullet scars. Ones from knives. What looked like whip marks. She hadn't seen his back, but if his chest was covered in scars, she had to assume his back would be as well. He was heavily tattooed. She wanted to trace those tattoos with her tongue. Press kisses over the scars just as he had over her three. Three bullet wounds had seemed a lot until she saw his chest.

Azelie forced herself to ask the necessary questions. The important ones. "Do you own a gun?" She had to know.

Her heart went crazy, accelerating far beyond what it should have. She found she was more fearful of his answer than she was of Billows and his threats. She wasn't falling for Billows. She was for Andrii.

She knew she was more than halfway there. Everything about Andrii appealed to her. He was sweet and caring. Very attentive. At the same time, he made her shiver with excitement, feeling the underlying power clinging to him. She had been on her own for as long as she could remember. Janine had taken her in when her mother had imploded, but she was expected to contribute to the household—even when Quentin wasn't.

She had often made decisions with Janine she didn't want to make. Neither woman had a choice when there was no one else to figure it out. She pushed herself to be definite and firm in her options, but her inclination was to put things off. Like Billows. She still didn't have a great exit plan. She kept putting that off until she made it through college. Who knew what she would do then?

But a gun in her home? Guns in the hands of the man she

might eventually live with? She wasn't certain she could overcome that particular roadblock. The thought was terrifying to her. She kept her gaze steady on his. "Do you, Andrii? Do you own a gun?"

Andrii didn't flinch or look away. "Several guns. And my guns aren't my only weapons. *I* am a weapon."

She touched her tongue to her upper lip, unable to decide how she felt about his admission. His tone was calm and velvet soft. He looked at her as if she were his world. Quentin had never looked at Janine that way, but he had professed to love her.

"Talk to me, Zelie. That's what we're doing here, being honest and communicating."

She had to be real with him. Tell him the strict truth. If he couldn't take it, they weren't meant to be, no matter how much she wanted him. "The idea of guns anywhere around me makes me uneasy," she admitted.

"Come here to me. I need you close when we talk about our future."

"I get lost when I'm too close to you," she admitted.

"I'll keep us on track. This is important to you. To both of us. Come here, baby."

His voice. So compelling. How could she resist? She moved into him, standing between his thighs. At once, he pulled her into his arms, onto his lap. She knew when he wanted her close, it meant on his lap. She didn't protest. She felt safer when his arms were around her.

He cradled the side of her face with his palm, his thumb sliding over her lips, sending shivers of awareness down her spine.

"Baby, I'm not Quentin. I know guns might seem scary to you, but you need to see who I am. I'm far more lethal than your brother-in-law could ever have been. He was a bully and a coward. He couldn't have loved your sister or his children or you. I would kill for you, but I would never do anything to harm you. You're my savior. My world. A treasure beyond any price. If things go bad between us, I would move heaven and earth to make them right. I would never, under any circumstances, consider harming you."

She touched the tip of her tongue to her suddenly dry lips. He had admitted to her he was trained as an assassin from an early age. She had no doubt that he was skilled in his craft. Just the fact that he was alive was a testament to his expertise. If she entered into a relationship with him, she would always know what he was capable of. It had never occurred to her that he wasn't telling her the truth. Looking at him, seeing him, lent credence to his admissions.

"What are you thinking?"

"You could have lied to me about your past." She didn't know what she was asking of him. Reassurance? How could he make her feel as if she wouldn't be living under a threat when he readily admitted he was a lethal weapon even without a gun?

"I could have, but I want our relationship to be about trust. About honesty. I need to know that you can accept me the way I really am. No fantasy. No overlooking my faults. To be in the relationship I need, you have to trust me. That isn't going to be easy, and I'm aware you'll be making quite a few concessions, so it's important to me to always, always, give you the truth. You will need to know you can depend on me, on my word, no matter what the circumstances are. If I can't tell you something right at the time you ask a question, I'll let you know why I can't answer and when I'll be able to."

Another red flag went up. Alarms sounded in her brain. That didn't sound good. Not answering her questions right away? She would have to have understanding for him if he decided he couldn't talk to her about some subject she was confused about. Or worried about.

Azelie made a move to get off his lap. His arms tightened around her, preventing the hesitant movement.

"We knew this wasn't going to be an easy talk, Zelie. It's necessary if we're going to have the kind of relationship we both want. Don't run away from me because you don't understand. We're going to keep talking until you do. Talk to me. Communication is necessary in our relationship, although when you ask me questions, I reiterate, I might not answer immediately. I might ask you to wait for answers. If that happens, I want you to know I have very good reasons for needing you to be patient."

Azelie didn't know what to think. He talked about communication but then told her straight up that he might not answer her if she asked questions. "You're confusing me, Andrii. You say you want us to communicate, but then in the same breath, you say you might not answer questions I ask." Azelie forced her gaze to meet his. "Are you a criminal?"

His gaze didn't waver from hers, but he remained silent for too long. Far too long. She sighed and tried to turn her head. He gently cupped her chin in a silent demand to keep her looking at him.

"Baby, I own a construction business with three friends. I play music in a band. Those are legitimate businesses and I get paid very well for them. I also do other things when the circumstances warrant it."

Her heart jumped. She felt instantly sick and, without thinking, pressed her hand tight over her rolling stomach.

"Don't you think me getting mixed up with Billows is bad enough? I didn't know who he was when I was sixteen. I'm not sixteen anymore, Andrii. Making bad decisions would be insane. I'm in over my head with Billows and don't see a way out. I know I told you I was just waiting to get out from under him, but I haven't really figured out how. Not and stay alive."

She looked down at her hands before once again meeting his gaze. "I don't need to jump from the proverbial frying pan into the fire. I'm going to take a wild guess and say you're still working with your dubious expert skills."

For one moment a hint of male amusement lit his gray eyes, giving them a slightly silver appearance. For some unknown reason, when she was certain she should be annoyed by his sense of humor, that look made her heart flutter. Not just her heart. Other body parts. She was *so* susceptible to him.

"Dubious expert skills? Are you calling my assassin skills into question?"

She scowled at him, but it wasn't easy. She liked making him smile or almost smile. He wore an expressionless mask most of the time, so when he showed her emotion, she felt as if he'd given her a gift. "I wish I didn't believe you had those skills, Andrii, but I have no doubt that you do. I think you're very good at whatever it is that you do. I just don't understand why you do it, and I don't think I can live with it."

Once more she made an attempt to get off his lap. She needed to put distance between them. Surrounded by his scent, feeling his hard body, hot and muscular, made her weak. This was self-preservation.

His arms tightened, locking her to him. "Where are you going?"

"I think it's better if I sit across from you and figure this out. You're scaring me, Andrii."

He shook his head. "Don't start lying now, Zelie. Not to me and not to yourself. *I* don't scare you. You know I'd never harm you. You know it in your heart. You see me. Into me. You know I'm not capable of hurting you."

"But you hurt others." She sat stiffly in his lap, refusing to relax against his chest. That way lay disaster.

"I hunt pedophiles and traffickers, Azelie. The men and women who slip through the cracks and are never brought to justice. I don't run drugs or guns. I don't participate in trafficking. I don't have a stable of women. Most of my time is spent building things. Crafting with wood. Playing music. But there are times when we come across information that has to be acted on."

She didn't know what to think or feel. He was so matter-of-fact, completely honest, telling her that he hunted criminals and then executed them.

"Can't you turn these people over to the police?"

His hand swept down the back of her head, and then his fingers slipped into her hair as he gently massaged her scalp and the nape of her neck. "You need to hear me, Azelie. Everything I say. Don't get stuck on the concept of what I am. We hunt criminals who aren't being caught or punished. Sometimes we manage to take back a child, and sometimes we shut down a trafficking ring. We follow a chain of activity online and off in order to do that. These people would never see the inside of a prison, or if they did, they would manage to get out immediately."

She worked at not reacting, but at listening and hearing what he said. "It's vigilante justice, Andrii."

"I'm aware."

He didn't apologize for what he did. He expected her to understand that the women and children he saved were worth what he had to do to rescue them. Had someone known about Quentin and his proclivities outside his marriage and the fact that he relied on Janine's money to stay afloat, her sister, niece and nephew might still be alive.

"I need to give this more thought. I don't like it, Andrii. I don't understand what drives you." But she did. She had followed the sound of the woman screaming in pain below the clubs, and she would have done anything to save her. If she'd owned a gun, she would have shot Quentin to protect her family. That was her nature. Despite her reluctance to make decisions, she would have been utterly decisive about emptying a gun into her brother-in-law if she had found out his plan. She would have done so before he pulled out a gun to shoot her sister.

It occurred to her that Andrii was hunting Billows. The thought had been growing in the back of her mind for some time. If that was the case, that meant Billows was into some extremely nefarious activities, worse than what she'd imagined. It also meant Andrii was using her to get to Billows.

"Your mind is working overtime. Share." He murmured it, his breath warm against the nape of her neck.

It was difficult to think straight when he was moving his

lips against her skin, sending little sparks of electricity dancing through her. She detested that she was so susceptible to him. Especially now, when she worried that he was using her to get to Billows and it was probable that nothing was real about his interest in her.

Why would he be interested? She saw the way other women looked at him. He could have anyone he wanted. She came with enough baggage for ten people. It was all beginning to make sense now.

"I have to think this through."

"Think out loud."

That was a command uttered in that same low tone he used so often, but one he meant. Her gaze jumped to his face.

"Okay then, but I'm going to reiterate I'm uncomfortable sitting in your lap with you kissing my neck while I'm trying to figure out what's really going on here." She didn't attempt to move but stated her preference.

"I get that, baby, but I think you need a little extra care and reassurance right now. This talk is far from over, and we need to get past a lot of hard issues."

He sounded so sweet. As if what she thought and felt mattered to him. She was reluctant to tell him what she was thinking for two reasons. If she was correct, she would be shattered. If she was incorrect, it might hurt him.

"Azelie."

Just her name but a clear prompt to get her talking. She sighed. "It has occurred to me that you started a relationship with me because I work for Billows, not because you were interested in me."

Her stomach knotted in anticipation of his response. She knew the answer. She absolutely did.

Andrii's fingers were firm on the nape of her neck, attempting to ease the tension out of her. He felt strong and safe when she knew better. She'd been such a complete idiot. She'd wanted to believe the fantasy, and she should have known better.

"Does it matter how you caught my interest when I ended up falling right off the cliff? You're an astute, very intelligent woman. You have good instincts. What are those instincts telling you?"

"That I caught your interest because I work for Billows, and you're very interested in him. That's the reason you're here with me now."

"That's hurt talking. Self-preservation. It isn't what you know in your heart. Tell me the time we've spent together isn't real for you. I'll think you're lying to us both, but you can say it if you really believe it."

She parted her lips to respond, but he had already caught her chin and tilted her face up to his. His mouth came down on hers. It was a claiming. A branding. Not sweet and gentle, but a takeover. He demanded complete surrender. When he kissed her, her brain short-circuited. All thought vanished and there was only feeling. Pure feeling. Fire coursing through her. Need building rapidly. She was drowning in him. Immersing herself. Going over that cliff without looking first.

She found herself clinging to his shoulders, chasing his mouth when he lifted his head. He didn't go far, just pressed his forehead to hers while looking her straight in the eye.

"Did that feel fake?" He took one hand and curled her palm around the thick, heavy erection he didn't try to hide. "Does that feel fake?" He brushed soft kisses down her cheek to her jaw. "When I tell you things I've never told anyone, does it feel fake to you? Do you think I'm making it up for sympathy? Or to impress you? Just to get at your boss? Do you really believe that of me, Zelie? That I'm playing you?"

She didn't believe it. That was the problem. She should. If she had an ounce of sense, she would, but he sounded so honest. So utterly truthful. He looked her straight in the eye. Everything about him screamed sincerity, yet the things he told her—and she believed—all pointed to him being right there with her because he was hunting Billows.

"Billows is a criminal."

"He is."

"You hunt criminals."

"At times."

"It stands to reason that you're using me to get to Billows."

His thumb slid over her lips, featherlight, but that brush of his hand set her heart pounding. She felt it as if it were a burning brand. She didn't want to give him up, but she was concerned her heart was at war with her head.

"It makes perfect sense," he agreed without hesitation. "But I'm not sitting in this apartment with you because of Billows. I'm here because I want you in my life permanently, and I'll do whatever it takes to get you there and keep you safe and happy."

She did believe that he wanted to be there with her. She had to believe that. She would shatter into a million pieces if he was with her and such a good liar that she couldn't read him. She'd been so careful to learn how to read other people, and she had to rely on her instincts. Her instincts told her that despite what Andrii said about himself, he was a good man.

She needed to drop the Billows question for now and wait until she could process better. There were other important things she needed to know about Andrii.

"Are you prone to violence?"

"Absolutely. I was raised with violence. If someone like Billows threatens my family or friends, my first thought is to make the world a better place and take him out. What I do not ever do is harm an innocent, and certainly not someone I care about. Having said that, you and I will need to come to several understandings. That's why we're talking now. You need to understand that while I would never harm you, that doesn't mean if you got out of line, I wouldn't punish you."

"Out of line?" She echoed the one thing that she could safely address. He had alluded to punishments before, and she'd put that out of her mind. She knew they would be discussing it eventually, but she needed her wits about her. Talking about punishments on top of everything else was way too much.

"Out of line. Don't listen when it comes to your safety. I told you that to function properly and safely in my world, I need control. That means I have to know the person I treasure most in the world is safe. I need to know she trusts me to keep her that way. And when I ask her to do something for me, it's because I have my reasons and she trusts me enough to know that whatever is happening, I'll explain when I can. Or maybe I'm asking something of you because I need reassurance that I matter."

Azelie frowned. "You're confusing me."

"You won't be confused. I'll lay out the few rules we have, so if you break them, I'll know you did so purposely. That earns you punishment."

"I'm not a child, Andrii. I like to think for myself, not just follow someone blindly." She meant it, and yet what he was asking for didn't seem too big a deal—without the punishment part. Punishment wasn't attractive at all in a relationship.

"I don't want a puppet, Zelie. I think you already know that. I like the way you think. You have a good mind. You're intelligent. You're able to laugh at yourself, and you find situations with me amusing when others would be afraid. I love all that about you. I wouldn't change anything at all. You want to tell me off because you think I'm wrong, you do it. But when I tell you something to do, such as don't move from where you are because it isn't safe, I expect you to follow orders, knowing I wouldn't give you an order like that unless it was necessary."

Her frown deepened. "I doubt you're going to give me unreasonable orders, Andrii, *most* of the time. But I might screw up, and I'm not a woman who would find punishments sexy."

"Punishments aren't meant to be sexy. They're meant to be reminders never to screw up again."

"*Exactly* what would a punishment entail?"

He didn't flinch or look away. "You over my knee. It won't be erotic or sexy. It would hurt, but we'll both know you won't forget the lesson."

"Spankings may sound hot in a book, Andrii, but I wouldn't like it." She was absolutely certain of that. Absolutely.

"You aren't supposed to like it. You're supposed to remember to do as you're told."

Her heart was back to pounding. Hard. "What if you get out of control?"

"Baby, sit on the floor for me. Right in front of me." He helped her slide from his lap but kept his hands on her waist.

She was happy to get a little space between them, even if it meant sitting between his legs on the floor. She sat tailor-fashion, staring up at him.

Andrii's eyes lightened in color, almost to liquid mercury. "Control. That's something we need to discuss further."

She didn't know what that meant, but she had to bite back a whimper. At least it wasn't a moan. The way he said *control*, the way his eyes went dark with desire, sent her pulse racing. Heat rolled through her veins and emptied into a pool of melted lava right into the pit of her stomach and lower. That didn't bode well for her, but he'd been in control of the two of them when he'd had sex with her, and she'd reaped the benefits.

"When I tell you I want to be the one in control, I'm not just talking about in the bedroom. You trusted me to satisfy you there, and I did. I'll give you whatever you want or need—eventually. I like to play. I know you're going to like playing. Some of the things we'll be doing might be a little scary to you at first, but if you trust me enough, you'll find you enjoy everything we do."

"With the exception of your punishments," she whispered.

"Then don't fuck up. If you do, do it knowing what you have coming."

Instinctively, she'd pulled back, but he reached down to take her wrist, pulling her hand to his thigh. His touch was gentle but firm. She knew if she pulled away, his fingers would tighten. He couldn't fail to read her elevated pulse or feel the fine tremors going through her body. She felt mesmerized by him, under a spell she couldn't quite get out from under.

"You're asking a lot of me, Andrii. You want me to take everything on faith. That's a lot of trust when I don't really have any idea who you are or why you're asking these things of me. You have to know that it feels very one-sided."

He sighed but nodded, suddenly looking serious. "I guess now is as good a time as any to discuss our needs. I thought a date or two might be a good thing before I tell you what's important to me in a relationship. I want to hear what you need, but I'll admit I'm very good at reading you."

She blushed. The heat was alarming under her skin. "I don't think that's good, Andrii."

"Because you're attracted to me? I like that you're honest. No games with you. When I ask you a question, you answer me, even if it's difficult for you. You don't pretend you aren't interested in me, or that you couldn't care less about a sexual relationship. You show me every time you look at me that you want me. Do you have any idea how that can make a man feel?"

"Arrogant? Overconfident?"

He burst out laughing and her heart nearly stopped. She found him utterly attractive when he wasn't smiling, but laughing turned her inside out. She slipped further down that slippery slope of no return.

"I *am* confident because I have reason to be. And if that makes me appear arrogant, so be it. Just know you can depend on me to take care of you. Men don't fuck up around me. You aren't flirtatious with other men. When you're with me, you look only at me, and I appreciate that trait in you. Everything about you appeals to me." He stretched out his legs on either side of her, satisfaction gleaming in his eyes.

"See, *Solnyshkuh*, I wanted you in front of me, looking up at me with your incredible eyes, and you sat on the floor without hesitation. Most women would think it was demeaning or that I meant it in a negative way, as if I put myself above you."

Azelie didn't know how to respond to that. She liked looking up at him. It hadn't occurred to her that he might be elevating his position over her. If she didn't like something, she would simply refuse to do it—unless she decided she wanted to do it to make him happy. In that case, she would weigh what it meant to him before she decided.

She waited in silence, her heart pounding just a little out of control.

"The fact that you're willing to do things for me is important."

Andrii rubbed the bridge of his nose, a small frown drawing his eyebrows together. It was the first time he showed that he was uncomfortable with the conversation. Reluctant even. That made her strangely happy. She knew he was going to share something about himself he didn't share with others.

"You said you needed to be in control at all times. Not just in the bedroom."

He nodded slowly. "There especially. But when we go out together, it is necessary that you understand I'm in control, and when I ask something of you, you do it."

Her eyelashes fluttered, hopefully concealing the way she was feeling. Conflicted. Scared. Excited. She moistened her lips. Took several breaths. He was conveying something extremely important that would affect her. He was explaining how their relationship would play out. She needed to hear him and understand what he was saying so there would be no misunderstanding later. She realized Andrii wanted her to know exactly what she would be getting herself into with him.

"You need to tell me what that means." She sounded as conflicted and as scared as she was feeling. She didn't bother to try to hide it from him. "I'm not certain I understand what 'at all times' means."

He reached out and slid his fingers through her hair. "It means exactly that. When we're together, and hopefully, eventually, we'll live together, because I want to be with you as much as possible. I had hoped to get you used to me before we had this talk, but I screwed up. I hadn't planned to take you to bed so quickly. I don't want just a sexual relationship with you. I want this chance with you. I think you want it too. That means we hash things out now."

She did want to explore the relationship; she just didn't know what he meant. What was expected. What she expected. She knew those fingers stroking caresses in her hair were meant to seduce her into doing as he wanted, but she was willing to feel every cell in her body coming alive. She was willing to be seduced in order to get the chance at a relationship that might be real when she'd only dared to dream of a man like Andrii.

"It means when I tell you to do something, I expect you to do it and not question me. I have my reasons, and you'll have to trust that no matter what I'm asking, I'll see to your protection and happiness. I need that level of trust from you."

She swallowed her nerves and looked up at him. It was a mistake to meet the vivid intensity of his eyes. His hand cupped her face and then slid around to the nape of her neck, sending a million goose bumps erupting all over her skin. Her stomach did one of those slow somersaults she associated with him, and she went damp, her sex clenching with need.

"That all sounds good, Andrii, until we circle back to your punishment. I'm not down with that at all."

Andrii's fingers tightened on her nape as if he could brand his fingerprints into her skin.

"If you disobey me, there will be consequences. Punishments. I need to know you're safe. I need to know you're willing to put me first, just as I plan to do with you."

Her breath left her lungs in a long rush, and she shook her head, an involuntary reaction. His fingers tightened.

"You need to know and believe that I would never hurt you. I'm not a man who would beat a woman." His fingers began a slow massage on the nape of her neck. "That doesn't mean a punishment wouldn't include pain."

She gasped and once more made the mistake of looking up at him. His eyes had darkened with desire. With lust. She could read the need in him for her to commit. To be part of him. There wasn't just desire and lust, there were hints of growing affection, maybe even more, although she couldn't understand how he'd developed genuine feelings for her so quickly. Just looking into his eyes made her want to give him everything he asked for without complaint or argument, but she wasn't that illogical or adventurous.

"Pain?" She echoed the word. Once again, her voice came out strangled.

Azelie did her best to ignore the way his touch soothed her. The way his eyes conveyed his need and desire. She was so scared, and yet at the same time, she desperately wanted to be with him, even when it made no sense to her.

"I told you I would have no problem putting you over my knee. Just know that the punishment wouldn't go too far, and afterward, I would see to your care. I'm not a sadist. I don't want to see lasting marks on your body, but I do want to know you would accept your punishment with grace if you fucked up."

She was involuntarily shaking her head again, but sadly, it wasn't because of the things he was explaining to her, it was because her body reacted in a way she didn't understand. She wanted to explore possibilities with him and that made no sense. The idea of him putting her over his knee because she'd chosen not to do what he asked, or she'd gone against him, scared the hell out of her. She wasn't down with that at all. She went her own way when she determined it was the right thing to do. She was bound to "fuck up."

"Baby, don't say no until you know how you really feel when I ask things of you. Giving up control doesn't mean giving up who you are. It simply means you trust that I'll take care of you and make the best decisions for us. You doing that for me, giving me whatever I need or want, means to me that you care about my happiness and you're willing to put me first. You doing that makes me want to give you everything you could ever possibly want or need. It also takes the burden of decisions from you. You don't like making them."

How could he know that about her? He was right. She was terrible at making decisions. She was the most indecisive person she knew. "But I'm working to overcome that flaw. I'm working hard at it."

Again, she looked up at him so he would see that improving herself meant something to her. She needed to feel empowered when for so long after her sister and the children had been murdered, when she'd been shot by a man who had helped to raise her, she felt worthless, alone and unsure of everyone and everything.

"I can help with that. You want to make decisions regarding our home, your school, your clothing—except when we're going out—I have no problem with that." He continued to cup her face with gentle fingers, holding her gaze captive with his. "Say yes."

"I want you to explain why you need these things from me, Andrii. It has to make some kind of sense when commitment for me is so scary."

"You commit to me, and I'll tell you as much as I can about myself. Anything you ask, I'll answer when I can, but I must have your word that you're in this with me all the way. Say yes. Be mine. I swear you won't regret it."

Her breath left her lungs in a rush. She couldn't look away from his compelling eyes. She forced herself to breathe. To think. No matter that he admitted to being trained as an assassin, she believed that he hunted criminals—ones falling through the cracks of the justice system. He found young children and women trafficked and freed them. Was what he did wrong? Probably. Vigilante justice wasn't a good thing, yet every instinct she had told her he was a good man. He hadn't exactly answered her when she asked him point-blank if he had approached her because she worked for Billows, but she had to admit that his question was a good one. What did it matter how he found her if what they had was the real thing?

She wanted to take the chance with him, when she'd never wanted to be with any man. The thought hadn't entered her head that she would ever trust someone enough to take that chance. But when she was with him, she found herself falling more and more under his spell.

She wanted to know about his past, what made him the way he was. She recognized that both of them had suffered trauma and at their core didn't trust anyone. Yet she found herself wanting to trust him. She wanted him to be able to trust her. Would it be so bad to at least try?

She started to nod, but he shook his head.

"Say it to me. Out loud. Speak it to me and the universe. Mean it, Azelie. Make that commitment to us."

"Yes." The word came out strangled. There were so many reasons to say no and very few to say yes.

"That's my brave woman."

The moment he gave her praise, she found herself responding even more to him. Was she so screwed up that having a man compliment her was all it took for her to want to give herself to him? She was agreeing to a relationship when she had no idea what that actually entailed. Azelie was caught in his spell despite her brain telling her to be cautious. To go very slow.

Andrii bent his head toward hers and her breath caught in her lungs. His kisses were killer. She wanted to get lost in his kisses, so she wouldn't have to think too much about what she'd just done. To her disappointment, he brushed his lips on the tip of her nose and released her. As he leaned back, his hand slid down her arm, causing a flurry of hot little sparks of electricity to dance over her skin. His fingers settled around her wrist, a bracelet, a handcuff, a tie between them.

THIRTEEN

"It's important that I disclose as much about myself to you as possible," Maestro said. "I know you're wondering why I'm so fucked up."

Azelie's eyes widened. "I don't think you're . . . well . . . messed up."

Maestro had to smile. How could he not? Most girls had no problem using foul language. It was second nature to him. It was to the other club members. Only Preacher was careful with his language because he had always looked after Lana, his younger sister, but even Preacher swore sometimes. Maestro thought it was hilarious that his woman couldn't say *fuck*.

He brought her palm to his thigh again and slid his thumb over the back of her hand, maintaining contact. "I don't talk to anyone about my past. I don't think it serves much purpose, but you're committing to us, willing to build a relationship with me. That means you hear about my past. I'm warning you, like yours, it isn't pretty."

He'd mentioned his mother's betrayal and briefly spoken of the school he'd been taken to, but there was no way she could understand him if he didn't give her the entire story.

It wouldn't be fair to her if he didn't give her something of himself. She deserved to know whatever he could share with her.

His thumb slid over the back of her hand a second time. "I'm saying again, baby, the things done to me in my past aren't for the faint of heart. If you'd prefer me to stay silent on the subject, I'm down with that, but understanding me will take some serious work."

"I want to know whatever you're willing to share with me, Andrii."

Bog. Those eyes of hers. He could stare into them every day and never get enough. Drown in them. He saw that look on her face and wanted to keep it there forever. No one had ever looked at him like that in his life. He saw the beginnings of love in her eyes. It was there, stark and real—for him. He didn't deserve that emotion from her, but he was determined to work every day to make himself into a better man for her.

"I told you my mother sold me so she could get her drugs." He found himself doing what was natural, what he'd trained himself to do from a very early age—distancing himself from the story he was telling her. He did so when he lived through it and whenever his mind insisted on returning to those memories. Mostly, he had closed that door and refused to open it. For her, he would.

Azelie deserved to know exactly what she would be dealing with. He understood her trauma even more than she realized. His club had researched her very carefully. Code was thorough. She didn't have that same advantage when it came to him. She would have to rely on whatever he chose to tell her. Maestro wanted her to know him intimately. To be able to accept him as he was, flaws and all. That didn't mean he wouldn't keep trying to overcome his failings, but he wanted—even needed—acceptance from her.

"What I didn't tell you is that I was barely able to walk when she started using me to get what she wanted. She had a sister, my aunt Anna, who was a year older. I thought Anna really cared about me. She fought with my mother all the time and eventually gave my mother money to allow Anna to keep me. That's when my life really turned into a nightmare."

Azelie gasped, her eyes widening with shock. "Both your mother and aunt?" She whispered it as if the treachery of their betrayal was too much to believe.

Maestro had watched Zelie for weeks before he made his move on her. She had been drawn to children. Laughing with them, playing, watching over them. Children who weren't even hers. It hadn't mattered to her. As a mother, she would be a fierce little thing, protecting her children—and him—with everything in her.

At first, he hadn't believed. He'd looked for ulterior motives. No woman could ever be that filled with sunshine, enough that she shared her light with everyone she came across. She seemed to look after the older people in the coffeehouse. She was the same with the owners. She nurtured others. Soothed them. Brought them serenity.

He knew she didn't see herself like that, a woman others gravitated toward. Since she'd lost her family, she held part of herself aloof. Because she was a naturally giving person, it made her feel guilty that she didn't give all of herself to others. Reporters and police had made her leery of sharing her story with anyone. He didn't think she realized just how much of herself she did give. The peace she brought people. The joy. The sunshine.

Billows was addicted to her. He might be a moody bastard, and it may have taken him time to realize she'd grown up, but he didn't want to give her up. Now that Azelie was in college full-time and around more men, it had probably occurred to Billows he might lose her. That didn't sit well, so he did what he always did—threatened and bullied to get his way.

Maestro realized threatening Azelie wasn't the best way to get her attention. If Billows had taken the time to get to know her, he would see bullying her would never work. Billows was used to dismissing women, using them for his business to make a crapload of money. Any man involved in human trafficking had zero respect for women. Having Billows' attention centered on Azelie was extremely dangerous for her. Having his man, McGrady, watching her every move was becoming annoying. Maestro intended to make certain Billows wanted to get rid of his spy.

"Andrii, you don't have to continue if the memories are too painful," she said softly.

He realized he'd taken too long with his introspection. He bunched her hair in his fist and tugged until she leaned closer to him. "I learned at a very young age not to believe anything a woman told me. My aunt had a business, and she was very sadistic. Her friends were sadistic. She pretended that she would take care of me and even went so far as to tell me how terrible my mother was, but she was far worse."

Her eyes went liquid. For him. Those tears were real on his behalf. She shook her head. "That's so wrong. A mother is supposed to protect and care for her children. Your aunt should have too. I don't blame you for not believing in women."

"Had it ended there, I may have survived intact." He doubted it, but who knew what little kids blocked out? Being sold to pedophiles? He didn't think so, but he wasn't around children other than Czar's and Steele's. Every one of Czar's children had been rescued from a trafficking ring or pedophile. They were traumatized but working their way through it. Steele's son had been kidnapped and subjected to beatings at a very early age. He had escaped the worst of what could have happened because the club was able to rescue him. He didn't point out that Azelie's drunken mother hadn't taken care of her either. She didn't need that reminder; he knew she was very aware of it.

"My aunt supplied children to a man named Sorbacov. He was very high up in the government. He worked for the president and wielded a great deal of power. He was married and had children. Few knew of his proclivities, including the fact that like my aunt, he was a sadist. I was too young to recognize what a sadist was. I only knew they hurt me, and I couldn't trust any of them."

"Andrii," she whispered his name, a small sob in her voice. She tightened her fingers on his thigh.

He needed that reassurance from her. Her touch kept him anchored in reality. He didn't slip back into those childhood memories of pure torture. He stayed disconnected from the past and remained with her—with Azelie. His light in the interminable darkness he had lived in for so long.

"Sorbacov must have felt Anna was too greedy. Whatever the reason, he summoned my mother and Anna to a meeting and offered to purchase me from them. I could hear lies by that time. I was very young, but I already had that gift, mostly from self-preservation, not because I was so talented. I didn't understand what he wanted from them or from me, but I knew that he wasn't telling them the truth. I should have tried to warn them, but I knew if I opened my mouth I would have been beaten severely."

"What terrible people. Seriously, Andrii, all three of them should have been executed on the spot."

He liked that she didn't say she thought they deserved to go to prison. She wanted them wiped off the face of the earth—just as he had wanted. He'd been five and already he knew suffering, betrayal, torture and death. He wanted all of them gone.

"My mother was quite willing to sell me again. Anna, not so much. I was worth more being sold daily than for just a onetime fee. My mother argued that I belonged to her, that I was hers to sell, and Anna should have nothing to do with the transaction. We were already at the school, although I had no idea what it was. Sorbacov had insisted the women meet him there."

"The school where he raised you to be an assassin?"

He nodded. "Not just me. I wasn't the only child there by a long shot. On the outside, the house appeared to be a huge mansion. The room where Sorbacov took us for the meeting was opulent, the furniture red-and-black velvet with gold braiding. I remember that very distinctly. Sorbacov had several men in the room with him. They were standing along the walls. He often had those men with him. They were quite brutal and thought nothing of raping women or children, both male and female. I didn't understand why my mother and aunt didn't realize they were in danger. The men were smirking. I could smell their arousal. By that time, even at that age, I knew all about sex."

Her long lashes fluttered, catching tears. She shook her head. "Rape, maybe, but not sex," she clarified.

He tried not to wince when she laid it out for him, showing him she understood what he was conveying to her. Using the term *rape*, while it was accurate, didn't sit well with him. Not when it was coming out of his woman's mouth. No man wanted his woman to associate him with pedophiles and rape in his past. He wanted to appear tough and capable, masculine and strong, to her.

Maestro forced himself to get beyond his protest. She was right to call it rape, but he didn't like it. He thought it best to ignore the definition and just continue telling her about his past before he shut down.

"Sorbacov whispered to me not to worry, that no matter what the *lying* women said, he wouldn't allow them to keep me. Even then I knew he was a liar. He was sadistic. He wanted me for the exact same reasons that my mother and aunt did. I had no worth as a person, only as a child to torture or have sex with. The women using me were every bit as bad as the men. Sometimes crueler—much, much crueler."

A small frown appeared. "In what way?"

"They would pretend to be motherly or sweet. They would promise to help get me out of Sorbacov's school. Several of them were that way. I wanted to believe them, so when I was a little kid, I did. They found it funny that I would be punished by Sorbacov for falling for a woman's lie. It always earned me whippings and beatings. They took special delight in that."

Azelie pressed her fingers to the corners of her eyes. "It's hard to imagine you escaped intact. What truly despicable people."

"I wish I could tell you it ended there, but my nightmare was just beginning at that school. As I grew up, I was trained to be an assassin for the government. Mostly, that meant I was Sorbacov's private assassin. If he didn't like someone's politics, he sent one of us. I wasn't the only child there. Along with learning languages and how to kill, we were all subjected to a multitude of sexual practices and expected to be proficient in all of them. We had to be in total control of our bodies as well as those of our partners. The idea was to seduce our targets."

Something elusive flashed across her face, into her eyes, and he just managed to restrain himself from cursing.

"I know how that sounds, *Solnyshkuh*. I know how you could interpret what I just said, especially since you're concerned that I'm here for Billows and not you."

She wasn't going to reply. He could see the conflicting emotions. She wanted to believe him, but he was asking a lot of her. He knew that.

"Baby, I only have the truth to give you. The truth of who and what I am. The last thing I want to do is come clean and have you change that expression on your face when you're looking at me."

Her long lashes fluttered, and he got that look—the one he was beginning to crave. He needed her to view him in that light. To see under all the bullshit Sorbacov and his cronies had heaped on him, shaping him into a mistrustful, lethal misogynist. He needed her to find good in him, to believe in him. She was someone worthwhile. She'd suffered the ultimate betrayal, and she still had a light shining so bright in her she could light up the world.

He bent forward to cup her cheek again, his thumb sliding over the bow of her mouth, over those silky lips. "If there is such a thing as loving someone, if that emotion is real, I feel it for you. I want you to think the best of me, not know the worst. I was betrayed over and over. I know exactly what it feels like, and I have no intention of ever betraying you."

"I don't know what to say to you, Andrii. Your life seems so harsh."

He heard the compassion in her voice—also the trepidation. She was intelligent and she knew there was no getting over what he'd experienced. It would always color his life. Without warning, his need for reassurance, control and obedience might spring up at any moment.

"What happened to your mother and aunt? Did Sorbacov pay them off?"

He had half hoped she wouldn't ask. He would never forget what Sorbacov had done to his mother and aunt. They were despicable women, but they didn't deserve Sorbacov's lesson in what women should be used for. Especially lying women, as he named them.

"Sorbacov loved to play with people and their emotions. It gave him great joy to watch others suffer. If there is such a thing as the ultimate sadist, it was Sorbacov. He wanted to see how long he could deceive someone. How many times they would let him go back on his word and then believe him again."

Azelie frowned. "Adults continued to fall for his lies even after he'd proved himself a liar?"

She sounded so shocked that Maestro knew immediately she had that built-in radar now. She'd most likely always had a warning system but had developed it much faster and sharper after Quentin had murdered her family. That would be a challenge. He knew the old adage "once bitten, twice shy" applied. He'd had chunks torn out of him, and he would forever look for betrayal. He would have to carefully go over every word he said if he had to dodge her questions, make certain he never lied to her. He might get away with the sin of omission but not an outright lie.

Trust was everything between them. He was so concerned

about betrayal he wanted to control their relationship—and her—in the hopes it could never happen. But he was in the position of committing a massive betrayal. She already suspected he had approached her to watch Billows.

She didn't realize he was after a specific item, her key to the underground offices. If she was aware he planned to search her backpack for the necklace holding that key, he knew she would view that as a betrayal. He wasn't certain how to get around that. He wanted to tell her the mission. He was sure she would go along with it, but he couldn't pull her out and hide her in a safe house without tipping Billows off that something was radically wrong. If he told her, she would have to act like nothing was wrong. She already was having a difficult time.

"Andrii?" She said his name, a gentle inquiry.

"Sorbacov didn't just deceive adults. His main targets were children. How many times they would rat on others. How many times, even after he refused to release them after his promises, they would believe him. That was the kind of shit he lived for. He did it every single day. No matter how many times I warned my female partners not to believe him, not to do as he said, they would tell him. Report me to him. I was trying to help them, stupid little girls who were desperate for Sorbacov's favor. I didn't deceive them, but it was him they trusted."

For the first time, he didn't sound distant from the past. He sounded bitter. He tasted bitter ashes in his mouth. Memories flooded his mind, sickening him. He broke out in a sweat. His skin felt clammy, yet he was hot—both symptoms that told him he was too close to the triggers that made him so dangerous at times.

"Honey." Azelie's fingers bit into his thigh muscle. "Just breathe. That's what I do. That's what you tell me to do. Just breathe through it. We can stop right here. I don't need to know any more."

Azelie was intelligent enough to know it was impossible

to fake post-traumatic stress, not when the symptoms were physical. But he worried it was just another way he would appear weak to her. She needed a strong man. Showing this side of himself could blow his chances, when he thought telling her about his past would help her to understand why he was so strange.

He forced himself to look down into her upturned face. Heat blossomed, spread through him. She was looking back at him with that expression he craved in her eyes. He didn't understand why or how that could be when he looked weak, but it was there. Adoration. Something close to love. Whatever connection they had wasn't just physical. He was betting his life on that.

"You can't look at me like that, *Solnyshkuh*, or we're going to end up back in bed. Right at this moment, I want you more than my next breath." That was the raw truth, and she had to hear it in his voice. She had to understand what she meant to him. "I don't know how to say the right words to you. I can lie to you. I had the best teacher in how to deceive, but telling the truth to the one person who matters is more difficult than anything I've ever done."

Maestro took her face between his hands. That face that was already more necessary to him than breathing. He was addicted to that look. He ran his thumb over her full, inviting lips. A faint smile curved her mouth beneath the light pressure of his thumb.

"I already let myself go a little crazy once. I'm not doing that again."

He couldn't help but smile. In the midst of a bad moment, she could shine her light on him and change his world.

"I think we're going to do that a lot, *Solnyshkuh*." He used his most compelling, velvet voice and watched the little shiver go through her with satisfaction. No matter how many alarms she tried to heed, she was very susceptible to him and their chemistry. He wanted everything between them to be real, so he was doing his best to give her what he could of himself, but he had a certain expertise, and as far as he was concerned, using it was fair. And they'd both reap the benefits.

"You think you have a poker face, Andrii, but I'm reading you right now. You're going to use sex to get your way, just because you know I can't resist you."

He brought the tips of her fingers to his mouth and bit down gently, enjoying the way her eyes went wide and goose bumps leapt over her skin. She could take away every nightmare and replace them with *her*. Her laughter. Her wide-eyed wonder. Her generosity and compassion.

"I absolutely intend to use every weapon in my arsenal to seduce you into choosing me for your lifelong partner. I'm not fucking around with you. I mean to do exactly what I'm telling you, so be warned."

Another shiver went through her body and her long lashes fluttered. "Unfortunately, I think you're up to the task."

His smile started somewhere deep as he quirked one eyebrow at her. "*Unfortunately?*"

"Yes, unfortunately. That means whenever you want your way, you're going to get it. That makes you spoiled."

"Think of all the pleasure you're going to have when I'm seducing you to get my way."

She gave a little shake of her head. "You're impossible. You have not one iota of remorse, do you?"

"Nope. Not if anything I do ensures I have you with me."

Azelie laughed. The sound hit him right in his heart. His chest ached and he rubbed his palm over the spot. He leaned in to take her mouth. That perfect mouth that sent roaring flames down his throat. That could be sweet with strawberries and honey or fiery like whiskey. No matter how reluctant her brain was feeling in that moment, when his lips touched hers, she gave him everything. Surrendered completely.

He lifted her and carried her right back to the bed. He needed to be inside her, connected with her. She wrapped her arms around his neck, all the while giving him her mouth. Somewhere in between taking off what little clothing she was wearing and stripping himself as well, as he kissed his way down her body, he realized she was giving him another gift. She had concerns about the two of them, about him. What he was. Why he was with her. Valid concerns. She'd decided no sex until she felt more comfortable with who he was, yet she was giving him this. It wasn't because of his expertise; it was because she knew he needed her.

Bog, his woman. He understood how the men in his club could become total pussies when it came to their women. Azelie could rip out his heart anytime she wanted. He didn't fuck her. He made love to her, making every single touch, every stroke, count. He wanted her to feel his love. Feel everything he felt for her.

"Do you understand, *Solnyshkuh*? Do you know what I'm saying to you?"

He threaded his fingers through hers and pinned her hands to the mattress on either side of her head as he moved in her. Long, slow, burning strokes. Each time he surged into her, fire raced up his spine and spread through his belly.

Azelie had tears in her eyes. Her teeth bit into her lower lip, and she nodded, not taking her gaze from his. He felt as if he were looking into her soul. Into the very essence of who she was. He saw her, this miracle that had been handed to him in the worst of circumstances.

"I understand what love is for the first time in my life." He kept moving, giving them both that slow-burning fire that seemed to roll them both in flames. Burning them together. Welding them until the ties were woven so tight, they would never loosen.

"Andrii," she whispered his name, her fingers tightening in his. Her blue eyes looking directly into his. She never winced from the raw intimacy. She held his gaze, allowing her to look inside him, just as he was looking into her.

"I mean it, Azelie. You've given me what I never had before, not one time, not from anyone. My brothers and sisters love me in their way. They're just as screwed up as I am. Victor tried to tell me. Hell, even Savin, a brother, tried to warn me I didn't know what the hell I was talking about half the time. I just couldn't get it. I didn't feel it, until you."

Maestro kissed her chin, nipped with his teeth, and then lifted his body enough to once again look into her eyes. "All the beauty that is Azelie Vargas is mine. All for me. Never had a fucking thing worthwhile until I bought my first motorcycle."

All the while he murmured to her, his body glided, cock pulsing with his heartbeat, surrounded by her. "I don't ever have experiences like this," he murmured, unable to look away from her blue gaze. "Never believed in heaven, baby. Lived in hell."

"Honey."

The blue deepened in her eyes, showing him more of the emotion she felt for him. Crazy. Impossible. He wasn't worth it. He never would be. He knew himself. He knew the results of lifelong betrayal were ingrained in him, a part of his makeup. He would forever be looking, maybe unconsciously, but no matter how hard he tried—and he'd try—he would fuck up and accuse her of things she didn't do.

He loathed himself. His tendency to mistrust everyone. His inability to understand his brethren when they consistently gave in to their women in situations Maestro deemed too dangerous. He'd never been hesitant about voicing his opinion, one that he now understood was absurd. Still, he would always need Azelie to listen to him when it came to matters of her safety.

He heard himself groan, and the affection in her gaze deepened even more.

"Didn't know angels were real. Met a few good women when my brothers found the ones for them, but I still didn't get it."

"I'm no angel." Her voice was breathless. Gasping. The slow burn was turning into a wildfire for the both of them. Her fingers locked tighter in his. "You want me to see you as you are, you need to see the reality of me."

He was looking at the reality. Feeling her. Seeing her.

She just didn't see herself the way he did. The fire was burning out of control, and he couldn't stop his body from reacting. Glides turned to surges. Hot streaks of lightning arcing between them.

Her lips parted. Lashes fluttered, concealing that look of heated desire mixed with the look he craved. Needed. Would give his last breath to see.

"Look at me, baby. Keep looking at me." He made it an order.

Her lashes lifted instantly, her gaze meeting his. He knew she would give him what he asked for. That was Azelie and why she was so perfect for him.

"You're my angel, perfection to me," he said. "*Mine*. Made for me."

With every powerful surge of his hips, her body rose to meet his. It felt as if she had been made for him, that they fit exactly. Every movement built the fire higher. Sent streaks of flames and vivid sparks of electricity rushing through his bloodstream. Looking into her eyes made for an even more intimate experience.

"Then you're mine," she whispered back.

His heart clenched hard in his chest. She had no idea how completely and utterly hers he was. Then it was impossible to talk. He couldn't think. The beauty of the experience and the overwhelming pleasure robbed him of his ability to do anything but get lost in her body. He took her much harder now, rocking them both.

"Not yet," he bit out, not wanting to lose the miracle of her body. Of their physical connection. He kept moving through the hot, slick silk, so tight he was strangled. A vise that clamped down like the tightest fist imaginable, stroking and squeezing, a fiery tango that had his cock jerking and pulsing as he drove into that scorching heat.

There was no holding back a wildfire, not when it burned so hot and out of control. They started slow but ended up consumed by the flames. Maestro collapsed over her, his body entirely blanketing hers. She felt small and utterly feminine, her heart wild, her body rippling with aftershocks as they both fought for air.

He was too heavy to blanket her the way he was, but it didn't stop him from sinking his teeth into her shoulder, marking her and then soothing the small bite with his tongue. Her body reacted with another rolling aftershock, gripping his cock, giving him more of her paradise.

It took effort to withdraw, the movement sending another wave of shuddering pleasure through him. He rolled off her, keeping one arm around her waist to hold her to him.

"Damn, baby, any better and I'm not going to survive."

He got her soft laughter, a little breathless, but that only added to the music. His gaze moved possessively over her face. "So beautiful. *Bog.* I look at you. I'm surrounded by you. I still can't believe you're real."

"I could pinch you," she offered.

The laughter in her blue gaze was contagious. That in itself was beautiful to him. That he could have these moments of intimacy mixed with humor and fun shocked him.

"I'd much rather you kiss me."

"Kissing you gets me in trouble," she pointed out, sounding more amused than ever.

"I think it's the other way around." He gave her the truth, although he was certain she didn't understand. That was perfectly fine with him. He didn't need her to know she would always have all the power in their relationship.

"You're going to have to go. I'm not moving," Azelie told him. "I would love for you to stay and chat, but I'm too tired. I'm going to just lie here and contemplate what an idiot I am for letting you distract me from our meaningful conversation."

He lifted an eyebrow at her. "We were having a meaningful conversation? Really? I thought you were attempting to find reasons not to be with me."

The blue of her eyes softened, amusement mixing with the beginnings of love. She wasn't all the way in yet. Reservations were still there, but that only affirmed his judgment that she was intelligent. Despite the overwhelming chemistry and the pull between them, because of her nature and his, she was still struggling with self-preservation. She understood he was totally fucked up and would, at times, be hell to live with.

"I don't have to find reasons not to be with you; just your views on punishment are enough to make me run the opposite way," she murmured. "Fortunately for you, I'm too tired to move."

He laughed. Not a smirk or a smile, an actual laugh. He wound his arm around her waist and tugged until her body was tight against his. "That *is* fortunate. I'm not leaving tonight. I think spending the night right here is best. That way whenever your fucked-up mind tells you I'm not good for you, I can kiss that thought away."

She giggled. It was a real girlish giggle that sent little sparks of joy streaking through him. He hadn't realized how much he needed laughter and joy in his life. It felt as if she gave him gift after gift.

"Your kisses are always going to lead to other things. And you can't stay."

"Those other things kissing leads to are good, and you like them."

"I love them, but that only means you get your way."

Her voice was drowsy. Sexy. Impossibly, his body stirred in response.

"You're going to love all the other things I'm going to be doing to you. We're just getting started. You might not mind me getting my way when I'm making you say my name."

Her lashes lifted and he found himself looking directly into her eyes again. So blue. So filled with laughter and that look of near adoration.

"Don't be so sure. You're already going to get your way because I like giving you everything. I don't need you adding to my problem."

He lifted his eyebrow at her again. "Problem? You think it's a problem that you want to give me everything I want from you?"

"You're already arrogant and demanding. Can you imagine how much worse you're going to get if I spoil you?"

He brushed his lips down her cheek to her chin. "No one has ever spoiled me, so no, I have no idea how much worse I can get." He inhaled her scent and then grinned at her.

Her eyes closed again, and she snuggled into him as she gave an exaggerated sigh. "I guess we're going to find out, then. As much as I want to wake up to you, you can't stay. Billows sends a man to watch me. I don't know why he started doing that, but he threatened any man I might date. His man can't see you."

Andrii couldn't help loving the little command in her voice. She was sleepy, exhausted, probably a little freaked out, yet she was looking after him. He was staying, and not just because he needed to search her backpack for the necklace with the chip that opened the door leading to the offices and possibly to rooms where women were held and trained as sex slaves. He wanted to wake her up in the middle of the night. He wanted to spend the night breathing her in. Feeling her next to him.

"Need to take care of you before we both fall asleep. I told you, leave Billows' man to me. He'll never see me."

She didn't hear him; she was already asleep.

FOURTEEN

"I'm going to see Andrii again tonight," Azelie reported to the merry widows. This time Doug Parsons and Carlton Gray were seated with the three older women.

Azelie set her drink on the table and scooted a chair closer to Blanc Christian. The ladies leaned in to hear every word. The older men crossed their arms and sat back in their chairs, regarding her with disapproval.

"Not a good idea," Carlton said.

Doug nodded his agreement with a jerk of his chin. "Absolutely don't date that man. In fact, never be alone with him."

The merry widows gasped in unison. China glared at them. "Seriously? You two don't have a clue what you're saying."

Azelie tried not to smile. She covered her reaction to the long-standing arguments between the five friends by sipping her iced latte. It didn't matter that they were not in agreement over her developing a relationship with Andrii; it was a standing practice for them to take opposite points of view on nearly every subject. She found it hilarious. If the women said the sky was blue, the two men would take great exception to that color and begin to describe the sky in any other

hue but blue. She thought it best to stay out of the disagree-
ment and let them go at it without her.

"We're men," Carlton pointed out. "We don't judge other
men by their looks."

Blanc did her best to look outraged when in fact, the hotter the man, the more she was all for Azelie to take a chance.
They'd tried to set her up with countless other males who
had innocently come into the coffee shop, unaware the merry
widows would be scoping them out for Azelie.

Azelie always hid in her books or writing, pretending she
had no idea what the women were doing. At first, their interference had been so upsetting she had nearly stopped going
to that particular shop, but it was close to her bus connection
to get to the college, the coffee was amazing, and it was
smaller and more intimate than one of the popular chains.
Once she knew the owners, Shaila and David Manger, she
had to support their small business. She liked them that much.
In the end, she was grateful she had stayed and gotten to know
the merry widows and Carlton and Doug. They provided
much entertainment when they weren't trying to set her up
with every available male who walked into the coffee shop.

"Looks? Do you think the only criterion we have for a man
to date our beloved Azelie is to be hot?" China demanded.

Doug nodded. "Absolutely. The three of you ogle every
man who enters this place and then you discuss whether or
not they are good enough for *our* Azelie. And you do it loud
enough that the entire coffee shop can hear every word, including Azelie and the potential male."

Carlton added his agreement. "The words *hot* and *gorgeous* and *OMG* are in your conversations quite often."

Azelie nearly spit her latte all over the table. The way the
merry widows exchanged outraged looks was hilarious.
Carlton and Doug were not wrong. In fact, they spoke the
strict truth.

"You've scared off many good men," Doug continued.
"And now you've got this Russian. He's *Russian.*"

Azelie stiffened, the laughter fading. "Okay, I'm going to have to object to the way that sounds prejudiced. You absolutely can't dismiss my man because he's from Russia."

"I don't care that he's Russian, honey," Doug said. "Only that he's from another country and looks as dangerous as hell. Not just looks it—he *is*. Any man worth his salt can see that."

"Oh my goodness," Penny exclaimed in an overloud whisper. "Do you think he's a spy? He looks like he could be a James Bond kind of man."

The Christian sisters nodded in agreement. "Super cool," China said in a breathy tone.

"If only," Blanc added. "Azelie, maybe he's a government agent. Wouldn't that be awesome?"

"Just the idea is sexy," China pointed out.

Azelie was back to stifling a full-blown laugh. The merry widows were ecstatic at the idea, already weaving a fantasy around Andrii. Doug and Carlton looked as if their heads might explode.

"I hate to burst your bubble," Azelie said. She had to press her lips together several times to keep from laughing. "Andrii is a United States citizen."

"What?" Blanc looked deflated. "That's too bad."

"Maybe not," China denied. "It's possible he's an agent for the United States. The boys are right; he does look sexy and dangerous."

Carlton choked until his face turned bright red. "I never said the man was sexy. That was the three of you crazy women. Good God, we're going to have to work to keep you in line. We were gone too long this time and left you alone with your conspiracy theories and your inclination to find men and pick over their bones."

Penny straightened her back and squared her shoulders. "We don't ever indulge in conspiracy theories. What are you going on about?"

Again, Azelie nearly spit out her iced latte at the outright

lie. Practically everything the merry widows talked anima-
tedly about was conspiracy theories or drop-dead, seriously
hot men. Even when Azelie didn't see any of the contenders
that way—with the exception of Andrii.

"Woman, the three of you watch too many crime dramas,
and you always think someone is a spy or a murderer," Carlton said.

"Unless they're hot, and then they become some kind of
fantasy hero," Doug qualified.

"I'm going to have you banned from our coffee shop,"
Penny declared.

"You've tried to have us banned at least once a month for
three years," Doug said. "Shaila and David aren't going to
kick us out because the three of you are wacky as hell."

"*We're* wacky?" China sputtered indignantly. "We were
sitting here calmly waiting for Azelie to give us a report on
her new man, and you shot her down, so now she isn't about
to share."

Doug instantly looked contrite. "I didn't mean to do that,
honey. It's just that men can look at other men and see them
for who they are, whereas women don't always have that
ability. Forgive me, but you're very young. Andrii is a good
ten years older than you, and he didn't get those scars from
playing in a play yard. I'm just worried."

Azelie could see the conflict on his face and hear it in his
voice. So could the widows. Their indignation vanished, and
the three women immediately sat straighter, appearing somber and interested in what Doug and Carlton had to say.

"What do you see in him that we aren't seeing?" China
asked.

"A couple of things," Carlton said. He glanced uneasily
at Azelie. "I don't want you hurt, honey. None of us do. You
aren't exactly experienced when it comes to men. Andrii is
the kind of man women fall all over. He looks like he plays
hard and then walks away. He's probably got a hundred broken hearts in his past."

Doug nodded, concurring. "Anything dangerous he's done in his past aside—and it's clear he's done dangerous things—just having women falling all over you and then dumping them breeds enemies. Excuse me, ladies, but you know very well women can hold a mean grudge."

He rolled his eyes toward the merry widows to indicate they all held a mean grudge. It was all Azelie could do not to laugh again. The women had to have seen his little gesture toward them, but it was clear he was trying to make Azelie laugh with his silent antics, and they didn't take offense.

"Do you really think one of his past women might harm Azelie out of jealousy?" Penny asked, speculation and anxiety in her voice. "He is a heartbreaker. I didn't think of that."

"He isn't a heartbreaker," Azelie corrected. "You have a false impression of him, when you haven't ever talked to him to get to know him."

"Women always think they can change a man," Carlton said carefully. "But leopards don't change their spots. He's a man women fall all over. They come easily to him, and he looks like he might know what he's doing in the bedroom."

Azelie felt color rising beneath her skin. Andrii certainly knew what he was doing when it came to sex. "Please don't worry. I don't rush into things with my eyes closed." She had her own concerns about the relationship, but not the ones they had, and she wasn't about to share. "I'm always cautious."

She fiddled with her drink and then decided to take the plunge. "I'm aware all of you have to know about my past. My brother-in-law, Quentin, murdered my sister, niece and nephew and shot me three times before he turned the gun on himself. I lived with my sister and her husband for a number of years. I can't say I thought Quentin was a great guy or a good man, but I did think he loved his children."

Her fingers inadvertently tightened around the latte cup, nearly crushing it. She wasn't as disconnected as she'd like to be. She thought of Andrii and what he'd gone through. He hadn't told her about the scars on his body, but she could imagine how he'd gotten them. Or maybe she couldn't. She didn't have that kind of imagination. How could adults be so brutally cruel to a child?

"Don't look so sad," Doug implored. "We did know about your past, Azelie. We just never brought it up. It's for you to decide you're going to share with your friends and what you don't feel comfortable sharing. Maybe we've gotten overprotective of you, but all of us feel you're important in our lives."

That was the nicest thing Doug could have said to her. Azelie felt the burn of tears behind her eyes. She had no idea he felt that way about her.

"You bring us joy," China said. "If you're in the room, it feels like you bring rays of sunshine with you, even on the stormiest days."

Azelie blinked rapidly to keep tears at bay. She wasn't a crier, but the sincere emotion China gave to her was overwhelming.

Blanc agreed, nodding solemnly. She placed her hand over Azelie's briefly. "I sometimes get very depressed when we're fogged in. You know San Francisco gets a great deal of fog. I always know if I come to the coffee shop and you're here, I'm going to feel so much better."

Azelie had seen Blanc depressed several times in the past. She would go very quiet and sit without speaking for long periods of time. Azelie would worry, and she often spent time telling funny stories about the antics of the children she babysat to make Blanc laugh. She had no idea Blanc deliberately sought her out to lighten her mood. That made her feel good.

"It's true," Penny said. "You have this way about you. I've seen everyone respond to it. Children especially."

Azelie considered that. Children did respond to her. She could easily stop a baby from crying when sometimes the parent couldn't. In the park, she got the children playing and laughing if they'd been fighting or arguing. Luke and Teddy Tudor, Bradley's five-year-old twins, had been considered little hooligans by most of the other parents who frequented the park. The moment Azelie arrived, they changed their behavior. Betsy, Abigail Humphrey's three-year-old toddler, would instantly stop fussing the moment she caught sight of Azelie.

"And seniors, older women and men," Carlton added. "I don't know anyone who doesn't want to be around you. You have an uplifting personality. Shaila and David have spoken of it many times with me."

Azelie was uncomfortable with so much praise. She wasn't used to compliments. Andrii gave them to her right and left. He did so casually, as if he were throwing out facts and she should just accept everything he said as gospel. Maybe compliments were catching, like a virus. Someone put them out in the air, and everyone around became infected and needed to hand them out.

In any case, she knew the things the merry widows and Doug and Carlton said were heartfelt. That brightened her world. She hadn't known others viewed her in such a positive way. It was clear they cared a great deal about her.

"Thank you," she murmured, not certain what else she could say. "What I was trying to say in a roundabout fashion is that I'm not a complete pushover. Andrii is a strong personality."

"Dominant," Doug said.

"Aggressive," Carlton agreed. "A fighter. He wouldn't hesitate to take someone out. I was in the service for a number of years, Azelie, and I've seen a few men like him."

"Were they protective of the men in their unit?" Azelie asked the question without challenge. She was genuinely curious.

Carlton sat back in his chair, folded his arms, and nodded slowly. "Actually, yes, they were, now that I think about it. They saved our butts a few times when the enemy swarmed us."

"That's right," Doug said. "Those kinds of men might be extremely dangerous in the right circumstances, but they do have a code and they protect their own."

"Aha!" China said. "So, we women are right."

"I didn't say that," Doug protested. "I didn't even imply it. He's still a Casanova."

"You don't know that," Blanc said. "You just want to justify your opinion because even you can see Andrii is hot."

Doug opened his mouth and then snapped it shut. He exchanged a long look with Carlton.

"The man has a sensual appeal," Carlton conceded. "But that's the problem. He's a woman magnet. Our Azelie doesn't need that kind of hurt."

"You're so certain that he'll cheat on me." Azelie made it a statement. Truthfully, she didn't have a lot of confidence in herself as a sexy woman. Andrii told her over and over that he found her sexy, but she didn't know the first thing about sex. She hadn't even kissed another man. That was how truly pathetic she was when it came to sex.

"Don't you dare undermine her confidence," China said.

"You don't get to make Azelie feel like she won't have the ability to hold a man," Penny added. "I know something about how that feels, and it sucks."

Doug and Carlton exchanged a horrified look. "Did I make you feel that way, Azelie?" Carlton asked. "I certainly didn't mean you couldn't keep a man."

"Men are going to fight over you," Doug assured her.

Azelie found herself smiling despite the insecurity she felt. "I very much doubt that."

"Why?" Blanc asked, expressing the curiosity reflected on the faces surrounding Azelie.

She could see they were genuinely puzzled. "I'm just me. I know you're my friends and you only see good in me, but there isn't anything special about me."

"You have to know you're beautiful," Doug said.

"Well, actually, no. I think I look okay, but I wouldn't call myself beautiful."

"How could you not know?" Carlton demanded. "You look in the mirror, don't you?"

"It isn't like I think I'm not pretty, just not the turning-heads kind of pretty," she clarified.

Doug threw his hands into the air. "What is wrong with women?" he asked Carlton.

"I don't know. I've never figured it out," Carlton replied, sounding every bit as exasperated as Doug. "We have four gorgeous women sitting right here at this table, and every last one of them believes the others are much more beautiful. Good God, girl." He glared at Azelie. "You have to be blind not to see what any male would see in you. Your skin and that hair. Doug and I considered hiring a bodyguard just to ensure men like Andrii didn't come around. We knew the minute he came into the shop with his friend he'd see right through your disguise and make his play for you."

"Disguise? I was wearing a disguise?" She was feeling a little faint. The two men were just on the edge of anger, and she didn't understand why.

"Sure you were. Your oversized sweatshirt that covers you up so no one can see you," Penny said helpfully. "We told you about your silly dress code."

The merry widows had spoken to her numerous times about the oversized sweaters and hoodies she wore. They had no idea she was hiding her body from Billows. Okay, maybe from everyone. She hadn't been ready to face the world. Bradley Tudor had freaked her out when he kept insisting they would be so good together. She had no intention of dating him and she despised hurting him. She didn't want to repeat that experience with anyone else. So maybe she had been wearing those clothes so no one would look twice at her.

"Maybe I have done that," she conceded. "But I'm not wearing the sweatshirt today. I still don't see men beating down the coffee shop door to date me."

"Doug and I make it known we're your uncles and we look after you," Carlton announced.

Azelie was back to laughing or nearly crying. She loved

these older gentlemen and the merry widows. How could she not? They were incredible, and they'd adopted her when she wasn't paying attention. They made her feel as if she had a family after all.

"That's so sweet. Although, thinking about it, that means you're running men off." She tried to scowl at them but knew she wasn't successful.

"Obviously, we didn't scare Andrii," Doug said, looking anything but pleased.

"Were you trying to scare him?" Azelie was shocked that she hadn't noticed the men posturing at Andrii.

"We only saw him the one time, when he first came in with his friend," Carlton admitted. "We saw both looking at you. As usual, you weren't looking back. Even so, we tried to give them the stare-down."

A smile slipped out. "Aren't they wonderful?" she asked the merry widows.

"You must not have understood him, dear," Penny said. "They were trying to keep your Andrii from taking notice of you."

"I heard." She flashed a smile at the two men. "Thank you for looking after me."

"*Attempting* to look after you," Doug corrected. "Evidently, we failed. You're going out on a date with him."

Azelie's smile widened. "That I am. I'm looking forward to it."

"Where are you going?" China took the conversation full circle in hopes that Azelie would tell them everything.

"I actually don't know," Azelie admitted. "He likes to surprise me. On our last date, he took me to a bookstore where Celine James was giving a master class on writing thrillers and murder mysteries. I have no idea how he managed to get last-minute tickets, but he did. The master class was sold out months ago."

Doug and Carlton exchanged a long look. "Andrii took you to a bookstore on a date?" Carlton wanted clarification.

She nodded, resisting the urge to burst into laughter.

"How could we be so far off base?" Doug asked. He narrowed his eyes at her. "Are you making this up?"

There was no resisting. Her laughter might be soft, but it moved through the coffee shop, turning heads. The merry widows laughed with her. Carlton and Doug reluctantly smiled. Azelie turned her head as the door to the coffee shop opened. The laughter died in her throat. There was no controlling her reaction, and both Doug and Carlton swiveled in their seats to see who had evoked her sober reaction.

Billows' man sauntered in, his gaze sweeping the room as he approached the coffee bar. Instantly, Carlton and Doug froze and then exchanged knowing looks.

"They knew," Azelie told Andrii. "They knew that man was following me and had been. Both took out their phones and snapped pictures of him when he was giving his order."

She was dressed in the long skirt and camisole top Andrii had given her. It fit like a glove. She knew it would. The color was a vivid royal blue, falling to her ankles in a series of ruffles. The camisole top matched the color and came to a V below the waist. She knew it flattered her figure, clinging to her curves, the soft material moving with every step she took in the most comfortable, beautiful boots she'd ever imagined. Dark-blue leather with a ruffle going up the back, the boots were not only stylish but so soft she felt she was walking on air.

"I don't know how long they've known he was following me, but they've clearly documented it. They're sharp, Andrii. Both were in the military for a long time. I don't know what either of them did, but they're very intelligent. I can't have them confronting Billows' man."

Andrii took his eyes off the road long enough to give her a narrowed glance. "Don't even think about going near that man, Zelie." He had poured command into his voice, and she instantly lifted her chin.

"You don't understand, Andrii. Doug and Carlton have

taken on the role of my guardians. So have the merry widows. I know they're aware of Billows' man following me. They probably think he's a stalker. It isn't like I can tell them about my job and what a scary boss I have. Maybe I could explain Billows is using him for security to keep me safe. What do you think?" Deliberately, she added the last to include him for two reasons. One, he was highly intelligent, and security seemed to be one of his specialties. Second, she didn't want him to think she was deliberately defying him and that his opinion didn't count. It did.

He took one hand off the wheel to take hers and place it on his thigh. "Babe, I was aware of the way Doug and Carlton felt about you the moment I entered the coffee shop. The two of them glared daggers at me. They definitely gave clear warning signs that I was to leave you alone."

"They did? Where was I?" The two men had admitted they had tried to dissuade Andrii from showing any interest in her, but she truly hadn't noticed.

"You were too busy pretending you weren't in the least interested."

She glared at him. "I *wasn't* interested. I thought you were the hottest man I'd ever seen, and it was scary to feel that kind of chemistry when I hadn't felt that for anyone before, not even a mild version—but I wasn't about to act on it."

He sent her a small approving smile. "I love your honesty. You're always so direct with me. No games. It makes me feel very secure in our relationship."

She loved the fact that he had enough confidence to tell her he needed to feel secure. Most men wouldn't have admitted it. Being with Andrii, seeing the way he focused so intensely on her, hearing the honesty in his voice, and his sharing things about his emotions and past all added to the feeling of intimacy. She craved that closeness between them. She needed it in a relationship.

"I had to work to get you to deign to acknowledge me," he conceded. "I planned out my strategy carefully. Fortunately,

I had the merry widows on my side. Also, Shaila and David. I was careful to cultivate a relationship with them so they would side with me and not with Doug and Carlton. I was also fortunate in that the two men didn't come into the shop when I was there after that first visit."

Azelie was stuck on his strategy. "You actually put together a plan to get me to go out with you?"

He sent her another quick grin. "Absolutely. I wasn't taking any chances that you would slip through my fingers. I was very aware Doug and Carlton would try to persuade you not to go out with me."

"They didn't know I was dating you until today."

He brought her fingers to his mouth, nuzzled, bit down gently and then kissed the tips before returning her palm to his thigh. The action sent little sparks of electricity dancing over her skin and down her spine. She was so susceptible to him, but she realized he was just as vulnerable to her, and he didn't mind her knowing.

"What was their reaction?"

Her laughter invited him to share her amusement at the situation. To her joy, it worked, Andrii laughed with her.

"That bad?"

"They had multiple reasons for me to consider not going out with you."

"Did you tell them we're already in a committed relationship?"

"We were still talking when Billows' man came in."

"His name is Andrew McGrady. He's scum. I really don't want you anywhere near him. He isn't the sharpest tool in the shed. He plays video games on his phone when he should be doing his job. He has a record a mile long, mostly for domestic violence. He doesn't mind hitting women. It wouldn't end well for him if he ever struck you."

A little shiver went down her spine at the menace—and honesty—in Andrii's voice.

"I don't want to get anywhere near him, but he's getting

bolder. He's never come into the coffee shop before. I didn't like the way he looked at the merry widows and Doug and Carlton."

"You have good instincts, Zelie. What was your gut telling you? Why did it make you nervous to have him see you with your friends?"

His voice was amazingly soothing. Calm. Steady. Andrii was a rock she could rely on. She thought back to the moment Andrew McGrady had turned around to stare at her group at the table. He had a look of satisfaction on his face. He leered at her, something she thought he would never dare do just in case she complained to Billows.

"It was the way he looked at them and then at me."

"Did you feel threatened?"

She had. Her fingers pressed into his rock-hard thigh. "Yes. But not because I thought he would report to my boss that I had friends Billows could threaten to harm if I didn't cooperate with him." She'd felt as if a snake slithered over her skin, giving her chills.

"He's wrong, Andrii. Billows is clearly a criminal with no code or remorse. He wants money and power and is determined to get it at any cost. He rules through bullying and intimidation. I don't think he would hesitate to kill someone simply because they were in his way."

She pressed her fingertips deeper into Andrii's thigh muscle as if clinging to him for support. He must have felt her dismay because he curled his fingers around her hand.

"That man. McGrady. He felt evil."

There was a short silence while Andrii drove through the busy streets. Headlights and stoplights flickered through the windows as the BMW smoothly and easily maneuvered around traffic.

"Billows is an evil man, yet to clarify what I'm hearing, you believe McGrady is the evil one."

Azelie wasn't certain how to explain how she felt. "I know Billows is an evil, corrupt man with no conscience.

His world is all about him. He doesn't see anyone else in it other than those he wants something from. He isn't nice about the way he gets what he wants either. I don't think his friendships are real. He uses people to get what he wants. He's a narcissist. He believes he's superior to everyone around him. I've heard him say he's smarter than anyone he's ever met."

Once more, Andrii's eyes met hers briefly. "Does he honestly think he's more intelligent than you?"

She found herself smiling, glowing even, at the obvious shock and disbelief in Andrii's expression. As if no one could think they were more intelligent than she was. He made her feel good about herself all the time. She might not think she was beautiful, but she did know she had an above-average IQ. She might even be considered a genius when it came to numbers, but her passion was creating stories. Mysteries. Thrillers. All with a touch of romance.

"Billows believes he's more intelligent than anyone."

"But you fixed his books. You're still fixing them for him."

"I'm a woman, so I can't possibly have a brain. I'm young in his eyes and don't know anything. And he's superior to everyone. You've met him," Azelie pointed out. "There isn't a doubt in my mind that you know exactly what he's like." She sent him a brief smile. "Doug and Carlton thought they knew what you were like, until I told them you took me to a bookstore on one of our dates. They were impressed."

"We can talk about Doug and Carlton later. I wouldn't mind their approval because they mean something to you, but it isn't necessary. I want to know what it is about McGrady that gives you a worse feeling than you get from Billows."

She thought that over before she answered him. "I don't think Billows cares one way or another about hurting someone. He doesn't seem to have feelings for anyone. He might pretend, but I don't think he's capable of feeling. That means he can be quite cruel and not ever think about it, but I don't think he gets off on it. He isn't sadistic in the sense he *needs* to hurt others. Or humiliate them. He just does whatever it takes to get what he wants."

"I understand what you're saying. That's a good assessment of Billows. What about McGrady?"

She glanced up at him, veiling her expression with her eyelashes. Andrii had been trained to read others almost from the time he was a toddler. He'd learned out of necessity as well as the training he'd received to become an asset to his government. He had to be able to size up his enemies in an instant.

"I feel a little ridiculous giving you my opinion on McGrady. I've been around Billows for years, so I know him fairly well, but I know nothing about McGrady."

"Other than your instincts, and baby, you have great instincts. I'm very interested in your opinion, or I wouldn't ask."

She sighed. "I think McGrady likes hurting people. Not only hurting them but humiliating them."

"You got that from him walking into the coffee shop and looking at you."

Had there been the least bit of amusement or scoffing, Azelie would have clammed up and not given her opinion again. Instead, Andrii sounded admiring. Pleased with her. She got that now-familiar glow inside just from his tone of voice. As if he approved of her, thought she was the most amazing woman in the world.

"Not just looking at me." She found herself gaining confidence. "It was the way he looked at Doug, Carlton, and the merry widows. As if he was assessing them and found them being with me amusing. I didn't want Doug or Carlton to give away the fact that they were onto him. They believe McGrady is stalking me."

"The moment he was spotted following you, research was done on him. Very thorough research. Your assessment of him is spot-on. I don't want you going anywhere near him.

He won't have a chance to harm your friends. Whatever he thinks he's going to get away with, he's not."

There was absolute conviction in Andrii's voice. She didn't ask him any questions about how he'd done the research because she knew he wouldn't answer her.

FIFTEEN

The club Maestro took Azelie to was small and intimate. He liked it because it was classy and the music was always great. He appreciated good music. He had a surprise for his woman, and he hoped she would get the message he was trying to get across to her. He was taking a big chance tonight, mainly because his woman was extremely intelligent.

Several of his Torpedo Ink brethren would be at the club. He wanted them to see Azelie, even if from a distance, but he was certain Lana would pull off the meeting while he was at the piano. Lana would be there with her brother, Preacher. Of course, he would be introduced by his given name, Kasimir Popov.

Other members—Keys, Master and Player—would be there as well. Maestro was in the band, Crows Flying, with the three men. He considered each of the men brilliant when it came to music. Seychelle, Savage's woman, often sang with them when they played at the Torpedo Ink Roadhouse, the bar the club owned.

They had rehearsed what they would say to make the meeting seem natural so they could sell the idea that they barely knew Lana. If Maestro and Lana were too close, Azelie would know Lana was part of a team. That would hurt and upset Azelie because he wouldn't be able to offer much in the way of an explanation.

At the moment, Azelie believed she met Lana through the college. They were becoming friends. Lana genuinely liked Azelie, but if she felt betrayed because neither Maestro nor Lana told her the truth, she might walk away from him. There was always that possibility hanging over his head.

Three times he'd brought it up to the club that he should just simply tell Azelie the truth. Unfortunately, running life-or-death missions, they'd learned the hard way not to take on anyone untrained. One slipup could cause a number of deaths. Azelie had acting skills when it came to Billows, but that didn't mean she wouldn't mess up. Each of this crew knew all about torture and how to hold out, if necessary, until their brethren came for them—and they would come. They would be certain the others would find them and get them free. Azelie wouldn't have that faith in them.

Maestro understood the necessity of keeping the truth from his woman, but he didn't like it. He refused to outright lie to her. That would be the one thing he could claim later when he was giving her the facts of their mission. *After* they'd found the women or at least shut down this link in the trafficking ring and gotten information to lead them to the next one.

Azelie looked beautiful, even more so than usual. She rarely wore a lot of makeup, but she'd given her eyes a smoky, exotic look. Her lips had a soft color on them, drawing his attention immediately. Her auburn hair tumbled down her back in long spirals and waves, so when the light caught it, copper and shades of red shone through. Her hair looked a little wild, adding to her striking, glamorous appearance.

The clothes were perfect for her, that skirt and fitted camisole accenting her very feminine figure. The camisole hugged her lush curves lovingly and showed off her small, tucked-in waist. The way the skirt fit over her hips and dropped to her ankles, moving with every step, added to her allure. He found himself proud to be walking into the club with Azelie on his arm.

More than one man turned to look at her as they walked in. Glancing down, he was pleased to see she was looking up at him as if he were the only man in the room. She smiled at him with that amazing smile she reserved for him. Her eyes were bright. Her expression was not just adoring but held a hint of developing love. He could see it, and it set his heart soaring.

He followed the hostess to their small table and pulled out Azelie's chair for her. He found he enjoyed doing little things for her. Opening doors. Seating her. Ordering for her. Hanging up her coat. Taking care of her after sex. All of it. He loved everything he did for her.

He knew he was already way too invested. If he lost her, he wouldn't recover. One of the things he knew about Azelie's character was that she was all or nothing. The moment she truly trusted him, he would have her devotion for life, but he had to earn it. He was on shaky ground. Each time he thought he was close, he remembered earthquakes.

Sea Haven and Caspar, where he resided, were right on a fault line. Earthquakes could turn things upside down if they were strong enough. They could damage property or completely destroy it. The things he was forced to hide from Azelie could not only damage but utterly and irrevocably annihilate their relationship. It was fragile. Just beginning. And she'd known betrayal the same as he had. If she had been using him to get to Czar or for any other reason and she lied, even by the sin of omission, he was certain he wouldn't forgive her, yet somehow he expected her to understand.

"You're doing it again, Andrii."

Her soft voice startled him, he'd been that deep in his thoughts. She leaned her chin into the heel of her hand, propping up her arm with her elbow on the table. Her eyes were filled with concern for him. That made his heart ache.

"What am I doing?"

"Frowning. Inside. Going quiet on me, which means you're worried about something." She made a little moue with her lips and then shook her head. "Not something. Me. Us. You're worried about us."

He wrapped his fingers around her hand, connecting them. "Baby." He kept his voice low and compelling so that she leaned forward to catch every word. "It's traditional for the woman to fall for the man and want to be with him. She might pretend she doesn't care if she's a game player, but she chases him and falls at his feet."

Her eyebrow shot up and a hint of amusement crept into her eyes.

"The man may or may not be interested, but he's the one with the power in the relationship because she wants him. He can take it or leave it. Traditionally, he couldn't care less about permanency, just the sex."

"That's tradition?"

He nodded solemnly. "You've got this entire thing backward. You're supposed to worry and be nervous I might run. Men run from the *relationship* word."

"Traditionally." She definitely sounded amused.

"Pay attention, *Solnyshkuh*. This is important information I'm giving you." He kept his expression solemn, as if he were imparting something life-changing. "There are certain rules we follow as men and women in a relationship, and we aren't supposed to mix them up."

The waiter came to the table to take their order. He sent her a small smile. "Do you want me to order for you, or do you have something in mind?"

As always, Azelie was thoughtful before she answered. "You order. I loved what you got for me last time. It's always fun to have a surprise."

"You don't like it, baby, we'll just order something else." He knew the menu without looking at it. He ordered her water without ice to start. "Azelie will have the khao soi soup and the shaved brussels sprout and Jonathan apple salad with avocado. I'll have the same salad and the ravioli." He flashed a smile at Azelie. "You up for trying wine? The club is famous for pairing wines with their food."

"I don't know the first thing about wine," she admitted.

"Neither did I until I started coming here. Great music

and excellent food. I took a chance on the wine and found I liked it."

"You'll have to order," Azelie said, turning the decision over to him.

He ordered her the wine suggestion that would be paired with her soup and then ordered himself a glass that paired with his ravioli.

Azelie gave him her bright smile, the one that lit up his world. He tightened his hold on her hand. "Getting back to what we were discussing, it's imperative you understand your role so I can be in mine. Right now, the roles are reversed."

He could see that he'd surprised her. She thought he'd been going for humor, and maybe he had been, but that was only because she'd asked him a question he didn't want to have to answer.

"Our roles are reversed?"

He nodded. "It pains me to say this, Zelie, but I seem to be the one who fell hard and fast. I jumped right over that proverbial cliff and I'm still falling, with no landing in sight. You, however, have reservations."

"I've fallen," she admitted, her fingers tightening in his.

Her voice was soft but carried a hint of anxiety, as if she had let him down. That was the last thing he wanted her to feel. He brought her hand to his mouth to run his lips along her inner wrist, right over her accelerated pulse. She didn't like him upset in any way. He'd known she would be like that, but seeing the proof right in front of him shook him.

"You have to go at your own pace, baby. I don't want you to ever feel as if you aren't sure about me. I don't like to feel as if you're slipping through my fingers, but those are my emotions, and I'm not used to having any feelings, so it's uncomfortable. The good news is, I feel like I can keep trying to be better for you."

"You're good enough," Azelie said.

"But you have doubts."

"Not about you exactly," she admitted. "It's more me and whether I'm capable of being what you need. Two people can be very different, but fundamentally, they should fit. I think it's good if we have differing points of view. I like hearing what others have to say. I don't want someone agreeing with me all the time, and I would hope you feel that way. Most of the time I think you do, but then you say things that can be alarming."

"Punishments," he said, knowing she really wasn't in the least on board with that.

She nodded slowly, thoughtfully. "That's a big one. If that's something you need to do because it's important to who you are, I wouldn't want you to change. Having said that, I don't want to be punished. It would be hard enough knowing I disappointed you without you treating me like a child, incapable of making my own decisions."

He fought down panic, but his expression didn't change. He knew he needed her. She was the one. There wasn't any doubt in his mind. How could there be doubt in hers? Was he being unreasonable?

"You're very fixated on punishments. What other things about my personality do you find difficult?" He didn't know if he could change, although she'd said she didn't want him to and he believed her. He'd asked the others to come, the ones who meant something to him. The ones who knew him. They couldn't bring their women, because it was a mission and no one ever took chances, but those coming would see him stripped bare. Would know he was all in, completely gone on this woman.

What did it matter if they knew he was making a complete fool of himself? Azelie was worth taking the risk.

She leaned her chin into the heel of her hand. "I don't find you difficult. You think you're far more difficult than you are. I like that you take the lead. Are you aware you always ask me first? You just did it here. You asked if you could order for me. Then you reassured me that if I didn't like what you ordered, we could order something else. Not that I would want to throw away the food. I know a few people who go hungry sometimes."

Of course she would know people who went hungry. He was beginning to realize Azelie would make it her business to watch over street people. "How often do you feed them?" The sincerity in her voice when she said she didn't find him difficult went a long way toward making him feel better about what he had planned for her.

Color swept up her neck to turn her face that rose color he liked. He found everything about her adorable. Azelie pushed at the hair tumbling around her face, tucking wild strands behind her ear. They were never going to stay, but he thought it was sexy. And cute.

"I don't cook for other people that much. If I have extra, I take it down the street to some of the kids. It would be silly to throw it away when others need to eat." She sounded defiant, as if she expected him to judge her harshly.

"Baby, I love that you do that. Did someone make fun of you for helping others? You sound as if you expected me to think you were being silly. It's admirable. One of my brothers from the school in Russia is with a woman who was raised in homeless shelters. She really looks after the homeless and has made all of us aware of how to take care of those living in bad situations. I admire the fact that you give what aid you can."

"I don't know why I always expect the worst from everyone." She sent him a look from under her eyelashes. "See? I'm not an angel. I think the worst of people."

"You don't, Zelie. You look for the best in others, and because you do, you find it. You have a sunny personality and people gravitate toward you."

That soft flush was back in her cheeks. "You have a way of saying the loveliest things to me. I'm not used to it, so I never know what to say, except thank you."

"*Thank you* is perfect."

"But it doesn't convey how I feel about you. Or the way you make me feel. Like bringing me here. This is such a cool place." She looked around her. "It's packed," Azelie pointed out. "Crazy packed. Like all the cool people come here. How did you find this club? Is it just the fact that you're hot as hell and cool as they come? Do they have a secret message they send out to the cool kids to invite them? Do you have a code to get in? A secret handshake?"

He found himself laughing. She made life fun. He'd sat in the club dozens of times and enjoyed the music and food, but he hadn't laughed. He hadn't looked around and noted the celebrities or the couples whispering to one another over their drinks. He just hadn't been alive.

Lana and her brother, Preacher, had come in. Master, Keys and Player followed. His three bandmates were seated at a table near the bar. Lana and Preacher were given a table for four in the shadows but close to the piano, exactly where they had asked to be seated when they made the reservations. Management was very aware one of the Crows Flying members had a special surprise for his lady. They were being extremely cooperative. It wasn't often they were able to get the band to come in and play.

Crows Flying stayed close to home. They were an internet sensation thanks to modern technology, but they didn't often take gigs outside of the roadhouse. They recorded, but only for themselves. Since Seychelle had been with them, lending her gorgeous voice, they'd made several new recordings, and all of them had ended up on the internet. For sale. Maestro suspected Code had something to do with it, but he never asked.

"I love music, and good musicians come here to play. I'm in a band called Crows Flying. We'll be playing tonight; that's your surprise. Part of it, anyway."

Her eyes went wide with shock and excitement. "Seriously? You're going to play here tonight?" She looked around the room again. "Did all these people come to hear you play?"

"We have a small following."

"Why haven't I heard of you?"

"We don't take gigs in too many places. Mostly, the music is online." He wasn't lying to her. He was determined to give her as much of himself as he could. There was the sin

of omission, but he was certain she would understand once
he was able to give her full disclosure.

Her eyes had gone soft, nearly liquid. He loved how she
looked at him. He sent up a silent prayer to whatever gods
there were in the universe to never take that from him. He
craved that look. Needed it. He went to sleep thinking about
her and woke up with her on his mind. Always, when he
imagined her, she had that look on her face.

"If I forget to tell you, in all the excitement of hearing you
play, thank you for the wonderful and unique surprises you
give to me. You're such an amazing man, and the way
you treat me is unlike anything I've ever experienced. I love
being with you."

Before he could answer her the waiter arrived, setting
their salads on the table. He had already given them both
water and told them the wine would be served during the
main course. He engaged with the waiter for a moment, giving him time he wanted to give only to Azelie, but he recognized the waiter was a fan of his music. He appreciated
those who enjoyed the band's music, and he wasn't about to
let them down.

He wasn't a man who easily shared himself with outsiders, but it was important to him to do his part for the band.
He knew being friendly and talking to people outside their
club wasn't easy for the others either. Unless they were playing roles, each of them stayed away from outsiders. Their
music wasn't a role they played. Their world was the music.
Opening themselves up where they were so vulnerable was
disconcerting.

Once the waiter left their table, he picked up his fork and
indicated her salad with it. The way she gave him honesty
was refreshing. Something he wasn't used to in women. He'd
found that the ones he knew outside of the club had a motive
for being with him. It wasn't about him—it was about them
and what he could do for them. He had money. He played in
a band. He had massive sex appeal.

"You give back to me more than you could ever know,

Zelie. There is a reason I call you my little sunshine. You've brought life to me. I feel alive when I'm with you. I swear I didn't know there was anything but cold and darkness until you came into my life."

Her eyes had that softness to them he'd come to rely on. She gave a little shake of her head, as if she couldn't quite believe him. He continued before she could protest.

"I had my music, my woodworking and the men and women that survived the school of horrors. I know that's far more than other people are gifted with, but I also have so many demons. I just couldn't trust anyone outside my immediate circle. At first, when I watched you, I couldn't believe you were true. I kept waiting to see you betray someone. Take a dig at them. Be ugly when the light wasn't on you. It was difficult to allow myself to believe you were the real deal. That's why you're my sunshine. You brought light to me. Hope. Most of all, you made a believer out of me."

He took a bite of the salad, which he always liked. With her sharing the table and eating the same salad, the flavors were even better. He enjoyed the food much more sharing it with her.

"I didn't even enjoy sex that much. It was more of a release than anything else. With the kind of work I did, I never turned to drugs, but I did drink in an effort to sleep at night without nightmares. It didn't work. I just woke up with a hangover and empty bottles strewn around my room. Fortunately, I wasn't an alcoholic, because it looked like I tried to be. That period didn't last long, but I'm ashamed to say I did my best to drown my sorrows."

He got those eyes again. She gave a little shake of her head. "Self-medicating is very common when you suffer trauma."

He arched one eyebrow. "Did you self-medicate?"

"My mother was an alcoholic," she reminded him. "Quentin used drugs. I didn't want any part of either one. I separated myself from the rest of the world as best I could and poured myself into college and the books I was writing."

"Baby, I just want to point out that you did a crap job of

separating yourself from the rest of the world. You have single parents and their children, street kids, three of the funniest older women I've ever encountered and two older men who all dote on you."

She sent him a small smile. "Yes, well, I doted on them but had no idea they returned the feeling."

She took a deep breath, her gaze clinging to his. He knew her so well now that it was apparent to him she was going to give him another revelation about herself. That was her way. He gave up information and she responded in kind, not wanting him to feel vulnerable. Looking out for him. *Bog*, he loved that about her.

"I never feel like anyone can love the real me. Or even see the real me. It makes me feel like a fraud. I had to hide my dislike of my brother-in-law once I was old enough to realize he was cheating on my sister, doing drugs, and living off the money she made. Then there's Billows. I'm working for a man who is part of some criminal ring. He isn't the only one involved. He has businesses, people who pay into his accounts. Most of them are not legitimate, but I'm doing his books and not telling a soul." She flashed a little self-deprecating smile at him. "Until you. I have no idea why or how I managed to give you the real me. I don't know how you see me under all the layers of guilt and survival instincts I have. Of course, I think you do have a tendency to glamorize me. I'm definitely not an angel, and I don't want you to be disappointed."

"You don't have to be everyone else's version of an angel. Only mine. My angel can have a bit of a temper, not that I see many signs of it. But it's all right with me. If you were society's standard of perfect, you never would be able to live with me."

"You always say the perfect thing to me."

He was grateful she thought so. At least she didn't think he was a controlling dictator. He spent the rest of dinner laughing with her. He was convinced she could make the mundane fun. Time was running out on him. It would be time to play with his band soon. He could see Player, Master and Keys making their way to the table.

"I'm going to give you a gift tonight," he said. "I wrote a song for you. It's yours. I'll be playing it on the piano at some point."

Her head went up, and again he got those shiny, liquid eyes. Eyes shining for him. "You wrote a song for me?"

He nodded. "Music is my way of expressing myself. I don't want you to have any misgivings at all about the way I feel about you. I've never written a song for anyone else. I write music and play it, but I'm no lyricist. This is my first time writing words to express my feelings. Usually, it's all about the music with me."

"You're too good to me, Andrii. I have no idea how to keep us equal in giving. I don't have any creative talent like you do with music."

He flashed her a grin to cover the real reaction to her genuine response. She was giving him so much already, she just didn't know. "It could be a disaster. You might hate it."

"I'll love it because you wrote it for me."

His three Torpedo Ink brothers made it to their table. He stood to meet them. "Let me introduce my lady, Azelie, to you. Babe, these are the men who own the construction company with me and are crazy music fiends, just like me."

He indicated the man she would be familiar with. Keys gave off the impression of a stalking jungle cat, with his fluid muscles, dark hair and piercing hazel eyes.

"This is Lazar Alexeev. Do you remember him coming into the coffeehouse with me that first time? Lazar is the man who knew about the place." He had known because he'd followed Azelie there.

Keys sent her a grin and gave her a little courtly bow. "Nice to finally meet the woman who captured Andrii."

That sweet color slid up her neck into her face, flushing her skin a wild rose. "I don't know that I've captured him, but I love being with him."

"You took him prisoner, woman. I'm Kir Vasiliev. Known

your man a long time, and I've got a wife who manages to twist me around her little finger. Don't know how she does it, but I see that same look on Andrii's face that stares back at me in the mirror when I'm trying to figure out how I got so damn lucky."

Kir Vasiliev could be a very intimidating man. He was big with a great deal of muscle. Scarred and tattooed. He looked as if he'd been to prison, which he had, many times. Azelie didn't look intimidated. She laughed at Kir's—Master's—comment. The tone was low and soft but sounded like a melody running through Maestro's head. He reached for her hand and brought it to his chest.

"Yeah, you did, babe. I think you cast a spell."

She laughed again, the sound inviting. "First he calls me an angel, and now I'm a witch."

"Love the way you laugh," the third man said. "Name's Gedeon Lazaroff. You have that same perfect pitch Seychelle has. Do you sing?"

Gedeon, aka Player, had striking blue eyes, was tall and muscular. He had light brown hair and wore a mustache and a small, barely there, beard.

Azelie looked horrified. "If I sing, the children put their hands over their ears."

"She can't lie worth shit," Keys said. "That's one thing you've got going for you, Andrii."

"They don't put their hands over their ears," Azelie conceded, "but I don't push my luck." She sent Keys a little smile.

"We're going to have to get this show on the road," Maestro said. "Are you going to be all right sitting here by yourself?"

"Of course. But I might go say hello to Lana. She's got a table right near the piano. There's four chairs, and it's just her and the man she came in with."

"I'll walk you over there," Maestro offered, and stood up to circle around the small table. Things were working out exactly like he needed them to.

Azelie took Andrii's hand as they walked around the tables to join Lana and the man she was with. Lana jumped up and hugged her. "I'm so happy you're here." Her gaze flicked to Andrii and their linked hands. "Hi, Andrii. We came to be supportive tonight. You know we're crazy about your music." She switched her attention back to Azelie. "I go to most of the Crows Flying gigs."

"I think everyone knew about the band but me," Azelie said. "I don't get out much."

"They're all over the internet," Lana said helpfully. She turned to the man who had stood when Azelie and Andrii approached the table. "This is my brother, Kasimir. He's not too bad until he gets in his bossy mode. Kas, this is Azelie. She goes to the college."

Kasimir Popov, aka Preacher, had curls no matter what he did to tame his hair. He looked far less intimidating than the band members because of those curls. That was deceptive, Azelie decided. He had muscle running beneath his clothing. He might look friendly, but he had that same reserve Andrii's bandmates had.

Preacher flashed a grin. "Someone needs to boss her." He shook hands with Andrii. "Would you care to join us? We have the room."

"I'll be playing shortly, but I'd appreciate your looking after Azelie."

"You got it, brother," Kasimir responded easily.

Azelie looked from Kasimir to Andrii. They knew each other. She couldn't tell with Lana, but she was certain there was a connection to Kasimir. Maybe it was the fact that Lana attended the Crows Flying gigs and Kasimir went with her. Still, Andrii didn't really look at Lana, and she was gorgeous. She was one of the most beautiful women Azelie had ever seen.

Andrii caught her chin and tilted her face up to his. "I'll

be the one playing either guitar or piano. You can focus on
me." He murmured the command against her lips, his tone
low, the words barely spoken aloud, but she heard them, and
it made her smile. Did he really think any other man in the
room could compare to him?

She licked along the seam of his lips, deliberately inviting his kiss. He was a member of a popular band, and there
were bound to be others watching them, but in that moment,
she didn't care. She wanted only to reassure him. Maybe it
was a mistake after all. He kissed her. Gathered her into his
arms, locked her against him and kissed her. Not gently.
Passionately. Claiming her. Demanding surrender, and she
gave herself to him because that was what he needed. That
was what she wanted. It was only when she was certain she
was going to burst into flames that he lifted his head. Even
then, his thumb whispered over her lips.

"Be good while I'm working."

She gave him her mischievous smile. "I'm an angel,
remember?"

"Stay that way until I'm with you," he cautioned and held
out her chair.

Azelie obligingly sank into it and watched him saunter
across the floor, threading his way easily through the tables
to join the other three members of Crows Flying.

"I love their music," Lana said. She waved her hand to
take in the entire bar. "You can see how popular they are."

Azelie wanted to enjoy the moment. Enjoy watching her
man play with his band for the first time. He'd set the date
up himself. Chosen to surprise her. The food had been delicious, and he had been totally focused on her, not paying any
attention to the female interest directed his way. She'd noticed, but he hadn't seemed to. Or if he had, he didn't care.
Azelie chose to put aside her questions about Andrii's
friendship with Lana and her brother until she was back
home and alone. Right now, she was determined to soak in
every moment of her dream date.

Lana grinned at her. "You like that man."

Azelie nodded. "More than like. I really hope he's real."

Kasimir made a sound like a growling wolf. "He's as real as it gets, honey. I've known him awhile now. I've never seen him look at anyone the way he looks at you."

Azelie resisted the urge to ask how Kasimir knew Andrii, mostly because she didn't want him to lie, and she had the feeling he might. Worse, he would do so convincingly. If he did, it stood to reason Andrii was doing the same.

She flashed a vague smile and turned her attention to the man announcing the band. The applause was thunderous when he said they were fortunate to get the chance for Crows Flying to play in their club. That much was true, then. There was a measure of relief knowing Andrii had told the truth about his band.

The band was well-known to some and clearly had a loyal following. The testament was the amount of people who seemed to know all the lyrics to the songs. Azelie found the band amazing. The music was incredible. They didn't play cover songs; all the music was their own.

Her heart beat far too fast when Andrii put down his guitar and went to the piano. He leaned into the microphone. "Don't sing as a rule. I leave that to Seychelle or one of the others. But tonight, I'll be playing a special song I wrote for my lady. First time playing it, so forgive me if it isn't perfect yet."

Azelie could barely breathe. He didn't have to announce to everyone in the room that he'd written the song for her. Or that she was his lady. He'd made the declaration in his compelling, soft tone, the one guaranteed to send heat down a woman's spine. Those in the room broke into applause. She could feel eyes on her and was grateful Lana's table was tucked into the shadows.

Then Andrii began to play. The music was moody at first. Then hopeful. So beautiful it brought tears to her eyes. And that was before he even began to sing.

I was once a broken man, who had learned nothing but hate.

A lonely fearful soul, who did not believe in fate.

There was a darkness around me, a blinding stormy haze.

No light could pierce the veil, nothing could bring the days.

Truth was just a stranger, and trust was just a word.

Empty promises were all I'd ever heard.

Then came the sun, there you are.

Then came the one, my shiny star.

Solnyshkuh, *a beautiful song.*

You sang to me, you're where I belong.

This is something real, this is something new.

Love took pain's place, and it's because of you.

Never had much of my own, never really needed it.

A soldier without a home, lonelier than I'd admit.

Never believed I'd have a life, not one worth living.

Not in this cold dark world, one so unforgiving.

On the brink of extinction, I fought hard on my own.

So few connections, betrayal was all I'd ever known.

Then came the sun, there you are.

Then came the one, my shiny star.

Solnyshkuh, *a beautiful song.*

You sang to me, you're where I belong.

This is something real, this is something new.

Love took pain's place, and it's because of you.

You lift me up and bring me peace.

Because of you, now I believe.

You show me love and how to laugh.

I finally found the missing half.

How could I know, how could I see,

Just what you would bring to me?

Little sunshine,

Love of mine.

Little sunshine,

Love of mine.

Then came the sun, there you are.

Then came the one, my shiny star.

Solnyshkuh, *a beautiful song.*

You sang to me, you're where I belong.

This is something real, this is something new.

Love took pain's place, and it's because of you.

The notes of the music faded and those in the bar applauded wildly. Azelie couldn't look at Lana, or anyone else. She could only see Andrii. Her eyes met his across the room and her heart stuttered at the way he was looking back at her. His face was usually a mask, expressionless, impossible for most people to read. Right at that moment, he was looking at her with open devotion. Even love. If she hadn't already been free-falling right off the cliff, she certainly was now. He was the most amazing man in the world as far as she was concerned. She didn't understand what it was about her that he found so wonderful, but it was evident from the song he'd written that he believed she was the one for him.

How could she not fall in love with him after that? How could she continue to hold part of herself back even when she knew he was holding back some truths? Lana made a single sound distracting her, then put her hand over Azelie's.

Lana leaned in close. "Isn't that the man who was at the bus stop when we first met?"

Azelie looked wildly around the room. Billows and a tall woman who looked familiar, like a model out of a magazine, were at the door being greeted by the hostess. Terror froze her in her place. For a moment, she couldn't breathe. She was risking Andrii's life for selfish reasons. What was wrong with her? Andrii deserved so much better, someone who would put his wants and needs first. His safety. He was thoughtful and protective. She couldn't allow Billows to know she was dating Andrii.

Azelie could only be thankful that Billows hadn't come in when Andrii was playing the piano and singing her song.

He was back playing the guitar. She knew he noted Billows the moment he entered the club.

"I'm not feeling very well," she told Lana. It was the truth. She texted Andrii that she'd meet him at her apartment. "I'll take an Uber home."

"We'll see you home," Kasimir said immediately. "We have a car."

It was too late. Billows headed straight to her table, while the host escorted his supermodel to their much more intimate table.

Azelie plastered on a smile. "Alan. How good to see you, although we were just about to leave."

"Alan Billows." Billows held out his hand to Kasimir, his gaze sweeping over Lana. "Azelie works for me."

"Kasimir Popov," Lana's brother replied. "This is Lana."

Billows gave Lana his charming smile. "Nice to meet you. I hope we have a chance to meet again. Azelie can give you the particulars, but any friends of hers are always welcome at either of my clubs." He handed Lana his business card. "Show that to the doorman. He'll contact me and I'll show you around."

Azelie found it significant that he gave his card to Lana, not her brother. She also found it extremely interesting that Billows didn't connect Kasimir with her, or if he did, he didn't respond with jealousy or threats. Was that because he'd brought a woman with him to the club and thought it would be inappropriate? That didn't seem to mesh with his personality. The Billows she knew couldn't care less about acting inappropriately.

SIXTEEN

His woman, protecting him again. Maestro let himself into her little studio apartment. Immediately, he heard the muted sound of her crying. His heart reacted, hurting. Aching. He desperately wanted to take her back to Caspar, to his home. Somewhere safe. They could put her in the Torpedo Ink clubhouse, and Billows wouldn't have a hope in hell of finding her. He knew he wasn't going to be able to take much more.

He'd searched her home and backpack numerous times for the key they needed to access the underground rooms. He wasn't the only one. Each time he took her away from her apartment, several of the others searched it. It should have been easy to find. She didn't have a car, and the apartment was tiny. They were well-versed in ferreting out secret places in floors and walls and even the ceiling. It was nowhere. He no longer believed she kept it in her home. But where, then?

She'd worn a necklace when she was at Billows' offices, but Maestro hadn't seen her with it on. She'd gone to the apartment, hung her backpack in the closet and spent the night with him. He was tempted to just ask her where the hell it was, explain everything and take her to safety. If he did and

Billows suspected something was wrong because she wasn't available, if the man was holding prisoners in his underground labyrinth, he would move them or kill them. Neither was a good scenario.

Maestro followed the sound of Azelie's soft weeping straight to the bedroom. "*Solnyshkuh*." He sank down onto the bed to remove his shoes.

"No." She sat up, trying to drag the covers with her, but he was sitting on them. "You can't be here. You can't, Andrii. You saw Billows come into the club. He was looking at my friend Lana in a way I really didn't like. If he knows about us, and he could have found out from anyone at the club that you were singing to someone, he could have you killed. I know he would. You have to believe me."

He simply reached out and picked her up, settling her onto his lap, his arms around her. Her face was wet with tears, swollen from crying so much. He bent his head and feathered kisses from the corners of both eyes down her soft, wet skin to her chin.

"Shh. You're breaking my heart."

"My heart is already broken. I was so selfish, Andrii. It was already such a risk with you coming here. I wanted to believe you could hide yourself from Andrew McGrady. You seem so capable, invincible even, and I needed to believe with your skills you could easily outwit Billows' man. But I knew better than to be seen in public with you."

He stroked caresses down the back of her head, massaged her scalp through the thick hair tumbling down her back in an effort to soothe her. The curls and waves were everywhere, a wild mess. He found it more appealing than ever.

"You aren't in the least selfish, Zelie. If you had your way, we would have remained hidden away from everyone. I was the one insisting you go out with me. I wanted to give you new experiences. It was important to me, and you knew it, so you pushed aside your reservations. You did it for me, not for you."

Azelie buried her face in the crook of his neck, her arms

winding around him, holding him tight. "I don't want to give you up, Andrii. I don't. But I can't have you in harm's way. I couldn't bear it if Billows managed to have you killed."

"Babe." He said it gently but with a hint of amusement.

He had to hold back a little snicker at the thought of Billows pitting his considerable bullying tactics and henchmen against an assassin trained from the time he was six or seven. Maestro knew more ways to interrogate, torture or kill than Billows could ever conceive of. Maestro had been trained by the cruelest of men. Experts in their field had worked with him and the others, never once suspecting that those children were already crawling through the vents and executing the worst of their brutal jailers.

She lifted her head and glared at him. A hard thing to do when her eyes were glistening with tears that dripped like diamonds off her long lashes. Her lips trembled slightly, just enough that he had no choice but to brush them with his to steady her. He tasted the salt of her tears and could have sworn there was a hint of strawberry on his tongue.

"Don't do that. Just because you believe you have skills, don't discount Billows. He's ruthless and cunning."

"Not nearly as ruthless as I am. He doesn't get to take you away from me. It won't happen. If you prefer to lie low for a while, tell him you need a vacation. I can get you somewhere safe where he won't be able to find you."

Her eyes widened with suspicion. "You do plan to do something to him."

"We're not talking about that. We're talking about you being on the verge of flight again. You need to make that commitment to us and stick to it. You need to believe in us as a team."

The moment the words were out of his mouth, he knew he'd made a mistake. She sat up, pulling a little away from him. Her blue gaze went cool like the liquid in a deep pool. A little stormy, as if a tempest was brewing out over the ocean.

"But we aren't a team, Andrii. You know Kasimir, don't you? And don't try to lie and tell me he follows your band."

"That wouldn't be a lie. Kasimir works as a bartender in the roadhouse where we play on a regular basis."

The intelligence in her eyes gave him a curious pride in her. He liked that she was so damned smart. Quick to figure things out. He really could worship her for her intelligence alone, although right at the moment that meant things were going to get dicey between them.

"You're looking for a way out because you're afraid for me, *Solnyshkuh*. Don't do that. Say you'll stay no matter what. I'm not easy. I'll never be easy, but I'm loyal, and I can promise you that no matter what comes our way, I'll be willing to work it out to both our satisfaction. I might need to be the one in control, but that doesn't mean I want to control you. I want to know you're safe and healthy and happy."

"That's what I want for you, Andrii. You aren't the only one in the relationship. We're supposed to be partners, but we aren't."

"Only because I can't give you all the answers you need right at this moment." He caught her chin, forcing her to look up at him. "I swear to you on our first child that as soon as I can, I'll give you everything. An answer to every question."

The merest hint of a smile curved her lips briefly. "You can't swear on our first child. You don't know we're going to have a child."

"We're going to have several children." He placed his hand over her belly, fingers splayed wide as if cradling his baby. "If you can't carry or don't want to, we'll adopt. I'm good with adoption. We can be like a friend of mine, taking in all the throwaways out there."

"You have a friend who takes in throwaways? What are throwaways?"

"Survivors of human trafficking. Young boys and girls with no families and no one who can deal with their trauma."

"But your friend does."

"My friend and his wife. His wife is the central figure in teaching all of us how to be better people."

"All of you?" she echoed.

He was wading into quicksand. He felt the earth moving beneath him, warning him subtly to be very careful. It was important to him that she know as much about him and the others as possible, so when the time came to tell her the things he was holding back, she would be more accepting. He would be more than grateful for her intelligence, knowing she would understand once he explained their mission.

"Throwaways like me," he said. "Children whose parents were murdered, and who were handed over to the cruelest people imaginable."

She was silent, her eyes soft. Lashes still wet. "Kasimir."

He didn't respond. She knew. She'd figured it out. She was accepting of Kasimir, but the blow was about to come. He saw her piecing it all together.

"Lana is Kasimir's birth sister. He has that curly hair, and her hair is straight and black. But they have similar features. She wasn't lying to me when she said Kasimir is her brother, was she?"

He remained silent. Hurt crept into her blue eyes and his heart stuttered. His gut clenched. He'd known this confrontation was coming. He'd assessed the risk and thought they could pull it off. They were all used to playing roles. The problem was he didn't want the members of his club to play a role with Azelie. They were his family, and he wanted her to know them as his family. That risk had been his. He'd tossed the dice and he lost.

"Lana is part of the throwaways, isn't she? Just like Kasimir. That makes it probable that she didn't just happen to have seen me at the college or to have rescued me from Billows at the bus stop. You had her watching me."

He listened carefully to her tone. There was hurt but no condemnation. He stroked one finger down her face, traced her cheekbone and then her ear. His fingers settled over her pulse. A little too fast, but steady.

"She was at that horrible school with you, wasn't she? If it was a school for assassins, she's most likely lethal, just as you are."

"I refuse to take chances that Billows is going to hurt you. Or that the maniac he has watching you decides to act on his impulses."

That wasn't exactly answering her, and yet it was.

"Why didn't you just tell me the truth, Andrii? I don't like being made a fool of. I believed Lana had befriended me because she liked me."

"She does like you. How could she not? You're genuine, Azelie. We don't get a lot of genuine."

"The probability is extremely high that Kir, Lazar and Gedeon are part of your family of throwaways." She made it a statement.

"Baby, don't be upset over Lana. That was my decision, not hers. She would have been happy to tell you the truth."

"But you felt it necessary to keep me in the dark."

"I don't know how good of an actress you are." He tugged on one of her curls. "I can read you like a book. I don't know if that's just our connection, or if everyone can."

"I can't ask you why, can I?"

"I'll tell you everything you want to know as soon as I can. You'll have to trust me." Maestro found he was holding his breath. He was asking a lot of her. How would he react if the roles were reversed? He'd just admitted that he'd had Lana deceive her. Never mind that it was for a good reason. It was his reason, unknown to her. Deception hurt.

Azelie liked Lana. She believed they had become friends because they shared the college experience. She'd been grateful to Lana for her timely rescue. Now, through no fault of her own, she would be leery of the friendship, not believing it was genuine.

"There's that word again. *Trust.* I seem to be the one having to give all the trust. You don't trust me though."

"Zelie." He said her name like a reprimand. "You know that isn't the truth. I trust you implicitly. I'm protecting you and a great many others. That's the most I can give you right now, and it's most likely more than I should."

She pushed back the heavy fall of hair, tucking wayward

strands behind her ear. The wild curls and waves simply escaped. There was no loud clock ticking, but he heard it anyway. The countdown to the bomb going off. Azelie didn't speak for a long time. She sat still in his lap, contemplating their future. Or her next move. He thought he could read her, but she felt closed off to him.

Then she let him have her weight, her head against his chest, back pressed firmly into him. "I think I need my head examined."

"What does that mean?" He stroked the pad of his thumb down her vulnerable neck and once more found her pulse. Beating too fast, but steady. That was his woman. She took her time thinking things through before she made a decision.

"It means I'm probably going to get my heart broken because I'm going to let you get away with not answering me."

Relief was overwhelming. He dropped his chin on top of her head, feeling her soft curls tangling with the bristles on his jaw. "You aren't going to ever have a broken heart, *Solnyshkuh*. I'm going to do everything in my power to make you happy."

"I am happy. I made a life for myself, and I've been happy in it."

"You forgot to include a future with a husband and children. Somewhere safe you can write your stories in peace. Those are important things, Zelie. I'm the man to give them to you."

He nibbled his way down her neck, scraping his teeth gently along the way. Tasting her skin on his tongue. Savoring that faint taste of strawberries. "Want you again, *Solnyshkuh*. I want to go to sleep with you in my arms and wake up seeing you first thing. I love to breathe you in."

He was making a statement. He wasn't leaving. She might be nervous about him staying, afraid of Billows and Mc-Grady, but he wanted her to realize he wasn't in the least bit worried. He wanted her to have that kind of faith in him—in them as a couple. They were stronger than Billows. They always would be.

"I want those things too, Andrii. But more than anything, I need to know you're safe."

This woman. He tightened his hold on her. "I'm a badass, baby. You don't want to believe it, but I am. Have a little faith in my abilities. I need to stay."

He waited. Watching her. He saw the capitulation in her eyes and then she turned to him and lifted her face to his. *Bog*, her mouth. She tasted like wildfire. It was Azelie who pulled back first. She tugged at the hem of his shirt, and he complied with her silent demand, removing it one-handed. Then he tugged off her little top to give him free access to her full breasts. He loved looking at her body. All those lush, feminine curves. To him she was beautiful.

Azelie placed little butterfly kisses over the hard muscles of his chest. Her mouth kept climbing, finding his throat, and then she kissed along his jaw. Little kisses. Barely there. He shouldn't have been able to feel them, but he did. Those featherlight kisses were like dozens of little flames leaping from nerve ending to nerve ending.

"I want to learn how to please you, but you'll have to instruct me. And you'll need your jeans off."

His heart leapt. Went crazy. He cupped her chin, forcing her to meet his eyes. She looked shy but determined. "Are you asking me to teach you how to suck my cock?"

That rose color he loved so much infused her skin, but she didn't look away. She nodded.

"It's important to me to learn how to please you. What gives you pleasure. You always give me so much, Andrii. I need to be able to do this. I want to."

"We might not be ready for that yet, *Solnyshkuh*, as much as I want it. When I have my cock in your mouth, I'll want to control the action. I like it a little on the rough side. That might scare you. It's important that whatever we do together, you have faith that I'm going to make it good for you. That means building up to the wilder things slowly."

Her gaze didn't leave his. "I want this, Andrii. It's important to me. I want you to control everything. That makes me feel safe. It also takes the burden off me of knowing what I'm supposed to do next."

His cock was already diamond hard. He needed to strip his jeans off just to get some relief. He could see the mixture of nerves and excitement in her eyes. Deliberately, he brushed his hands down her shoulders to the full, inviting curves. He loved the sheer beauty of her breasts. Her nipples were tight buds but sensitive, reacting to his play. He'd been very gentle with her, introducing her to sex as lovingly as he could.

"You're certain this is what you want to do?"

She nodded. "More than anything I want to learn the right way to do it, to give you pleasure."

"Your mouth on me is going to bring me all kinds of pleasure, Zelie. There isn't a right or wrong here."

"There're ways you like sex, Andrii. There are ways you might prefer to be in my mouth. I want to learn those ways. Anything you like. But you have to teach me because I don't have a clue what I'm doing. It's important to me."

He didn't wait for her to keep explaining. He could tell it was difficult for her, and he was proud of her for communicating her desire. More, his body raged at him, impatient for her mouth.

"Take your clothes off, *Solnyshkuh*. Strip. Fast. I don't need a show right now; I'm not taking chances on getting any more aroused than I already am."

She slid off the bed and dragged down the drawstring pants she was wearing, and he was grateful she'd changed from her gorgeous club clothes into the more simple ones she wore to bed. He kept his body facing hers. Without a shirt, the Torpedo Ink tattoo would be very prominent on his back. He didn't want anything to mar this special moment.

"Lie on the bed with your head hanging over the edge. Spread your legs wide for me. I need to see how hungry you are for my cock."

She crawled up onto the bed and lay down sideways, so her neck was over the very edge, tipping her head back. She did as he commanded, spreading her legs for him.

"Wider." He bent over her, and without preamble worked two fingers into her hot, slick entrance. She gasped and lifted her hips. He slid his fingers out again, deliberately trailing the pad of his thumb over her clit. She made a little sound of startled pleasure. He flicked her clit hard, and he saw the answering ripple of her belly muscles as her sex contracted.

Holding her gaze, he licked his fingers, savoring the subtle strawberry flavor. "You are hungry for my cock, aren't you?"

She nodded. Andrii shook his head. "Say it. I need to hear just what you want."

He knew forcing her to tell him what she wanted would up the anticipation. He'd noticed from the beginning of their relationship that she responded to rough language and even cruder suggestions.

"I'm very hungry for your cock," she admitted in a low voice. The moment she did, her entire body took on a rosy glow.

"Where do you want my cock?" He kneaded her breasts and tugged and rolled her nipples. At first, he was very gentle but began to slowly increase the pressure of his play.

"In my mouth."

He loved the expression on her face—a shy look mixed with a darker lust. He could see her pussy gleaming at him, droplets of liquid caught in the fiery tangle of curls at the junction between her legs. She was responding to the rougher play, a good thing when rough was often his preference.

"What do you want in your mouth, baby? You didn't say."

Deliberately, he shoved down his jeans, standing close so that his straining cock was just out of her reach. Immediately, her gaze locked on to the prize. She moistened her lips with the tip of her tongue. Her breathing turned ragged, and her nipples tightened even more, so erect they appeared to be two stiff little candlewicks waiting for him to ignite them. *Bog*, but he found her beautiful.

"I'd like your cock in my mouth, please, Andrii."

Her voice was breathy, a thread of sound, but it managed to vibrate through his body, pushing him into a brutal need. The broad head wept pearl droplets. Fisting the thick shaft, he smeared the drops over her lips. Her lips were soft. She looked sexy lying on the bed, eyes on his cock, waiting for his instructions. He didn't want to disappoint her.

"I want you to slide your hands down your body. Feel your breasts, tug on your nipples. Don't be gentle." He watched her obey him, her small hands following the path he enjoyed. The sight made his cock jerk and pulse. More droplets welled up. "Lick the head of my cock while you're giving yourself pleasure. Just lick up the drops."

Her tongue felt like a living flame, branding him. He couldn't decide which was sexier, watching her hands kneading her breasts, fingers tugging on her nipples, or that hot little tongue sliding over the head of his cock, sending streaks of lightning through his shaft and balls. He might not survive. It was important to him that she felt the same way.

"Slide your hands down to your pussy, Zelie. Bury your fingers deep. I want you getting yourself off." His voice was that smooth velvet he used to compel her, but he knew he was on the verge of losing control. He wasn't going to last long if she had her mouth around him.

It was her gift. The need to give to him. The trusting look she gave him. Or the near adoration when he didn't deserve it. She wanted this for him—not for herself. The excitement and trepidation mixing together only added fuel to the fire burning in him.

⌒

Azelie glanced up at Andrii's face and her breath caught in her lungs. He was partially in the shadows, but his features were carved with stark sensuality. He looked like sin incarnate. Beautiful, like a long-lost warrior claiming his victory. His eyes were hot silver crystals moving possessively over her body as if she belonged solely to him. And she did. She knew there would never be another man for her.

Her skin under her fingertips felt soft and wholly feminine. Everywhere she touched herself, she left behind the feeling of flames dancing over her, licking at every nerve ending.

"Fingers in your pussy, baby. Need to see you giving yourself pleasure."

"It's distracting." Her voice was husky. Not her own. "I want this for you."

"Follow my instructions, *Solnyshkuh*. I'm in control here, not you. This is what I want. Trust me to know what you need to do."

The crown of his erection felt like hot satin as he rubbed it over her parted lips. The taste of him was exquisite, salty, but not at all bitter. She wanted his cock. She wanted to give him something back for all the things he'd given her. It felt strange to her to be the taker, not the giver, and this was something important that she knew if she learned, she could always give him when he was having a difficult time.

Her fingers moved almost of their own volition, finding the small bundle of nerves Andrii was so good at locating and driving her insane with. Every movement sent more heat spiraling through her. No matter how tight that coil in her stomach wound, her entire focus was on Andrii. She kept her gaze fixed on his. Every line in his face was carved deep with lust—for her. That realization sent waves of happiness and satisfaction rushing through her.

"Open your mouth, *lyubeemaya*."

Just the way he gave the command, his eyes going to that piercing steel, his breath coming in raw heaves, sent more flames licking over her. She moistened her lips with the tip of her tongue and slowly parted them. Her heart pounded. Her sex clenched around her fingers in sudden fiery excitement. He slid the broad crown along her tongue, letting her taste the unique salty flavor that was wholly his.

She had never wanted to do something right as much as she wanted this for him. Andrii had given her pleasure beyond her imagination. He made her feel beautiful and sexy. He made her feel as if she was truly someone special. She wanted to give him back that same feeling. The trouble was, she had no idea what she was doing. Even now, it felt as if he was giving her more pleasure than she was giving him.

Her body was on fire, her hips rocking with each stroke of her fingers. She tried to tell him with her eyes that she needed to focus her entire attention on him. Very gently he caught her jaw, slipping his cock deeper into the hot haven of her mouth. He wasn't very far in, but he took up so much space she felt as if she couldn't breathe. But there was a look on his face she'd never seen before, and she relaxed, needing his expression to never change.

One of his hands went to her head, fingers fisting tightly in her hair so that her scalp ached. A growl escaped his throat. Excitement and joy burst through her. His control was slipping. She wanted him to keep giving her commands. The sound of his voice was mesmerizing to her.

"I love to see how wet your pussy is, Zelie. Knowing you're getting off on this makes the experience even better for me."

His skin was hot to the touch. She could smell his arousal and his primitive, wild scent. She found his taste addicting. The idea that she might be able to please him the way he brought pleasure to her would go a long way to making her feel she was on equal ground with him in their relationship. For her, it wasn't about the sex. It was about giving him complete surrender. Complete focus. Needing to take away his demons in a way no one else could ever do.

"Explore with your tongue. Get to know the shape and feel of my cock. You'll know what feels good. Don't like teeth, but that tongue of yours is perfect. Pay attention to my balls."

She never took her eyes from his, so she was able to see every shudder rippling through him. She wished she knew how he felt.

As if reading her mind, he gave her that. "Fire racing up my shaft to my belly and spreading through my body like you may have detonated a stick of dynamite. Even my balls are burning, but feel free to take your time learning."

She ran her lips up and down his shaft, trying to memorize every inch of him. Her tongue lapped at his balls and then once again curled around his shaft and moved back up to the sensitive crown. Another groan slipped out. A growl. His fingers tightened in her hair.

"Take me deeper, baby. Suck hard. I want to feel the pull of your mouth."

That usually velvet voice had dropped another octave, sounding a little hoarse. There was a distinct rasp to his voice she'd never heard before.

Elated that she was getting to him, giving him pleasure, she did as he said, doing her best to take him deeper. There was a lot of him to take, but she focused on the shape and feel of him. On giving him her complete attention. She was very good at details, and her tongue had mapped each zone where he was highly sensitive.

She loved what she was doing, giving him an experience. He may have had the same thing a thousand other times, but she was the one who wanted to bring him the most pleasure she possibly could.

He swore under his breath, exciting her more. She loved that she was getting to him, shaking his control. She moaned around his cock, sending a delicious vibration through him. She worked at each of his most sensitive places, getting her reward when his body shuddered and his cock grew hotter and thicker.

"Never felt anything like this, Zelie," he praised. "You're working me and giving me something I've never had. All because I matter to you." He sounded a little shocked that he could matter to her.

How could he not realize he had fast become her world? She would try to find a way to give him the moon if that was what he wanted.

"You really do want to please me. That shocks the hell out of me." That soft velvet tone gave way to a sexy rasp. "Perfection. Seriously. You're so damned beautiful."

She loved that he thought so, but she loved what she was doing. Her mouth on him. The taste and scent of him. The way she could make his body shudder with pleasure when she tightened her mouth around him and sucked hard or used

the tip of her tongue to dance along the sweet spot that had
his hips making shallow, almost frantic mini-thrusts.

"Need to take over now. I'm going to go a little deeper.
Don't panic on me. Trust me to give you the air you're going
to need."

She did trust him. She loved that he was decisive. That he
was commanding. She needed him to take control and tell
her what to do.

"Want you looking at me and nowhere else. I can read
you, baby. I'll know if you start to panic or want to stop."

She couldn't imagine wanting to stop. She actually felt
powerful and as if she were giving Andrii something special. She loved that, and she loved looking into his eyes while
he was feeding his cock to her. She could see the dark, car-
nal lust mixed with something too close to adoration. And
love. It was there, stark and real, for her to see.

"Suck and use your tongue and relax for me."

She was very wet between her legs, her body on fire.
There was no way she would take her gaze from his, not
when he had that dark hunger carved deep into the lines on
his face. His eyes were hooded and vividly intense as he
slowly withdrew. His hands went to either side of her head,
positioning her the way he wanted. Then he pushed his cock
into her mouth again, holding her still.

He filled her mouth, pushing deeper. She never would
have been able to do such a thing on her own. Never. His
cock felt heavy on her tongue and filled the space in her
mouth, stretching her lips. He held himself still, allowing
her to suck hard. Very hard. She needed to give him this
pleasure more than she needed air.

Her gaze clung to his to see his reaction, and she was instantly rewarded when a fine sheen of sweat covered his chest.
When every muscle stood out in definition. When his eyes
went molten. He looked like the epitome of sensuality to her.

He pulled back, allowing her to breathe, and then he
pushed in again, thrusting this time, the action causing a
rush of hot liquid between her legs. She used her mouth and

tongue as best she could, catching his rhythm so she could suckle hard and tight. That got her feral growls. The sounds made her aware of her breasts aching and her body burning up in a fever of need. Tremors ran through her. For a moment she was tempted to use her fingers again, but he was far more important to her than her own satisfaction.

He sank deeper, so scorching hot he felt like a brand. So thick she worried she might not be able to use her tongue the way she wanted on the underside of the broad crown. She hollowed her cheeks, feeling his cock pulse. Jerk. His body shuddered, his thigh muscles rigid. He withdrew abruptly, and she made a single sound of protest.

"Want your sweet little pussy, baby. Get on your hands and knees. Hurry." His hands were already moving her, spinning her around, yanking her hips up and shoving her head down toward the covers. He kept one hand between her shoulder blades as he surged into her. A hard, claiming thrust. That was all it took, and she detonated. He kept pounding into her right through her first orgasm and then her second.

She came close to screaming his name when her body clamped down on his cock on the third orgasm, sending them both rocketing into sweet oblivion.

SEVENTEEN

"Be right back, babe," Andrii said. "I'll start the bathwater."

Azelie couldn't keep the smile from her face. Not only had she done a rather spectacular job giving him a blow job for the first time, but their sex was off the charts. Now he was doing what he always did, taking care of her. She lay on the bed, hands behind her head, not bothering to try to cover up. She was as limp as a dishrag and so happy she couldn't think straight.

"I have Andrii fog," she announced.

He grinned at her, leaned over, and brushed a kiss on the top of her head. "You're going to contribute to my smug arrogance if you keep that up."

"I can't help it if it's true." She smiled up at him. "You're better than brain fog."

"It could just be sex fog," he teased.

She loved making him smile. He seemed relaxed and very happy. "It could be, but if it is, it's still Andrii fog, because you're the one providing awesome sex."

"I suppose that makes sense to you. I think it's the other way around. You provided for me." He turned to walk away from her.

Azelie stared at his broad back in a kind of shock. She sat up slowly. She knew he had tattoos. He had them all over his chest and arms, but he usually was dressed, and the other times they'd had sex, she only saw him from the front. He pulled on a shirt after. He woke before her when he slept in her bed. She'd never seen his back tattoos. The main ink on his back was a large piece done predominantly in blacks and grays. The central part of the tattoo was a tree with many branches. Crows sat in the branches or flew above them. Mixed in the roots of the tree were numerous skulls piled high. Some were scattered on the ground near the roots, as if they'd tried to escape. A rocker above the canopy of the tree said "Torpedo Ink." The one below said "Sea Haven–Caspar."

"You're in a motorcycle club."

He stuck his head around the door frame. "Yeah?" A distinct challenge. His expression had gone hard. "You have a problem with that?"

"Well, yes." She wrapped her arms around her middle. "That means you ride motorcycles. You're probably really good on a motorcycle. Like an expert rider or something."

He looked puzzled. "Not following you, babe. You're going to have to spell out your objection."

"Sheesh, Andrii. Do I have to spell it out for you? Is there anything you can't do? Anything you're not good at? I'm saying you're most likely a badass on a motorcycle. You are, aren't you? Just own it. Just admit it."

She knew she sounded a little hysterical, but every time she thought she might be able to give him something of equal value, bring something to the relationship, she found out more about him. Everything she found out was over the top. He was like a hero in a fantasy book, larger than life and impossible to match.

Andrii studied her face, the harshness in him fading. "Baby, you're not making any sense. I've ridden motorcycles for years. You'll never have to worry when you're on the back of my bike. I'll keep you safe. Are you afraid of motorcycles?"

Naturally, he would think she feared being on a motorcycle.

More than likely, prior to thinking she was afraid, he had thought she was upset that he was in a club. He didn't understand the disparity between them. It would always be there, this huge gap she would never be able to close. She despised that she had no experience, that she'd been a coward and hid from life because of what had happened.

She pressed her hand over the scar closest to her heart. She'd been afraid to take a chance with Maestro, pretending to herself she was afraid of his past, but the truth was she thought she would never be able to keep him. He would realize after a short while that she was no match for him.

Azelie turned away from him. She couldn't even look at him when he was so ridiculously gorgeous. He didn't seem to care in the least about his nudity, comfortable in his own skin, where she often wanted to hide. She knew she'd worn baggy clothes from a young age because Quentin had drilled it into her that she wasn't to show her figure. She wanted to blame her lack of confidence on that but was afraid she simply lacked self-esteem in every department.

She heard Andrii swear under his breath, his voice soft but close, too close. He moved like the air, silent and deadly. He was on her before she could defend herself, catching her up in his arms and cradling her against his chest.

"Baby, you're crying." He swung around, stalking back to the bathroom, where the water was running into her small bathtub. "Told you before, don't want you crying unless you're in my arms. Cry it out, and then tell me what's going on so I can fix it."

She didn't know what to say or do. How could he fix the wide gap, ever growing, between them? "It's not like you can suddenly turn into a nerd, Andrii. Or goofy. Or sexless. You're always going to be you, and I'm always going to be me." She choked, hiccupped and pressed her wet face against his bare chest. "Even after crazy sex, you smell good. You can't stop that either."

"That's a good thing, Zelie, not a bad thing." He rested his butt against the sink, holding her close as the water filled the tub. "I don't think you'd be attracted to me if I was the smelly type."

"Don't get me laughing. I don't want to laugh. This is so bad between us. There isn't any way to fix it. There's just no way."

He set her feet down in the small bathtub. "There's always a way to fix something, baby. But if you're worried about the two of us, we're solid. We're always going to be solid, even when we run into little hitches."

His voice was soft, a brush of velvet over her skin. Worse, there were notes in his tone that had goose bumps erupting everywhere. She wanted to curl up into a little ball and weep forever at her lack of confidence. How could a man like Andrii hold her with such tenderness? So gently. So absolutely certain they would make it.

"You don't understand," she blurted. "I don't think it's possible for you to understand."

"Despite being ridiculously arrogant, I am intelligent. I can figure it out. Get all the way into the water, Azelie."

He stripped the robe off her, and she sank down into the hot water obediently, drawing up her knees and gripping them so tightly her knuckles turned white.

"I really don't like you being so distressed."

She laid her head on top of her knees. "It's just that you're so extraordinary." She looked up at him, seeing he was shaking his head. "Don't dismiss what I'm telling you. You are. You have so much experience in so many areas. Anything you choose to do, you're not just good, you're amazing at it."

Her hair was all over the place and she swept it back, annoyed that she hadn't put it up. The moment she pulled it back from her face, Andrii took over, bunching her thick hair in one fist and deftly twisting it into one of the many silk scrunchies she had on a mini-tower next to her sink.

"You're even good at putting my hair up."

"I'm good at reading your distress level. You needed it out of your way. I was close to your hair ties, so I put it up out of the way."

She glanced at him again. "You're good at everything."

"I'm not. I couldn't write a book if my life depended on it. I can't make a roomful of senior citizens light up when I walk into a coffee shop. I certainly am not going to take on a couple of little boys or a baby girl. Quite possibly, they'd eat me alive. I have certain skills, but not one of them will lend itself to any of those things."

She continued to look at him. He meant what he said. He just didn't get it. "Andrii, I'm falling in love with you. When you open your eyes and realize I'm boring and scared and I'll never be your match, you're going to get restless. You may stay with me because you're loyal. I see that in you. I don't believe you're a cheater, but you aren't going to be happy, and I couldn't bear that."

For a moment he looked very upset, and then he crouched down beside the tub, where he could look directly into her eyes. "Azelie, look at me." He waited until she managed to raise her gaze to his. "You need to hear me. Really hear me. I've had countless women in my life. That was part of my training. Even missions I went on involved seduction of a target. I'm not telling you any of my past because I'm proud of it—just the opposite. You need to understand I'm not normal. I'm never going to be normal. I don't have natural erections as a rule. As in never since I was a teen. Everything in my life has been about control. I didn't ever feel alive. I went through the motions because I believe in what we do. I've experienced trafficking, and more than anything I wanted to be part of an organization to stop it. But I wasn't living. I didn't enjoy great food or drink. I didn't enjoy the women I fucked. It was a release for me, nothing more. Some days, it was damn tough to find a reason to keep going."

He had to stop. Her eyes burned with tears. Not for herself, but for him. He was giving her the absolute truth of his life and it wasn't pretty.

"It doesn't matter how experienced I am at sex if I'm not enjoying it. Killing people isn't a gift, it's a curse. My life was a total fucking mess until I laid eyes on you. You don't have to understand that you brought me back to life, but you do need to understand there will never be another woman for me. Not ever. You're the one or it's no one."

He never once shifted his gaze from hers. How could she not believe him? He was right, she didn't understand the how or why of it, only that Andrii believed what he was saying with his entire being. She tried a smile to reassure him. She didn't know why she was reassuring him because to her he was as perfect as a man got.

"I don't know how you see yourself like that, Andrii, but I'm going to take what you say as an absolute."

"I won't lie to you, Azelie. I haven't lied to you. Not about my past and not about what I want for our future. If there comes a time when I have to ask you to wait for explanations, have faith in me. Trust me to look out for us."

"I have faith in you, Andrii. It's me I feel always falls short."

"Stop feeling that way. It's you I want. It's you I'm always going to want. They say no one can promise forever, and that's fucking true because we're all facing death. I can promise you that when I take my last breath, I'll be thinking of you. It's always going to be you."

There it was. Complete conviction. Her heart nearly exploded at the look in his eyes. Stark love. That was what she saw looking back at her. She wasn't used to love, but there was no other way to describe what she saw etched into the lines on his face and in the depths of his eyes.

He was amazing. The fact that he had genuinely developed such intense emotions for her in so little time shocked her. Elated her. There was no way she could have poor self-esteem and sabotage what they had if he looked at her that way. She would never be worthy of him if she wasn't willing to fight for them the way he was.

"It's always going to be you, Andrii," she admitted. "There's no one like you in the world. I know I don't want anyone else. I've never looked at anyone else."

He swept his hand down the back of her head. "You have to stop running from me. I'm doing everything I can to show you what you mean to me. Maybe it isn't enough. I'm new to relationships, but I swear, baby, whatever you need so you're absolutely certain of us, I'll find a way to give it to you."

"I think you just did, Andrii." She sounded breathless, choked up, mainly because she was. There was a lump in her throat she couldn't quite get around.

"Your parents programmed you to believe you aren't worthy of love. I may not go to counselors, but I've heard Blythe telling her children that they were programmed by the people who took them. When you meet her, you'll see that Blythe makes sense. Once we broke out of that school and were out from under Sorbacov, I never wanted to view myself as a victim, so I tried not to hear her. But she makes sense. We're going to run into these glitches sometimes, not through our own fault, but because past experiences shape us. I know I'm going to need reassurance at times. I know I'm going to be a moron and test you, but I'm aware that I do that shit and it isn't fair to you, so I'll fight those tendencies."

Her heart melted at his admission. She loved that he would let her know he expected to fail at times. It made her feel as if her continual battle with self-esteem could be acknowledged and hopefully overcome.

"You could let me know when you're having a difficult time, Andrii."

"I think that's a very good idea. A wise man once told me good communication is the key in a relationship. When you need extra reassurance that I find you the most beautiful woman on this planet, inside and out, you let me know. We can do this, Zelie. I know we can. You just need to believe in us the way I do."

Azelie found it interesting and a little sad that he was all in, seemingly without reservations, and she was such a coward she kept throwing roadblocks in their way. There were reasons. She was intelligent enough to know Andrii was holding back something huge, but at the same time, she found that she did trust him. Something in her responded to him.

She knew she had good instincts when it came to judging

people and their motives. She could determine whether they were liars and what kind of character they had. The bottom line was she believed Andrii and she wanted to be like him— taking a deep breath and jumping in with both feet.

She nodded her head slowly, determined she was going to let go of her fears.

~

"He wrote a song for me," Azelie announced as she flung herself into the chair beside China. "Andrii plays in a band, and he wrote a song and played it for me. Right there in the club. He told everyone the song was for his lady."

She couldn't help sounding breathless. Andrii made her breathless. He'd been so loving and sweet, holding her all night, whispering the most outrageous things to make her laugh. There were no nightmares when Andrii slept in her bed with her. There was no room for them because Andrii made sure of it.

Penny's breath exploded from her throat. She patted the tabletop beside Azelie's hand. "A band? He plays in a band? And wrote a song for you? Musicians are the *best* lovers. It's their artist's soul."

Doug groaned and slapped his palm against his forehead. "Don't tell her such nonsense, Penny."

"What are you doing encouraging her to be a groupie?" Carlton demanded. "And musicians aren't necessarily the best lovers. Any man who pays attention to his partner's needs is a good lover."

Penny rolled her eyes. "You don't understand the significance of a man with a poet's soul. His very artistry gives him a superior skill right off the bat."

Doug made a noise in his throat that sounded like a cat dying of strangulation. Then he began a coughing fit. Azelie politely pushed the glass of water she hadn't yet touched to him in the hopes of saving his life. He had turned an alarming shade of lobster red.

China and Blanc hid their smirks behind their hands. Azelie

glanced toward the counter, where Shaila was serving a customer. At least she acted as though she were serving a customer, but in reality, she was listening to the conversation right along with half the coffee shop. The discussions between the merry widows and their two male friends were legendary.

"Penny." Carlton did his best to sound reasonable, but his voice shook with the effort. "That is quite possibly the most ridiculous thing that's ever come out of your mouth. And over the years, you've managed to spew a lot of insane nonsense. It's a wonder you haven't been committed."

"Ha!" Penny returned. "You're just jealous because I took an entire year and followed several of the top bands."

"You didn't follow them," Carlton objected. "You had sex with all the band members."

Penny nodded, completely without one iota of remorse. "Which, may I point out, makes me an expert when it comes to musicians and their sexual prowess."

Doug choked some more. He took another drink of water and glared at Penny. "You will not encourage our girl to follow bands and sleep with the members."

"Of course not." Penny turned her entire focus on Azelie and gave her a very straight-faced lecture. "Honey, you don't *sleep* with musicians, you have *sex* with them."

China and Blanc both erupted into giggles. Half the customers in the coffee shop followed suit, although they tried to muffle their reactions.

Carlton threw his hands into the air. "That's it, Penny. I'm officially banning you from talking to Azelie. You've spent half your life corrupting the young."

China sobered quickly. "That's going *way* too far, Carlton, and you need to apologize."

"That's so true," Penny said. "I only managed to corrupt a few other girls, introducing them to a rollicking good time with the best lovers *ever*." She blew on the tips of her fingernails. "I like to think I've made women aware of the differences between bad sex, decent sex and fantastic sex. All women should know."

"There's no talking to you, Penny," Doug declared. He switched his gaze to Azelie, his features softening. "Half the things she says are pure bullshit designed to make our heads explode, Azelie. It gives her great joy to watch Carlton and me lose it over her nonsense."

"If you know I'm spewing nonsense," Penny challenged, "why does your head explode?"

Azelie thought that was a very good point. She was very aware everyone in the coffee shop was listening to the conversation. She was glad they were no longer discussing her date. She didn't want to answer questions about Andrii in front of everyone. She still feared there was a good chance word would get back to Billows and he'd find a way to harm Andrii.

She considered Billows' odd behavior at the club when he'd come in with his supermodel trophy displayed on his arm. When he'd come over to the table, he hadn't been looking at Azelie, he'd been looking at Lana. He'd all but ignored the fact that there was a man at the table. There didn't appear to be jealousy or anger toward Kasimir at all. When she went back over every detail, she realized he'd barely glanced at Azelie.

Carlton sighed very loudly. "Someone has to keep you in line, Penny. The statements you make have grown outrageous."

Penny's eyebrow shot up. "Now you're my keeper?"

Doug and Carlton exchanged another look. It was Doug who assented with a nod of his head. "Yes, Penny, we look after you, China and Blanc. Your antics could get you in trouble. You perform at that seedy little theater the three of you seem to love. It's not in the best part of town. You're attractive, funny and very vocal. It isn't like anyone could ignore your presence. Each of you lives alone, and if someone follows you home and breaks in, what then?"

The merry widows had mixed reactions to Doug's revealing statement. He sounded very matter-of-fact, but it was clear the two men knew the women's habits intimately.

"Do you follow us around?" Blanc asked. "Like stalkers?"

Azelie decided it was time to intervene before the merry widows worked themselves up. She leaned across the table toward Doug. "That's the sweetest thing I've ever heard." Smiling at the women, she indicated the two men. "It sounds like they're your personal bodyguards. Coming from their backgrounds, you three are so lucky to have them. And you don't even have to pay them."

The women closed their mouths on a protest, looking mollified. China was the first to recover. "Now that you put it that way, Azelie, you're right. We are lucky. Thank you, Doug. Carlton. It can't have been easy keeping track of us."

"You really were being sweet," Blanc added.

The door opened, bringing in a draft of cold air. Andrew McGrady waltzed in as if he owned the coffee shop. Azelie's heart dropped. They couldn't continue their conversation in front of him.

"Stop," she whispered. "Don't talk, not with him here."

Both Doug and Carlton had already noted him the moment McGrady opened the door. They seemed to always be on alert. The merry widows ceased their laughter, heads coming up, eyes following Billows' man's progress as he sauntered to the counter. The entire length of the room, McGrady kept his gaze fixed on the table where Azelie sat with her friends. He had the expression of the cat that ate the canary.

Azelie's first inclination was to get up and leave, hoping McGrady would follow her out. She bunched the straps of her backpack into her fist in preparation. McGrady pulled out his cell phone, held it up and began taking photos of the merry widows, Doug and Carlton and her together at their table. Her heart went into overdrive.

"I'll see you later," she told the others and dragged her backpack from the floor. If McGrady didn't follow her out, she could always return on the pretense she'd forgotten something. She was determined to have a few words with him one way or the other.

"Put that away," Doug snapped. "You have no right to take our pictures."

"Shut up, old man," McGrady ordered.

Azelie rose instantly when Doug and Carlton stood up. "Don't you dare talk to them like that."

McGrady's laughter was sneering, not at all humorous. He sounded as if he was deliberately goading the older men.

"You need to leave this establishment and not come back," Shaila declared.

Shaila's husband, David, came from the back room to stand beside his wife. He held a cell phone in his hand.

"I've got 911 on speed dial," he told McGrady. "If you don't leave, you'll have a police escort to help you off the property."

"You ban me from your coffee shop and when it mysteriously burns to the ground because you don't have protection, you'll know you caused it."

Azelie stormed up to him, snatching his phone from his hand while his attention was on the shop owners. She backed up several feet from him while she found his photos and quickly began to delete the pictures of the merry widows, Doug, Carlton and herself.

"You little bitch." McGrady crossed the distance in two long strides. He brought up his fist.

"Go ahead," she taunted, holding her own phone up. "I'm sending to Billows everything you're doing. You hit me and you know there's going to be hell to pay."

McGrady's face twisted into a maniacal mask. He couldn't seem to stop his aggressive behavior. At the last moment, he opened his fist, so it was his palm that hit her in the face.

"You dare threaten me? When Billows is tired of you, who do you think he's going to give you to? I'll remember this and treat you accordingly. I always have access to his women when I want them."

Everyone in the coffee shop stood up as Azelie reeled

backward. She might have gone down, but Doug caught her before she fell.

"I've called the police," David announced.

"Got it on video," several voices claimed. "We need to keep him here until the cops arrive."

"Try it," McGrady snarled, already moving quickly to exit the shop. He shoved Doug and Azelie out of his way as he stalked out.

Shaila handed Azelie an ice pack for her face. She took it absently as she watched McGrady get into his car. He stuck his hand out the window and flipped off the coffee shop.

"Shaila, he might really try to burn down your business," Carlton said. "He's a vindictive little bastard, if you pardon my language, ladies."

Azelie found herself shaking. She sent the video to Billows before she thought it through. Before she was too afraid to do so. **What does he mean?** she texted. The moment she hit send, she decided that might not have been the best idea. It would bring on a confrontation with Billows she wasn't ready for. But when would she ever be ready? She couldn't have McGrady threatening the merry widows or Doug and Carlton. She followed up with a text telling him the police had been called and she planned to press charges. Everyone in the shop was a witness to what McGrady had done, and she had no choice.

Billows texted back **WTF** but didn't answer what McGrady meant when he claimed Billows shared his women with McGrady. She thought that silence was significant. Billows had some kind of arrangement with McGrady. There was too much confidence in McGrady. He'd publicly struck her, knowing others were using their phones to record everything he said and did.

A chill went down her spine. Andrii had warned her that McGrady was vindictive. He'd told her the man had gone to prison on several occasions for domestic violence, yet he was always able to get out. To her, that meant Billows aided him. Billows had money and clout. He knew people. He paid people off. Cops, maybe even the district attorney. Not only had she put herself in harm's way with McGrady, but quite possibly with Billows as well.

She had no choice but to follow through and press charges against McGrady, however. Everyone in the coffee shop had witnessed what happened. McGrady was long gone, but Doug and Carlton had the license number of his car. The police would be able to find him quickly. She sighed. There was no going to her classes today. And she wasn't going to work, no matter how many times Billows called her.

More than anything, she knew she would have to face Andrii. He would most likely regard this as one royal "fuckup." It turned out to be a very long afternoon talking with law enforcement.

❦

Maestro had never been so terrified for another human being in his life. The moment he saw the security feed Code sent to him from the coffee shop, his heart nearly stopped and then went into overdrive. He had studied McGrady, the way he did every target. The man was unusually cruel and vicious to any woman in his life. It didn't matter if he dated them for a night or a month, the results were always the same. The woman ended up brutalized, often so badly she was hospitalized. He'd gone to prison a few times for domestic abuse, but he always seemed to get out. Clearly, Billows had political pull.

What the hell was Azelie thinking confronting the man? Calling the cops on him? Swearing out a complaint? He'd made it clear that they would take care of the man. Now, if McGrady turned up dead or just disappeared, as Azelie's man, Andrii would be considered a suspect. The police would want to interview him.

Swearing under his breath, he unlocked the door to Azelie's apartment and stormed inside. She sat in one of her comfortable chairs facing the entrance, clearly expecting him. He wasn't about to be moved by her tears. Ignoring the way his gut knotted at the sight of her looking so miserable, he stalked across the room to sink into the chair beside hers.

"Do you remember what I told you about fucking up?" he demanded.

He could barely look at her. She looked devastated. Totally shattered. He could see her distress wasn't about the day's events. Azelie looked up at him without flinching, but he could see that overwhelming emotion, the one that was so second nature to her. She'd disappointed him. Gone against the one thing that meant the most to him—keeping herself safe. She knew she'd screwed up, but even the threat of punishment didn't seem to be the defining criterion.

Andrii didn't want to read that look on her face or see the utter devastation in her eyes. He wanted to yank her across his knees and carry out the threat he'd professed he believed in to his brothers and sisters in the club. A physical punishment would impress the weight of the sin on his woman. She would be far more apt to remember never to do such a thing again.

"Yes." She whispered her answer, still looking straight at him. Not flinching.

Azelie had declared numerous times that she didn't go along with corporal punishment. She didn't believe it was right. She wasn't into pain. What had she said to him?

It would be hard enough knowing I disappointed you without you treating me like a child, incapable of making my own decisions.

He scrubbed his hand down his face. His hand shook. "You scared the holy hell out of me, Azelie. Don't like the feeling."

She pressed her lips together and brought her knees up, tucking her feet onto the cushion of the chair. Protecting herself. She thought he was going to yank her across his lap. Strangely, he'd lost all desire to punish her. That look she had on her face was testament to him that she knew she'd fucked up and she detested that she'd disappointed him, just as she'd told him would happen. He had no idea what to do or say.

"I'm sorry, Andrii. Really, really sorry. My temper got the best of me. Temper and fear for my friends. My brain short-circuited for a few minutes, and by the time I could think straight, it was too late."

"Has Billows reached out to you?" His tone was harsher than he intended, and she winced, but she didn't look away.

She shook her head. "I texted him at the time, demanding to know what some of the things McGrady said to me meant. He didn't answer me." She rubbed the pad of her finger across one eyebrow. "I'm terrified to see him. He knows I spoke with the cops. I really made a mess of things."

Maestro made up his mind. The team had decided they were going to raid Billows' building and look for any signs of abducted women. At the same time, they intended to interrogate Billows.

"You're going to stay home tonight and tomorrow. Not leave this apartment. And you're going to tell me where you keep the key to the underground rooms," Andrii declared. "I know you have one. You keep it in a charm that looks like an envelope. It's nowhere in this apartment."

There was silence. She remained huddled in the chair, knees drawn up protectively, her eyes large, watching his every move. He couldn't imagine what was going through her mind. Doubtless nothing good. He'd just made his demands and hadn't given her an explanation. His anger was still roiling in his belly, and he didn't know where to put it.

"Don't you fucking look at me like that. We're a team. You signed up for this shit when you took me on. Clearly, I signed up for a rough ride when you lose it and don't think about your safety. I need to know where the key is."

He didn't take his gaze from hers. He needed to see every expression crossing her face. Everything. Did she trust him? Was she going to give him what he needed even though she had to have a million legitimate questions?

She pressed her lips together and then they parted. He found himself holding his breath, waiting for condemnation.

"When I exit the club, there's a small knot that's hollow

in the hall panel just as you reach the door. I place it there. I don't want any reminders on me anywhere."

Her voice was very soft, but she didn't falter. She just gave him the information, no questions asked.

"You're to stay in this apartment for the rest of the night and all day tomorrow. Wait for me to come to you. I don't care if you have important classes. We'll find a way to make them up. Just be safe. Lock yourself in."

She nodded.

"I have to go, but I'll be coming back to you."

She nodded again.

Maestro stood, towering over her where she sat, knees drawn up, her blue eyes fixed on his face. "I'm coming back," he said again and leaned down to brush a kiss along her temple. He didn't dare do anything else. She looked forlorn. Abandoned. Frightened. He didn't have the time to reassure her. His team was going in for a rescue mission and to take Billows alive in order to interrogate him. It was extremely important for them to get the names of those higher up in the ring.

"Don't forget there are bombs under the floor," she murmured.

"I'm aware. I'll be safe. You don't forget that I'm in love with you. Stay safe."

He turned and left her there. His heart ached, but he did it. Time was a huge factor, and his brothers and sisters were waiting to make their raid.

EIGHTEEN

"We need to find McGrady," Maestro announced to the Torpedo Ink members gathered around the large table where they had carefully planned their mission. Steele was team leader, and he never left anything to chance. Not the slightest detail. They had plans for anything that could go wrong and then more plans just in case those steps went awry as well.

Code looked up from one of the seven screens set up in the room. "Billows had him picked up. The men who took him from his garage weren't very gentle either. I had his place wired, complete with cameras, and I could see very plainly he was in fear for his life. He stepped over a line, and Billows must have decided to take him out."

"Did you follow up on the car's route through traffic intersection cameras?" Steele asked. "I need to know McGrady's not going to be breathing down our necks."

"The car took him to the location I've indicated on this map." Code brought up the map on the largest screen hanging in the room. "We all agreed there had to be a way to bring the women to the training area that we were certain was located beneath the two clubs. Billows would never have been able to get away with trafficking for so long if he brought women in through the club. Someone would notice eventually."

Maestro could easily see the large red X Code had placed on the map. The road was narrow and unpaved, looking as if it was a part of a park or land reserved for a park.

"You believe there's another entrance to the underground rooms?" Steele asked Code.

"There would have to be. How could Azelie work for Billows for seven years and never see evidence of women coming and going if her boss moved them through the club?" Code said.

Maestro nodded. "I suspected as much when she told me about hearing the woman scream. Her boss wasn't in an office, she was certain of it, yet he appeared out of nowhere. How did he get down there without her being aware?"

"When Maestro told us Azelie's story, he mentioned then that there would have to be another entrance," Code explained. "Beneath the city, there's a maze of underground tunnels. It didn't surprise me to see Billows' men taking McGrady to a different location to enter his underground rooms. Suffice it to say, McGrady, if he's still alive, is in a holding room below the Adventure Club."

"Thanks, Code," Steele said. "We're going to run this mission by the numbers. Always be aware of the clock; time's moving fast on us. Billows normally shows up in the underground office around three-thirty or four A.M. Code, do you have eyes on him?"

Code nodded. "At the moment, he's at home with a very accommodating blonde. They never spend the night with him. He doesn't sleep with them. He has very rough sex with them and then sends them home."

"Let us know when he's on the move," Steele said. "We're on the clock. Let's move out."

The team was made up of eight members, plus Steele at the lead. Lana, Preacher, Keys, Maestro, Master, Player, Ink and Code trained consistently together. In this case, Savage and Destroyer from team one had joined them because they were the best at interrogation. It was imperative to get names from Billows to continue the quest to find those higher up in the trafficking ring.

They left their transportation a good block away, and, like wolves, the pack circled around the huge building to come at the entrances from several sides. They couldn't take the chance of guards getting behind them.

Cameras weren't normally a problem. Code identified each security camera's location, and he took over the cameras remotely. Code and his information were essential to both teams. He'd never let them down, not once, and Maestro knew the responsibility for the lives of his brothers and sisters weighed on him.

Each had a role to fulfill, and the lives of the others depended on them getting their job done. Lana was a marksman, rarely missing a shot. Maestro had never known her to fail in bringing down a target or protecting them from a distance. She was their eyes on scene, going high and establishing the best place to protect them from any hidden dangers.

Preacher moved around the building to find each security guard. He went to the left and Ink went to the right. If they encountered a guard, they killed him quietly and hid the body carefully so it wouldn't be easily found. There were four stationary guards and one roving. Neither had much time to take the guards out and hide the bodies. Fortunately, when they ran the plan repeatedly, they knew the position of the guards, even the roving one. They had established ahead of time where to hide each body. That was due to Steele's meticulous planning. When he ran a mission, no detail was too small, which was why their missions tended to run smoothly.

The most important guard was the one stationed at the entrance to the private hallway marked *For Employees Only*. If Billows came into the building via the clubs, he would use that route. A guard had to be present at that door, and one had to be sitting at the desk where Bobby Aspen usually was on duty. His replacement during the daylight hours was a man named Alex Right. It didn't matter which guard sat at the desk, he had to be replaced with a team member. Preacher had that role.

Once he disposed of the security guards outside the building, Ink would remain dressed as one of the outside guards on roving patrol. Preacher would take Bobby Aspen's place. He was adept at adapting his body image to appear however he needed to look. They had taken the precaution of making masks of both guards to be on the safe side.

As a precaution against being recognizable, every member wore a silicone mask. They were used to wearing them, changing their appearances and even their walks, with the roles they played, when necessary.

"Guard is down," Ink reported. "In place."

Preacher made his approach with Maestro toward the employees-only door. A guard stepped in front of the door, one hand on his gun, his chest out. He looked impressive, his features set in lines of command.

"You can't . . ."

Maestro threw his favorite small throwing knife with deadly accuracy. It didn't take a huge blade to kill a man. One needed to know precisely where on a body to hit, have the training and do so without hesitation. They were on him before his body went down. Maestro dragged him behind a wall of hydrangea bushes, concealing the body. Very little blood seeped down the neck to soak into the shirt and jacket.

Preacher wore a jacket with the security emblem on it in

preparation for his role. He removed the keys and small radio as well as a cell phone from the guard's pockets. Maestro opened the door and stepped inside as if he owned the place. The entrance was mostly dark, lit only by a single bulb. Much farther down the hall, he could see the desk was manned by Bobby Aspen.

Maestro stopped just inside the door to lay his hand on the wooden panels that made up the wall. Immediately, he felt the connection in the way he did, the gift he'd been born with. The knot was only inches from his fingers. He felt Azelie's presence strongly, as if she stood right there in that hall with him. The wood remembered her, felt her connection with it.

He found the necklace in the knot, scooping it out with one finger, his body covering the movement from Bobby. He suspected the guard's desk was too far away to see what he was doing. That was why Azelie had chosen—or been given—that particular spot to conceal her key. She was adept at putting it in the hole and retrieving it, which meant she'd practiced somewhere else until she was extremely fast at it.

"Who the hell are you?" Bobby demanded, belligerence in his voice. He stood, gun locked in his fist, aiming at Preacher.

Preacher kept walking toward him, a friendly smile on his face. "New security guard. Weird you didn't get the memo that I'd be introducing myself to you."

Preacher was nearly at the desk by the time Maestro had the key in his possession. Bobby's attention was centered solely on Preacher. It was clear he believed him to be the real threat. He thought Maestro was too far away, Preacher blocking any access to Bobby's body. Neither Preacher nor Maestro had a gun out.

"Stop right where you are. I need to see your ID and scan your prints. This is a restricted area," Bobby continued.

Maestro used Preacher's body as a shield, coming up behind his Torpedo Ink brother in a deliberately slow stalk.

Movement attracts attention. Preacher deliberately shuffled his feet, threw his hands up and out while he talked, spoke rapidly and interjected laughter into his monologue to keep Bobby off-balance.

"Isn't it just like Billows to forget to send an important memo? Guess if he loses one security guard, especially a new one, he won't lose any sleep over it." He laughed as if he'd told a huge joke.

Preacher no longer moved forward toward Bobby, but he was the epitome of a very young man with ADHD, unable to stay still. He threw his arms around and punched his fist into his palm and turned this way and that. Bobby's attention was riveted on him.

Maestro stepped around Preacher, putting him to the left side of Bobby. Almost simultaneously, he threw his favorite knife, the same one he'd retrieved from the outside guard. He didn't ever leave his weapons behind if it was at all possible to recover them. Bobby reeled back under the impact, gurgling and choking. One hand came up to his neck as if he didn't quite know what happened. The gun in his hand fell to the floor.

Preacher was on him, snapping Bobby's neck, not waiting for him to bleed out. With the ease of long practice, he dragged the dead guard into the darkest part of the hallway. Billows kept the hallway dimly lit so there would be no chance of an employee seeing where the door was seamlessly woven into the woodwork. Even knowing it was there, the members of Torpedo Ink would have had a difficult time finding it. Fortunately, Lana had counted the steps Azelie had taken from the guard desk to where the opening of the door was.

Maestro measured out the steps while Preacher dragged Bobby out of sight and retrieved Maestro's knife. Maestro placed his hand on the ornate wooden panel, feeling the instant connection. The lock was inches from his palm. He had Azelie's fingerprints on his fingers using silicone, and he mimicked the way she palmed the tiny chip. His hand was much larger than hers. It took a moment to get the chip centered before he placed his fingers carefully on the pad woven into the wood. In all the years they had run missions and encountered heavy security, he'd never seen such a clever device.

"Keys, I'm in," he announced. "Building's as secure as it's going to be."

"Right behind you," Keys assured him. He entered quickly, saluted Preacher, who had pulled on the silicone mask of Bobby's face and a ball cap and sank into the chair Bobby had vacated. He was their first line of defense so no one could come up behind Maestro and Keys as they descended into the lower floors.

Maestro waited for Keys, allowing him to go first. The stairway was narrow, lit only by LED lights. Before stepping onto each stair, Keys patiently crouched low and ran his palms just above the next stair down. Both were aware of time passing, but they didn't attempt to hurry the process. They knew how many stairs they had to descend to reach the floor where the offices and potential prison for the women were. Knowing there were bombs in the floor, both realized bombs could be placed beneath the stairs as well. It was entirely possible Billows activated the bombs when he wasn't there, but if he knew Azelie was coming, he'd have made certain there was no chance of them going off.

"Player said he'll have a main switch in the office he uses," Key said. "And he'll most likely always carry a manual switch on his person. When he's taken, we'll have to strip him to ensure he can't blow us all up."

Maestro wasn't worried about Billows' chances of killing them, not when Savage and Destroyer would be there to take care of the interrogation. No matter what self-preservation instincts Billows had, the two men were guaranteed to get around them. They'd been trained in every aspect of interrogation from the time they were young boys. Both had exceeded the expectations of every instructor.

Keys found four bombs beneath the floorboards in the

maze of seemingly dead-end hallways, but none of the four were live. They'd simply been placed there.

"While you find an entrance to the other rooms, I'll check Billows' office for a switch for the bombs and also to see if he has the same kind of chip to unlock the door in the wall."

That was the one thing Maestro was most worried about. If Billows had rested on his laurels and programmed the lock to be the same as the one for the door leading down to the underground floor, it was possible Azelie had access to every lock without realizing it. Billows had her so intimidated she hadn't tried to explore the environment. That was smart on her part. Billows had been lulled into a false sense of security by Azelie's compliance.

Maestro followed the same path Azelie had taken when she had tried to locate the woman screaming. She'd told him how the hallways narrowed and would dead-end straight into a wall. The floor was dimly lit with LED lights along the ceiling in places, but they hung down in a rope, causing shadows to move ominously. It was disorienting and gave off the illusion that the walls crept in, closing in on him as his hand whispered along the wood. It would be a terrifying experience for a young woman alone.

Torpedo Ink had a member, Player, who was a master of illusion. He could create entrances and exits or throw up false walls they could hide behind. The toll was tremendous on him for using that talent, but he'd developed it into a real weapon that had saved their lives on many occasions. Maestro wasn't thrown by illusions. He was good at telling the difference between reality and tricks.

The swaying ropes of light had been set up deliberately to give the illusion of the walls closing in on anyone walking around. It was a good trick and required a professional to manage it. Billows most likely had done it knowing Azelie worked in an office below the clubs. He didn't want her exploring. The illusion hadn't stopped Azelie when she believed another woman was hurt and needed help. Billows didn't know Azelie nearly as well as he thought he did.

The wood panel whispered to him as he made his way steadily toward the wall solidly in front of him. He felt Azelie's presence, although the incident had taken place months earlier. Her fear and determination were impressed into the grains in the wood. That made Maestro love her all the more. She'd been unwavering in her resolve to find the unknown woman even though she was terrified. Azelie was courageous, even if a little foolhardy.

He located the lock in the carvings along the wall. Keys came up behind him just as he was trying Azelie's chip and prints. He did so smoothly, as if just by believing, the chip would work—and it did. Billows hadn't gone to the trouble of removing Azelie's prints and key from the lock. He'd just used the same one.

"He has all this elaborate security, and yet he reused the same door lock," Keys muttered. "Sometimes people make no sense to me, Maestro. None at all."

"It goes with Billows' personality. He believes he's too intelligent for anyone to catch him. Ego tends to be the downfall of men like him. His device is so secret he doesn't need more than one."

The door opened silently. Maestro peered into the darkened corridor. This hall was much wider than the one they had followed to get to the door. Reluctantly, he stepped back to allow Keys to precede him.

We're in, he reported to Steele. They had the small radio earpieces in their ears, but because they had been unable to get audio when they were following Azelie's progress into the underground rooms, they thought it would be better to try to communicate using telepathy. Some were better at it than others, and distance could screw things up. The radios were for backup if telepathy didn't work.

Steele responded, *It's quiet out here so far, but clock is ticking.*

Maestro knew they were taking a little longer than antic-
ipated, searching for bombs beneath the floor and in the walls.
They couldn't afford to take any chances, especially if women
were being held captive.

The corridor had several doors leading to rooms. One
was slightly open. No light shone through and there was no
sound. Maestro stepped to one side and pushed the door
open another two inches with one finger. The scent of blood
hit him. He was very familiar with the smell. The fact that
there were no lights and there was the scent of blood didn't
have him jumping to the conclusion that the room was
empty. That kind of thinking only got a person dead. They
could have accidentally tripped a silent alarm they knew
nothing about.

He slid into the room without disturbing the door further.
It wasn't as easy as he would have liked. His chest slid across
the door frame, a whisper of sound, but that was enough to
get one killed. He had too much muscle for tight places. He
naturally put on muscle. That sounded good, but in his pro-
fession, it wasn't always a good thing.

"It's Andrew McGrady," he told Keys. "He died hard.
They didn't just execute him. Billows was pissed as hell over
the attention he brought to Azelie. He doesn't want the cops
anywhere near her."

Seeing McGrady's dead body worried him for Azelie's
safety. Billows easily could decide the job she did wasn't
worth the risk to him. She knew more about his finances than
anyone else. She had to know the names of his colleagues.
Torpedo Ink had already discussed the best way to go about
debriefing her, trying to learn other names that would lead
to the heads of the trafficking ring.

Steele, is Rock watching over Azelie? Rock—Fatei
Molchalin—hadn't gone to the same school as the founding
members of Torpedo Ink. He'd attended the school Gavriil
had gone to. He had come to Torpedo Ink as a prospect, willing to put in the time and effort so the members would know
he could be counted on. That he was loyal and always had

their backs. Once made a full-fledged member, he had continued to prove to them he believed in their causes. They had voted to take him along on team two, Steele's team. For now, they used him mainly as a guard. He hadn't trained with them, and when the members of the team worked, they were a smooth-oiled machine. Having anyone new could throw them off their game.

She's still in her apartment. No one has come near the building other than the normal tenants, Steele replied. *Rock won't let you down.*

Maestro knew he wouldn't, it was just that he would have preferred his woman to be in Caspar, at the clubhouse or at Czar's home, where she could be under guard, eyes on her directly, not just her apartment building. He'd prefer her to be anywhere but in San Francisco. Billows didn't know him or the members of Torpedo Ink. He had no idea they were hunting him. He did know Azelie. Billows had associates and men loyal to him. If he suspected he was in jeopardy, he would get rid of any threats to him.

Maestro continued down the hall, trailing his palm just above each door as they passed it. The rooms were empty until he came to the fifth door. He signaled to Keys, who was going down the hall checking the doors on the opposite side. Keys took his place in front of the door, lifting both palms toward the entrance. He had a gift for seeing through walls. Maybe not actually seeing, but he had developed senses, whether he saw heat imaging or just felt the presence of others. However that gift worked, he could tell how many enemies were in another room and their exact location. He hadn't failed since he'd become a teen.

Two women. Both are hurt. One's in the far right corner, on the floor. Man standing over her. His partner is shoving the other woman away from the first one. Second woman just went down in the middle of the floor. Her assailant is kicking her.

Maestro stood to one side of the door, while Keys was directly behind him. Keys tapped his shoulder and Maestro

opened the door, stepped to his right and shot the man standing over the woman in the far right corner. He fired one shot
straight to the middle of the forehead. Simultaneously, Keys
shot the man kicking the woman. Keys didn't miss when he
aimed at someone, and neither did Maestro.

Maestro held up his hand to the women on the floor. "Don't
scream. Need to know if there are more of you. More guards.
We've come to get you out of here."

The woman in the middle of the floor sat up, looked him
over carefully and then crawled across the room to put her
arms around the second victim. Keys ignored the torn clothing strewn around the room and handed her a shirt he'd
brought with him. "You have decent clothes somewhere?"

"In the holding rooms. They brought us here to have a
little private fun, they called it," the woman said, taking the
shirt. She began to put it on the woman crouched on the
floor. "Paula, it's okay. They aren't going to hurt us. I think
they're here to help."

"We're in a time crunch," Maestro said. "I don't want to
push you, but we need to get you somewhere safe. You both
need medical assistance." The one she called Paula looked
as if she'd been in a train wreck. Clearly, she was terrified
and nearly comatose. He'd seen that look hundreds of times
before. Human beings pushed beyond their minds' ability to
accept the trauma happening to them.

"I'm Cecily." She took Maestro's hand so he could assist
her to her feet. He wrapped her in a shirt he'd brought. They'd
learned victims often didn't have clothes. It was one of the
ways their captors stripped them of dignity and made them
feel vulnerable.

Maestro crouched down beside Paula. She looked young,
still in her teens. "I know this is difficult, Paula." Deliberately he called her by her name. "We're going to get you and
Cecily out of here. Can you walk? I'd carry you, but we have
to clear the rest of the rooms."

"Everyone else is down in the holding room," Cecily volunteered. "There's a tunnel. They brought us in through that

way. We've never been anywhere other than the room they hold us in, the training rooms and now here. This was the first time anyone took us here."

If Maestro had to guess, the two men assaulting the women had most likely been the ones to kill Andrew Mc-Grady. They were probably celebrating.

"How many other women?" Keys asked.

"Six," Cecily answered readily. "Paula, baby, we have to go. I'm right here. I'm not going to leave you."

"I'm putting my hands on you," Maestro said, "but only to help you get to your feet. Think about getting out of here." He sent up a silent prayer that whatever powers might be would give the girl the strength to tolerate his touch.

Paula's gaze clinging to Cecily, she let out a little sob as she gave a barely perceptible nod. Maestro didn't wait. He lifted the girl to her feet. She shuddered with pain and nearly collapsed. *Broken ribs for certain*, he informed Keys and included Steele. *This one can't be out of her teens and she's in bad shape.*

We have the hospital we use standing by. Clock is ticking, Steele reminded them. *Get them out of there before Billows makes his rounds.*

"We've got to go, ladies," Maestro said. He signaled to Keys to lead the way. He'd bring up the rear. Keys was the man who could see through walls. "Tell us where the opening to the tunnel is." He kept his voice soft and compelling.

Cecily wrapped her arm around Paula's back. "You have to go down to the very end of the hallway. There's a lock on the wooden panel." She looked and sounded alarmed. "They have a special way of opening the lock. They shut the door, so it automatically locked."

"We'll get through," Maestro assured her. "Keep moving."

The progress down the hall was excruciatingly slow. He wished he could carry Paula, knowing every step she took hurt like hell, but he needed his hands free.

"You're up," Keys said.

Maestro moved around the women to hover his palms an

inch from the paneling. The screams and cries of women mixed with male arousal and ugly visions drowned out the intricacies of the lock. He was going to have to touch the wood. His gut knotted at the necessary decision. He knew childhood memories would flood in, bursting open the doors he'd sealed shut in his mind. He clung to Azelie, using her as a buffer. The lightness of her. The sunshine in her. The joy she had for life and the people she surrounded herself with.

Despite the vicious, brutal memories locked in the grains and carvings of wood screaming at him, he was able to find the lock and open it with the same ease as he'd opened the previous one. After they went through, the door closed automatically behind them.

The tunnel was cold and drafty, the walls dirt and rock with only the occasional two-by-four to hold chicken wire that had been strung to keep the dirt from crumbling. The tunnel was a disaster waiting to happen. One good earthquake could easily collapse the roof, which was leaking and had roots hanging down like poisonous webs.

Maestro exchanged a look with Keys. They'd spent their childhood in just such an environment. Damp. Cold. Miserable. No clothes to help with warmth. Injuries were untreated until Steele, a very little boy, had shown signs of his tremendous talent and ability to soak up the knowledge in medical books they found in the mansion's library. Even then, they didn't have supplies unless they managed to crawl through the vents and steal them. These women had no chance of crawling through vents.

"How many guards?" Maestro whispered to Cecily.

"There were three that I observed when we were brought in. One at the door to the room we're locked in. One in the tunnel just down from the room. Not leading up here but leading to the outside entrance. And at least one guard is at the outside entrance. He seems to stay in the tunnel for shelter. At least, I caught glimpses of a couple of chairs just inside when we were being brought in."

Cecily was extraordinary. She had to have been scared. She was intelligent enough to know what was going to happen to her, but she kept her wits about her and observed as much as she could.

"Nice job, Cecily," Maestro praised. "The information you're giving to us will help."

"We're getting close. The first guard stationed in the tunnel might be able to see us."

"We've got you two, and they'll believe we're bringing you back."

Kill the lights in forty-five seconds. Maestro sent the instructions to Code. "Both of you keep your heads down. We can't afford the guard at the entrance to the tunnel to hear gunshots."

At least one guard just inside tunnel entrance. Come in from that side but be cautious. My source only saw the one when she was coming in.

Maestro took the lead. He was the best at throwing knives. Keys was good, but they would be without lights, and the first guard would have to go down while Maestro was moving on the second one.

As they rounded the bend, Maestro saw that two men were in the center of the corridor talking together. He quickened his pace, noting the position of each as he palmed his throwing knives. The lights flickered and went out. Instantly, without hesitation, he threw the knives, one after the other, the clear vision of his targets embedded in his brain. He sprinted forward, Keys with him as they reached the men, ensuring they were dead or dying, at least unable to draw a weapon. Fortune had favored Maestro in that the two men were facing each other, which made the artery he needed to sever an easy target. On the other hand, it was dark, and reaching the bodies before one of them had time to fire off a round if he was still able wasn't easy.

When he reached them, both men were slumped in the dirt. One was gasping for air and trying to stem the blood pouring between his fingers. The other stared up at Maestro with shock in his eyes. Keys removed their weapons, just to be safe. Maestro drew a third knife that had been resting in a scabbard between his shoulder blades. He drove it into the back of each of their skulls, severing the spinal cord.

"We need those women ready for transport to a medical facility, Cecily," he said as he and Keys dragged the bodies away from the door.

Lights, he ordered.

Code complied almost instantaneously.

Guard at entrance down. Bring them out, Steele said. *Player is shadowing Billows. He's on the move, heading this way. Savage and Destroyer are inside the building.*

"We've run out of time, ladies," Maestro said, making a show of looking at his watch. "Billows is on his way to the club. Does he always check in first thing?"

Cecily indicated the door. "Open it fast. It has one of those locks. And yes, he's the worst. You never know what you're going to get with him. He's been known to whip a woman nearly to death when he's crossed."

Maestro unlocked the door, allowing Cecily to rush inside, calling out to the women to hurry, that they were being rescued but they had to go *now*. The other women and girls were in various states of physical distress and injury. They helped one another out the door to stand in a semicircle around Maestro. The room was horrific—no toilets, no shower, just the way he'd been raised. The stench told him there were a couple of women with infected wounds. That was another thing he was well versed in.

"I'm carrying you," he informed Paula. "Cecily will walk right beside us, but we have to hurry. We have medics waiting to help. You'll be taken to a safe house. At that time, the cops will be involved. We prefer you don't talk to them about us. No descriptions; simply say we wore masks." The women would never know they were already wearing masks. If someone did eventually talk, the descriptions would never match a single member of Torpedo Ink.

Maestro was as careful as possible when he lifted Paula into his arms. She gasped and jammed her fist into her mouth. "Sorry," he whispered. He hoped Billows died hard.

Several members of Torpedo Ink met them in the tunnel to aid the women with the worst injuries. They had long shirts to cover them so when they emerged from the tunnel and got into the two vans waiting for them, they wouldn't feel quite so vulnerable.

Billows pulled into the club parking lot, Player announced.

Maestro lifted a hand toward Cecily. Then he turned and jogged back through the tunnel, racing through the maze of corridors to get upstairs before Billows entered the building. Ink's disguise as the outside guard hopefully would pass muster. Billows, as a rule, didn't speak with his guards often.

He's coming up the walkway toward the door, Ink announced.

I have him in my sights, Lana confirmed. *You're covered, Ink. Unless I miss.*

Very funny, Steele said.

Maestro managed to make it up the stairs and took up a position deep in the shadows behind the guard's desk, where Preacher sat looking bored.

I dropped my cell and had to fish it out of the brush so he couldn't see me clearly, Ink reported. *He's going in. Savage and Destroyer are waiting for the door to be opened.*

Billows strode straight up to the desk. "You're looking lazy tonight, Bobby," he greeted.

Preacher stretched his arms out and deliberately yawned.

Billows grinned. "You need to visit the rooms downstairs more. You won't be so bored."

Preacher gave him the thumbs-up and then fished for his cell as if he had a call. Billows stepped around the desk, heading toward the concealed lock on the door. Maestro waited for him to open the door before he was on him. The blow to the head stunned Billows. Maestro flung him to the floor facedown, half in and half out of the doorway. He and

Preacher searched him after they restrained his arms and legs, tying him as if he were a steer at a rodeo. They removed the switch for the bombs, along with his cell phone and three guns.

Savage and Destroyer entered and followed Maestro and Preacher, who were dragging Billows not-so-gently down the stairs. The entire way, Billows threatened them, mainly concentrating on Preacher, still believing him to be Bobby.

It took less than an hour for them to get the information they needed before they killed Billows. They left the body in the room where his men had tortured and killed Mc-Grady. As usual after a successful mission, they all met back at the Airbnb they had rented to go over every move they'd made. It was considered necessary to spot any flaws in the planning. Thirty minutes into the debriefing, Maestro glanced down at his vibrating phone. **911.** That was all, but it came from Azelie's number.

His heart climbed into his throat. "Is Fatei with Zelie?"

"We pulled him off when we took Billows," Steele answered, looking up from the videos they were going through. They always went over a mission while it was fresh in their minds. "He's headed back to Caspar."

Maestro's throat got tight. His phone rang. Doug Parsons calling. "Don't have time, Doug," he barked.

"Billows dragged Azelie from her apartment and took her away in a black SUV. Carlton and I are following. The widows insisted on coming along."

"That can't be. Billows is gone."

"I'm looking right at him. I wasn't the only witness. Several people from her apartment building saw him take her."

"Doug says Billows has Azelie," Maestro reported to the others. "He's following the SUV right now."

Every head snapped up, and all eyes were instantly on him. Code sank into a chair in front of one of his screens. "Tell me streets so I can pick them up."

"Billows is dead," Savage assured everyone in the room.

He looked at Destroyer for confirmation. "We fucking killed the bastard."

"Put him out of his misery after he finally gave up a few names and where to locate them. Once he started talking, he couldn't say enough," Destroyer added.

"Someone who looks a hell of a lot like Billows just took her," Maestro declared. "Doug, we need that information now."

NINETEEN

Azelie knew she was in trouble. Real trouble. Alan Billows was smoldering with fury. He'd burst into her apartment, strode across the small space and punched her right in the face before she could even speak. Her cheekbone felt as if it had exploded. She had the presence of mind to hang on to her phone as she went down. He kicked her twice in the thigh, deadening her leg, but she managed to get a short message to Andrii, hoping he understood her 911. Billows ripped the phone from her hand and flung it across the room before dragging her up by her hair.

To her absolute horror, when he pulled her down the stairs to the street, he pressed a gun to her neck. Instantly, memories of bullets tearing into her sister, niece and nephew flooded her mind. She could feel the shock and pain of the three bullets smashing into her chest all over again. The memories were vivid. Terrifying.

Azelie was certain Billows was so incredibly angry that he would pull the trigger before he told her what was happening. She sent up a silent prayer that Andrii was safe. He shoved her into a black SUV and climbed into the back seat after her. The driver turned his head, and to her horror, there was a second Billows at the wheel. Twins.

She pressed her lips together to keep from saying a word. That there were two of them certainly explained the mood swings and personality changes. It was no wonder she could never figure Billows out completely.

"Who did you give your key to?" Billows roared the question in her ear, his fingers biting into her arms as he shook her.

The driver floored the vehicle, muttering a curse under his breath. "Several of the people from the apartment saw you put her in the car, Derrick."

"I don't give a rat's ass who saw me," Derrick Billows snapped, giving her another shake. "There was no other way for anyone to get into the maze or tunnels. It had to be her, Patrick."

Patrick? For a moment she couldn't think, and then it hit her. Alan had distinctive personalities. She'd even considered the possibility of him having some disorder.

"Where's Alan?" She sounded like a forlorn frog croaking.

Derrick shook her again, this time hard enough that her head hurt. "Not here. Dead, you bitch. As if you didn't know."

She gasped in alarm. Triplets. Three, not two. Why hadn't she figured that out? Alan hadn't known how much money she made. He kept acting as if they were going to be a couple. He treated her differently than either Patrick or Derrick. Clearly, Derrick didn't have social skills and didn't want to have them. He was vicious and cruel, most likely the one she'd observed being abrupt and rude to his employees. Patrick had to be the charming one, who went out on dates with known celebrities and influential politicians. He enjoyed mingling with those in positions of power. Each of the triplets had played a role in their rise in money and influence.

"Alan's dead?" she echoed. Derrick would never believe her, but she had a slight chance with Patrick. "But he . . .

we . . ." She trailed off and pressed her fingertips to her mouth. She didn't have to fake fear or the tears in her eyes. She didn't want to appear defiant, but rather as if the news had crushed her.

Patrick glanced at her through the rearview mirror. "How did someone get your key, Azelie?"

She shook her head, allowing tears to track down her face. "I always put it in the same spot, that tiny knot in the wooden panel. I've never carried it out of the building. Not once. I thought it was safe with Bobby and whoever the security guard is in front of the door." She sobbed again and ducked her head. "It doesn't make sense that someone would know where my key was hidden. Alan is the only one who knew."

"We knew," Patrick declared. "I personally showed the knot to you."

"You're right, you little slut. No one else knew, but they used your key to get in," Derrick snapped. His fingers were vicious, biting into her arm. She would worry about bruises later; right now she had to think about how she was going to stay alive.

"How do you know Alan's dead?" she whispered. "Maybe he's not. Maybe he's at home." Her voice shook naturally from fear and stress. The hope she poured into it was acting. She knew Alan had to be dead for his brothers to act the way they were. They had to have seen him. Did that mean Andrii had killed him? Were they aware of Andrii? She was certain they were going to kill her. She might have had a chance with Patrick but not with Derrick. He was still in a killing rage.

"We saw his body and what those fuckers did to him before he died," Derrick snarled. "If you had anything to do with this, every single thing done to him I'm going to do to you. I know ways to keep you alive even when you're begging for death."

"Why would I want Alan dead?" That seemed like a fair enough question. "None of this makes any sense." She wailed the last, sounding scared and bereft.

"You tell me why you would want my brother dead," Derrick demanded. "He was pissed as hell on your behalf when you went running to him about not getting enough money. Every chance he got he stood up for you, but you turned on him. Was it because you saw Patrick at the club, and he was with someone else? You got jealous and had him killed?"

"You're absolutely crazy to think that," she whispered. "Insane."

Derrick slapped her right on the same cheek where he'd punched her earlier. Her face felt like it had exploded. She didn't make a sound. Even her tears stopped. She might know it was prudent to be scared and give them anything they wanted—as long as it wasn't Andrii—but all Derrick was doing was making her want to fight back.

"Derrick." Patrick's tone was cautionary. Reasonable. "We're coming up on the club. I've beefed up security on the outside and closed both Pleasure Train and Adventure for the rest of the week. We need to find out who our enemies are and take them out before we reopen. No one else has been down in the offices."

The fact that Patrick used the term *offices* gave her a tiny bit of hope. He was still trying to act as if things were more normal than they were.

"We know someone stole our money. *She* does the books," Derrick said, but he sounded less threatening.

"We can talk about that when we're inside," Patrick said. He drove the SUV up close to the private employee entrance.

When Derrick hauled her none too gently out of the vehicle, she caught sight of three guards in uniform as the two Billows men took her straight up to the door and unlocked it. Derrick slammed it closed on the startled faces of the guards and went straight to the knot where her key should have been. It wasn't there.

"They may have to disappear," Derrick announced as he shoved Azelie down the hall toward the door leading down to the offices.

He said it so casually she realized that for Derrick, making people disappear was commonplace. It also meant that those three guards had seen her with Derrick and Patrick. They would remember if she disappeared and the cops went looking for her. His statement made her believe they were going to kill her; otherwise why threaten perfectly innocent security guards? Also, the fingers surrounding her bicep were biting into her flesh viciously. Derrick was deliberately inflicting pain.

Azelie refused to give Derrick the satisfaction of her crying out in pain, nor did she try to fight as they took her down the stairs to the rooms below. Instead of taking her into her appointed office, they hurried her along the same corridor she had taken to try to find the woman screaming out in agony so many months earlier. She thought about the woman now. Which of the triplets had come out to confront her? Someone, maybe all of them, had been with that woman, and they'd hurt her. Maybe killed her. She felt terrible that she'd let that woman down.

Derrick opened the lock in the wooden panel and marched her down the corridor until they came to a room with an open door. She smelled blood. He shoved her inside and snapped on a bright overhead light. The bodies of two men lay like broken life-sized dolls in one corner. Close to the center of the room, Bobby Aspen lay next to Andrew McGrady. McGrady had clearly been tortured before he died, while the two men in the corner and Bobby appeared to have been killed quickly.

Derrick gripped her arm and forced her forward, stepping right into blood on the floor. Blood and fingers. Her stomach lurched as he stopped, looming over the body in the center of the room. Alan Billows had been tortured too, but what he'd gone through looked to be far worse than what McGrady had been put through. It was Billows' fingers strewn all over the floor. Whoever had tortured Billows knew what they were doing. She tried to drown out Andrii's voice telling her he was a trained assassin. He had learned how to take people apart at an early age. She found herself praying Andrii hadn't been the one to do this horrible, cruel thing to Billows.

"I'm going to be sick," she whispered.

"Be as sick as you want." Derrick was entirely unsympathetic.

Azelie didn't blame him. The man, who looked as if he'd been carved up like a turkey, was nearly unrecognizable, and he was their brother. She was positive they would kill her now. How could they not? She would want to kill someone who did that to someone she loved. She had to brace herself for what would come next. No matter what they did, she could never reveal her connection to Andrii.

There was a very uncomfortable chair bolted to the floor in the center of the room, just behind Alan's body. It appeared as if he'd been in that chair when he was tortured. There was blood and what looked suspiciously like urine on and below it. Fingers were strewn on the floor around it.

Azelie tried to hold her breath so she wouldn't take in the horrendous stench. Derrick shoved her toward the chair, and for the first time she couldn't overcome her panic and horror. She struggled against him. There was nowhere to go, no possible way to run, but her fight instincts kicked in and she couldn't stop the hysteria welling up.

Derrick backhanded her, punched her stomach to double her over and slammed her into the chair. Azelie froze when her bottom landed on the seat, which was covered in the blood and urine of a dead man. Her stomach lurched again, protesting the smells and the vicious punch. She leaned over the steel arm of the chair and vomited.

Derrick swore and stepped back, but Patrick went to the sink, wet a cloth and brought it to her. He wiped her face with surprising gentleness.

"Derrick, cool off. We have no idea if Azelie is involved. It could be that someone took advantage of her. That man at the club, the one with your friend, do you go out with him?"

"No. I met him for the first time that night. He's Lana's

brother. The only thing I know about him is that he works as a bartender. I don't even know where."

"How do you know Lana?"

"From school. She goes to the college and takes fashion design. We ride the bus together sometimes to get to the school. I had no idea her brother would be at the club, but she told me he's older than she is and is protective of her."

"What about your good friend Bradley Tudor? Could he have found out about the key?"

She realized everyone she knew was going to be in trouble. The merry widows, Doug and Carlton, Shaila and David, maybe even Abigail Humphrey and her little three-year-old daughter, Betsy. All because she worked for Billows.

"He doesn't even know where I work. I babysit his kids when his regular babysitter has appointments or is ill. Otherwise, we don't really associate at all."

The surveillance Alan had put on her in the form of Mc-Grady would bear that out. He had to have reported to the Billows brothers. All of them. He might not have known there was more than one, but surely over the time he watched her, more than Alan had gotten a report.

Derrick pushed forward. "This is bullshit, Patrick. She knows more than she's saying. Don't fall for her sweet little innocent act the way Alan did. Look at him, his guts spilling out of his body. He didn't deserve that."

He stepped around his brother and hit her in the face again, the same cheek, this time splitting open the skin. He punched her breast hard. There was no way to stop the cry of pain as agony exploded through her body.

"Talk, you little bitch. You have no idea what's coming."

She could barely see him through the veil of tears, but it was just as well. What she did see appeared to be his features twisted into a demonic mask. That added to her mounting terror. She was going to die a terrible death. She prayed she would just become unconscious and they would kill her outright.

"Derrick." Patrick sounded like the voice of reason. "Back

off. We were getting somewhere, weren't we, Azelie? You want to tell us the truth. You cared a great deal for Alan. Anyone could see it. He was always loyal to you, trying to make certain you were safe. He was so enraged when he found out McGrady hit you. And threatened you." He gestured toward McGrady's body. "That was done for you. Because McGrady dared to strike you."

It hadn't been Andrii who had done those terrible things to McGrady. Could she honestly say she was sorry McGrady was dead? No. He'd threatened the merry widows and Doug and Carlton. He'd threatened her. But did she want him to die in such a hideous way? No.

A small sob escaped before she could stop it. Her gaze clung to Patrick's. She knew what the brothers were doing. One was good, the other bad. They would play her like this, one giving hope, the other taking it away. She reminded herself over and over, a chant in her mind, not to believe in Patrick. He had no intention of saving her.

"You knew someone stole from us." Patrick made it a statement, switching subjects. "Alan said you believed it was an elite hacker, someone who may have been hired to harm us. He said you were still going through the books looking for a lead. Did you find one?"

Her mind was in complete chaos from sheer terror. If she was going to stall in the hopes of being rescued, although she had no idea how she would be rescued or who would rescue her, she had to pull herself together. Her body was almost numb from the blows Derrick had delivered. She realized he could have hit her a lot harder. He knew where to strike her to scare her, humiliate her and cause pain without damaging her. That only reinforced the possibility Andrii had raised that they were involved in human trafficking.

She took a deep breath, but that only dragged the stench into her lungs. She felt like her entire body was covered in blood, sweat and urine from the dead in the room. Now that coating was inside of her, where she would never get it out.

"I was still searching." Was that even her voice? "You

have a lot of business associates. Alan was going through them with me to tell me which were the most likely to be able to hire that kind of hacker. It would take a lot of money. I don't know any of his—your—associates personally. Alan didn't want me around them."

"But you did meet a few," Patrick persisted. "Derrick brought them into your office."

It made sense that it had been Derrick, not Alan, who had allowed the men into her office. Alan had always been adamant that she stay out of sight. It hadn't made sense to her at the time. Now she could see Derrick doing it, mostly as a silent threat.

Her biggest fear was that she would inadvertently blurt out Andrii's name if she became too disoriented. He would come for her. She knew he would. He would have no idea that Alan was one of triplets or that his brothers were even more vicious and cruel than he had been. Andrii believed himself capable of handling men like the Billows triplets, but he didn't have all the facts. She didn't want him to come, as much as she needed to believe he would.

Now she was even more afraid for Andrii. He would come, and she didn't want him to. She prayed he wouldn't find a way in. These vicious men would kill him for certain.

━━━━━━

"We run this by the numbers, like any other rescue mission," Steele said before Maestro could leap from the truck.

"Then fuckin' get the numbers down," Maestro said. Code had provided them with feed from the cameras he'd tapped into. "She's a mess. You know they're going to kill her."

He glanced at Savage and Destroyer. Killing wasn't the worst that was going to happen to her. The blows she'd been receiving were nothing compared to what was coming. Derrick would inflict more pain and damage, and Patrick would act as if he were trying to calm his brother. It was a method used often in the trafficking business to force their victims into cooperation. It was possible they would even use drugs on Azelie.

"The guards outside the club must be taken out. Code said they were hired from a private security company, which means they aren't part of the Billows' business. Some may be, but you can't take the chance. That means put them out, but no kills unless you have no choice."

Maestro's hand tightened on the door handle. "We know the rules of engagement. Every second we're waiting is time they have with her."

Steele ignored him. It was stating the obvious, and Maestro knew it wasn't Steele's fault. He was team leader and responsible for the safety of every member of his team. Steele had felt the same anxiety when his son had been kidnapped. Steele was right: they had to keep the team safe, or they wouldn't be any good to Azelie.

"Sorry, Steele." He rubbed his chest, over his heart. "We're coming, sweetheart. Have faith that we're coming for you," he added, murmuring aloud.

"Code says she hasn't so much as whispered your name, Andrii," Lana said. "She's going to protect you. She was dismissive of Preacher as well, as if he couldn't possibly have anything to do with this."

"She knows what's coming, and she still won't give you up," Savage said. He looked over Maestro's shoulder to the quick sketches Steele had thrown up on the screen, giving them their assignments.

"What are we going to do about Doug, Carlton and the widows?" Keys asked. "They're in the way, and they aren't about to leave without seeing that Azelie is safe."

"Let them distract the guards," Maestro suggested. "Those three women can talk the ears off of anyone. They can be an asset if they're told what to do to keep safe."

"I'm on it," Lana said. "They've seen me."

"Need you protecting our people," Steele reminded her.

"It won't take but a moment," Lana assured him. "Give me three minutes with them and then I'll go high."

"Grateful, Lana," Maestro said. "Those five are her family, or as close as she's got. They matter to her."

"Parsons and Gray were a big deal in the military," Code said. "I could hack into their records, but most of it will be redacted. Even so, I don't need to see the records to be aware they know what they're doing. They might have gotten old, but don't discount them. They can be lethal. Penny is the daughter of a cop. After he died, she spent years on the shooting range at her mother's insistence. The other two, the Christian sisters, lived with them. I'll bet both have concealed carry permits. I haven't checked, but I wouldn't be surprised."

"Let's do this," Steele said. "Be safe, but you bring her back to us. We don't need information from either of those men. Get in, take them out, and get Azelie out of there. Be mindful that either or both of those men could have a manual switch to the bombs. We haven't pulled the plug on them yet. I figured it would be better for the cops to find everything intact."

Maestro flung the door open and leapt out, ducking as he ran toward the tunnel entrance. Keys, Master and Player were right there with him, spreading out, running the way they had on so many missions. Reminiscent of a wolf pack. That was Czar's teaching. He'd taught them to be wolves, to work together to bring down prey.

They made no sound as they moved through the grass, brush and rocks toward the tunnel entrance. Maestro was lead. Two guards were stationed on either side of the entrance. Neither wore the security company jackets with the logo that would have told him they were recently hired. The Billows brothers hadn't taken any chances with their tunnel. They were using their own men to guard it.

Two guards outside, and they're on full alert. They're not rentals, he warned the others.

Keys, get close enough when the guards are taken down to vet the tunnel entrance inside, Steele cautioned.

Maestro detested that Keys would be in harm's way. As

an asset, he was worth his weight in gold. But he was also Maestro's closest brother.

Maestro went down onto his belly and dug his elbows and toes into the ground to propel himself forward, staying low as he stalked his prey through the brush. He'd learned the maneuver from his childhood, when it was always life or death if there was a whisper of sound. A grass blade moving or a rock disturbed could earn a vicious beating with a whip, not just for him, but for the other members of his team. As children without medical aid and living in dirty conditions with rats and insects, always cold, the more they had open wounds, the more likely it was that someone would die. Maestro, like his other team members, had learned to move through the brush without detection.

He used the stalk of a leopard, moving and then freezing if his prey had looked toward him. The guard was a fairly large man, bulky in his oversized jacket. He carried a semi-automatic and had extra magazines strapped to his waist. A knife hung from his belt, blatantly large, the blade slightly curved. It was clear he meant business. He didn't smoke or pull out his phone. He was very much on alert.

"All clear, Dwayne," he reported to someone.

Someone has surveillance on these guards, Maestro said. *Ink, we need eyes in the sky.* He was frustrated that he couldn't just take the guard out. He was only a few feet from him, but someone was watching over them. The moment he killed the first guard, the Billows brothers would be alerted, as would any other guards on the property.

"Check in with Bam-Bam, Conway," came the terse reply.

Ink was their go-to man if they needed aid from birds or other animals. He had a way of connecting with them that, again, like Keys' talent, Maestro had no understanding of how it worked. But his gift was valuable and had saved them many times as children. He'd been instrumental in shielding Steele's young son, Zane, during their rescue of the child.

The flutter of wings heralded an owl swooping low, skimming along the grass, talons stretched toward the earth. The bird seemed to come out of nowhere and was large, like most of the great horned owls. With its four-and-a-half-foot wing-span and the shape of its wings and softly fringed feathers, the bird could fly in near silence. This great horned owl was gray and white in coloring, making it appear to materialize out of the San Francisco fog, looking for all the world like an apparition. With the large tufts on its head resembling horns, round yellow eyes and wicked beak, the predator was unnerving.

The owl streaked, talons outstretched, looking to lock on to prey hidden in the grass close to Conway's feet. Conway swore, stumbling back as the owl pulled up and seemed to fade into the fog.

"Did you see that?" The guard sounded shaken.

"Yeah, what the hell just happened?" Dwayne demanded.

The team leader is sitting in the oak tree, the tallest one, with the bent, twisted branches, Ink reported.

I'm on it, Preacher said. *Give me a couple of minutes*.

"Did you see that owl, Bam-Bam?" Conway asked, apparently shaken. He rubbed one hand up and down his thigh. "I nearly pissed myself."

The second guard, pacing just outside the entrance, gave a sneering laugh. "You sound like a girl, Conway."

Conway swore at Bam-Bam but then laughed. "I wish I had my phone out and got a picture of it coming out of the fog."

Dwayne is down, Preacher advised. *You're clear to go*.

Maestro didn't wait. *On three*. He didn't have to look. He knew Keys was in position. They'd run this particular drill hundreds of times. He rose up, slashing with his knife, severing the arteries in the thighs, groin and under the arms in less than a second, slamming one hand over Conway's mouth to prevent him from crying out. Maestro lowered him to the ground, stripping away the gun. Keys had mirrored his actions with Bam-Bam and was already hurrying away from the body to approach the actual entrance to the tunnel.

Maestro covered him as Keys ducked inside the darkened passageway and approached the door that had been built to block entry. Keys held up his hand and then held up two fingers.

Two just inside, but I feel the presence of more. We're going to have to take them down fast, so the others hidden along the corridor won't be alerted.

Maestro swore under his breath. It stood to reason that the Billows brothers had secreted their own men inside the tunnel rather than have them patrolling the grounds of the club. The rented security was for show only and to create a distraction if any rescue party showed up.

The second we go through that door, we'll have to kill them both, Maestro said. *Give me the exact position of both men. They can't have time to get a warning off.*

Keys stood in silence for what seemed an eternity to Maestro before finally nodding. *One is taller than the other by quite a bit. He's on the left side of the corridor leaning against the wall. His back is to us. The other is sitting, but I can tell he's very slight. His chair has been turned partially toward the other man. The one sitting is older, and he keeps moving like his hip hurts. He's the one I'm worried about. If he moves when we go through the door, you're going to miss.*

I won't miss. Azelie's life depends on a clean throw. Maestro was confident because he had to be. This would be the most important throw of his life. He had to make that blade fly true. There was no room for error. He had no doubt that if Billows was sent an alarm, he would kill Azelie. *Give me the exact coordinates again. Once I have them, we go in fast. No hesitation.* He couldn't afford for his target to shift positions.

Keys waited, hands toward the door, and then he told Maestro exactly at what angle the guard was leaning. Maestro had already unlocked the door in preparation. He shoved inside and threw three knives in rapid succession. Simultaneously, Keys rolled into the tunnel to come up directly behind the taller guard. He slammed his blade hard into the back of the guard's neck, severing the spinal cord.

Maestro followed his knives to his target to ensure the man was dead. He was gone, his eyes wide open. Maestro retrieved his blades, wiping the blood on the guard's clothing. Keys was already moving down the tunnel at a rapid pace but stopping at each door along the way, checking either side. They were halfway to the room where McGrady had died when Keys signaled that the rooms on either side of the corridor were occupied.

Another delay. Another possible alarm for Billows. Maestro shared a long look with Keys. He indicated the door on the left side of the hall. He held up three fingers, bent down and drew stick figures in the dirt, marking the position of all three precisely. He drew them in chairs seated around a small table.

Cards. He circled one of the chairs and the stick figure. *I'll take this one. You take the one on the end. We'll both go for the guy in the middle.*

Three. That would take precision kills. Maestro's target was the farthest from the door, but he had skills when it came to throwing a knife. He planned out his attack, going through the moves in his mind. It was imperative to take out his first target immediately and hit the second one before he could react. He had to be fast. Very fast. There were men in the room directly across the hall. There couldn't be a sound, certainly not a gunshot. That meant the men at the card table had to die before they were aware they were under attack.

Once more, Maestro went over each move in his mind before he signaled to Keys it was a go. It was Keys who shoved the door open, giving Maestro the momentum of his throw. The easiest and best results when throwing a knife came from being square with your target, stationary, feet planted, shoulders pointed toward the target, elbows tucked and wrist locked. Follow-through was extremely important.

Maestro had practiced thousands of hours, throwing on the run. Each step was calculated, his feet squaring his shoulders in the perfect placement to his target. He had force behind his throw, so the blade penetrated the neck, slicing through the artery. He was throwing the second knife before the first had struck his target. He hadn't dared to slow down; he had to reach his prey before either could recover from their shock enough to attempt to raise a gun or shout for help.

Normally, if the carotid artery was severed, it would take only five to fifteen seconds for death to occur. It was the one target Maestro practiced nearly daily to hit with efficiency. The artery was only one and a half inches below the skin. He didn't have to carry huge knives to get the job done. He simply had to be accurate and extremely fast.

Keys had taken his man out as well, and the two of them left the dead behind, closing the door after themselves. Keys immediately went to the door across the hall, holding his palms close to the wood and dirt.

Code fed them information. *I had to dig deep to find evidence of triplets. They weren't born in the United States. Their parents were from here, but their mother went to Haiti to have them. She left their father and joined a cult, very enamored with the leader of the new religion. Her husband fought for the children, but he had ties to the local Mafia, and she claimed he beat her. She stayed in Haiti with the cult leader, a man who called himself Seradieu, which means "will be God."*

You can guess how those kids were treated, and the mother allowed it. She died under suspicious circumstances, and they came back to live with their father. That's how they got into this business they're in. By the time they came to the States, they were in their teens and already pretending to be one person. Their father left his estate to Alan Billows, his only son. He went along with their deception.

Keys held up his two fingers. Again, he drew stick figures in the dirt, positioning them exactly.

Maestro didn't care about the information Code had given him on the Billows brothers. He didn't need to know what had made them into monsters, he only knew they were monsters.

Every member of Torpedo Ink had been tortured, had had
family members murdered, had been subjected to physical,
emotional, mental and sexual abuse. They didn't traffic
other human beings for money. They didn't harm children.
They were men and women who could shut off emotions
and kill, but they didn't kill indiscriminately. They had a
code and they stuck to it. What Maestro cared about was
getting to his woman and freeing her from monsters.

Two men were quite a bit easier to take down than three,
but there could be no misses, no warning shots.

Get a move on. Code's voice was tight. *Derrick Billows
is getting seriously ugly with Azelie. She isn't giving you up,
Maestro. She didn't even throw Preacher or Widow under
the bus. She's taking everything they're dishing out and
looking innocent as hell. I'd believe her.*

Maestro didn't give a rat's ass if the world believed her.
The Billows brothers weren't going to stop torturing her until she was dead. They had to kill her. They could never trust
that she wouldn't turn on them, not after the things they
were doing to her.

He signaled Keys, pushed open the door and threw his
knives, a quick one-two, killing both men before Keys could
get into the room. He retrieved his knives, made certain both
men were dead and hurried out, closing the door behind him.

Go, Keys, fast.

*You go ahead of me, and I'll check the doors leading to
the room where she is*, Keys said.

I'm in, coming up behind you, Player said. *I'll back up
Keys. You go, Maestro.*

The fact that Steele had changed the plan meant the situation was dire. Maestro sprinted through the tunnel, not making noise, but only because it had been ingrained in him not
to. He trusted Keys and Player to have his back.

The door to the room where McGrady had been killed
and Alan Billows interrogated was cracked open. He could
hear the agony in Azelie's voice as she tried to answer multiple questions Derrick shouted at her. Patrick's voice was

more calming, encouraging her to answer. He knew Azelie. She wasn't thinking about answers to their questions. Uppermost in her mind was protecting the people she loved. He was one of those people.

Derrick made it impossible for her to answer. His purpose was to terrorize her, and he was doing so in a vicious, cruel way. The man had a knife in his fist, and the blade was bloody. Maestro didn't make the mistake of looking at Azelie to assess the damage. There were two men assaulting her, and both were dangerous. Both were close to her. She couldn't dive out of the chair, even if he shouted to her. Her wrists were zip-tied to the arms of the chair. There were blood and fingers on the floor around the chair. His heart dropped.

He pulled a gun from his belt and took aim at Derrick, going through the second shot to Patrick over and over in his mind until he could will the bullet to hit exactly where he needed it to. Both men were likely to have a manual switch to activate the bombs and blow up the building. They'd do so without hesitation if they knew they were dying.

He moved to the right of the door to keep Azelie from the line of fire, squeezed the trigger and shifted aim to Patrick, firing a second bullet. He followed the shots with two more to ensure both men were dead. As he fired the second rounds, he sprinted across the room to Azelie.

He wouldn't have recognized her swollen, bruised face. Both eyes were nearly closed, and her lips were cut. Derrick had used his knife to cut into her thighs, slashing lacerations into the muscles.

"I'm here, *Solnyshkuh*. You're safe." *She'll need your skills, Steele. He beat the shit out of her, but he also cut her with a knife several times. Thighs.* Maestro cut through the zip ties to free her wrists. "Stay still, baby. I've got you now."

The sound of gunshots had her crying out, her fingers forming a fist in his shirt, holding on tightly.

"The boys have this," he said with total confidence. "They're mopping up, clearing the way to get you out of here." While he assured her, he turned his body slightly to

make certain he blocked her from the door while he in-
spected the wounds in her thighs.

Arterial blood?

*No, not deep, just quite a few. He cut the muscle in both
thighs. I doubt she could get far if by a miracle she got away.*

He lifted her, cradling her close, whispering how sorry
he was that he was hurting her. It didn't matter that she was
covered in blood, urine and sweat. He'd grown up with open
wounds and the disturbing physical ramifications of torture
on the human body. It sucked that he was well versed in
those things, but right now, when his woman needed comfort and care, he knew the right things to say and do.

Keys and Player met him at the door. Keys led the way
back through the tunnel at a run, Maestro following smoothly
and Player bringing up the rear. Steele waited in a van, his
medical bag already open. He had treated hundreds of children, teens, men and women for the types of wounds and
trauma that Azelie had experienced.

Maestro climbed in beside her, retaining possession of
her hand. "Steele's got you, babe. I'm right here and you're
safe."

TWENTY

"I wish I could have seen the way the merry widows distracted the outside security guards," Azelie said. "It must have been hilarious."

Maestro was finding it hard to retain a sense of humor, even though Code had footage of the three women flirting and acting like tourists when they approached the security guards. Doug played the part of China's long-suffering husband while she prattled on about dancing and what was the difference between the Adventure Club and the Pleasure Train.

The swelling had gone down quite a bit on Azelie's face, but she was still heavily bruised, and her lower lip was a mess. She would have scars. She had stitches in both thighs, three places in her right thigh. One laceration had been deep enough that she'd had to have stitches inside and outside.

He was happy to have her in Caspar at his home. The first few days she'd been on the coast with him had been spent in Steele's home, where Steele could watch her closely for infection. Knife wounds tended to become infected. Sometimes the stab wound wasn't that deep or in any way life-threatening, but the bacteria on the blade was deadly.

"Code has video with audio," he told her, trying to contain restless energy by pacing up and down the length of the bedroom.

He hadn't thought about decorating his home when he'd first bought it, other than with his piano and other musical instruments. He had an extremely large workshop that was well stocked with every kind of tool he could possibly want or need. But his house . . . He hadn't really considered it home, and he rarely stayed there.

While Azelie was at Steele's, he had a very good bed brought in, along with a few other items Lana and Alena helped him choose. Breezy, Steele's wife, sat with Azelie while he was gone, reassuring her that she was safe and so were her friends. His brothers and sisters in the club hastily put his house together, including stocking the pantry and refrigerator.

Maestro wanted the chance to be alone with her. He liked taking care of her, but now that she was there, looking pale beneath her bruised and swollen face and body, he feared he might have insisted on bringing her home too early.

"You're frowning."

He wasn't. Inside maybe, but he had on his expressionless mask she wasn't supposed to be able to read. He deliberately scowled. "Zelie, you aren't supposed to be able to read me. *I'm* the one that reads *you*."

She flashed a small smile and then gasped, putting her hand over her lower lip where the gash had been sewn. "Don't make me laugh."

His scowl deepened. "You're supposed to take the things I say very seriously. There are rules in place for a reason."

"Well, give me the reason, because I always know when you're frowning. I don't like you upset and need to do something to make things better."

"I'll look like a fuckin' pussy if I show too much concern. You have no idea how I've already had to eat my words, thanks to you. If the others have any idea how you've wrapped me around your little finger, I'll never live it down. At least pretend you can't read me."

She tilted her head and studied the mask that settled over his face. He might joke with her in an effort to put things right between them, but how was he ever going to make what happened to her right? He couldn't. Her eyes were still a little swollen and very bruised, but she still gave him that penetrating look of hers. She knew he was bullshitting her, trying to throw her off the subject.

If he voiced his underlying fear aloud, it would give her an opening to tell him she wanted to leave as soon as she was able. The worst of it was he knew the merry widows and Doug and Carlton were on their way from San Francisco. Doug had called and made it very clear that they were coming to see "their" girl, whether he approved or not. It wasn't said in so many words, but the resolution was there. She would have a way back to San Francisco if she wanted to leave.

He knew the merry widows would take care of her. They'd be more than glad to have her in their homes while she was recovering. He might be able to convince them the doctor didn't want her traveling yet, that the danger of infection was still too high.

"Talk to me, Andrii." Her voice was very soft. Persuasive. Loving.

"I can't lose that."

"What can't you lose?"

"The way you look at me. That tone in your voice."

"What's wrong?"

"I'm waiting for you to tell me you're out of here the moment you're able to fend for yourself," he admitted. "The widows are coming with Doug and Carlton to see for themselves that their little chick is alive and well. You know they would do anything to be the ones to take care of you through this."

"And you think I'd want to go with them?"

He couldn't read her this time. Not even her speculative

tone. "I told you I'd protect you, and I didn't. I thought Billows was dead and you were safe. They pulled your protection and didn't tell me. I should have checked that Rock was still on you, but I went to the debriefing with the thought that once it was over, I could get back to you. It didn't occur to me they'd send Rock to look after the women."

She didn't ask who Rock was. She didn't ask about the women or what that meant. She looked at him, her eyes looking like two bruised flowers pressed into her face.

"You haven't asked a single question, *Solnyshkuh*. Not one." He ran both hands through his hair in agitation. "It stands to reason you aren't asking because you're leaving me. You don't want to know because, like with Billows, you know things I do aren't exactly legal." Harshness crept into his voice.

She sighed. "I haven't asked you any questions, Andrii, because I've been in so much pain and I didn't want to think about what happened. I know my fingerprints are in the club, and once the cops sort through everything, they're bound to think I was involved with whatever the Billows family had going on. I wanted to enjoy the way you were spoiling me, not making me think about anything that happened or was going to happen. I figured you would talk to me about everything given time."

He turned away from her, swearing at himself under his breath. "There you go again, baby. The voice of reason. That's supposed to be me."

He got her laughing with that absurd statement. The sound was low and cut off with a gasp that had him swinging around to face her again. "Don't laugh, *Solnyshkuh*."

"Don't make me laugh."

"I love you." He blurted it out like an idiot. "As in real love. The real thing."

Her expression changed. He got that look from her he craved. So loving. Almost adoring. She didn't seem to think he was being a pussy when he confessed insecurities to her.

"I didn't know I was capable of feeling love. I didn't even know if such a thing existed until you came to me. I saw Czar with Blythe and Reaper with Anya. And others with their women, especially Savage and Seychelle, but I still didn't get it." He knew she had no idea who he was talking about, but he wanted her to understand how overwhelming, just how big it was that he realized love was real. That *she* was real.

"We'd been tracing a human trafficking ring for well over two years. We finally got the names of a couple of people the women were sent to after they were taken. Billows' responsibility was to train them as sex slaves before they were auctioned off. After they were trained, they were shipped to the next rung in the ladder, the man holding the auctions."

"That's where I came in," she murmured.

He nodded. "We got into the clubs but couldn't find a way to get to the underground rooms. In researching, we discovered you. We focused our attention on you, and after three weeks, I made my first contact with you."

"But you still had your suspicions I was involved."

"You were the bookkeeper. Your office was below the Adventure Club. It stood to reason that you knew what was going on. But then I met you. I was already halfway falling before I ever made my approach. Just watching the way you were with other people convinced me you couldn't possibly have anything to do with human trafficking."

"You asked me out to look for the key to the offices." There was no accusation in her tone, just a neutral acknowledgment.

"Full disclosure, when you would leave your apartment, it was searched by various members of the team. No one could find the key. We were afraid if we waited too long, if Billows did have women he was training, he'd ship them off before we could find them. Once they're gone, you don't have a very large window to retrieve them, and at that point, we didn't have any way to track them."

"Were there women in the rooms I couldn't get into?"

"Yes. There's a tunnel system leading to that subterranean

floor. The women and teens were brought in through the tunnel. They never went through the club."

She looked down at her hands. He followed her gaze to see her twisting her fingers together until they were white.

"I left her there." She said it softly. With sorrow. "That woman I heard screaming, I just left her there. She was probably sold and is in a situation she can't ever get out of." She lifted her anguished gaze to his. "If they were treating her the way they did me and then sexually assaulted her, she would have been desperate. I felt desperate. I was terrified that they wouldn't just kill me outright."

He should have known she would feel guilt for not being able to rescue the unknown woman. "If you had gotten to her, the Billows brothers would have taken you too. They couldn't afford to allow you freedom if you knew they were sex traffickers. We don't give up on the victims, Azelie. We'll continue to look for the ones they sold. It takes time to sort through the information we acquire and find a new direction to get to the top, but we don't stop. All of us experienced atrocities at the hands of offenders, and we're committed to stopping as many as possible."

"We don't even know who she was," Azelie said. "I can't even give that to you as a starting point."

"Have faith, baby. That's all any of us can do."

"Thank you for risking your life to help those women," she whispered. "I know you must have felt you were risking your relationship with me. I love you even more that you would make such a personal sacrifice. I know those decisions had to have been difficult for you."

She was his everything. She seemed to be able to be there for him, no matter what. Wrong or right decisions, and he had no clue sometimes which was which. When he felt insecure, weak, the pain of his past swamping him, she was there, standing for him. Loving him. How could it be?

"I did my best to give you truth. To give you the real me. I didn't want you to ever wake up one morning and feel used. I want you to feel loved, Zelie. I may not always go about it the right way, but I want you to feel loved even when I'm a complete ass."

She started to laugh and gasped again, her hand covering her lip. "Stop making me laugh. Seriously, Andrii, I thought we were going to be positive about ourselves."

"No. You're supposed to be positive. I can say whatever I like about myself. And most of my brothers and sisters call me Maestro. We call one another by our club names. We left most of who we were behind when we escaped Sorbacov's school."

"But your birth name is Andrii?"

"Yes. You're the only one who has called me that in a long time."

"You know the cops are going to question me. You killed the Billows brothers. You can't be anywhere near the cops."

"Baby, even the women we freed will give a different description of their rescuers. We wore silicone masks to alter our appearances. You were rescued by the same men. You have no idea who they are. When you're questioned, you'll have a lawyer present. He'll shut down anything he doesn't want you to answer. I'll give you a full description of what I looked like, what Keys and Player looked like. They were the only ones you saw."

"What about the merry widows and Doug and Carlton? They had to know it was you who came for me. Especially since you brought me here."

"We used the tunnel entrance. They weren't anywhere near the tunnel. They were at the club, distracting guards. We told them you'd been rescued by some team and brought to us because we had a doctor waiting."

She kept her gaze steady on his. "They won't believe you, Andrii. They think you're James Bond. Doug and Carlton especially won't believe you."

"Doug and Carlton would never betray us. They wouldn't because they wanted someone to rescue you, and they knew they could never get in. They're coming here and will meet some other Torpedo Ink members. They wouldn't take a chance on crossing us. They can read what we are. The widows will love believing they're putting one over on the cops. They can honestly say they didn't see anyone."

"You sound very sure the police aren't going to try to get you and your friends for this."

"Fortunately, we have alibis. We're very good at planning. Any time I go out on a mission, I want you to remember that."

She looked around her. "This is a beautiful home."

"Perfect for writing your books. And we aren't that far from the widows. We have plenty of room for them to visit."

"You want me to move in with you?"

"Yes."

She was silent for a minute. He pressed his hand to his chest. *Bog*, this relationship shit was fraught with land mines. He'd given her honesty and had no idea if what he wanted from her would drive her away. Was it too soon? Why hadn't he studied romance the way he'd studied kill tactics? He should have at least read a few books. He knew if he voiced his thoughts, she'd laugh, and it would hurt, so he remained silent.

"I do want to move in with you, Andrii, but I have to finish school first. That's important to me. I'm in my last semester, so close to getting my degree." She made a little face. "This has probably set me back. It isn't like every professor I have is the understanding type."

"They'll understand." He kept his tone very mild. Velvet soft. He didn't fool her for a minute.

Her gaze jumped to his, and she narrowed her eyes. "I know you aren't thinking of talking with my teachers."

"I had Absinthe meet with each of them separately and explain your situation. They were very understanding and sympathetic."

"Who is Absinthe?"

"He's one of the brothers and our lawyer. Very soft-spoken, but he can be persuasive."

"I suppose I should question you more about this, but I'm

too tired and sore. And I think you're rather wonderful to remember how important my classes are to me. Thank you for letting the school know I was attacked."

Maestro decided he may as well go all in. So far, she was with him every step of the way. She seemed to believe she loved him. It was there in the way she looked at him, her lack of condemnation for his actions. Her protectiveness. She hadn't even considered giving him up to the Billows brothers to spare herself pain.

He pulled the little jewelry box from his pocket and crouched down beside the bed.

Her eyes widened. "What are you doing?"

"Marry me, Azelie. Be with me forever. Grow old with me. Take your last breath with me. Have our children. I love you more than life. I sometimes can't breathe without you. Just say yes."

Her gaze moved over his face, feature by feature, and then dropped to the open jewelry box. She gasped. "Andrii."

"Ice is a jeweler, and he made it for you. I picked out the design and stones. The blue reminds me of your eyes. Such a gorgeous color."

He loved the vintage look of it, and it was reminiscent of the things he loved about Russia. The main stone was a rare blue Russian diamond with extraordinary color and clarity. The stone was set in white gold. Going up both sides of the ring was scrollwork made of very small blue diamonds. Three blue diamonds representing suns were set on either side of the ring just below the larger diamond. The ring was dainty looking, even loaded with all the tiny blue stones.

"Marry me."

"I might have to just for that ring. It's amazing. And perfect."

"Say it."

"Yes."

He actually choked up. To cover his idiocy, he pushed the ring onto her finger. "Looks like it was made for you, which it was. One of a kind, a rare beauty just like you."

"Take a picture with my cell phone. I want to send it to the widows."

"They'll be here shortly."

"I know. I love it and want to share. They'll go crazy and scream in the car and make Doug and Carlton crazy."

He took the picture with her cell phone. "They might put those women out on the side of the road. You're an instigator."

She giggled and hastily tried to stop. "I know. I shouldn't encourage them, but I can't help myself."

She sent the photograph of her hand with the ring prominent. It looked perfect on her if he did say so himself.

"If I forget anything important to you, let me know. I like taking care of you, *Solnyshkuh*. With what you give to me, it's very little in return." That was Maestro being honest.

There was a knock on the outside frame of the master bedroom door, and Lana stuck her head in. "You feeling up for a visit? I know the widows are coming, so I promise to make it short."

Maestro assessed Azelie's features. She was tired, but he could see she wanted to visit with Lana. She touched the stitches on her lip with her fingertip.

"I look a little like Frankenstein, but if you don't care, I don't either."

Lana flashed her high-wattage smile. "You look great to me. I saw you several times in the early days, and your face is looking more like you and less like a shattered pumpkin."

Azelie laughed, gasped and covered her mouth.

Maestro scowled at Lana. "Don't make her laugh. It hurts."

"That's going to be difficult, especially when the widows get here. Azelie laughs at everything. She makes life fun."

"The *widows* make life fun," Azelie corrected. "I just sit in the coffee shop and laugh. Most of the customers come there to eavesdrop on their conversation as much as for the coffee."

"That could be true," Maestro said. "They're a little addicting."

"A *lot* addicting," Azelie corrected.

"She's waving her hand under your nose, Lana. You're supposed to be very observant," Maestro said.

Lana caught Azelie's hand and stared at the ring. "It's beautiful and unique. I'd recognize Ice's work any day. I absolutely love the scrollwork." She let go of Azelie's hand. "Are you certain you want to tie yourself to Mr. Bossy Pants?"

Azelie burst out laughing, this time interrupting the beautiful sound with a gasping cry.

"I told you not to make her laugh." Maestro glared at Lana.

"Sheesh. You see what I'm saying, Azelie?"

She didn't seem in the least fazed by Maestro's stern look.

"Alena is cooking dinner for your guests," Lana said. "She'll have it here around five or six, whichever you prefer. She said to let her know." Lana sat on the edge of the bed. "Wait until you meet Alena. She's supersweet and the best chef I know. Well, I don't know a lot of chefs, but I've eaten a lot of food, and hers is spectacular. She owns Crow 287 in Caspar. People come from all over to eat there, and she's never advertised."

"That's so nice that she'd bring dinner for my friends," Azelie said.

"Those women are a hoot," Lana said. "Have you seen the video of them?"

"Not yet. Andrii said he'd play it for me. More than likely, they'll want to see it too. If for no other reason than to have Doug and Carlton lose their minds."

"They should have a reality show," Lana said.

"Don't give them any ideas," Maestro said. "They'd do it just to tweak Doug and Carlton. Those men have enough on their plates trying to watch over those three firecrackers. And we're not introducing them to the Red Hat ladies." He pressed his palm to his forehead, horrified at the thought. "Those women are out of control as well. Lana, we need to get a handle on our senior citizens."

"I'm going to be just like them when I get older," Azelie warned.

He sighed. "You already are. I've decided wrapping you in bubble wrap and keeping you pregnant is the only safe thing to do."

Azelie tried to make a face, but she was on the verge of laughter. Maestro wasn't that certain he was joking. Lana knew him well enough to know he was half-serious.

"He's obsessed with babies," Azelie said. "Even though he's admitted kids would probably eat him alive."

"That's because he's a pushover with them. Not so much with women, but kids run all over him," Lana said.

"He's kind of a pushover . . ."

"*Don't* say it. Don't even think it. The alarm was triggered, which means your friends have arrived. Be prepared to be mobbed. And I'm going to be interrogated and lectured." He was resigned to his fate.

Azelie giggled and pressed her hand to her mouth again, sobering.

"That's my cue to leave." Lana bent forward to brush a kiss on top of Azelie's head. "I'm so happy for you and Maestro. Thank you for being so perfectly wonderful. Someone had to tame him."

"Not tamed," Maestro muttered as he walked her to the front door.

"How is she really?"

"Nightmares. A lot of pain. She doesn't talk about it. She hasn't once condemned me or considered any of it my fault, including the fact that I didn't protect her."

"That's because you found one of the good ones. Like Blythe and Seychelle and Soleil. They have this light in them and manage to find a way to make our lives so much better."

Maestro hadn't been wrong when he said he would be interrogated and lectured. He showed them through his house, noting that all three of the widows observed he had very little furniture.

"A beautiful home," Blanc commented.

"But a bit sparse on décor," Penny pointed out.

The speculation in her voice and the way the three women

exchanged suddenly bright looks had him sweating. Little kids ate him alive, and it seemed that older women did as well. They looked as if they might rush right out and buy every piece of furniture they could find.

Doug saved him. "Clearly, he wants Azelie to find the things she likes when she moves in with him." He pinned Maestro with a stern eye. "She apparently has a ring. We know this because all of a sudden three women started shrieking at the top of their lungs. We almost wrecked."

Blanc rolled her eyes. "You're always so dramatic."

"I didn't believe it because no one asked Carlton or me for her hand. That's mandatory."

"I have no problem with formally asking you," Maestro said, "but only if you're going to give me the green light. Azelie would love it, but I'm not giving her up. She's rare and wonderful."

"We know," Carlton agreed. "And she deserves the best."

"You're aware lookin' at me I'm not the best man in the world, but I'm going to make her happy. No one will love her the way I do. Or need her as much. Azelie must be needed to be happy. It's essential she has a buffer between her and the world. She may have experienced trauma, but she still doesn't protect herself the way she should. She sees the good in people. It takes a lot for her to see the bad."

Maestro wasn't a man to explain himself, but these five people were Azelie's only family. They obviously loved her. He felt they deserved the respect he gave to the women his brothers had married. They were family.

"Good you see that," Carlton said gruffly.

"I love that woman and want to spend my life with her. I can swear to you I'll do everything in my power to make her happy."

The merry widows squealed so loud he winced. All three put their hands to their hearts. "Well said," China approved.

Doug and Carlton simultaneously rolled their eyes. "You don't quite get the seriousness of this moment. The three of you are utterly impossible."

"He means yes," Blanc interpreted.

"Ask again so I can record it on my phone," Penny said. "I wasn't ready."

"He isn't asking again," Carlton declared. "Yes, you can marry her. But you'd better take care of her and make her happy."

Maestro led the way to the master bedroom without further comment. He might need to take up smoking. Or try drinking again.

Everything changed the moment the widows stepped into the master bedroom. They forgot all about him. Joyfully and tearfully, they surrounded the bed with both squeals of happiness at seeing Azelie and tears over her appearance. China dared to sit on the edge of the bed to put her arms around Azelie.

"Tell me if my hugs hurt," she said through a sob.

"Hugs never hurt," Azelie lied.

Maestro cleared his throat. "She has multiple wounds in both thighs, and her ribs were cracked. Movement can be painful."

"Honey," Blanc said, her voice gentle and sympathetic. "What can we do?"

"You're here," Azelie said. "You drove all the way to see me. I love that you came." She looked up at Doug and Carlton. "Thank you. It makes me so happy to see you."

Doug reached down to cup the side of her face. The gesture was fatherly. Loving. It made Maestro's heart lurch. These people loved his woman. They really did think of her as their daughter. He realized none of them had children. They had given their love and loyalty to Azelie.

"We had to see that you were healing, honey. All of us were worried," Doug said.

"Andrii kept us informed on your progress every day," Carlton added.

Azelie lifted her gaze to Maestro. There it was, that look he craved so much. He could fall into her eyes and drown in her love, and he'd be perfectly happy. He loved her so much. More than he'd ever thought possible and growing every day.

"Show us the ring," Blanc said. "It looks so beautiful in the photograph."

"Andrii designed it," Azelie said proudly, lifting her hand so they could admire the ring. "It's absolutely perfect. He chose the stones as well. He has a friend who is a jeweler who made it for him." She smiled up at Maestro, her heart in her eyes.

The women exclaimed over the ring with *ooh*s and *aah*s, giving their approval.

"We have the security tapes from the outside of the club," Maestro said, to cover the unexpected burn in his chest. "Azelie wanted to see how you handled the guards at the club, distracting them so her rescuers could get inside without detection."

China, Penny and Blanc clapped their hands in delight while Doug and Carlton made a show of groaning.

"We've already seen their outlandish behavior," Carlton declared. "China and Blanc showed off their dancing skills to the guards. China tried to get Doug, who played her husband, to jitterbug with her."

"That wasn't even the worst of their behavior," Doug said. "Penny chased one of those poor guards around a tree because he gave her a compliment."

The three women erupted into laughter. Penny sobered, managing to look demure and innocent. "It's called acting, Carlton. The three of us regularly star in plays at the theater. I managed to distract not only him but three others as well. They fell over themselves laughing at the darling boy. He was very young to be a security guard. I targeted him on purpose."

"You targeted him because he was considered hot. How do I know this?" Carlton demanded. "Because the three of you went on and on ad nauseam about how truly hot he was."

"Well, he was," Penny defended them. "If I'm going to

flirt and proposition a man, he'd better be hot or why waste my talents?" She patted Azelie's hand. "I sacrificed for you, dear."

"Sacrificed?" Doug spluttered. "You were having so much fun harassing that poor boy you forgot what your mission was."

Maestro was listening to the familiar teasing between the widows and their male friends, but mostly he was watching Azelie's face. She was happy. For those few moments, she'd forgotten the bruising and pain of her lip, thighs and ribs, enjoying the bantering between her friends.

"We're immortalized on the video," China declared. "I'll want a copy of it to show to Shaila and David. They come to all our plays."

"It was truly our finest acting," Blanc agreed.

Carlton threw his hands into the air. "Save me, Andrii. Show me around your property while the sex-crazed lunatics review their performances."

"I'm going with you," Doug declared.

Maestro stepped between China and Blanc to gently cup the side of Azelie's face that wasn't so swollen. "Text me if you need me. I won't be long." He straightened. "Ladies, she tires easily. If you see she needs to rest, come into the living room. A friend is bringing dinner, and we have rooms available if you'd like to spend the night instead of driving all the way back to San Francisco tonight."

He got the look from Azelie, her eyes adoring, her features soft with love. His heart nearly exploded in his chest. He had that beauty when he'd never considered it possible.

"Love you, *Solnyshkuh*. Be good while I'm gone."

"I love you too, Andrii. The three of you behave yourselves."

That brought laughter from all five of her friends. *Bog*, but he loved that. She'd already turned his cold house into a home. He'd gotten a miracle after all.

In the distance, dark clouds gathered over the sea in an angry roiling boil. The wind slammed hard into the surface, creating rough, hazardous waves that rushed toward shore like angry stallions. There was little beach between the sea and the vast forest that stretched almost to the very shoreline. The canopy swayed and rocked, rustling tree branches and sending leaves and needles swirling through the air like weapons of destruction.

Darkness brought out the creatures of the night. Bats wheeled and dipped as they feasted on insects. Great round yellow eyes blinked from some of the higher tree limbs as the owls surveyed the forest floor, and the voles and mice rushed through rotting vegetation to get home. The merciless wind swept in from the sea, slamming into the stoic trees, bending them, causing creaks of protest, but the trees held as they had for hundreds of years.

The village of Nachtbloem rested on the outskirts of the forest, so close that the wilderness crept forward as if to recover the site that had been carved from the woods. Night flowers grew wild in every meadow, tipping their faces toward the moon. The village was situated near the river and close to the ocean where many of the inhabitants made their living fishing or sending their wares to neighboring countries via the sea route.

Often, fierce storms brewed over the ocean and crashed over their homes, pouring water into the river so that it reacted like a snake. The river would swell up, a thrashing, roaring serpent, spewing the frothing, maddened water from its banks to flood the roads. With the roads impassable, the people were trapped in the village until the abundance of water soaked into the ground or they managed to fix it. It had happened often enough in the last two years that it no longer fazed them.

Silke Vriese knew storms like the ones Nachtbloem experienced weren't normal. Everyone in the village was aware the weather wasn't normal even though the storms came consistently in the same months. It rained often in Holland, but in comparison to other countries, the weather was rather mild across the land. Living on the coast, they shouldn't experience such violent storms.

With one arm, Silke circled a tree trunk while she watched the ferocity of the waves pounding the shore. In the distance, waterspouts leapt across the choppy surface of the water, the towering columns ominous as they spun wildly, forming more and more geysers as they hurtled toward shore.

"Doesn't look good," Tora Kros said, standing on the other side of the tree. She was tall and willowy with shining dark hair and gorgeous emerald green eyes.

"I think of these storms as tests," Silke said. "Look into the clouds, Tora. You can make out the faces of our enemies."

Tora followed her gaze to the dark clouds laced with lightning. As each cloud rolled and boiled as if in a cauldron, eyes glowed from the jagged lightning, demonic faces staring malevolently at the shore, forest, and village. The faces distorted eerily as the clouds roiled and churned. Each face twisted and turned, but it was clear the glowing, malevolent eyes were marking the village and forest, attempting to see everything they could.

"A war is coming," she whispered aloud to her best friend. "I read it again in the cards this evening, just as the cards have warned me for the last two years."

The tree she held on to was solid, although slenderer than quite a few of the others. She needed the grounding when she was all too aware of the land shifting under her feet. In days long past, mythical creatures and demon slayers were considered part of everyday life. Now they seemingly existed only in video games. Movies were made about vampires and evil demons. Television shows depicted supernatural beings. No one believed in these things in modern times; at least, it seemed that way. Those living in Nachtbloem knew better.

Three hundred people, give or take a few when elders died and babies were born, resided in the village of Nachtbloem. Although many people in Germany, the Netherlands and even Belgium claimed to be fully Frisii, the people living in that remote village were direct descendants of those from Germania times. The story of the battle between the Frisii and Roman invaders was always kept fresh in their minds, handed down from generation to generation during storytelling time.

In AD 28, the Frisii were the only people able to defeat the Roman army when their land was invaded. At first, the Frisians lived alongside the Romans without rancor. When new leadership of the Romans demanded taxes be paid in forms the Frisians didn't have, wives and daughters were sold into slavery in order to satisfy the leader of the Romans. The Frisians rebelled and decided, with a small force, to attack the fortress where the leader was hiding. The Romans fought back and even managed to get reinforcements.

The Frisii were a people who, once riled, refused to quit. They got the job done. The Romans had an overpowering force, so the villagers pulled back to the forest they were so familiar with and prepared for battle. The forest held its own secrets, only known to those people long ago and to many of the villagers in the present day.

"The demons are looking to map out the land. To see the

best way to attack us," Tora said. "Notice they are particularly studying the forest."

As the stories of that epic battle unfolded, much was lost in the translation of accounts. Many simply believed that the woman leading the battle and aiding the small army was mythical. Unreal. She was called Baduhenna and named goddess. The suffix *-henna* often denoted a female deity. The prefix *Badw-* or *Badu-* meant battle. Baduhenna's daring and skills became the things of legends as she became known as the Frisian goddess of war and battle.

To the villagers living in Nachtbloem, Baduhenna was very real. In the stories, Baduhenna led her small army into the darkened forest. There, crows aided her, flying through the woods or circling above. The cries of the crows instilled fear in the hearts of the enemies as the sounds pierced the absolute quiet just before the battle ensued.

Many believed another goddess, Morrigan in the form of a crow, aided Baduhenna. She helped to bring panic and confusion to the enemy. The small force of Frisians using only light weapons, such as hand axes, had killed over nine hundred Roman soldiers in a day. In their confusion and paranoia, the Romans had killed an additional four hundred of their own men before they fled, making the Frisians the only people to defeat the Romans.

The villagers living in Nachtboem were extremely proud of their ancestors. They also believed the rest of the legend— the part history left out. That the Romans had been aided by demons from the underworld in their invasion. Without Baduhenna and Morrigan to aid them, even with their fighting skills and the affinity they had with the forest, they would have been defeated.

Legend said history would repeat itself. They would be invaded again. This time the battle wouldn't be for their small village but for all mankind. No one knew how they could defeat a modern-day army aided by creatures from the underworld; they just knew they would have to do so.

"I suspected these storms covered the movements of

those sent to spy on us," Silke said. "I can't command the weather the way you do, but I've been practicing."

Silke was a demon hunter. A slayer. Her mother had died in childbirth, passing her gifts, her responsibilities and powerful tarot cards to her only daughter. Tora and several elders in the village had begun her training when she was a child. Most of the techniques for killing demons known to her female ancestors had been passed on to her at birth. She had to perfect each one. Learn the names of demons, what they were capable of, and how best to slay them.

She knew there was a hierarchy among demons, and some were far more powerful than others. Tora had three friends who knew demon slayers. They didn't live close, but like Tora, they were guardians of the gate and the Carpathian species. Carpathians were nearly immortal, existed on blood, and slept during the day in the rejuvenating soil. The other three women were very generous in passing the information on fighting demons to Tora, who shared it with Silke so they could better defend their people when the time came.

"You don't want to draw their attention to you," Tora cautioned. "I've been very careful to counter their storms with a gradual decline, so they don't notice it's waning any way but naturally."

Silke wished she were as adept as Tora. Tora had centuries of experience on her. Her Carpathian heritage allowed her to shape-shift and fly through the air, which Silke very much wanted to do. That was one gift she was especially envious of. Silke had discovered she had a small talent for manipulating weather, but it was underdeveloped. With all she had to do—after all, she had to eat and wear clothes, which meant working a job—time was an issue. She trained as a slayer from the moment she rose to when she finally allowed herself to sleep. In that time, she had to fit her day job into the mix. That left little time to refine the gifts she needed to develop.

"We want to keep every advantage that we can," Tora added.

Silke nodded her agreement. "I sealed the ground beneath the village the best I could after we found Albert Friesorger dead. His body looked as if animals had torn him apart, but it was a pack of small demons. I tracked them to the edge of the sea as if they found their way to us via water, but I know they came from underground."

Tora was much older with a vast amount of information on the hunting demons; guarding gates and destroying vampires didn't argue with her. She trusted Silke as the slayer, with hundreds of years of knowledge passed from mother to daughter. She trained with Silke nightly and knew her abilities. That alone gave Silke confidence in herself, but she also was very aware of the buildup of the enemy. They were becoming much more aggressive, the storms more frequent and much more violent.

"Testing us," she murmured again.

"We have to continue to look as if we fail to spot them," Tora said. "The only thing we have going for us is the element of surprise. They can't know our strengths or weaknesses. We must outsmart them and hope our reinforcements get here on time."

Silke knew they needed the Carpathian warriors to aid them. There was no hope of winning an intense battle, even in the forest of secrets, without help. She was very conflicted over who would be coming. Every year from the ages of two to twenty-three, Silke had opened a package on her birthday containing recordings from Astrid, her mother. Prior to giving birth, she must have had a premonition that she wouldn't survive. Silke came from a long line of women with special gifts. All who knew Astrid testified that she'd had special talents in abundance.

Silke had been fourteen when Astrid's now-familiar voice had told her to go to Tora and ask questions about a species of people called Carpathians. Silke always looked forward to listening to her mother's voice and hearing her advice. This was the first time the recording hadn't been about personal advice from mother to daughter. There weren't her usual thoughts on the recording or even tips on fighting demons. Astrid detailed how important it was for her to learn about the Carpathian species and reiterated several times that she was to rely on Tora to educate her.

Silke had grown up speaking an ancient language, one that Tora referred to as Carpathian. She'd asked, of course, where the origin was, but Tora had simply said she would reveal all to her in time. Silke was so busy learning everything from fighting skills to other languages that she had stopped asking. Now her mother had specifically instructed her to learn what she could about the Carpathian people from Tora.

Tora had been her best friend almost from the first day Silke could remember, even before she could walk. Tora was kind and patient, and Silke considered her family, a sibling. Since both her parents had died, as a child, Silke had clung to Tora. She'd always seemed older, although when they were children, she couldn't have been more than five years older—at least that was what Silke had thought at the time.

"When I first asked you about the Carpathian species, you told me they were warriors, hunting vampires," Silke said to Tora. "At that time, you said they slept in rejuvenating soil and drank blood without killing their donors. You told me they had tremendous powers, including shape-shifting and flying. When you told me that every gift comes with drawbacks, and you explained that Carpathians were nearly immortal but would become paralyzed during daylight hours and come out only at night, I realized you were Carpathian. You visited me at night, never during the day. Only once in that conversation did you mention demons and Carpathians in the same breath. I thought you meant vampires, but you didn't, did you?"

Tora shook her head. "Carpathians view vampires as just that—vampires. They're wholly evil and prey on every species on this earth they can. They create flesh-eating puppets and ruin the land. They have made alliances in the underworld recently. Banding together and making alliances is new, from what I'm told."

That didn't explain the demon reference Tora had so casually made all those years ago. Silke knew where vampires came from. When she'd turned fifteen, she'd learned that, aside from that of being a demon slayer, her mother had also passed on another responsibility—a huge one. Silke guarded the soul of a Carpathian warrior. If that wasn't fantasy, what was? When a Carpathian male was born, his soul split. He retained all the darkness, and somewhere, a female child was born with the other half of the soul, made up of his light. His task was to find her and bind their souls together. It wasn't easy to find a lifemate, and many of them succumbed to temptation, turning vampire, forcing friends to hunt them. The woman could die, and the soul would be born again and again for as long as the Carpathian male still existed.

The thought of such a responsibility at fifteen was disconcerting. Still, at fifteen, none of the things Silke had learned about Carpathians had seemed real. They were larger-than-life heroes, hunting vampires and keeping mankind safe. They were warriors fighting for others despite the constant whisper of temptation to kill while feeding just so they would feel a rush. Those were facts she'd learned from Tora.

Tora had told her that male Carpathians lost their ability to see in color or feel emotions. They lived in a bleak, gray world century after century. She'd also revealed that Carpathians choosing to give up their souls to feel the rush when they fed became vampires. Silke had lain awake often over the years thinking of how horrible it would be to live with honor for centuries and then, in a moment of weakness, become the very thing you hunted.

She was responsible for guarding the soul of a Carpathian warrior. It was told in the stories handed down from her ancestors that he would come with others to help them in their final battle with Lilith's demons from the underworld. She feared he wouldn't arrive in time. She was also very nervous. The idea of a stranger having a claim on her bothered her immensely. And there was that casual line about demons Tora had mentioned when Silke was fourteen. Tora wasn't volunteering an explanation.

Once more, Silke looked up at the black, rolling clouds. The edges seemed frayed, as if the vicious wind would suddenly reverse directions and rip at the clouds to pull them apart before once more aiding the demons in their quest to spy on the village and forest.

Tora had covered the forest in a shroud of dense magic weaves that appeared as fog, so that even with the canopy swaying in the wind, it was impossible to penetrate through the layers to see inside the forest. Silke had done her best to seal the ground to make it impossible for demons to enter that way. They needed the forest to remain a mystery to their enemy. It would be their chosen place of battle, just as it had been in AD 28, when their ancestors fought off the Romans.

"Tell me what you're afraid to say about Carpathians and demons, Tora." She wasn't going to be a coward, and she needed as much information as possible.

Tora sent another wave of capricious winds to counter the violent storm, this time toward the waterspouts whirling their way toward shore. The wind shifted at her command, stilling just on the surface beneath the spouts, so the rotating winds propelling the spouts abruptly ceased and the spouts collapsed.

"Stay still," Silke advised. "I feel their scrutiny. They're wondering if something or someone is countering their commands."

"They won't be able to detect my touch," Tora said with confidence. "They can try, but I'm hidden from them."

"One of them is a sniffer," Silke cautioned. "That isn't his official demon name, but I call him that. He has a long snout, and the others depend on him to ferret out their prey when they fail. If you left any trace of yourself behind, there's a good chance he'll catch your scent even if he can't track you."

Tora tilted her face up to better look at the faces in the clouds. The wind she'd sent pulled more of the clouds apart, so the faces were even more distorted than before. "I thought I knew a lot about demons, but your knowledge is much more than mine."

"It's the only area where I might have an advantage on you," Silke conceded. "I was born with the knowledge of my ancestors imprinted on me. Every demon slayer in the family contributed until I was a walking encyclopedia of demons." She made a face. "That's not a good thing when I try to sleep."

Tora had a strange expression on her face, one that indicated guilt. Or at least she was anxious, which was so unusual for her friend that it alarmed Silke.

"We're back to what you don't want to tell me," she said. "Just say it, Tora. We'll figure it out."

Tora reached for her hand. "You're my family, Silke. I love you the way I would a sibling. Or even a daughter at times. I'm always proud of the way you face every new threat. You have such courage."

That little speech didn't bode well, although she knew Tora meant every word. She waited in silence for Tora to explain. The heavy rains lessened along with the wind. The overhead clouds lightened from ominous black to a dark gray. The faces faded as if they'd never been, but Silke wasn't deceived.

"They're still there, hidden in the gray."

"For demons, they have quite a lot of power," Tora observed, speculation in her voice.

Silke frowned, the puzzle pieces turning this way and that in her head. Those particular demons were at the top of the hierarchy, but they couldn't command weather. They had various skills, such as the one she'd named Sniffer. Two others had excellent vision. One had amazing hearing. All together, the skills would allow them to ferret out secrets or find their potential prey easily. Silke and Tora had unusual training, allowing them to hide from the demons.

"Someone else is controlling the weather," she mused. "That must be the answer. As powerful as each demon is alone, even together they couldn't possibly do that. Someone else with your skills, Tora, is most likely commanding the weather we've been getting."

Tora dropped her hand and rubbed her hands back and forth on her arms as if suddenly cold. Silke knew Carpathians controlled their body temperatures. More than once, Tora had done so for her.

"You know about the gate I guard. That's why you have the tarot cards. There are four gates, and a Carpathian woman guards each of them. You have the ability to keep demons from escaping the underworld, and together the two of us have kept that gate intact."

Silke had been to the gate on several occasions to ensure no demon had found a way through. Time and again, she'd sealed the ground around the gate. Lately, she knew Tora was concerned that whatever was behind the gate was weakening the ancient wood and the spells. She'd never seen whatever was being held there. Tora referred to him as a beast.

Another Carpathian woman, Gaia, lived in the underworld and seemed to be Tora's friend, but Silke had never seen her. She knew the area the beast had at his command was tremendous, stretching from Siberia, Italy, and Algeria around to their little village. The beast and his companion seemed to travel from gate to gate. Silke didn't understand how he could be so dangerous if a Carpathian woman was his companion.

"It's difficult for all of us guarding the gates to comprehend just how lethal the beast is. His name is Justice; at least, that's what he was called when he chose to save members of his family and remain behind in the underworld. He fought off the demons while his family escaped. All of them were horribly wounded, as was Justice. He blocked the portal and shut it down so the demons couldn't go after his family, thus trapping himself in the underworld."

"He sounds like a hero, not a beast," Silke said.

Sorrow flashed across Tora's face. "He is a hero. He was the thing legends were made of, even in my world. Justice was Carpathian at one time."

"I don't understand. Is he vampire? Did he turn while he was trapped in the underworld? How could your friend stay with him?"

Tora shook her head. "Justice isn't vampire. Our species can live very long lives. Some believe we're immortal, but we can be killed, as you well know."

Silke had seen Tora after several battles with vampires. She'd been close to death on two of those occasions. Silke had managed to aid her in dispatching the vampires before attending to the wounds and giving her friend blood. Several times over the years, they had gone into battle together and prevailed, but their wounds had been numerous.

"After centuries of a gray, emotionless existence, when life has been nothing but hunting and killing your friends, family, and other Carpathians who turned vampire, seeing the horrific things vampires did to their victims takes a tremendous toll."

Silke imagined that the life of the Carpathian male was grim and endless. She was surrounded by people she loved in the village. She was an orphan, but she'd always been cared for. She had Tora as well as the elders in the village, who were generous with time, attention, and advice. Fenja Reinders, a single woman in the village, had always wanted children. She had taken Silke in when her mother had died. She was the local midwife, assisting women giving birth, and had been present when Astrid had slipped away. The village had decided she would be the best choice for raising the orphaned infant, and she'd readily accepted the task.

Silke loved her as she would have her birth mother. Fenja had raised her with kindness and love. Silke couldn't remember a single time when Fenja had yelled or lost her temper. She had lovingly told her the stories of the Battle of Baduhenna, making them exciting and every hero or heroine larger than life. She'd taken Silke to the forest and introduced her to the plants and trees, carefully and patiently teaching her which were poisonous, edible, or could be used for medicine. She'd taken Tora into her heart and given the girls plenty of time to train in the skills Silke needed as the demon slayer.

"I can't imagine what kind of life those men have led." Silke's heart ached for the warriors. In modern times, the stories of Carpathian males hunting vampires and sustaining near-fatal wounds, yet going back over and over again to do the same thing, should have been more like a grim fairy tale, but Silke had always considered those stories reality. Perhaps it was the way both Fenja and Tora regaled her with tales of the past so often that those stories became believable to her.

Tora sighed, glancing upwards toward the sky again. The clouds had drifted closer, no longer out over the sea, but nearly directly above the forest. Now, rather than angry, dark and boiling, the shapes were intact and the color various shades of charcoal.

"They're back," Silke announced.

"They're so predictable," Tora said. "You called it when you said they hadn't left. Do they think we're going to fall for their tricks and reveal ourselves to them?"

"Tora, whoever creates the storms had to have been like you at one time. Why would they be in the underworld?"

"A vampire was a Carpathian," Tora reminded her. "Once destroyed, they very well could be trapped in the underworld and subject to Lilith's bidding. She's a cruel and exacting mistress, from everything I've been told. There have been three battles with her armies. She used vampires and mages to aid her demons."

"This beast you guard, could he be the one building the storms for them? Would he have that kind of power?"

Again, the look of anxiety crossed Tora's face. "The reason he's locked behind the gates is because even Lilith fears him. She wants to find a way to control him, as do other factions. That's why you need to guard the tarot cards so carefully. Like the soul you're keeping safe, the cards must be kept safe and away from others as well."

Silke took her gaze from the clouds gathering over the forest to study Tora's expression. Tora was an absolutely beautiful woman. Her skin was flawless. Her hair was dark, thick, and shiny. Her eyes were shaped like a cat's and colored a deep emerald green. Every man who met her, young or old, was enamored with her, and it was easy to see why. Not only was she beautiful, but she had a mesmerizing quality to her. Just being in her presence was soothing.

"Tora, clearly you're worried about my reaction to whatever it is you're holding back."

Tora rubbed along the bottom of her chin with her closed fist. It was one of the few things she did when nervous. To others, she would never give that telling sign away, but she knew she was safe with Silke, even if she had withheld something important.

Silke didn't hold grudges. Not ever. She sometimes got even, as she had when two young boys tried to push her around in school when she was eleven. That hadn't ended well for them. When one tried to push her so the other could steal her lunch, she beat them up right there in the schoolyard. She told them that until they apologized, bad things would happen to them. It only took three days of insects crawling all over their bedrooms, clothes, and toys before they gave her the apology. After they apologized, she brought them fruits and baked goods often, because Fenja told her the boys didn't have a lot in the way of food. Their father had gone on a fishing trip and never returned. Their mother struggled to make ends meet. That was when Silke realized that although the village was filled with happy people, some struggled.

"It's your lifemate, I know he's one of the ancients." Tora made it sound as if she were confessing a great sin.

Silke frowned, trying to comprehend her meaning. Obviously, that revelation was supposed to be significant. She shifted her gaze to the clouds when she felt the buildup of energy. "They're going to rain lightning on us in an attempt to penetrate the veil you are protecting the forest with."

Tora gripped her arm. "Honey, did you hear what I said?"

"I figured out that if I was guardian to a soul, he would have to be a Carpathian warrior living the kind of horrible life you told me about. This doesn't come as a shock."

Again, Tora rubbed her arms as if cold. "He's ancient. Your lifemate is one of the *very* ancient Carpathians. There were a few who held out far longer than others. They became . . . more. From everything the others guarding the gates told me, these ancients have much battle experience and powerful gifts developed over two thousand years of going into battle. In that time, they made numerous kills. Even when one doesn't feel, killing takes a toll. Living in that endless void takes a toll."

Silke was trying to understand what Tora was not telling her. "But they haven't chosen suicide, and they didn't choose to become vampire. It seems they are extremely strong. Isn't that a good thing?"

"They have a code. They believe they owe it to their lifemates to remain on earth searching until they find them. These men secreted themselves in a monastery in the Carpathian Mountains to keep from going insane or turning. Each battle, each kill, brought them closer to the brink, so it seemed a good idea to lock themselves away. Your lifemate did that. He's considered extremely dangerous, Silke. He's powerful and has gifts many other Carpathians don't, and most hunters have tremendous talents. Already it is whispered that, should he turn vampire, few if any could defeat him."

Silke found herself frowning, still trying to puzzle out Tora's concern. She wasn't certain what Tora was trying to tell her. It was very unlike Tora not to be direct, especially with Silke. They were very close. Silke tended to follow where Tora led, trusting Tora to show her the things she needed to learn to better defend their people. More than that, she allowed Tora to take the lead because she loved and trusted her. Tora had never let her down.

"Justice, the beast we guard, was Carpathian." Tora frowned. "*Is* Carpathian, or has remnants of his Carpathian code. Gaia would never stay with him otherwise. Gaia was brought to the underworld as a child. An exchange was made with Xavier, the high mage. I think Lilith wanted her for her ability to talk to animals. When she couldn't mold Gaia to her likeness, she allowed demons to terrify her. Gaia hid in the beast's territory, inside the gates with him. He protected her and made it known she was under his protection. That was how their friendship began."

"Again, he sounds like a hero to me."

Jagged lightning ripped through the sky, sizzling and crackling as, almost simultaneously, the roar of thunder shook the forest and ground. The strike was directly overhead, yet it never penetrated the canopy. Ground to sky, the energy couldn't build because the heavy layers of fog were impenetrable. As if the lightning were dozens of swords and spears, the bolts rained down, seeking an entry.

The veil held, despite the relentless battering.

"You would think they would recognize the touch of a Carpathian," Silke said. "If Lilith has vampires at her disposal, and I can't imagine that she doesn't, why don't they recognize that the forest is protected by a Carpathian?"

Tora gave her an enigmatic smile. "I was a young woman when the Battle of Baduhenna took place. Over the years I have learned many, many things. It seems that most Carpathians trained under the high mage, Xavier. The spells they learned to safeguard; even using just one weave that is familiar to vampires would quickly identify a Carpathian, but I had no such experience. Everything I learned was through trial and error. My weaves are natural, all about the earth. I learned mainly from nature and all the creatures I came across from the time I was a child."

"You never talk about your parents."

"I was very young when they passed. My father hunted a

vampire, and he was killed." Tora's voice was very matter-of-fact. "The vampire followed the trail back to my mother and me. My mother defended me, but he would have killed us both if it wasn't for your ancestors. A group of women heard my screams, and they came running. My mother knew them and was able to tell them how to aid us in defeating the vampire. It was your ancestors leading the way fearlessly. They took me in and raised me when my mother succumbed to her wounds."

Silke knew the battle and the death of Tora's parents had happened centuries earlier. Tora acted stoic about it, but Silke sensed her underlying sorrow.

"I'm so sorry, Tora. It's never easy to lose one's parents. I didn't know mine, but if I were to lose Fenja, I know I would never get over the loss. I'm so happy it was my family that took you in. You're my sister. I love you very much."

They didn't often express their affection for one another, although they showed it in the things they did for each other.

"This Carpathian warrior who is your lifemate," Tora blurted out. "Like I said, he's one of the ones who were in the monastery. He's lived longer than I have. I'm told he's extremely dangerous. Even other Carpathians who were in the monastery are leery of him. He has developed gifts that would make him nearly impossible to defeat in battle, just the way Justice has developed them."

"What are you saying, in plain language? Do you believe the man I've been promised to is like the beast you and the others have kept behind the gates?"

Tora frowned and rubbed her chin. "I don't know. No one knows, only that when you live so long and fight so many battles, something happens to you. It isn't vampire, but more like a demon. Not the type of demons Lilith commands. One with all the knowledge of centuries of battles. Scary strong."

Silke stared at her friend for a long time in utter astonishment. Then she burst out laughing. "You're telling me the soul I guard could very well belong to a demon? I'm a demon slayer. He's supposed to be my husband. I guess that's very fitting. If he gets out of hand, I'll be the one who is supposed to take him down."

"It isn't a laughing matter," Tora scolded.

"It is. You really need to see the irony of a demon slayer having a demon as a husband. Sheesh, Tora, what could be funnier than that?"

CHECK OUT THESE UPCOMING TITLES FROM
#1 *NEW YORK TIMES* BESTSELLING AUTHOR

CHRISTINE FEEHAN

SCAN ME
or visit
prh.com/christinefeehan